Reign of Shadows:
Masks of the Fallen

T.S. COLUNGA

To Pauline.
This adventure wouldn't be the same without you.

The Reign of Shadows series is dedicated to my brother, Eric.
Role model. Hero. Best brother ever.

3

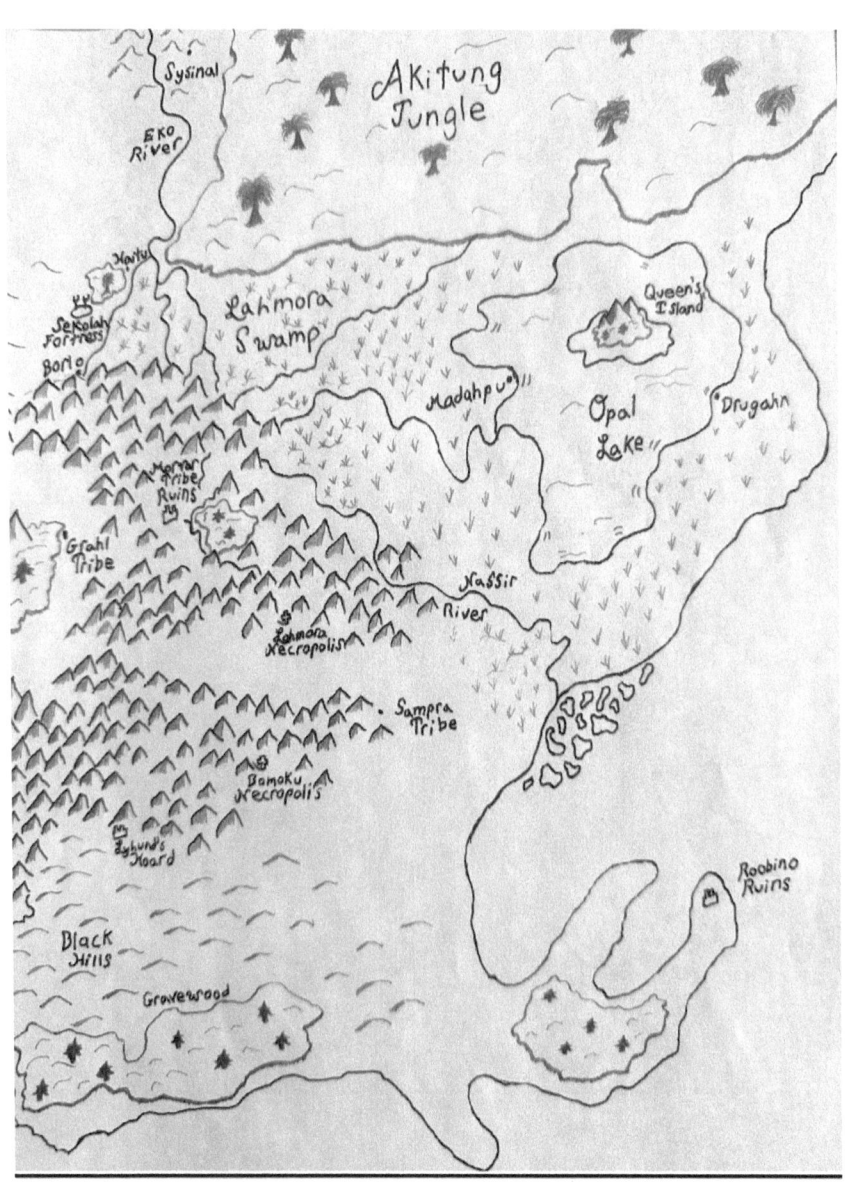

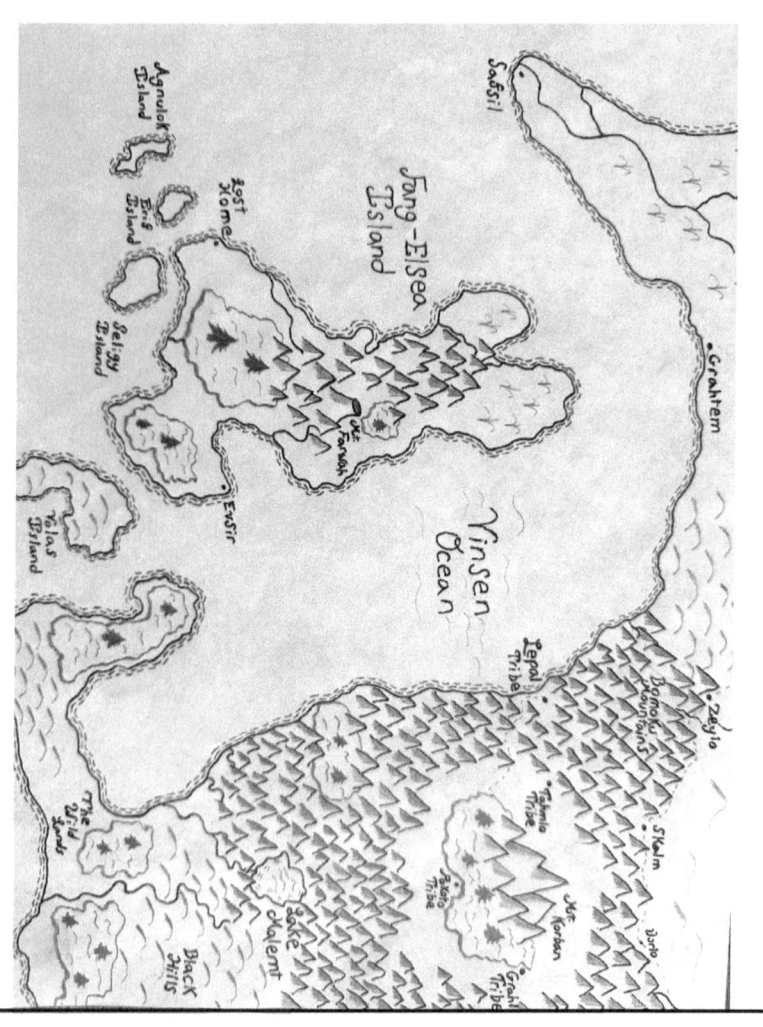

Table of Contents

Chapter 1: The Boy in the Tree

Lepal Tribe, Bomoku Mountains, Alutopek

King Vanarzir howled like a beast. Two years he had to wait. Two years he had to watch as the world around him prepared. He married the commoner, Valkayto, in hopes to settle the rising whispers of rebellion. He even went along with her plan to wait two years before continuing to collect and enlist children. Not to mention letting some of the youngest and oldest of those he had already gathered go home. Fortunately, he had his servant, Nekvaz, stop most of them from leaving. Until he, too, disappeared.

From his castle in Detnu he would receive reports of villages and towns east of the Eko River preparing for war. Even on the night of his proudest moment, him becoming a father, was filled with treachery. He recalled tying and locking up Valkayto, unsure of what to do with her. It didn't take long to produce a plan to deal with her, and possibly the heart of the rebellion all in one stroke. It was just a matter of time now. "Tick tock." He growled under his breath as the ship he was on made it to shore. The devilish grin grew as he imagined her punishment, and this oncoming battle.

The two years were up. Instead of marching through the Gateway Mountains, or sailing into the Silent Sea, he went south. The first handful of islands had few people and were easy to sweep. Making his way back to the mainland he saw a peculiar sight. Smoke wafting into the air.

Now, a single column of smoke wasn't anything to concern oneself with. Maybe not even two. He counted at least a dozen separate fires swirling and spiraling into the air, creating a gray haze before blending into the ebon dome he had placed over all Alutopek. More worrisome was the smell of metal permeating around the Vinsen Ocean.

The Fohdorsha, or dragonborn as they were commonly called, were preparing for war.

He had sent emissaries and others to speak to these primitive peoples, but few returned. And those who did never spoke of metal work and claimed they had faces that weren't human. They were more monster than man. That wasn't much of a deterrent for King Vanarzir. He ordered for his ships to head towards the smoke and prepare for war. It was finally time to finish what he started.

His army, the Kylix, gave the appearance of the living dead, as their armor was made to resemble bone. But his favorite soldiers were the Kylika. Soldiers with talent, or a magic ability, that made them even more dangerous. To tell them apart from standard soldiers they wore skulls more bestial than human. A long snout like a wolf, thick horns that curled to a point near the mouth, and glowing eyes. They had proven themselves worthy two years ago by defeating a necromancer. Nothing could stop them. Especially with the full might of the Kylix behind them.

"Are you ready?" He asked his favorite of the Kylika.

Krista nodded. "I am." She brandished her sword and stamped her feet, letting out a guttural growl.

"What are you doing?" Vanarzir asked.

"Getting ready to fight." Krista stammered; the excitement she showed now erased.

The king shook his head. "Know your place. You may know how to fight, but you're a healer."

It was fortunate Krista wore the Kylika helmet, as the face she made would have made the king angry. She bit her tongue, pausing, letting the pain become nearly unbearable. "Yes, my lord." She said, tasting blood with every syllable. An instant later her tongue was healed, never showing a sign of abuse.

The Bomoku Mountains, and everything south of them, belonged to the Fohdorsha. Few traveled here. It was aptly named the Wild Lands since nobody knew what to expect. As the Kylix stepped off their ships and onto the sandy shores, everything was quiet. The nearby trees were just yards away but felt like an expanse that could last a lifetime. It was like the never-ending hallway from nightmares.

As they marched onto shore an arrow whistled through the air, piercing a Kylix soldier in the leg. Krista hurried over, ripped out the arrow, and healed them. Vanarzir didn't give any sign of acknowledging this and stood facing the forest. He hollered for shields as a volley of arrows erupted into the sky from nowhere.

The rain of arrows pummeled the soldiers from above as the front lines had their bellies slashed out of thin air. Their collapse startled others, and murmurs of magic spread among them. King Vanarzir growled, shoving his way through the soldiers. He stared at the ground, noticing impressions in the sand. At the last moment he kicked the air, and a loud 'oomph' sounded nearby. In one swift motion Vanarzir yanked out his sword, twirled it, and stabbed the ground.

A gurgling noise along with blood leaking onto the blade came next. The king knelt, padding the ground and air. It was like he was trying to be a mime. He grabbed something nobody could see and ripped it off. In his hands was a metallic mask, and beneath him a man dying. The king glared at the man before turning his attention to the mask.

"Very interesting." He said, marveling the craftmanship. It was clearly made from some sort of metal, but something about it didn't feel right. It wasn't like the blade of a sword or nails from a smith. Something within it felt alive. Like a surge of energy just waiting to escape. As he held it up to his face, a hammer swung at him, knocking him to the ground and the mask out of his hands, shattering it. A peculiar green smoke wafted out from the shards of the mask along with a ghostly and shrill hiss. The blow also came from thin air. The king scrambled to his feet and yelled to attack.

The world around him erupted into chaos. The Kylix fought at nothing but air, making their way into the forest and towards the columns of smoke. If one were to witness this battle, they would think the soldiers resembling the dead were fighting imaginary creatures. Some slashed high, others low, while others jabbed their spears forward. Yet at the same time, soldiers fell. Their skull helmets crushed, their sides suddenly spewing blood.

The battle couldn't have lasted for more than a handful of minutes. Though the Kylix stood victorious, one couldn't tell since only their bodies were strewn across the sand. As the living tried stepping over their fallen brethren they stumbled, tripping over what couldn't be seen. "Search the bodies." King Vanarzir ordered, motioning his hands through the air before finally finding another corpse. He ripped off the mask and felt the familiar living energy within the metal mask. "What else are you hiding?" He asked, turning his attention up into the forest.

The masks were a peculiar thing. If the Kylika tried wearing one, splitting headaches suddenly seared them, causing them to collapse in a horrible scream. Even with King Vanarzir the mask fought back, leaving him unable to use its power. Others noted the presence of energy within the mask, but to them they weren't attacked. As they removed their skull helmets and donned the mask, they marveled as the energy coursed through their bodies. Like a bolt of lightning rippling through them. Moments later they faded in and out of existence, claiming to be in a strange, shadowy world of distorted colors. Each mask looked the same, much like the skull helmets of the Kylix army. And each one who wore a mask faded from view as they tried to control this newfound power.

Vanarzir gave a devilish grin. Maybe it was good to pick back up collecting children here. Especially if there were more of these masks hidden within the Bomoku Mountains and Wild Lands.

"What's the plan?" Krista asked, handing a mask she grabbed to her friend, Taygin.

"We march to the Fohdorsha. Don't kill them if you don't have to. We need to learn more about these masks and where we can find them." King Vanarzir said. "Take the children." He turned his attention to the columns of smoke now fading from view. A horn echoed in the distance, and the air fell quiet.

"What was that?" Taygin asked, still struggling to control his mask. As he spoke bits and pieces of him would fade.

"They know we're here." Vanarzir said, shoving Taygin out of his way. "It makes no difference. Just be on alert. There could be more of these invisible soldiers."

"Over there!" Taygin shouted. His head was missing from his body, his hand pointing to the nearby forest. A couple soldiers dashed over there, hacking at the thin air with their blades. It wasn't long before they both fell to the ground, dead.

The air grew silent, but the Kylix could feel eyes on them, deep within the woods. The Kylix soldiers now wearing masks claimed to see the ones hiding while they, too, had vanished. It was agreed that they stood guard around them, as a plan was quickly devised. The first line of defense would be those with the masks. They could lead the way and help spot those invisible to everyone else. King Vanarzir would oversee everything. Commander Mahlix would lead the Kylika, while Commander Jinuk and others led the rest of the Kylix. It would be wave upon wave of living death against this primitive people and their masks.

Two long years in waiting, finally coming to an end. And the Fohdorsha were going to feel his wrath.

The Fohdorsha didn't have cities or villages like the rest of the people of Alutopek. There were once eight, but now seven, what they called tribes. Long ago, before the Black Wall, before even the Four Kings, there were eight tribes of Fohdorsha. Each tribe descending from one of the eight colors of dragons. With so much time since their creation, tribes mixed and mingled. Though they kept their names, the tribes were now a little of everything and everyone.

It was called the Lepal Tribe, Vanarzir learned from a Fohdorshan who was dying. The Water Tribe. He wasn't sure what to expect. The man who was dying resembled any other man. Though he had darker skin than Vanarzir, he wasn't blue, or sported blue hair or eyes. In fact, the king felt disappointed staring at the dying man.

For ages people of Alutopek told of the unnatural beings of the Fohdorsha. They didn't have faces of men. It was said they moved as invisible as the wind, could creep quieter than shadow, and slither into any crevice. Demons in distorted bodies of man, who worshipped the nearly extinct dragons.

Yet, here was this man. Dark skin, his eyes a tint of gray. Even the blood trickling from his mouth was red like anybody else's. King Vanarzir spat on the man as he died.

"The only thing that makes them special are these masks." King Vanarzir said, gesturing to Taygin who was slowly learning how to control this new power. They are just men and women like you. Men and women so misguided in their beliefs, they've shut themselves away from the rest of us, making us fear them. Making us avoid them and believe them to be monsters. They are but men. If they wish to be monsters, then we will slaughter them like the beasts they worship!"

The cheers of the Kylix erupted. Peace in the Wild Lands was over.

Lepal Tribe was a sprawling town made of differing shades of limestone spreading in every direction. It wasn't until King Vanarzir stood atop a nearby hill that he saw the genius of the city streets. It was like art made for the gods. The streets were the lines of an artist, while the buildings were the texture giving the masterpiece life. What seemed like random placements of homes now made sense. The Lepal Tribe was in the shape of a dragon.

The king held out his hand, tracing the streets through the air as he drew the dragon. He ended at the dragon's mouth where the smoke had been earlier. Dust kicked up below the king. Vanarzir gripped his sword, ready to strike. A moment later one of the Kylika kneeled before him.

"My King." The speedster said. "I finished scouting the place."

"Good boy, Haloro." Vanarzir cooed, patting the boy's head as if he were his pet. "What did you find?"

"Everything is deserted. Most everyone left, and they didn't leave a trail where they went. But my guess is to another nearby tribe." Haloro said. "The only people left that I could tell are in the center of town."

"Take me to them." The king ordered.

Haloro nodded and sped away, leaving the king behind. A second later he returned. "I'm so sorry, my lord. I forgot."

Vanarzir swatted at Haloro, striking him across his helmeted face. The Kylika fell, slowly getting back to his feet. "I don't care if you're sorry or not. Do that again and you'll regret every breath you ever took, boy."

Haloro gulped. "Yes, My King. Of course, My King." His voice quivered and cracked. He turned, ensuring every movement was slow and deliberate, as he led the king to the few people left in town.

"Stay away from my mom!" A boy screamed in a heavy accent. He held a peculiar staff with a hook at the end. "We're not leaving." He stood in his doorway, his mother standing firm behind him. The look on both their faces was that of stubborn anger. One would have better luck convincing a donkey to dance than to move these two.

"Silly child." Vanarzir said, keeping eye contact with the boy's mother. "We don't want your mother. We've come for you."

In a blink of an eye the mother yanked the boy back into their home. "You're not taking him."

The king nodded and a dozen Kylix soldiers wearing masks suddenly appeared in front of her. She gasped, her eyes for the briefest of moments went wide and filled with fear. The next moment they turned back to a shining gray, boiling over with guarded fury.

"You're not taking him." She repeated, the cold in her voice almost giving the king himself chills.

"I don't recall ever giving you a choice." The king said. "Give him to me, and you will be allowed to live. Make me cut you down and I'll make sure your boy will live long enough to curse your name for defying your king."

The woman smirked. "Times change, old one. We know of Xeo. We aren't afraid."

With a lunge quicker than the eye could see Vanarzir struck the woman, sending her back into her home. Not skipping a beat, he picked her up with one hand and threw her across the room. She let out a gasp as she hit the brick wall. Before she hit the floor the king was on her, kicking her. Her boy jumped on the king's back, which he shook off with ease, sending him into another room. "That *child* is dead." He hissed, his voice dripping with malice. "Much like yours will be."

Nobody had seen the king move that fast. Outside of his armor he looked like any other old man. Sunken in eyes, a jaw that quivered when not clenched shut, and a body that showed he was once strong and powerful, but now a husk of his former self. But this, this brutal assault, showed he was still capable of moving when he wished.

"No!" The mother cried as King Vanarzir turned, his eyes set for the boy who was now cowering in the corner of the other room. "No. Leave him alone. Let him stay here. He belongs here."

King Vanarzir stopped mid stride. Only the boy saw the devilish grin on his face. "You're in luck, you pathetic swine. I'm feeling charitable. Seeing your boy here, I believe you're right. He belongs here." The king turned to leave, not saying another word.

"My King." The scrawny and squawking voice of Jinuk called as the king left the small home. "My King. I don't mean to question, but you said all children. Is that wise, leaving one behind?"

Vanarzir smirked at his commander. "As the mother said. He belongs here. Forever. And maybe we can use her instead. Setup camp here for the night."

The army that resembled the dead spread throughout the Lepal Tribe. They had collected 42 children, not touching the one the king promised could stay. The parents and adults who remained glared from tilted heads and quivered as armored boots approached them. The air was filled with raucous shouts of the victors and alcohol wafted on the wind.

It didn't matter that most of the townsfolk fled to who knows where. The Kylix were sweeping across Alutopek like a plague, and it was just a matter of time before everyone was found. The children would be forced to serve one way or the other. And nobody could hide under the Black Wall.

As the celebrations went on, others looted homes. They found food, weapons, clothes, even some texts in their own language nobody could read. But nowhere were the masks. No matter how the Kylix asked, or where they searched, the masks were gone. More than once, they caught some of the Fohdorsha trying to steal the ones the Kylix had already claimed.

Even through torture, and publicly executing a dozen of the Fohdorsha, nobody spoke of where anymore masks were, or how they acquired them. Jinuk screamed and gritted his teeth as he ordered the last execution. He didn't want to let his king down, but these people refused to talk. The only one who was calm about this was the king himself. He was confident that by morning they would have all the answers they wanted. And with his confidence, most of the Kylix turned to celebrations rather than interrogations.

Several soldiers passed out where they stood from the night's festivities. Fohdorshan rum was much stronger than most other drinks any of the Kylix soldiers had drunk.

Lepal Tribe was as silent as the start of a gentle snowstorm as the light in the east reflected off the Black Wall. And just like in the winter storm as it picks up and howls to life, so to, did everyone within the tribe. A blood curdling scream echoed throughout the area. Kylix soldier and Fohdorshan alike jolted from their sleep, feverishly searching back and forth for the cause of the sudden panic.

It was at the heart of the Lepal Tribe that a new tree had grown, seemingly overnight. The trunk was thick, branches scraping the sky. Unlike the other autumnal leaves of the area, this tree was bright green, teeming with life. What was even more peculiar, was the tree itself. If one examined it closely, they would find something…off. On the tips of some branches that were bare the bark resembled fingers. As two branches were closer to the center of the tree, the bark resembled arms. And at eye level for a child was a knot in the tree. But this knot resembled the boy's face who Vanarzir agreed could stay. His eyes screamed with agony as they could faintly be seen under a thin layer of bark, shifting back and forth. His gaping mouth, a hollow portion of the tree, bellowed a groan that caused the tree to shake. And at the trunk of the tree, was the mother, crying and wailing.

King Vanarzir stepped out of the shocked and fearful crowd, walking up to the mother. He smiled that devilish grin as he placed his hand on her shoulder. "You are right. He does belong here."

"What have you done?" The mother asked between sobs. "What have you done to my baby?"

"I did exactly as you asked. I've left him alone. I have no qualm with trees. And you insisted he belonged here."

"Ch-change him back." The mother cried, watching the eerie way her son's eyes moved from beneath the bark.

"What's your name?" Vanarzir asked.

"Kaliboon." She sobbed.

"Well, Kaliboon." Vanarzir sighed, not even hiding his twisted and cruel smile. Every word was like venom dripping out of his mouth. "I have a deal for you. Once the last of the leaves turn color and fall, your boy will be a tree forever. I can change him back, but I need something from you first."

"Anything. Anything for Dahsho." Kaliboon sobbed.

"Such a wonderful mother you are, Kaliboon." King Vanarzir laughed, and Kaliboon winced as he said her name. "You are going to tell me everything. Where to find more of these masks, where your people ran off to. Everything. And once I'm satisfied that I know everything, your little boy, Dahsho, will be returned to you."

Kaliboon nodded. "I'll tell you everything."

Chapter 2: Blood of the Covenant

Dark Tribe, Mahparry

Rafik could hardly recognize himself in the mirror. When was the last time he saw his reflection? Thinking back; the memories returned like water breaking through a ruptured dam. Two years. It was two years ago he had seen his reflection. Two years since he had lost his mother and sister. He was in rags then, compared to now. He clenched his fists, his nails cutting into his palms as he recalled back to that time. King Vanarzir and the Kylix sweeping through his home. Finding a cursed sword. Fighting a necromancer. Waking up to...this.

Mahparry. The World Beneath the World. Hidden away from the king, Rafik was trained by mythical beings, the Immortals. But now, whether they liked it or not, his training was over. He watched Xeo sparring against five Immortals, which wasn't an easy feat. Immortals were said to be one of the two cursed tribes of men. With the body of man, the mouth of a bird, and massive wings to match, they were formidable. Add that they could control one of the elements, and even just one was a force to be reckoned with.

He watched two hovering in the air while a third dived in on Xeo. Two others flanked him. The two swords Xeo had to defend himself with were a blur of motion. Echoes of steel against steel reverberated back.

"Ow." Rafik hissed, wincing, and forcing his attention away from the battle.

"I told you it would sting." Neypa, an Immortal with translucent white feathers signaling she was from the Air Tribe said. She dabbed the wet cloth on Rafik's face again, cleaning the cut he had just received during his final sparring match. "You did well."

"Not well enough." Rafik sighed. He had managed to fend off three Immortals before blood was drawn, Neypa being one of them. "How does he do it?"

Neypa shrugged. "He is well-versed in combat. But you have talent of your own."

Rafik nodded, staring at his hands. While Xeo spent the last two years fighting constantly, his time was split between sparring and mastering his talent of psychometry; the power of viewing objects' memories. "I guess so."

As Neypa washed the wound Rafik turned his attention to Xeo once more. This time as he watched he imagined how much better he would be with his cursed sword, Blaridane. The thoughts of the possessed sword didn't consume him like when he was first here, but they still lingered. Festering in a corner of his mind. Though the Immortals insisted he had been 'cured' of his addiction to the blade, he knew if given the chance he would snatch it in a heartbeat. The thoughts of having the sword and having to hide in this foreign land felt as if they were driving him more into madness than the thoughts of losing his family.

A bell sounded and a sixth Immortal swooped into the arena. This one all black, an embodiment of shadow itself. Sayros. Rafik watched the Immortal of Shadow attack. He was what Master Agam called a 'Life Tracker.' He could sense life across all Alutopek. And even he couldn't find Anza. The last connection of his family. His father had died nine years ago, and his mother two years ago. He was officially an orphan.

Lost in his hurricane of swirling memories and thoughts, Rafik didn't notice Xeo get beaten down. He only returned to reality as a louder bell sounded. He saw three blades at Xeo's throat as he was flat on his back. "It's about time." He muttered.

"Now, now." Neypa laughed. "Jealousy won't help make you better."

"You heard me?" Rafik asked, eyes wide. "I'm sorry. It slipped. Didn't mean to say that out loud."

"Don't be sorry, young one. It's only natural for two teenage boys to constantly strive to be the best. Just don't let your ambition keep you from him. Xeo, Tragi, and yourself are brothers by circumstance, not by the flesh. If you nourish that connection, it will be stronger than any other bond." Neypa said.

Rafik shrugged. "I'll have to take your word for it, since I don't have a sister to compare it to anymore."

"Well done!" A booming, crackling voice said, entering the arena. This Immortal was tall, with bright orange feathers intertwined with his red hair. It was like solidified fire erupting out of his head. The Master of Fire ushered for Rafik to return to the arena as he helped Xeo to his feet. "You two have done marvelously well."

"Thanks." Xeo said between breaths. "I thought you were going to kill me Sayros."

The Dark Tribe Immortal nodded, giving a smirk. "I was told to not hold back."

"Way to go, Xeo and Rafik. To allow the title of warrior an Immortal must fight off two others at once. Rafik, you fought off three before falling to the fourth. Xeo, you did five. I cannot even begin to say how proud I am of both of you. To think it's only been two years! And without wings, no less! Truly remarkable. Remarkable!"

"Now we're heading back, right?" Xeo asked, ignoring the praise. "Back to Alutopek?"

Agam frowned, lowering his head and nodding. "I'm afraid so. If it were up to me, you would stay here for another two years at least. Sadly, destiny doesn't wait for your convenience. King Vanarzir is on the move again, and he must be stopped. We don't have any time to continue training."

"I think we're ready." Xeo said, sheathing a sword. He yanked the cloth an Immortal was using to clean where he was cut and pressed on the wound himself. "Right, Rafik?"

Rafik nodded, smiling. "King Vanarzir doesn't stand a chance between us."

"You know," Xeo said. "King Vanarzir would lose in a day if all of you helped. I'm sure people would be thankful for that."

"We've been through this." Agam said, his crackling voice sounding more irritable than he actually was. "Immortals aren't allowed to help in Alutopek. Not yet."

"You helped us." Xeo pressed. "That means you're willing to break the rules sometimes."

"That's different." Agam said. "Saving a child from death is different than overthrowing a king. Especially when we were ordered to do so."

"By whom?" Xeo asked.

"If I were allowed to tell you I would have already." Agam sighed.

"When will we know?" Rafik asked.

"When the king wishes it." Sayros interrupted, his voice more of a hiss than usual. "And not a moment sooner."

Mahparry. The World Beneath the World. Arriving here two years ago, it was almost unbelievable discovering it. The second tribe of men cursed by the gods, who had turned into bird like creatures were forced to live in the underground world until the curse lifted. It was a cosmic joke to be allowed to fly, but never reach the heavens. The Immortals had lived here since the curse and established their own world below everyone's very feet. Including a king. One the boys had yet to meet. Though, they didn't get to travel that far out of the Dark Tribe unless being chaperoned by an Immortal.

"Ready to go see Tragi?" Neypa asked.

"That's why I let Sayros beat me." Xeo smirked. "I wanted to see my brother's ceremony."

"Excuses, excuses." Sayros spat. "I beat you."

"I'm with Sayros on this one." Rafik laughed.

"We can all go together." Agam cheered. "Your brother needs all the support he can get, I'm afraid."

"I'll catch up." Sayros said, backing up from the crowd. "I need to attend to something first. Dark Tribe matters." Before anyone could say goodbye Sayros launched into the sky and flew away.

"Are you ready?" Gyre asked. His dark hair mixed with bright blue feathers of varying shades. It was like running water frozen in motion. Running along the sides of his arm were tufts of sky-blue hair.

Tragi nodded, removing his robe as he sat cross-legged in the center of the theater. The room was massive. Before sitting down Tragi noticed he could barely see the walls of the other side. It was the domed center of a temple at the heart of the Dark Tribe village. Running along the sides of the dome were seats one could only get to by flight alone. Tragi had given up imagining what it would be like to fly. He had grown content with his own body. For these last two years he learned that's all he needed.

"Are you ready?" Gyre asked in a more impatient tone.

Tragi looked up; his eyes scrunched together as he nodded. He met Gyre's eyes before lowering his head again. This was it. His final test.

Gyre smiled. "Good. Was just testing you. You know the rules. Utter silence. Not a peep. Not a word. Not a scream or a sneeze. Doing so, you will be shunned in silence for a year. And all you have trained for will be for nothing." The Immortal explained.

Tragi nodded. For the last two years he had been trained as a peacekeeper. To know the laws of the land as well as the gods. Not just of the Rhine-Pa religion, but all religions. More than once Xeo and Rafik joked at how boring it was. At first Tragi agreed. Dragging his feet to lessons and not paying attention when he was there. Slowly, just ever so slowly, his temperament changed. He learned of myths and legends, ancient histories, and how to communicate with others. He smiled, remembering how he tricked Xeo into giving up food for two days.

This was the final test. To have him be officially recognized not just as a peacekeeper, but as a priest of the Rhine-Pa religion. He would be given the mark of the peacekeepers. But if at any time he moved or made a noise, the mark would be changed to an emblem of disappointment. He would forever be marked as a failure for all to see.

These ceremonies weren't that popular. A handful of Immortals may show up to watch. Possibly even try to provoke them. But already Immortals were flying and swooping into their seats. Out of the corner of his eye Tragi noticed several holding fruits in varying stages of rot. He clenched his teeth, refusing to even breathe out of his mouth. Several Immortals didn't like the three of them in Mahparry, and this would be their chance to bully while it being perfectly allowed. They just weren't allowed to physically touch him.

"I won't lie to you." Gyre sighed, picking up an awl. He twirled the small pointy tool between his fingers as he spoke. "You will feel every dot. And you aren't to move. Some places will hurt more than others. But if you manage this, I'd say you're stronger than your brother."

Tragi smirked at the thought. Xeo didn't think this was important. Another piece of evidence that he was meant for this role over his brother as he gripped tighter the water damaged and worn-out book he was given when first arriving. Tragi took a deep breath, closed his eyes, and nodded once more. It was finally time.

Xeo and Rafik arrived just as Gyre began to speak. They both cursed, seeing the eager Immortals ready to make Tragi fail.

"Welcome everyone." Gyre began. "We are gathered here in hopes to welcome another into the brotherhood. Tragi has proven himself more than capable for this task. And at only 16? He is one of the youngest in recorded history to be given this honor. With every dot punctured into his skin, it represents the souls he will save in this life. The symbol, once finished, will show he is a man of peace. Not violence. That he can be trusted to remain neutral among friends, and do what is right by law, and by the gods.

Tragi, while bestowing this gift upon you not one sound can be uttered. Not one movement made. Let this gift flow into you and fill you like a vessel of peace I know you to be. You know the punishment for failing, and you wish to continue?"

Without looking up Tragi nodded.

24

Gyre smiled. "Let's begin." The Water Tribe Immortal took a brush and lightly began drawing on Tragi's back. After making the sketch he picked up the awl, dipped it in ink, and with his other hand was a small mallet. "This is going to hurt."

Tragi winced, clenching his teeth, hoping that movement wasn't noticed. Gyre wasn't lying when he said it was going to hurt. Like a needle poking him relentlessly along the spine. Just as he thought he could handle the pain, the tip of the awl struck a nerve, shooting electric shocks throughout his body. All he could do was sit there and wait it out. He was stronger than this. He had come this far. He couldn't give up now.

The crowd of Immortals erupted into cheer, tossing their rotting food at Tragi. A potato zoomed through the air, hitting Tragi in the side of his head. Xeo sprang up and cursed, screaming at the Immortal who didn't even notice him.

"Xeo stop!" The crackling voice of Agam echoed around the theater. "You cannot interfere."

Rafik was quiet, touching the scripture of a nearby priest, watching Tragi intently. His eyes flickered. Though his body was here, Rafik was somewhere else. Viewing the memories of the book of the priest. His eyes shot open a moment later, jumping to his feet and grabbing a shield.

"What do you think you're doing?" Agam asked.

"Well," Rafik smirked. "After doing some research of my own, I've learned his loved ones can protect him. They just can't touch him. Isn't that right, priest?"

The elderly Immortal scrunched his eyes, glaring at Rafik before letting out a nod. "In some rare cases, where the crowd has been most unruly, family has been allowed to protect him. But that's been the case for Immortal, not Nomad."

"That's all I needed to hear." Xeo smirked. He yanked a shield from beside a guard watching the ceremony and dashed to his brother. He lunged into the air, swatting away a rock that almost hit Tragi's head. The crowd had run out of food to throw.

Rafik and Xeo circled Tragi, swatting away anything that came near him. The crowd jeered and cursed at the boys while the

25

rhythmic noise of the mallet tattooing Tragi behind them echoed. The rabble quieted and attention turned to the far side of the theater. Five hooded figures were walking towards them.

About halfway to Tragi the hoods lowered. Five Shadow Tribe Immortals marched; their swords raised. "Sayros." Rafik cursed, noticing the one in the middle.

Two Immortals jolted into the air, while another two flanked the boys on either side. Sayros charged head on. He screamed, his orange eyes nothing but slits as he glared at them.

"You ready?" Rafik asked, watching the Immortals fly around.

"They won't even touch my brother." Xeo said. He tapped Rafik's sword, and the two nodded. Before they could make a move, the theater was shrouded in darkness. Immortals in the crowd screamed, and the two boys could feel them flying above, diving and swerving. They couldn't tell which was part of the panicked crowd, and who were the enemies.

The two saw the orange eyes first, peering through the darkness. As one they moved to strike, Xeo aiming high while Rafik low. Sayros took a step back as an Immortal crashed into them. They scrambled to their feet, pushing the Immortal, whoever it was, off them as fast they could.

"Keep near your brother." Rafik ordered. "I got this."

Xeo nodded, hoping he was stepping in the right direction to his brother.

Rafik felt the cold tendrils of solidified shadow slither towards him. He twirled his blade, hacking at one and another, slowly advancing on the Immortal creating them. As he finally made it Rafik stabbed his blade forward. The Immortal lurched to the side, and the surrounding darkness disappeared. It was Sayros he was facing.

Sayros snarled at Rafik, blasting him with bolts of shadow. Rafik managed to block the attack, but an Immortal swooped down, yanking away the shield. In this battle they seemed more aggressive than in the initiation ceremony. More coordinated with their attacks. Rafik glanced back, seeing Xeo had his hands full with three of the Immortals.

He bit his cheek, crinkling his brow, realizing he was just fighting two and thinking *that* was difficult. The flying Immortal dove for him again as Sayros fired another bolt. Rafik lunged in the air, rolled, and sprang to his feet. Without looking he threw his sword behind him. The sword cut through the air, slicing the Immortal's wing. He pivoted, losing balance as he climbed on the back of the Immortal trying to fly, and fell to the ground.

Faster than he thought possible, Sayros was standing over him, blade at his throat. "Can't even defeat two Immortals." Sayros laughed. "Pathetic."

Rafik glared at Sayros. Out of the corner of his eye he saw Xeo in a similar situation. Gyre, however, was still tattooing Tragi meaning he still hadn't moved or said a word. If the soon-to-be-priest hadn't given up, neither could he. "I was going easy on you."

"Even I can tell you're lying. You're weak. You don't belong here. None of you do!" Sayros snarled. "So long, Rafik of Datz."

A circle of fire surrounded the two and Agam landed with a resounding 'thud.' "What are you doing, Sayros?"

"Doing what you should have done a long time ago." Sayros said, keeping the sword at Rafik's neck, but turning his attention to the Master of Fire. "Eliminating the Nomad scum."

"I never knew you felt this way." Agam replied in a calm tone, his voice still crackling like fire. "What else are you hiding?"

Sayros spat at Agam, and turned, plunging his sword downward. Rafik rolled to the side thanks to the distraction and kicked at the Immortal. Within moments Agam had Sayros subdued. The Immortal of Shadow screamed, cursed, and snarled. Where Rafik was defeated a moment ago, his luck had turned, as other Immortals came to their defense.

"Nomads don't belong down here with us. It goes against the word of *my* king." Sayros said.

Agam paused. "Your king? Who do you serve Sayros?"

Sayros stayed quiet, glaring at the Master of Fire.

"Who do you serve?" Agam asked again, holding a sword, the edge of the blade rippling with flames at his throat. "Tell me."

Sayros glared at Rafik before turning his attention back to Agam. "I serve the true king. The Forgotten One. And I know he lives like you and me. He will cast this world into never ending shadow. It will be so great even the gods will be left quivering in the darkness. And all will bow to the glorious Forgotten One."

Agam's eyes widened. "The Forgotten One?"

Sayros smiled, laughing. "Heard of him? Best you join us now. I can put in a good word for you, fire spitter."

The Master of Fire shook his head, and with his free hand sent a searing column of fire near his head. The malicious glint in Sayros's eyes faded as his eyes closed, his smile drooping to the familiar frown they all knew of Sayros.

"Did you kill him?" Rafik asked, getting to his feet.

Agam shook his head, pointing to the scarred ground beside Sayros. "No. I blasted the ground near him. He passed out from the heat. A little trick I learned."

"That's a cool trick." Rafik said.

"You don't become Master of Fire without learning all the tricks." Agam smiled.

"Who is The Forgotten One?" Rafik asked.

"He's an old Shadow Tribe legend." Agam replied. "After the ceremony I will tell the three of you what I can about him."

After the ambush from the five Shadow Tribe Immortals, what was left of the crowd was quiet. They watched as Tragi was slowly tattooed the mark of the Immortals, and that of a Rhine-Pa priest. The sign of the Immortals, Rafik had recognized before. Back in the tunnels when he was first escaping Datz. A pair of semi circles facing back-to-back. At each end of the hemisphere another half circle capped it off. At each end those were capped, slowly getting smaller. To Rafik, it was like an intricate flower designed by man. Between the two main semicircles a line sprang up from either end, sprouting into three lines before also being capped off by the semicircle design. Just above the top of the

Immortals' emblem, was the sign of the Rhine-Pa religion. This one was simple, a triangle with a sun in the middle of it.

The process took hours. More than once both Xeo and Rafik had dozed off to sleep, watching Tragi slowly get poked. One dot at time. Agam jostled them awake as Gyre put down the mallet and awl. 19 hours later, it was done.

"We have a new peacekeeper, and priest to Rhine-Pa!" Gyre announced. "Tragi of Kristol, you may rise and speak again."

Tragi looked to Rafik and Xeo and smiled. "Thank you."

The Immortals remaining in the crowd were cheering. The five would-be murderers had been taken away hours ago. The three noticed an Immortal they had never seen before cheering among the crowd. This one looked older and wore a crown.

"Who is that?" Rafik asked.

"Anak-Turin." Agam said. "King of Immortals. He's here to see you three."

"Why us?" Xeo asked.

"This can't be good." Rafik said.

"I agree with them." Tragi said. "Any time anybody with authority wants to see us, we're in trouble."

"I have authority." Agam said.

"You don't count." Xeo said. Rafik and Tragi laughed.

"Now, would you three step forward?" Gyre asked, gesturing for them to return to the center of the theater.

The three boys looked from one to the other, then to Agam who nodded. They weren't told about this part. Gyre's face held no sign of pride like it did before. It was like he was about to convey horrible news. They had never seen him this serious before. "Are you alright, Gyre?" Tragi whispered.

Gyre nodded but didn't acknowledge any of them. He hollered to the crowd watching. "You know, I was with Agam when we picked these three up. Xeo's hands were severely burned, Tragi unsure of himself, and Rafik lost in grief and anger. But look at them now. Two years with us Immortals. Two are warriors and one is not just a priest of Rhine-Pa, but also a peacekeeper of Mahparry."

The crowd clapped and cheered. Gyre paused until the noise died down.

"For two years they've been with us. Going on adventures, training, learning. Becoming men. Dealing with adversities all along the way. Even today, marred with an attempt at murder, which wasn't a plan mind you. Yet you three persevered. Together."

Once again, more cheers erupted.

"The blood of the covenant is thicker than the water of the womb." Gyre said, turning his attention to the three boys. "Although two of you are born as brothers, all three of you are brothers by what you've been through. Rafik, you were looking for a family, but I'd say you've gained at least two brothers on this journey."

Rafik looked from Xeo to Tragi, both nodding and smiling. For the last two years he had felt at ease with them. Possibly even at home. But, with how anyone close to him died, he never considered extending his heart and the rank of family to others. Rafik smiled. He had a family without even realizing it.

"Stay with each other. Trust one another. You may squabble, but don't let that tear you three apart." Gyre continued.

Chapter 3: Legend of Syrus

Dark Tribe, Mahparry

While living in Mahparry the three boys had witnessed several initiation ceremonies. Rafik and Xeo especially enjoyed watching Immortals becoming warriors. But no matter which ceremony it was, the ending, if it was successful, was always the same. A great celebration with a seemingly endless supply of food. The World Beneath the World celebrated so heavily the three often wondered if those up in Alutopek could feel the earth shake beneath them. And tonight, was one of the biggest celebrations they had ever seen. And it was for them! Though Tragi insisted it was also because the king was here as well.

The beating of drums reverberated off the walls. Musicians used this to add another layer to their music, creating a hypnotic and vibrant rhythm. Even while sitting and eating one would bob their head or tap their feet. Immortals danced on their feet and in the air doing acrobatic twirls with one another.

Tonight's feast was larger than most, but also the crowd was much larger too. The Dark Tribe was known to be a quieter place. Being covered in shadow, most other Immortals didn't care to be there. But tonight, the Dark Tribe Immortals made an exception, lighting up their village for the first time in the two years they had been there.

"Where are the lights?" Rafik asked, turning from one side to the other trying to find the source.

"Lights?" Gyre asked, his face scrunching in confusion. "I've never heard you use slang like that before, Rafik. You mean the Immortals of the Light Tribe?"

Rafik shook his head. "No. The lights. You know, like what fire gives off. Or the light stones." This whole time the entire village had been covered in darkness, save for posts with large light stones placed throughout the village for the three to walk around. "Now, suddenly, it's as bright as any other place down here."

"Ah. I see what you mean now." Gyre smiled. "When an Immortal is content or comfortable, they can release some of their powers without even knowing. Fire Immortals radiate heat, while air ones just float in place without using their wings. The Dark Tribe emits shadow. With so many in one place, it just cloaks their portion of the world in endless shadow. Since they're hosting so many, it was agreed, they would consciously make an effort to keep the shadows at bay so everyone could enjoy themselves."

"Wait, if that's the case," Xeo paused, swallowing a chunk of meat he just tore off the bone.

"Learn to chew your food!" Tragi said, rolling his eyes.

"Thanks, Mom." Xeo said, before turning back to Gyre. "Does that mean you just drip constantly or something? You're from the Water Tribe, right?"

Gyre burst out laughing, slapping Xeo on the back. "That is a good one, my non-winged friend." The Immortal chuckled as he tossed a few cherries into his mouth. "If you excuse me, I think I see someone who needs a dance." He launched himself from the table, and the three watched as he cut in, dancing with a girl who was previously dancing with someone else.

"Even at 300 years old that child still has no manners." Agam said, taking Gyre's seat.

"300 years?" Xeo and Rafik asked in unison.

Agam smiled. "Yeah, he's still a young little thing."

"How old can you get?" Rafik asked. "I know you're not really immortal like your name implies."

Agam nodded. "You are right, Rafik. We aren't immortal. But most of us live to be about 1,000 years old. 2,000 if we're lucky."

"Is Anak-Turin 2,000" Xeo asked, pointing to the king.

The king of Immortals sat on the far side of the room, on a higher table than the rest. It reminded Rafik being back in the Sekolah Fortress, seeing King Vanarzir on the raised table. Where Vanarzir emitted unease, Anak-Turin gave off the aura of happiness. His smile lit up the room, his graying feathers were all that was left on his head, his hair had escaped him long ago. His

32

eyes were a deep mocha, nearly black, not sharing the weathered appearance he had. Even his beak, which to all Immortals were sleek and smooth, maybe having an occasional chip or scratch in it, appeared old. Brittle, almost.

Agam smiled before answering. "He sure looks it, doesn't he? Even his wings are so frail he can no longer fly. No, Anak-Turin is much, much older. He's around five, maybe 6,000 years old."

"That's as old as the Four Kings." Rafik gasped.

"Is he immortal?" Xeo asked.

Even Tragi, who had been focusing on eating and not the conversation was beginning to show interest.

"No." Agam said, shaking his head. "Anak-Turin is pretty secretive about it. All he has said is that it was a gift from a gray fox. He will die when Syrus has returned."

"The mythical being Syrus?" Tragi asked, perking up. He had read about him in one of his texts.

"The very same." Agam said. "His health was doing fine until about 16 years ago, give or take a year. Now he's declining fast. Most believe either Syrus is coming, or the king is finally dying, and his story was a ruse to inspire people."

"Who is Syrus?" Rafik asked.

"Do they not teach you anything in Alutopek?" Agam asked. "But I guess I should be happy they don't. Because that's a nice way to tell you the king wants to see you three. He has a history lesson for you."

"Rafik, can't you just touch the history book and tell me later." Xeo asked, still gnawing on a leg of meat, and scooping in potatoes between bites.

"He could. But the king requires all three of you." Agam said, yanking Xeo up by the collar of his shirt.

The three followed Agam, taking them away from the celebrations and into a barren room, lit by a handful of candles running along the middle of a table. The four each took a seat, and moments later an Immortal entered the room, suited in armor. They hadn't seen an Immortal in a suit of armor before. Moments later

Anak-Turin hobbled in. The king was hunched forward, his arms shaking as he walked with a cane.

"If I may offer some advice before we begin?" Anak-Turin asked as he heaved a sigh of relief once sitting down. "Never get this old. You feel your own body betray you, and your bones turn to dust." With the last bit he heaved, a hollow, breathless laugh. His wings shook and fluttered, and more feathers drifted to the ground.

"Nice to meet you, King Anak-Turin." Tragi said, bowing.

"Oh, you must be the new peacekeeper." Anak-Turin said. His voice was shaky. "I saw your ceremony. Shame some had to try and ruin it."

"Sayros and the others are in custody, my king." Agam said. "We'll get to the bottom of this."

"If it's one thing I've learned throughout my years, is that all things will reveal themselves in time." Anak-Turin said. "Now." He snapped his fingers, his fingers and hand popping as he did so. "Bring me the book."

Another Immortal stepped forward, dropping a thick tome on the table. The massive book had signs of it being rebound a handful of times, as there were holes from previous threads, stitching the dark leather cover to the book. Across the front was the emblem of the Immortals; the semi-circular lines each glowing with different lights fading in and out.

"Aren't you glad you didn't have to read that?" Xeo asked, smirking.

"This is the King's Journal." Anak-Turin explained. "It is the king or queen of Mahparry's duty to write in this book. It tells of everything that ever was. And here, I have a tale to tell you. Though I know it by heart, so if anyone wants to fact check me, you're more than welcome to do so."

Tragi began to grab the book when Agam kicked him underneath the table. The Master of Fire feverishly shook his head. Nobody fact checks the king.

"My king." Agam interrupted as Anak-Turin cleared his throat.

"Yes?" Anak-Turin asked, taking a deep, wheezing breath.

"These three don't know who Syrus is. You may need to start at the beginning."

"Very well. It was long ago," Anak-Turin started. He turned his head, staring at the wall behind Rafik, Xeo, and Tragi. "Before the Black Wall. Before the Four Kings, or even the Dragon Wars. It was at...the very beginning.

"The Age of Monsters was ending, and the Age of Heroes began. Not counting the Fohdorsha, who even then kept to themselves, there were three tribes of men. The first were the Taktor. A seafaring people who were very territorial. Anywhere they went, the land was theirs. No one could stand up to the might of the Taktors. They were feared barbarians and thugs. They didn't see a need in education. If they could destroy it, they didn't need to learn about it. They considered themselves kings of Amlima. The chosen tribe to rule the world.

"The second tribe were the *Immortals*. They branched off from the Fohdorsha and wished nothing more than to learn everything about the universe. They were scholars and managed to unlock some of the powers imbued within themselves. Most called the *Immortals* devils, or demons in human skin. Even being called such names and worse, the *Immortals* wished no ill will on any living thing.

"The final tribe didn't have a title like the *Immortals* or Taktor. They were simply nicknamed as the Wanderers. Nomads who went from place to place seeking shelter. They weren't scholars or murderous brutes, but somewhere in between. Some would say they had the worst traits of the other tribes. They would learn about their prey, whether beast or fellow man during war, and use the weaknesses they discovered against them. Although they didn't have the same military tactics as the Taktor, many still feared them.

"The three tribes lived peacefully for hundreds of years. *Immortals* watched from the hills over the land. Watching and learning. The Taktors lived among the coast, sometimes marching deeper inland to hunt. The Wanderers went everywhere. But the mutual happiness between the three tribes was destined to end.

"It was the harshest winter not just in Alutopek, but all Amlima had ever seen. Oceans froze and trees were encased in ice. Even the sands of the Biodlay Desert iced over. Chunks of ice and snow hailed down from the heavens constantly for months. Animals froze within minutes to the harsh environment. It was a miracle anyone survived.

"The three tribes were reduced to scavenging, like ancient times long forgotten. The Wanderers could no longer live on open land, and created shelters made of ice and snow to keep warm. The *Immortals* copied their technique and were beginning to thrive as well. It was during this time the Wanderers began receiving talent and discovering magic. Nobody knew how this discovery was achieved, but most blamed the *Immortals.* However, where the *Immortals* controlled the elements, the Wanderer's magic varied greatly.

"The Taktors heard about this and began their invasion. They wanted this magic, and the shelters that kept the people warm. The warrior people attacked anyone who wasn't of the Taktor Tribe. The *Immortals* fled, not wanting to be a part of the violence. The Wanderers stood their ground. And thus, man's first great war had started.

"Years passed, and the war between the two were still ongoing. On one day it would seem the Taktors were winning, the next the Wanderers. The *Immortals* buried themselves in studies, trying to think of how they could help. They weren't warriors and knew they couldn't stand against either tribe. People in all three tribes prayed to the gods to intervene. But nothing happened. Believing the gods had abandoned them, the *Immortals* began devising a plan. For centuries the *Immortals* had watched and learned. They had unlocked their inner powers and found other secrets to their world no one would have expected. And finally, they decided to put their knowledge into a defensive weapon.

"They devised two powerful books to end the violence. One promoted life, the other peace. The powers contained within the books were unimaginable and rivaled the gods. The wielders of these books began to change the war entirely.

"It only took a few instances for the Wanderers and Taktors to realize what power they contained. Both sides coveted them and turned their attention to the *Immortals*. The scholars hid away the books before it was too late, hoping that would be enough, praying no one would find them. Even after word got out that the books were gone, the two opposing forces kept attacking.

"Within the *Immortals* a wicked and mysterious faction was growing. One who wanted to profit off all this violence and bloodshed. They were corrupt, not caring about others, but just bettering their own standing. In secret, these *Immortals* created two more books. Instead of peace and life, these two were of chaos and death. And just like in the titles, chaos and death poured onto the land tenfold.

"Taktors fought for land and any of the books they could get their hands on. The Wanderers, although wanting the books, pestered at the Taktors like fleas on a dog. They believed they could pry the books out of their cold, dead hands later. And by now, even the *Immortals* were fighting back. The creators of the last pair of books abused their powers.

"If the continuing violence wasn't enough, a plague broke out. The plague didn't know any boundaries and attacked everyone. The few religious people left believed it was the gods trying to end all the madness and violence once and for all. Though some believed it was from one of the books, which collectively were now called the Master's Books. The ones who could still hold a sword fought for the books, trying to gain their power.

"From the heavens the gods stared down at them all in pity and disgust. Man squabbled like birds after fruit. They had agreed not to intervene, hoping the sickness would be enough to settle the childish qualms. But now it seemed like the only thing they were capable of was destruction. As the plague ended, war continued. Desolation in the icy world was nearing. But still, they refused to intervene. Mankind would have to learn to come together or fall divided. This was something they had to learn.

"One god didn't want to sit back and watch. He tried to find a way to help. When the other gods found out he was stripped of his godhood. He soon died, though his spirit lived on. The wandering spirit of the former god went throughout the tribes, trying to find a worthy host. It searched throughout the *Immortals* and found no one worthy of the wisdom that it would bestow upon them. It watched the Wanderers and realized none would last without using their power for selfish reasons. Their hopes rested on the Taktors.

"Hiding in a stable was a slave. Where he had come from, the spirit wasn't sure. Even the slave could no longer remember. This man refused to fight others or take what wasn't his. The slave no longer had a name and was treated like any other work horse or beast of burden. It was a cruel fate, as even pets and other animals had names. But to the Taktors, slaves didn't deserve one.

"The spirit entered this slave, melding with their own, and gave themselves the name of Syrus, meaning 'hero.' Syrus broke free of his bonds, freeing the other slaves along the way. He marched into the middle of the battlefield, with only a staff in hand. Arrows flew towards him but missed. Others tried hacking at him with swords, but he managed to avoid every blow.

"The clear morning sky darkened with storm clouds. Thunder roared for miles around, sounding like it were the gods themselves laughing at these warring men. Fear crept into every man as they watched Syrus float into the sky.

"'The Gods gave you time to save yourselves.' He spoke. 'But you wasted it, trying to kill each other. They sent me, Syrus.' He proclaimed. His voice echoed over the thunder. 'And from this day forth you will all be cursed. You, your children, and your children's children, will bare this mark until the world's end.'

"Syrus held out his staff, and everyone below him radiated an eerie light. He turned and spoke to the Taktors who were glowing the color of a raging sea. 'You want more land, Taktors? I will give you more land. From this day forth you will be cursed to roam the seafloor, only able to step on dry land for short periods of time.'

"As Syrus declared these words the Taktors began to change. Their skin grew scaly and their ears turned to fins. Their arms and legs grew out thinner fins while their noses slowly shrank back into their heads, leaving two slits. The screams from their changing were unbearable, but no one could move.

"The Taktors screamed and fled, gasping for air they could not breathe.

"Syrus then turned his attention to the *Immortals*. 'And you just want to learn? To achieve this knowledge but stay out of the world you live in. And when you do you created a weapon far worse than any smith could ever achieve. From this day forth, I curse you with what you wanted. I curse you with long life to gain the knowledge you so crave, but never to share. Further, you didn't want to be in this world, well, you are no longer part of it.' His voice echoed across the frozen landscape. 'To everyone else you will no longer be called *Immortals*. Everyone will forget you and nickname you as Immortal. Though I promise you're not.'

"The *Immortals* fell to their knees, screaming in pain. Feathers sprouted from their arms and heads. Their lower half of their face grew outwards and hardened into a beak. And jutting from their backs were enormous, angel-like wings. But before they could fly away, the frozen ground tore open beneath them, and swallowed them whole.

"Syrus then turned his attention to the Wanderers. 'Nomads. I leave you as you are. Alone. Your own greed will be a curse for you, leaving you as you are should teach you to accept others, as they once looked like you. Not only greed, but vanity and lust surge through your veins. And that's worse than anything I could bestow upon you.'

"It was many, many years later that Syrus left this world. He vowed to return when the world needed him most and lift the curses he placed on the Taktor and *Immortal*."

"While growing up my uncle, Gorik, would tell me about the Taktors." Rafik started. "How they were once men, but now cursed by the gods because of their greed. They were to teach us that we could end up like them. He never told me about Syrus. I even met one just before coming here."

Anak-Turin managed a twinge of a smile before coughing. "History has a way of changing facts and truths. What was once truth becomes rumor. Rumor becomes legend. And, if the story persists, the legend becomes a myth. A tale to tell children. We take out what we don't want and leave what works for us. Soon what's left is a twisted tale with a hidden grain of truth somewhere within."

Tragi scrunched his brows, looking from the ancient tome to the old king. "I've spent the last two years learning history, and nobody has told me this."

"You think you can learn everything in two years?" The king laughed. "Even among us *Immortals* this is considered nothing more than a legend. To explain why such a great people with wings allowing us to scrape the sky are stuck in the World Beneath the World."

Every time Anak-Turin said "Immortal" Rafik could see his beak make a word of something else, but a deep voice in his head uttered 'immortal' instead. It was further proof this story was actual history. "Is it true? The Master's Books? Syrus? The curse?"

Anak-Turin smiled and shrugged. "I honestly don't know, Rafik. It is a nice story, and gives one something to believe in. But I don't know. When I received this gift from a gray fox I believed in Syrus. Throughout the years, I see troubles rise, some worse than others, but mankind, Taktorkind, and our kind always seem to make it. Now in my old age, I'm beginning to think Syrus was a myth. A story to give the lost and weak hope."

"Then why did you tell us this?" Xeo asked. "I could still be eating right now!"

"Please excuse my brother." Tragi sputtered, shooting daggers at his brother. "He's not used to royalty and probably has nine stomachs with the way he eats."

The king smiled. "It is a valid question. Because, young ones, what happened today stems from this story. Rafik, tell me again what you heard Sayros say."

"That he served the true king. The Forgotten One." Rafik replied after a moment.

The king nodded. "Yes. The Forgotten One. You see, he was an *Immortal* from the Dark Tribe a long time ago. He believed he was Syrus, and would achieve supremacy and godship if he had the Master's Books. A war erupted, nearly crumbling Mahparry in the process. He was finally stopped by his brother. Me."

"You?" The three boys and Agam gasped at once.

"The Forgotten One was so cruel and horrible. He almost won, too. With his power so great, somehow, he couldn't die. So, he was locked away. Just north of the throne in Mahparry-Haitu. I feared some would try to find him, so I erased his name from history, and he became known as the Forgotten One. Stories of this *Immortal's* greatness and power spread. The Dark Tribe *Immortals* moved from their original home of Mahparry-Haitu, which is the capital of the World Beneath the World, to the northern most part of this land in hopes to find him. Though they never did, the Dark Tribe settled here, and it became home to them."

"Do you think Sayros found The Forgotten One?" Rafik asked.

Anak-Turin frowned. "I don't know. The Forgotten One is still shackled where I left him, and nobody else knows where he is that's still alive. I haven't cared to visit him in centuries, though I know the way to his prison is still shut. But he is powerful. I'm sure even now. I hope he didn't find a way to send tendrils of hate into the minds of the weak. The Order of Syrus, as they were called then, could easily be forming once more. Under our very beaks."

"What can we do?" Xeo asked.

"Nothing you three need to concern yourself with just yet." The king said. "I was going to tell you three you had to stay longer, study from each tribe to become the best you could possibly be, before letting you leave to fight Vanarzir. After today, I don't believe it is safe in Mahparry for you any longer. If the Order of Syrus is returning, war could be on the brink in Mahparry. And that's a war you don't need to concern yourself with. Agam will lead others to search for these zealots. You three are not to speak of this world you've lived in for the last two years. I wanted to share this story, and explain some of our history, so you understand what I am now doing. For your own safety. Until one of us comes to collect you, you are hereby banished from Mahparry."

Rafik always imagined if one were exiled, they would be dragged to the borders and thrown out like trash. A slight pang of disappointment clouded over him as he was politely escorted to his rooms to gather everything.

"We'll miss you." Neypa said, standing in the doorway to guard, though he didn't try to escape.

"I'll be back." Rafik smiled. "I always planned to come back."

Neypa flashed a smile. "If anything takes longer than a tree to grow, it's an *Immortal*. These are scary times, Rafik. I don't know when the other zealots will be found. They could slink back into the shadows like they have for so long, and nobody would know. I don't think you'll be coming back."

Rafik frowned. It never occurred to him that the place he had called home for two years would be gone from him forever. "They may have been hidden for a long time," Rafik said. "But they revealed themselves now. They can't go back into hiding." Even as he said it, he could feel in the pit of his stomach that this was a lie. And not a very convincing one at that.

"There were attempts across Mahparry at other initiation ceremonies." Neypa explained. "It wasn't just the Dark Tribe participating in this rebellion. Things have changed."

"Well, let's hope you never do." Rafik said. He glanced over and noticed she was standing on her feet. It was the first time he had ever seen her not float in air. "As soon as we take care of Vanarzir we'll come back and help. I don't mind being bait if it will draw them out."

"You've been hanging around Xeo too much. That's a stupid plan." Neypa laughed. "Come on, I'll walk you out."

Rafik left his room, Neypa placing a hand on his shoulder. He noticed Gyre do the same to Tragi, and Agam to Xeo. He was expecting their goodbyes to be joyous. They would defeat Vanarzir, possibly return, and see one another again. But with this new threat, it didn't seem like any of the Immortals expected to see them again. Their grim expression and silent walk behind the three transferred to them. Their time in the World Beneath the World was over.

The three watched from one spot to another. The Dark Tribe had been their home for two years. They saw the spot where they first started sparring, and where Tragi first took interest in reading and becoming a peacekeeper. Immortals around them bowed as they walked by. The feeling of reverence and fear on each of their faces.

The Dark Tribe was sprawling with dark domes made of stone. Bright yellow light emitted from them marking who was currently in them. It reminded the three of the Black Wall. Where the Black Wall made one fearful and doubtful, these shined with the sense of warmth and home. Throughout their time here among the streets there were large poles with massive light stones perched atop them. They were wrapped in rope and tethered to the pole. For the two years they were here these lights helped guide them through the village. As the three passed one, an Immortal would come by and cut down the pole, extinguishing the light stone.

For two years the Immortals that thrived and loved the darkness lived among the light for these three. Tears streamed down Rafik and Tragi's face as they both realized this.

They learned the Dark Tribe wasn't evil, like they first believed when coming here. Darkness was the absence of light, but it didn't make one evil. It was a different beauty to their homes here, and to the people.

Even with The Forgotten One and Anak-Turin. Two brothers from the Dark Tribe, one Immortals revered, and the other they feared. The boogie man of this world.

The six arrived at a staircase, leading up into the sky. There wasn't a railing, or any sign anyone used this. What was called darkbrush, a violet-colored bush with crimson flowers, littered the stairs. "I guess this is it." Agam said, leaning against the last of the light posts.

"I guess so." Tragi sighed. He smiled at Gyre and then to Agam and Neypa. "Thank you."

"I don't remember thanking you for healing my hands." Xeo said. "But thanks. For everything."

"You didn't." Gyre laughed. "Better late than never."

"Be safe up there." Neypa said, hugging each of them.

"We always are." Rafik laughed.

The three waved, giving one last look at the Dark Tribe before beginning the stairs, taking them farther away from the village. They had never noticed this part of Mahparry before.

"Follow the stairs." Agam said. "You'll get to Alutopek again. And, in case you ever do need us, we'll leave this light up for you."

A burst of intense heat, followed by a frigid wind and the sound of water raining down happened all at once. The three looked back to see their three mentors gone. The light post was now encased in earth, steam still hissing out of some crevices.

"Well boys," Rafik smiled, turning back to the stairs. "Let's go home."

Chapter 4: Out of the Darkness

Datz, Nyler Peninsula, Alutopek

In the Dark Tribe the shadows and darkness didn't bother the three boys. There was a sort of warmth to them. That at the end of the day, no matter how badly bruised and beaten you were, the darkness was there. To envelope you in its peculiar chill that felt warm and cold at the same time. It provided them the comfort they needed, and the silence and solitude to sleep.

But here, back in these tunnels, the darkness was much different. Something was watching them. Waiting. The shadows didn't offer comfort, but suspicion and dread instead. The darkness didn't call for safety, but for danger. Something was lurking out there. Watching.

Tragi was the first to speak up. "Anybody else feel a little…"

"Creeped out?" Xeo finished. "Oh yeah. Don't worry. We'll protect you." He and Rafik both had their hands on their swords, waiting for the moment to yank them out of their sheath.

Tragi rolled his eyes. "Just because I wasn't trained as a warrior as much as you, doesn't mean I can't protect myself."

"Of course not. Just like we aren't trained to be a peacekeeper as well as you." Xeo said. "Right, Rafik?"

Rafik nodded. "Xeo's right, Tragi. Something isn't right here."

Before Tragi could speak, they heard chains slithering across the ground. "Tiris." The three said in unison.

"You don't happen to have a lightstone, do you?" Xeo asked.

Rafik shook his head. "Don't even have Blaridane." The memory of the last time he heard these noises filled Rafik. Escaping the Kylix, his uncle Gorik led the Datians through these tunnels. If it weren't for the lightstone and the cursed sword, they all would have died.

"Shouldn't be a problem. He let us go last time." Tragi said. "Remember?"

Xeo nodded. "Yeah. Next time we see him we had to have somebody with us. What was their name? Hopefully it was Rafik. Sorry, Rafik. Don't know what this monster wants with you."

"It wasn't me!" Rafik snapped.

"Swayfir." Tragi said. "His name was Swayfir."

"We haven't found him yet." Xeo said. "May help knowing where he is."

The shadows lightened slightly as a silhouette of a figure appeared. Rafik recognized the monster instantly. The nubs jutting from his back where the wings used to be. His beak crushed in, almost like a hammer fell on it after an attempt to rip it off. And leading from each of his fingers were tentacles of chains. In a raspy voice like rocks cracking in half, the monster spoke. "His name is Swayfir. Find him."

"We will." Tragi said. "Where is he?"

Tiris slithered a chain closer to the boys. "Everywhere."

"We can't find him if you kill us." Xeo said.

The monster's eyes glowed for a moment before retreating into the darkness. "Your final warning."

"You know, I think he's nicer this time around. He must be warming up to us." Xeo joked.

The air grew colder and darker than any had experienced. In an instant they were separated, isolated by a thick wall of shadowy fog. Rafik yelled, spinning, and searching for any sign of Tragi and Xeo. He called for them, but his voice seemed dampened by the dark. The heavy fog suddenly settled around him. He could hear the faint voice of Blaridane, shouting at him to kill. To swing and attack wildly without remorse. The sounds of screams as the Kylix finally took over Datz were next. He could clearly see the face of his mother as she fell to a volley of arrows. The screams of Skage as his arm was severed. The gurgling struggle of Salina as she took her last breath, before shrieking and rising, attacking the Kylix. Every fear he ever had echoed around him. Sweat streamed down his face as he shouted at the nightmares. His yells soon

46

became cries, and the darkness swallowed him. The final images of the small boy, Nayflin, murdered by an invisible hand. He couldn't do this. "Help!" He finally managed to yell out. Or at least he thought he did, until everything fell silent, including his thoughts.

The darkness got lighter. His fears had retreated into the recesses of his mind. There, far away, was a light. He just had to crawl towards it. Where Tragi or Xeo were he wasn't sure. But he didn't want to stick around within this abyss of shadow any longer. Rafik hobbled to his feet and ran towards the light, hoping it would be the exit he so desperately craved.

Dragon's Roost. A name that's been haunting Kryn and Ziri for two years now. Kryn stood in front of a wardrobe, tracing the shapes of objects engraved on the doors. The more she touched them the more detailed the images became. One was a bag, another a sword, an eye, and a chalice. "I think they were here." Kryn said, clutching the bag with her other hand. She brushed her blond hair out of her face and held a fire in the palm of her hand. The shapes grew increasingly detailed now. "I know this bag is one of them. I don't know about the others, though. Like that cup."

Ziri shrugged. "I'm sure they were here. But they aren't here now. And there's nothing here showing it's Dragon's Roost."

"I know!" Kryn shouted, spinning around, letting the fire twist and spiral around her, pushing Ziri away. "You don't think I can't see that? Does this look like a place where dragons even stay?"

"I agreed to help find Anza because Rafik was my friend, too. I didn't agree just so you can snap at me every time we don't find her."

"I'm sorry, Ziri." Kryn said, the flame protecting her now diminishing, crawling back into the palm of her hand. "I thought we would have found her by now."

"Do we even know if Dragon's Roost is a real place? Or the real name of it?" Ziri suggested for the millionth time.

And for the millionth time Kryn shrugged. "I don't know. But that's all we have to go on. Would Gorik make this up in his last breath?"

"I didn't really know him." Ziri said. "Shallon said he mentioned it, though. So, it has to be real."

"Yeah. Some help he was." Kryn spat, clenching her fist. The fire within her wanted to grow and roar back to life thinking of him.

"He said if we figured out this message, he would help us." Ziri said, holding up the letter. Soon after the Sarason Fortress collapsed, and they were scavenging the rubble for Rafik, a crow delivered them this letter. Shallon, who was helping at the time, received one as well from another crow. He soon left, telling them he would help again if they deciphered the message. What confused them both was what was there to decipher? It was a letter from an unknown person, telling a story of how a dog found a treasure during a storm. To Ziri, it seemed like a chapter to a much bigger story. To Kryn, a fairy tale. In either case, neither of them could figure it out. Their only hint came from Shallon. The truth is written in silver. But if that were to mean anything to either of them, the hint was lost.

For two years they scoured the Nyler Peninsula looking for Dragon's Roost or any sign of Anza. They evaded the Kylix, and were soon declared dead, being lost at the battle of the Golden Gate.

"While you're investigating this, I think I'm going to roam the streets more. Maybe I'll get lucky and find something." Ziri suggested.

Kryn nodded. "Don't forget to take the stones."

"Yeah, yeah." Ziri said, already snagging two of the elemental stones. She held up a hand showing the two before disappearing up the stairs and out of the cellar.

The city of Datz was empty. After the fall of Skage few returned to the city. And the ones who did soon left. It had survived countless millennia, even the formation of the Black Wall, but not King Vanarzir's might. Rafik had told Ziri how the

Kylix swept through and took all the children. Those who managed to escape sailed away. As snow drifted down, the ghost town was an eerie place to walk. Night was settling in, and thanks to the twilight glow of the Black Wall, the ruins gave off twisting and unnatural shadows.

By now Ziri was positive Anza wasn't here. Not in Datz, let alone any part of the Nyler Peninsula. Could Gorik have found someplace in the desert? Or did he manage to go somewhere else? He was in Sysinal, after all. And that's bordering the Akitung Jungle. Maybe Dragon's Roost was somewhere around there? Kryn didn't want to hear those suggestions. She was adamant Anza would be here. Though to Ziri, it seemed more like wishful thinking. She was beginning to think Kryn didn't want to leave Datz for another reason. Rafik.

They had grown close in the limited time they knew each other. But being ripped away from family to be trained as killers, one took family where you could find it. And to Ziri, she and Rafik had become family. She was sure Kryn felt the same way. And it was hard letting go of family. Knowing they're gone.

"I need to talk to her." Ziri said to herself. It wasn't healthy to obsess and dwell over something that couldn't be changed. Rafik was dead. And waiting for his ghost to appear wasn't going to bring him back.

Deep in thought, Ziri didn't hear the noises at first. A crashing sound from a nearby tower half toppled over. She jumped back as the door to the tower exploded off its hinges and slammed into the ruined wall across from it, shattering it to pieces. In one hand it enveloped in water. In the other a fist of fire. "Show yourself." She demanded, straining her voice as she spoke in more than a whisper. Her talent of poison left her barely able to speak.

A young man with shoulder length hair stumbled forward. He took three steps, half falling, as if he were drunk, before collapsing to the ground. He groaned, pushing himself up and shaking his head. Ziri hurried over to him. The man got to his feet with wobbly legs and shook his head. He finally noticed Ziri and smiled. "Oh, hello there."

Ziri yelped, shooting a ball of fire at his feet. The boy fell backwards, holding up his hands in surrender, saying something she couldn't hear. "What did you say?"

"I mean no harm." Tragi said. "My name is Tragi. And I'm guessing you're Kryn?"

Ziri glared at him before shooting another fire ball at him, this time at his chest. Tragi rolled out of the way and sprang to his feet. "Did I say something?"

"What makes you think I'm Kryn?" Ziri asked. "What do you want? Shouldn't you be with the Kylix?"

"The fire is a dead giveaway. I don't think anyone else has that talent." Tragi reasoned. "And no. I escaped them. Just like it seems you did, too."

"How come I've never seen you before?"

Tragi glanced at the tower from where he came from. "That's a bit of a long story. Have you seen anyone else around here?"

Ziri glared at him, clenching her fist tighter making the fire glow brighter. "No. Just me."

"Oh no! This isn't good." Tragi gasped. He took a step towards the tower and again Ziri shot a ball of fire at his feet.

"You aren't going anywhere." Ziri said. "What's in that tower?"

"Nothing. Well hopefully nothing. I'm not sure." Tragi said, frowning and holding the back of his head. The look of genuine confusion on his face.

"You're a good actor, I will give you that." Ziri said. "But I can smell a trap a mile away."

"Well, that's nice. Let me know if you sniff out anything. Ya shire, now I sound like my brother." Tragi said.

"What did you say?"

"That I sound like my brother?" Tragi asked.

"Before that."

"Ya shire?" Tragi said. "You're right. I'm so sorry. I shouldn't be cursing in front of women. That was incredibly rude of me. I'm sorry to have offended you."

"Where did you hear that?"

"I was raised with manners, ma'am. Not to mention you have me outmatched with your fire. Kind of don't want to upset you." Tragi said, holding up his hands.

"No. Ya shire. That's not a common phrase." Ziri said.

"Oh." Tragi blushed. "From a friend of mine. I think you know him. Rafik. He told me all about you, Kryn."

"You're lying." Ziri said. "Rafik is dead."

"Well, not when I saw him last." Tragi said. "He should be around here somewhere."

"Rafik is dead!" Ziri repeated, shooting fire at Tragi. "You're a Kylix spy come to find us."

"Us?" Tragi asked. "I thought you said it was just you?"

Ziri didn't answer. In one hand she let out a stream of fire, while in the other a torrent of water, tackling Tragi to the ground.

"Fire and water?" Tragi gasped. "How is that possible?" He raised his hands in surrender as Ziri raised hers for a finishing blow. The next moment she was tackled, the elemental stones clattering to the ground and out of reach.

"See what happens when I'm not around?" Xeo asked, getting to his feet.

Ziri glared at Xeo, kicking his shins as she scrambled to her feet. She lunged forward, snatching the firestone and blasting the two brothers.

"Whoa, Kryn!" Xeo said, holding up his hands. "We're friends of Rafik."

Ziri got to the waterstone, blasting them both. As she dived into an alleyway and the brothers ran for cover. This wasn't good. Some Kylix spies had finally found them. And worse, they claimed Rafik was alive. She was positive Kryn would fall for this, and she had to be found and warned before it was too late.

Rafik was crying. He stood in the middle of his home he had nicknamed The Nest. The pile of blankets was still huddled by the fire. The fireplace cold and lifeless. Behind him was the blanket covering the only room in this small home, his parents' bedroom. The last time he was here he heard Anza giggling as she and their mother talked. If he had known it was the last time he would have been here, he probably would have joined them rather than skulk off and pout. Everything had a layer of dust and dirt. The windows broken, and a chill air wafted through. This was as much a tomb as anything else. The silence was eerie, and memories of his childhood echoed through his mind like a dream just out of reach from memory.

He was told upon waking up in Mahparry that Anza was gone. Several nights he would cry, missing his family, wishing Anza were still alive. Seeing The Nest empty, devoid of any sort of life or happiness, it finally hit him. He was alone. "I'm sorry, Anza." He whispered softly, choking back tears. "I tried to find you and save you. I failed. I'm not going to fail again."

Rafik tightened his fists, clenching his jaw. The tears stopped and his brow creased. This was King Vanarzir's fault. If the Kylix hadn't come, they wouldn't have had to escape. She wouldn't have gotten lost in that tower. He knew Vanarzir had done terrible things, but this was it. His reason for joining a war in a much larger world than he ever knew existed. And he was going to find Vanarzir and make him pay.

A bright light caught his attention out of the corner of his eye. Out the window, for the briefest of moments, he thought he saw a flash of fire. Puzzled, he turned and watched, waiting for it to happen again. It didn't take long. Moments later a plume of fire erupted into the sky. "Kryn?" He hurried out the creaking door and ran towards the fire. If, anything else, there was life still in Datz, and he had to find it.

He dashed through the ruins of Datz. What may seem like a labyrinth of road and ruin to outsiders, he knew like the back of his hand. Even after being gone for two years. Rafik weaved through one street, darting down an alley before popping out onto another road. He was getting close. He could hear it. Sounds of two men yelling, and grunts of somebody attacking. It had to be Kryn. Who else had the talent of fire? But why would she be here?

The men shouted for her to stop, but another blast of fire lit up the darkening sky. Winter had settled early in the City of Ruins. Snow drifted down from the Black Wall, and a gnawing chill crept through him. The freezing wind wasn't blowing hard, but still packed a bite that tore through his clothes. If it wasn't Kryn, maybe he could at least convince the person to keep them warm until morning, and then go their separate ways. He didn't want to disturb the memorial that was The Nest.

Rafik turned the corner, confident he would find the battle, but nothing was there. He saw the scorch marks, and the familiar patterns in the ground of a struggle. It seemed like one person was chasing two. Where they were he wasn't sure. Everything was quiet now. The fighting, the fire. All of it gone. If it weren't for the burn marks, he would have thought he imagined it all. A phantom of his past. His last day in Datz before his return.

He knelt, examining the hints of the chase.

"What's your problem?" A familiar voice said behind him, though the sword at his neck kept him from spinning around instantly.

Rafik held his breath. Not because of the sword, but from the voice. Could it be? He raised his hands, slowly inching back to his feet. All the while the sword didn't leave his throat. "Of all the things you could have said." Rafik finally said. The sword left his neck. It was a moment later he was brave enough to turn around.

He recognized her instantly. The intensity in her green eyes. Her dirty blond hair. The slender nose. More than once, he dreamed of her while in Mahparry, and never thought he would see her again. "Kryn." He said before throwing himself into her arms. He felt Kryn lunge slightly forward, believing she was about to do the same. The two held each other, not saying a word for what seemed like a lifetime.

Kryn finally broke off the hug, pushing Rafik, and slapping him. Without saying a word, she turned and walked away.

"What was that for?" Rafik asked.

She gave him an obscene gesture with her hand but continued walking away.

"Wait, Kryn!" Rafik shouted, running to catch up with her. "What's wrong?" When she didn't stop Rafik stepped in front of her, holding her shoulders and forcing her to.

"What's wrong?" Kryn spat, holding in a laugh. "What's wrong? For two years everyone said you were dead. And I didn't believe it. For two years I've been trying to find your sister and secretly hoping you're still alive one day. And then I finally do see you, huddled in the middle of a street, and acting like nothing is wrong? What's wrong with me? What's wrong with you? Where have you been? Why show up now? What do you want? How dare you leave in the first place! How dare you leave! We were a team and you just left! And you expect everything to be how it was? It's been two years, Rafik! Two years! Where have you been? Why did you go? Why did you leave me?" The last question wasn't in anger like the rest of her rant. She burst into tears.

Rafik pulled her into his chest. "I'm so sorry, Kryn. I'm so sorry. If it means anything, I missed you. Thought about you a lot. I wasn't allowed to leave."

"Where were you?" Kryn asked through sobs.

"I wish I could tell you."

"Why can't you?"

Rafik paused before answering. Technically he never promised. He was just ordered not to. By an ancient king over a race of bird-like men who had the power over the elements. It probably wasn't best to test them. "I promised." He answered.

"Did you escape? Was it Skage? Is he still alive?" Kryn asked.

Rafik smiled. "I think we have a lot of catching up to do. Are you with anyone?"

Kryn nodded. "Follow me. You may be able to explain a couple guests we ran into."

Rafik didn't think he would ever see this room again. It was the cellar he and Anza had found with the wardrobe in it. Where everything started. Beside the cellar he smirked, seeing Xeo and Tragi tied up, sitting on either side. In front of the armoire was

Ziri. She looked just as he remembered, though slightly taller. "Hey Ziri." He smiled.

"Rafik?" Ziri gasped in her version of a yell. She leaped forward, wrapping her arms around Rafik, burying herself into his shoulder. "Is this really you?"

"It's me, Ziri." Rafik said, returning the hug. "It's so good to see you."

"I've missed you. We thought you were dead." Ziri said.

"I hate to break up the reunion, but does somebody want to untie us?" Xeo said, holding up his hands that were bound together.

"I'm surprised they caught you." Rafik laughed. "How many Immortals could you fight off?"

"Immortals?" Kryn and Ziri said in unison.

"Yeah, well, the blonde ambushed us. They both can shoot fire. And the redhead has the power over water, too." Xeo said.

Rafik laughed. "The element stones?"

Ziri smiled and nodded. "We have those and the bag. Gorik gave them to us before he died."

"It sounds like we have a lot to talk about." Rafik said, kneeling and untying Tragi. Kryn leaned over and singed the rope keeping Xeo bound. He jumped to his feet, holding up his fists ready for a fight.

"Relax, tiger." Kryn laughed. "Who are these two, Rafik?"

"We can speak for ourselves, thank you." Xeo said.

"Then stop arguing about it and tell us who you are." Kryn snapped.

"I apologize for my brother's manners." Tragi said, massaging his wrists. "I am Tragi, and that is my twin brother Xeo. Both from Kristol."

"Wait." Kryn paused. "The Xeo? The one who dueled the king, almost won, and disappeared. The one everyone believes now to be dead or didn't exist at all."

Xeo flashed a grin of overconfidence. "The very same. I would have won, too, if Tragi didn't pull me away from it. And, as you can tell, I'm still alive."

"He just pushed you into a fire. If I didn't you would have died." Tragi argued. "We've been through this. I think we started off on the wrong foot. I thought you were Kryn. Seeing her now, I know I was wrong. It was the fire that made me think you were her. I'm guessing you're Ziri?"

Ziri nodded. "That was the plan. Just in case we ran into any Kylix. Though most don't come around here anymore."

"Why not?" Rafik asked.

"The peninsula is empty." Kryn answered. "After the Sarason Fortress collapsed the Kylix swept through here. Anyone up here was sent away, either voluntarily or by force. From Kristol to Datz, it's a ghost town. We evaded them, all the while trying to find Dragon's Roost."

"What? Like an actual dragon's roost?" Rafik asked. "I've never heard of that place.

Kryn frowned, Ziri lowered her head looking defeated. "When Gorik was dying he said Anza is safe there. We just don't know where that is."

"Anza is alive?" Rafik gasped. "That's impossible."

"Just like it wasn't possible for you to survive." Kryn said.

"No. I met a life tracker." Rafik said. "He said he couldn't sense her."

"Maybe he was making that up." Xeo suggested. "It was Sayros, after all."

"Who?" Ziri asked.

"Somebody we aren't allowed to talk about." Tragi said, raising his eyebrows and giving his brother and Rafik a look. "I've never heard of Dragon's Roost."

"Tell me everything." Rafik said. "I can find her. She needs me."

Chapter 5: Frozen in Time

Dragon's Roost, Biodlay Desert, Alutopek

Anza quietly closed another book. She had lost count on how many she had read. Some were more boring than others. She had read histories of the Silver Council, books about herbs and other plants and their medicinal purposes, even a handful of spell books. It wasn't as exciting as it sounded. Though she read them all, it was Izamar's strict instruction to not be practicing anything while trapped within the portrait and mirrors. If any of the mirrors cracked, or the picture frame she came from dislodges from the wall, she could be gone forever. With all this knowledge just at her fingertips, though, she didn't want to read another book. Amazingly, she could remember every page, every word. The warnings and consequences of everything. Before she was stuck in here, she always had a good memory and inquisitive mind, but nothing like this.

She stared across the room to the reflection peering between books. The wizard clad in gray was thumbing through a book before placing it back on the shelf and starting another. This was his library, in the heart of his secret stronghold of Dragon's Roost, a lone mountain in the middle of the Biodlay Desert. Though he had died centuries if not millennia ago, she wasn't sure, thanks to the Mentor's Mirror and his enchanted library, he could spend his afterlife reading these ancient tomes. Every wall of this library had a mirror on it, even if it was behind the dozens of bookcases. This allowed the two to wander the room within its reflection and interact with everything within. If it weren't for this, she was positive she would have gone crazy being cooped up in the picture frame long ago.

Just above one of the mirrors was an empty portrait. The necromancer, Skage, had tricked her, and swapped places with her. This left her a prisoner within the portrait while he roamed free. And who knows how long that had been. Time was peculiar here. She had read who knows how many books now. But it still felt like not even an hour had passed by. Yet in the next moment it seemed as if a lifetime had already come and gone. And if the latter were true, she hadn't aged a bit. But if it was more like just a moment, how could she have read so much?

"I'm assuming you don't want to leave anymore?" A deep voice growled, pulling Anza away from her thoughts.

"What?" Anza asked, shaking her head. She was staring off into space, slowly realizing Izamar was speaking to her. Beneath his gray, wide brimmed, floppy hat, was his old and gnarled face. Bushy gray eyebrows almost hiding his eyes, and a bulbous nose that capped a long gray beard. "I'm sorry. No. I do. Trust me, I do. Was just thinking."

"Something you read disturb you?" The wizard asked, changing his tone to that of concern.

"No. Well, kind of. More like everything I've read has me wondering." Anza said.

"And what's that?"

"How long has it been since I've been down here?"

The wizard stroked his beard and let out a hum before answering. "You know, Anza, I don't rightly know. Time works differently for you."

"What do you mean?"

"I discovered the portrait of Skage while trying to find him. The likeness to him was uncanny. I didn't think it was him, but I wasn't certain. So, I hid it within the endless bag, in front of the Mentor's Mirror." Izamar began to explain. "What you have explained to me, it seems like Skage either created this to prolong his life and escape punishment or found this and switched places with whatever was inside. In either case, he was frozen in time until he got out. And now you have that fate. You are still as old, or as young, as healthy, or as sick, as you were when you got in there. So, everything that transpires between now and when you get out will be as if it happened in a blink of an eye."

"I could be stuck in here for as long as he was and not even realize it?" Anza asked, mouth agape, her face losing color.

Izamar nodded. "Unless we find a way to get you out, it's entirely possible."

"What about Gorik and Rafik? Will I see them again?"

Izamar frowned. "I'm sorry, little one. I don't know the answer to that. It could only be a few minutes since Gorik left Dragon's Roost."

"Or a couple centuries." Anza said, staring at the pile of books she had read.

"Yes, or a couple centuries." Izamar agreed.

"I need to find a way to get out of here."

"Yes." Izamar laughed. "Now you understand."

Anza fought back tears. There wasn't a point to crying in here. The only person that could save her was already trying. Before she was reading haphazardly. To pass the time until Gorik and Rafik returned. But maybe she shouldn't be waiting for them? Maybe she could do it herself. As she picked up another book and read the title 'Practical Uses of Magic,' she interrupted Izamar's reading. "If I find a spell or something to help me escape, will I be able to use the magic?"

Izamar glanced up from his own book with a wicked smile. "I won't let you practice magic in here and potentially break this little reflection world, so I will be doing the magic. But, once you're out, I don't doubt you will."

"I don't have any talent." Anza said. "Not like Rafik."

"Magic is a funny thing." Izamar sighed. "It's all around us. The air we breathe, the lives we interact with, and the land we touch. Even between your toes, magic is hiding. Yet, if you don't know how to access it, magic will never be found. It's like the air we breathe. We know it's there, but we rarely see it."

"So, if I read these books, I could do magic?"

"With a good enough teacher to properly educate you, without a doubt." Izamar said. "Magic touches others in different ways. There's the Fohdorsha, or Dragonborn. Said to be descendants of dragons themselves, magic comes naturally to them. Then there are those with talent. Also, the Immortals, who can master a certain ability or element. After that are the ones who are born to be natural magic users. Unlike Immortals or the Fohdorsha, they must study and work for their magic abilities. These are the Bordin."

"Bordin?" Anza asked. "I've never heard that word before."

"Bordin is from the ancient language. It means regular, non-magical people." Izamar said.

"Oh." Anza frowned.

Izamar laughed. "Even Bordin can learn magic. Look at me for example. It takes a lot of time, decades even, to learn certain spells or potions. Because of this, most just focus on one type of magic or another. Others attempt more. The only problem with Bordin magic users is once magic is used it needs to be replenished. You can't use it constantly like those with talent or the Fohdorsha. And just like people who are drawn to cooking, crafting, or sailing, some are drawn to magic. And they excel at it more than others."

"Do you think I'm drawn to it?"

"I do." Izamar smiled.

"If Rafik can have talent, I'm going to be the best witch Alutopek has ever seen." Anza said, eagerly yanking another book off the shelf and opening it with such force she nearly ripped off the cover. She skimmed the first page and glanced at a hand drawn picture of a pair of hands holding long needles. A long strand of yarn dangled between them. "Um, Izamar. I don't think this is a book on magic." She turned the book back to the cover. 'Knitting for beginners. The magical craft.' On the inside of the cover Anza noted the name, Haxama of Drugahn. "And who is Haxama?"

"Who?" The gray wizard asked, striding over to Anza. His face soured with every step. "I personally added every book into this library. I know every tome and every author. Knitting?" He picked up the book and tossed it onto the floor. "This is a study of magic. Not needle craftwork. Though some works knitters make I'd say can be argued of some sort of magic. Twisting yarns to create is an art that often baffles me."

"Oh, come on, Izamar. I'm sure you can knit a wonderful sweater." Anza teased, suppressing a laugh.

"I do, actually." Izamar smiled. "Enchanting needles to do the work for me, I've knitted plenty of sweaters in my time. But I don't recall this book. And my skill with the cursed needles is beyond beginners to be needing this book. Let's see…Haxama. Haxama? Of Drugahn." He scratched his chin and stroked his beard, his eyes staring off into the distance. To a time long ago, well before Anza, or her parents. Before the Black Wall, even.

"It's alright if you can't remember. I have a hard time remembering things sometimes, too." Anza said.

"A good witch or wizard never forgets." Izamar snapped. "Ah, yes! Haxama. She was a young girl in the town of Drugahn. Very superstitious place. If you visit there make sure you carry a piece of silver on you at all times."

"Why?"

Izamar shrugged. "The reasoning has been long forgotten. The townsfolk are caught up in not having bad luck they have strange rituals and traditions even they don't understand. But silver is regarded as a pure metal, even holy at times. I wouldn't be surprised if it stemmed from that. I wonder, if I got her book, which of mine does she have?"

Chapter 6: Making a Plan

Datz, Nyler Peninsula, Alutopek

Rafik stared into the Pond of Memories. It was in the center of town, and once a great temple. After an earthquake, before the Black Wall, it collapsed and flooded, becoming this ruin. The people of Datz memorialized it, and it was then known as the Pond of Memories. A reverent place. A place to reflect and ponder one's life. The night before this whole adventure began, he was here to remember the loss of his father. And after the Kylix attacked the City of Ruins, he and others escaped by diving into the depths of the pond. It was a peculiar feeling, being back here. Alone.

Now he sat beside a crackling fire, and just learned Anza was still alive. Gorik's last words were to Kryn, telling her of Dragon's Roost. He never mentioned that place before. But he never mentioned he was part of some sort of rebellion either. Something Kryn and Ziri learned from Shallon soon after the battle at the Sarason Fortress. How much did he actually know about his uncle and father's best friend?

After hearing what had transpired in the last two years, Rafik excused himself from the group and came here. He had agreed to stay in Mahparry because his family was gone. Anger, sadness, confusion, and happiness swirled within him. His body shook, and his grin changed from a smile to a scowl in an instant. The tears streaming down his face he wasn't sure if it was for him, Anza, or the entire situation. Let alone if they were tears of happiness. Yes, it's great she's alive. But she's been alone for two years. How could he forgive himself for that? Forgetting her and trying to move on.

"Need some company?" Ziri asked, startling Rafik out of his well of emotions.

"No, not really." Rafik answered bluntly. He wiped away tears that were drying on his face.

"Oh." Ziri said, pausing midmovement. She finally sat cross-legged next to her friend and let out a long sigh. Snow drifted down above, melting as the flames lashed at them. Her breath tinted red, noting the poison that was within her. "I think when somebody says that that's when they need somebody the most."

Rafik shook his head. "I can't believe she's alive. What am I going to do?"

"What you've done since I've met you." Ziri replied, a slight smile creeping in on the edges of her face.

"What do you mean?"

"Since I've met you all you've wanted was to save your sister. At the same time, you've wanted to stop King Vanarzir like so many others. You have a good heart. You didn't even lie when it would have saved your life during Salina's trial." Ziri explained.

"I feel like I'm being pulled in two different directions." Rafik said, reaching out and poking at the campfire with a stick. The flames crackled and burst, sending ash to mix with the snow as sticks collapsed. "I need to go with Xeo and Tragi. We were trained to fight and stop the king. But I can't leave Anza behind."

"Do you know where Dragon's Roost is?"

"I've never even heard of it." Rafik said.

"Exactly. So why punish yourself staying here, wondering what to do? We can join the rebellion and stop the king, maybe find Dragon's Roost along the way. Maybe find somebody who knows the place. For all we know, Gorik could have sent her away."

"What do you mean?"

"Gorik's your uncle. And if he cared about Anza even half as much as you do, do you think he would keep her nearby while fighting a necromancer and his minions?" Ziri asked.

Rafik smiled. "No. He would try to keep her safe. Even if she wanted to fight."

"We met with Gorik in Sysinal just before the battle. Anza wasn't with him. At least that Kryn or I noticed. And to hear he was part of a rebellion? Maybe he had contacts and sent Anza away. Who knows, we could have passed her while on the Eko River. She could be with the Fohdorsha."

"You think so?"

Ziri shrugged. "We know she's not in the Nyler Peninsula, at least, that's for sure. But if she's in a place called Dragon's Roost, maybe we should start searching where the people of dragons live?"

"And that's going to be where King Vanarzir attacks since he didn't two years ago!" Rafik said, his voice rising and smile growing. "Ziri, you're a genius!" He jumped to his feet, brushing himself off. "We should get going!"

Ziri looked up at Rafik, noting his smile and the light in his eyes returning. That was the Rafik she remembered. "I think we need to figure out how to get there first. And maybe wait until morning when it isn't as freezing." She poked at the dying fire, now mostly glowing embers.

"We should probably leave the fires to Kryn." Rafik suggested.

"Unless we have an elemental stone." Ziri said, opening one of her hands to reveal the reddish orange stone. Wisps of fire glowed within.

"You had that, and didn't use it?"

"We were having a moment. Didn't want to ruin it by shooting fire from my hands because your fire kindling skills need work." Ziri smirked.

Rafik laughed, helping his friend to her feet. "Let's go tell the others we have a plan." As the two walked away from the pond Rafik glanced up, noting his favorite constellation of Quellor, and silently promising he would find Anza.

The group wasn't sure when King Vanarzir would begin his attacks again. But the two years were up, so it was only a matter of time. Where would he strike first? According to Kryn, he sent her aunt and others to build a fortress in Syro. Maybe the Kylix will sail there and spread across eastern Alutopek southward like a plague? The home to the Kylix, in Haitu, was on the Eko River. They could sail eastward and spread from there? Or head south to the Bomoku Mountains? Xeo even suggested going from

Safsil or Grahtem in the Ohmrang Fields, onto Fang-Elsea Island and eastward across the Fohdorshan lands.

"I think we can agree we have no idea what his plan is, or where he'll start." Rafik said.

"Or where the rebellion will meet him." Kryn added.

"How about we don't make our plan off of that." Tragi suggested.

"What do you mean?" Xeo asked.

The group huddled around the map of Alutopek, tracing their fingers here and there as they suggested plan after plan. But without knowing King Vanarzir's, nobody could agree on where to go. Tragi reached towards Datz, tapping it on the map. "We're here. And the king is going to attack somewhere here." He circled the entirety of eastern and southern Alutopek. "We don't know where he is, but we need to get out of here first. Our plan should be how do we get to one of those places."

Xeo nodded. "That's smart. I think the easiest would be to sail. We could leave Datz and go towards the Akitung Jungle."

Rafik shook his head. "In ancient days, that could work. There are so many sunken ruins surrounding Datz now, it's nearly impossible to sail around. We would need my uncle's chart showing everything. Did he give you that?"

Kryn shook her head. "I don't think so."

"Ya shire." Rafik cursed. "I know how to get us to the Golden Gate, at least. We could go there, use the Eko River and head south to the Bomoku Mountains. That might be smarter than randomly choosing a spot to cross the river and hope we run into them."

"The Golden Gate is crawling with Kylix soldiers now." Kryn said. "And they think we're all dead. We should probably keep it that way."

"I guess that only gives us one option. To head west." Tragi said, tracing his finger along a path from Datz, to the Bruin Fortress, and into the Biodlay Desert.

"That's a lot of walking." Kryn groaned.

"We could run?" Xeo laughed. "That would be less walking."

"You're not helping." Tragi said.

"It was a joke." Xeo argued, shoving his brother.

"Hey!" Kryn shouted, snapping her fingers, a small flame sparking to life for an instant. "Don't make me separate you two."

"Sorry, Mom." Xeo said.

Kryn glared at Xeo.

"That could work." Rafik said, ignoring the argument. "We could go to the Bruin Fortress, sneak around, and head west, going along the foothills of the Gateway Mountains. Nobody has used that path since ancient times, so it should be unguarded. When we make it to Lynn, we could find somebody to help us get to the Bomoku Mountains."

"I second this idea." Ziri said almost the instant Rafik had finished speaking. It was the first time any of them could agree on anything.

Kryn studied the map before finally nodding. "I think this is our best option. There isn't as many Kylix there, at least."

"Let's go!" Tragi and Xeo said at the same time.

As first light hit the Black Wall the five had packed and were leaving. Having the bag with a secret room came in handy, as most things were stored in there. Kryn even collected the chains and locks of the wardrobe before departing. Rafik took one last look of his home, the City of Ruins. He wasn't sure when or if he would be back. It was a somber walk, going through the streets as they made their way to the city gates.

The nickname of Datz was aptly named. As ruins littered the city. Toppled towers, burned buildings, and ravaged roads were everywhere. To Rafik, it was home. Memories flooded him from every direction. Some good, some bad. His heart felt as if it was in his stomach as he made his way through. But to the rest of the group, it was a maze of destruction. A land that should be left to rot.

Rafik noted the cursed forest, just beyond Datz. Said to have the spirit of an angry vengeful child guarding over it. Tragi suggested to keep to the shore for as long as possible to not get lost.

"I can't get lost here." Kryn boasted. "Last two years searching for Anza, I know this place better than my own home now, I reckon."

"I didn't explore much of the peninsula." Rafik said. "I preferred sailing and playing in the ruins."

"Tragi and I didn't make it out this far either." Xeo said. "We hunted in a forest near our home called Fogwood. Farthest we made it was Kirahka La Bruna Ruins. Remember that place, Tragi?"

"Of course I do. That's where you dueled the king and I had to save you." Tragi said.

"No, before that." Xeo laughed, ignoring the part where he had to be saved.

"Oh, yeah. Kay was so angry with us. Instead of helping tend the farms, fields, and orchards, we sneaked off."

"Who is Kay? And what are those ruins?" Ziri asked. "Kryn and I saw those but didn't really explore them. The place made my skin crawl."

"Kay is our sister." Tragi said. "Valkayto is her full name. I hear she's queen now. Not sure how or why that happened."

"We'll figure that out when we talk to her." Xeo said, sounding annoyed. It was obvious this conversation had played out countless times between them. "The Kirahka La Bruna Ruins are a forbidden place."

"Why?" Kryn asked.

"It's said when an army marched on Queen Kristol she convinced the wildlife to attack them. All that remained were their camps they had made to last the winter. Everyone within the camps were either dead or turned to stone." Xeo said.

"And the ruins are now guarded by bears. Monstrous bears that could fight dragons, according to legend." Tragi added.

"Is that why Bruin Fortress is called Bruin?" Kryn asked. "For the bears?"

Xeo nodded. "Bears used to be everywhere in the Nyler Peninsula."

The winter storm came in waves. For several hours, the snow would spin and swirl through the air, blocking their vision. Then the next little while it would drift slowly through the air, like feathers, becoming a calmer wintry snowscape. The snow didn't stop, and it didn't take long for the group to be trudging through mounds of snow, then the sands of a beach and rocky, uneven paths on foothills.

As night crept in, the darkness grew colder. Every breath felt like needles. An eerie fog, with the tinge of violet swirled around the group, making their path harder to see. It was agreed that as soon as it got dark, Rafik would hang the endless bag on a tree branch, and they would all climb in for the night. It was much warmer, drier, and everyone could sleep at once instead of taking turns standing guard. Rafik would stare at the wall where the mirror used to be. The mirror and portrait of Skage were gone. According to Kryn and Ziri they never saw them. To Rafik, that was more evidence Ziri was right. Gorik must have sent Anza away, and with those two things to keep out of Skage's hands.

By the fifth day of constant walking the storm had finally passed. Where the wind blew the snow brushed away from the road to either side, creating large banks like a miniature canyon. It was easier to walk on these paths, but they learned the hard way it wasn't easy to get out of. It was during a lull of conversation between the five, about to turn a corner, when they heard voices.

"Hide." Tragi whispered, climbing one of the snowbanks. He kicked and flailed, finally making it to the top before disappearing to the other side. Xeo helped Ziri over, and then Kryn. Rafik and Xeo jumped and scrambled, just making it over the edge as Kylix soldiers came into view.

The soldiers, resembling walking skeletons, held a spear in one hand, and a shield in the other. If they noticed any disturbed snow, they didn't stop to investigate. The four soldiers continued walking, laughing, and joking about how easy their position was.

"That was close." Tragi said, once the soldiers were out of earshot.

"I thought you said there weren't any Kylix soldiers here." Xeo said, glaring at Kryn.

"No, I said there aren't as many." Kryn answered, returning the glare.

"Do you still have your armor?" Rafik asked, looking from Ziri to Kryn.

The two shook their heads. "After we learned they thought we were dead, we sank them. Our armor is somewhere in the Tahlbiru." Kryn explained. "Why?"

"If you did, you two could sneak through." Rafik said. "Scout ahead, maybe find a safe route for the rest of us to go around."

"We can just sneak around once it's night." Xeo suggested.

"Simple." Kryn said.

"What's wrong with simple?" Xeo snapped.

"If you would let me finish," Kryn said. "Simple, but not a bad idea."

"Oh. Ugh...thanks." Xeo stammered.

"I could turn you all in." Tragi suggested. "I have the markings of a peacekeeper. They wouldn't think much of it."

"And then what?" Rafik asked. "The plan was to avoid as many Kylix as possible. Why get caught now?"

"He'll leave us to rot." Kryn said.

"Hey!" Xeo and Tragi said in unison.

"I take offense to that. He wouldn't leave me behind. Being his twin brother." Xeo said, puffing out his chest. "The rest of you...maybe."

"I'm not planning on abandoning anyone." Tragi said. "I could release you all, and we could take the fortress. I'm a peacekeeper, so they won't find it suspicious I'm not part of the Kylix and turning you in."

"We aren't staying." Rafik said. "Why would we take something we have no intention of holding?"

"It could draw more Kylix soldiers here." Tragi said. "Possibly even the king. It would give us time to get ahead of him."

"Or just waste time taking over an outpost that isn't necessary in this war. The Nyler Peninsula is abandoned. There's nothing up here." Kryn said.

Rafik held his chin, staring towards where the Kylix soldiers had come from. The Bruin Fortress was nearby. They could easily maneuver around it like Xeo suggested. Tragi's plan offered something else. They could find out where King Vanarzir is. "We'll do both, Xeo's and Tragi's." Rafik finally said. "We'll use the chains Kryn grabbed from the wardrobe, and Tragi will take Ziri and I into the fortress. Xeo and Kryn, you scout on ahead. If we're not back with you by the end of the day, come rescue us because something must have gone wrong."

"Are you sure that's smart, splitting up?" Ziri asked.

Rafik nodded. "I'm not saying we can take the fortress, but I think we could be a thorn in their side. Ziri with your talent you could make people think there is a sickness. We can discover Vanarzir's plans, and escape."

"As long as I'm not the one in chains, I like this plan." Xeo laughed.

Chapter 7: The Ally in the Dungeon

Bruin Fortress, Nyler Peninsula, Alutopek

"I don't like this." Ziri whispered, glancing down at her hands now bound in chain. It was already freezing before, but the snow and cold winds made her hands numb. Much longer of this and she would be happy to be near the fires within the Bruin Fortress, regardless of company.

"Probably not the smartest plan." Rafik said. The chains were bound by the enchanted locks. Testing them didn't summon a spirit of the person tied to them like when Rafik had first unlocked them, but they still unlocked without a key. It would be easy for them to escape, even if things didn't go according to plan.

"Maybe we should have just walked around." Ziri said.

"If we did that, we wouldn't get the chance to find out what King Vanarzir is doing." Rafik said, mentioning it more to himself than anybody in particular.

"Trust me." Tragi said. "It'll be fine. I promise."

"That's easy for you to say. You aren't in chains." Ziri said. She raised her hands and clanged the chains together.

"If you want to spend hours training to become a peacekeeper, and then several more hours in silence as you get tattooed, dot by dot. Be my guest." Tragi said. "Until then, we each have our role to play, and unfortunately yours is the prisoner."

"Still easy for you to say." Ziri said.

Before either could respond the three turned a bend in the road and saw the fortress. The wall was built in two parts. The lower half was of stone and said to have deep dungeons beneath. The upper half, thick pines ending in points giving the fortress the appearance of a fanged lower jaw. In the center of the fortress was a single tower. Even from here guards could be seen leaning up against a mound of logs used for a call for help if lit. To Rafik's knowledge, the beacon had never been lit.

As the three approached a horn sounded and the Kylix soldiers on guard duty straightened up. They counted about a dozen soldiers. If Ziri could poison even just a quarter of them, it should cause enough panic they could escape.

Tragi raised his hands, signaling his peace and surrender. "Hello!" He hollered to the soldiers atop the wall.

"Are you lost, child?" One soldier asked.

Tragi smiled. "No, quite the opposite, really. I hear King Vanarzir is collecting children for his army, is that not correct?"

"It is." The soldier replied.

"I'm a Rhine-Pa peacekeeper. Been traveling through this land for nearly two years now searching for lost souls." Tragi explained. "About to give up when I came across these two. They put up a bit of a fight, but in the end, I got them subdued."

"And why shouldn't we be taking you, too?" The soldier asked. "I've never met a peacekeeper that young. And if you aren't one, then you belong in the army as well."

Tragi lowered the hood of his robe and turned around, moving his hair to the side. The tops of the insignia could just be noticed on the nape of his neck. "If you want a better look, I can show you, but I assure you, I have gone through initiation."

The soldiers disappeared behind the wall without saying another word. A moment later the rickety gates opened. Rafik sighed. "Are you ready?"

Ziri nodded.

"You must be one of the youngest peacekeepers in history." A Kylix soldier said, removing his skull helmet. He was a balding man, his cheeks sagging. "Thought there was a rule or something about that."

Tragi smiled and shook his head. "No rule. My name is Tragi."

"Commander Yomin. And these two are?" He added after Tragi shook his hand but didn't mention the prisoner's names.

Tragi laughed. "I didn't care to ask. Saw these two wandering about, and to my knowledge the king wants children to raise in his army."

Commander Yomin nodded. "Raising children to be soldiers, instead of taking men in. Who knows, maybe in 20 years it'll be worth it. Just seems silly now."

"Are you not enforcing it?" Tragi asked, eyebrows raised.

"You may be a peacekeeper, monk, but I won't have you be questioning my loyalty under my own house." Commander Yomin snapped, his sagging jowls waving back and forth as he shook his head.

"I apologize, Commander." Tragi said. "That wasn't my intention. Just never heard a soldier talk about it like that before."

Commander Yomin grumbled, cursing under his breath. "Tell me, peacekeeper, where did you find them?"

"In the ruins of Datz. That place is like a labyrinth. No wonder they were able to hide." Tragi said, glaring at Rafik and Ziri.

"I see." Commander Yomin said. "And you, peacekeeper, where do you come from?"

"Originally Kristol, from what I'm told. I've spent quite some time away from there becoming a peacekeeper, not sure if I can still call it home." Tragi sighed.

As if satisfied by the answer, Commander Yomin nodded and smiled. "Well, I'll have my men take these two into the dungeons. They'll be carted off soon enough to where they belong. You can spend the night here, peacekeeper, but you must leave in the morning."

"Your generosity is more than I could have wished." Tragi said, bowing his head. He winked at Rafik before walking away in step with the commander.

Rafik and Ziri were shoved from behind, being told to 'get moving.' More than once they were shoved and jabbed in the shoulder or back if they went the wrong way. Rafik bit his tongue, wanting to tell them it would be easier to be led to where they needed to go instead of assuming they knew. He glanced over at Ziri who seemed to be sharing the same thought.

The Bruin Fortress was mostly a massive wall, with a courtyard, and a tower in the center. There weren't many places to hide. Coming to the tower there was a second, smaller door beside the main one etched into the stone. Once opened, it led to a darkened stairwell, leading into the bowels of the fortress. The only light came from the torch one of the Kylix soldiers held. The stone stairs extended to the walls of the fortress, and then spiraled downward. With every step it got colder. Before even making it halfway Rafik and Ziri were both shivering.

Finally, at the bottom of the stairs, were rows of cages. At the far end a roaring fire. The nearest of them held food, drink, and supplies the soldiers would need to last the winter. Beyond that were mostly empty cells. Near the fire was a larger cage holding a single prisoner. The Kylix soldier shoved Rafik and Ziri into that cage, and slammed the door shut behind him.

"The prisoner will tell you the rules." The Kylix soldier said before walking off, snagging a bottle of whiskey as he left.

"Did you do it?" Rafik asked, ignoring the prisoner now standing up. The prisoner was nearly as tall as the cage they were in, and large. Every bit of him that he could see in the firelight was hard muscle.

Ziri nodded. "When he first shoved me I was able to. Just a little bit. He should be feeling sick in about an hour."

Rafik smiled. "I guess now we wait for Tragi."

"Are you sure about this plan?"

Rafik shook his head. "No. But, it was worth the risk."

The prisoner laughed. The deep guttural laugh echoed throughout the mostly empty chamber. "Two children planning to escape. Good luck. We're so far down I'm pretty sure we're on the rooftop of Soboribor by now."

"I think we have a lot farther to go before we are in the underworld." Rafik said. "Can't make it too easy for spirits to try and escape."

The prisoner smirked, stepping into the light, revealing an emerald embedded on his right hand and the tattoo of a crescent moon over his left eye. "You have your father's wit, I see."

"Shallon!" Ziri gasped. "How did you end up down here?"

"You knew my father?" Rafik asked.

"I got caught smuggling dransbian steel from the mines. Not sure how long I've been down here." Shallon said. "It's always cold down here."

"We're about to break out." Ziri said. "Will you join us?"

Shallon smiled. "If you manage to break free and escape, I would be happy to join in that adventure. But after, it depends. Where are you going?"

"We're heading south, to the Fohdorshan Lands. Going to see if Vanarzir is there and stop him."

Shallon nodded. "You still haven't figured it out yet."

"Figured what out?" Rafik asked.

"Your uncle told them to read what's written in silver before he died." Shallon said. "I'm assuming you know how to already?"

"I don't know what you're talking about." Rafik said. "Gorik didn't tell me anything. What do you mean what's written in silver? And you knew my father?"

"Gorik didn't tell you anything?" Shallon gasped. "What a shame. And of course, I do. I helped him escape to the island in the Silent Sea."

"He didn't get lost at sea? He's alive!" Rafik gasped. "I knew it! What's he doing there? What should Gorik have told me?"

Shallon opened his mouth and paused. Finally, he spoke. "Your father is resting. Gorik gave you the ink when he died?"

Ziri nodded. "It's still in the bag. We haven't figured it out. And the letter we received didn't make any sense."

"Until you learn what's written in silver, I won't be joining you, nor you me." Shallon said. "But we can work together in breaking out."

If anything more was said, Rafik didn't hear it. His head was spinning. For nine years he believed his father to be dead. Everybody said he was. Even Gorik. And now this stranger of a man claims he knows his father, and helped him to safety? Why would he be resting for so long? Is he hurt that badly? Is he stuck there? Why hadn't Shallon helped him return? Not only was his sister still alive, but his father? Was Dragon's Roost the name of the island? Is that it?

"Where is Dragon's Roost?" Rafik asked, interrupting Shallon and Ziri's argument. She was trying to get more hints about how to read what was written in silver.

Shallon shrugged. "I've never been to that place. Your uncle mentioned it once."

"Is it the name of the island in the Silent Sea?" Rafik suggested.

Shallon shook his head. "Not that I'm aware of. According to legend, that island must never have a name. Giving the island a name will curse you, and anyone with you."

"Why? What's on the island? Never heard of that before." Rafik said.

"Nobody knows. Several different stories about it. But I've met several who did give it a name and died horribly. I'll leave it that way. I intend to die in battle, not by a curse." Shallon said. "Look on every map of Alutopek. Not one gives the island a name. And for good reason."

"So, it isn't Dragon's Roost?" Rafik asked.

"You can call it that if you want to be cursed." Shallon said. "But I never heard of Dragon's Roost until speaking to Gorik two years ago on the outskirts of the Akitung Jungle."

'Maybe it was a secret name that Gorik discovered? My father is there. If Gorik knew he was, maybe that's where he sent Anza. It must be.' Rafik thought to himself.

"When will we know we're breaking out?" Shallon asked.

"The Kylix soldier who took us here, and another who shoved us when we arrived," Ziri started. "I used my talent on them. They should be feeling sick from poison within the hour."

"And that's your plan?" Shallon laughed. "Two soldiers getting sick? They would leave us down here if anything else."

"There's only 12 of them here." Rafik said. "They can't afford two to be sick. And they should realize something is going on."

Shallon lowered his head, putting his fingers between his eyes as if he were hurting from a headache. "You children have a lot to learn. If you see 12 in a fortress manning the walls, it's the general rule to multiply that by three. I know when I was first caught there's at least 50 soldiers here. Two soldiers being sick won't cause any issue. And if they believed you to be the cause, they wouldn't release you. Probably just kill you. You're stuck down here." He shook his head, looking from Ziri to Rafik, letting out a long sigh.

"In our defense," Rafik said, "It wasn't our plan, but Tragi's."

"But you went along with it." Shallon said. "That just makes you a pawn."

Rafik bit his lip, glaring at Shallon. If he had Blaridane with him, he would cut him down where he stood. He could feel the itching, the longing, for the sword. The voice whispered in the corners of his mind, encouraging the violence. He could see it now, Shallon falling to his knees for calling him a pawn. And harboring the secret of his father still being alive! How could he?

Shallon placed his hand on Rafik's shoulder, the emerald atop his hand glowing. "Are you alright?"

"What?" Rafik asked, staring up at the giant as if it was the first time seeing him. "Yeah. Just lost in thought." The sudden urge of anger and violence was gone just as soon as it happened. "We need to find a way to get out of here."

"You shouldn't have allowed yourself to get caught." Shallon said. "Could have just gone around under the cover of darkness."

"We were hoping to get information." Rafik said. "We are going to stop Vanarzir, but don't know where he is."

Shallon nodded. "Well, until you learn to think, going after a king may not be the best idea if you want to live. This wasn't a smart plan."

"Yeah, this is the last time I let myself get caught." Rafik said. "Even if it is supposed to be a trick."

From down the row of cages, into the depths of darkness, a door clanged open. Coughing and vomiting echoed. "And you said it was a dumb plan." Ziri smirked.

Minutes later two Kylix soldiers arrived, Tragi standing between them being dragged. "I didn't do anything!" He shouted. "Let me go!"

The soldier that wasn't sick opened the gate to a cage beside the others and threw Tragi in. "Until you learn to tell the truth, you're staying down here. Peacekeeper or not."

Without another word the two left, the sickly one throwing up at the base of the stairs. "Great job." Shallon said. "I can feel the cool wind of freedom on my face already."

"What happened?" Rafik asked.

"Commander Yomin caught me in a lie." Tragi said. "Couldn't exactly say where I was the last two years."

Rafik nodded. "That's ok. According to Shallon, here, he said our plan wasn't going to work anyway."

Tragi looked up at the giant. He had the tattoo of a crescent moon over one eye. That was the sign he had seen some other peacekeepers wear instead of the tattoo he had on his back. "By the sun I stand guard."

"By the moon I watch over." Shallon said, nodding. "Haven't seen a peacekeeper so young before. My daughter was to be one. Though, that seemed like a whole lifetime ago."

"I'm sorry, friend." Tragi said. "What happened?"

"She was murdered." Shallon said behind gritted teeth.

Rafik looked to Ziri who shrugged her shoulders. "I take it you two know each other?"

"Never met the guy." Tragi replied. "I'm sorry about your daughter. I do have good news, though."

"What's that?"

"The cart that will take you to Haitu should be arriving tomorrow. Apparently, they had sent one for Shallon." Tragi said. "Commander Yomin told me. Not sure if I'll be in that prison wagon, though. Least you three won't be freezing to death down here."

"That's not good news." Ziri grumbled. "I want to be free."

"We'll find a way to escape." Rafik assured Tragi and Ziri. "I promise. And we won't be going to Haitu, either."

"How do you know?" Tragi asked.

Rafik flashed a smile. "Because I say so."

Tragi shook his head. "We're all going to die."

"Yep." Shallon sighed.

Rafik assumed it was nighttime by now. The great fire sitting outside their cages was dying. Shallon said they fed the fire once a day. By the time they would come to rekindle it, nothing but embers would glow in the freezing darkness. It was a deterrent, to help keep the prisoners from escaping, being too cold to move. The door opened above, and an angry howl of wind gushed through the dungeon.

Two soldiers appeared in the dying light, each carrying bowls of food. "Oh, good, I'm starving." Ziri said.

"Don't get too excited." Shallon muttered.

They couldn't smell it until the bowl was under their noses, but Shallon was right. The porridge, if one could call it that, had a foul odor. Like the stench of rotting cabbage mixed with wet dog. It was cold, and the spoon made a disgusting, wet noise as it pushed into the slop. The consistency of their food made Rafik gag. "And you've been eating this?"

Shallon nodded. "It was either this or starve. After starving for so long, it didn't seem so bad."

"This is disgusting." Rafik held the bowl over his head and turned it upside down. The food barely moved within the bowl.

"I never said it's good." Shallon said.

"Never and always —" Rafik started.

"Are two words you always want to remember never to use." Shallon finished. "I know. Your father would say that constantly."

"You knew him?" Tragi asked.

"Oh, yeah." Rafik said. "Turns out he's been on the island in the Silent Sea all this time. Shallon and Gorik just left him there."

"That's good, though, right?" Tragi asked. "You could still see him."

Rafik shrugged. "I don't even know if I want to anymore." On one hand he was ecstatic his father was alive. He could see him again. But on the other, that meant he was gone for nine years. Nine years he chose to be away from his family. Why would he want to see someone who chose to abandon them?

"Oh." Tragi said. "I saw my father die. If I knew he was still alive, I'd want to go to him. No matter what."

"I'm not you!" Rafik shouted. "Can we just change the subject?"

"I'm sorry, Rafik." Shallon said. "I thought Gorik told you."

"No. He didn't tell me. He didn't tell me anything. And now he's gone. My sister is missing. My father is stuck on some island. Hopefully his rest was worth leaving all of us behind. Not like we needed him or anything." Rafik snapped, throwing his bowl of frozen porridge across the cell. The bowl shattered against the bars, and the food fell with an unsettling 'squish' noise. He turned away from the rest, facing the corner, allowing the darkness and dying flames to hide his pain.

"So...any idea when they were supposed to be back? Thought they should have by now." Xeo asked.

Kryn shrugged. "Ziri said her poison would take effect an hour after they got caught and would be out soon after."

"I'm fairly certain it's been longer than that."

"I think so, too." Kryn said. The two had hiked into nearby woods and went around the fortress. They scouted ahead, and didn't notice any other Kylix soldiers, or living person for that matter, on the road. Everything was blanketed in untouched snow. Trees would still tower over the white landscape, but everything else was like a blank canvas. More than once, they had stubbed their toes on buried boulders and walked into ruins. Winter was in full swing in the Nyler Peninsula. It almost seemed unbelievable that a two, or three, day journey south of here it would be a barren and blisteringly hot landscape.

The cold didn't touch Kryn much. It just seemed semi cooler than it usually was. Her talent over fire gifted her an internal furnace that always ran hot. Surviving in the Nyler Peninsula for the last two years in the wilderness proved the cold didn't affect her. At this point she doubted it ever could. Where others shivered and clung to blankets, she put on a light jacket and was already burning up.

Xeo rubbed his arms, taking a deep breath and blowing it out, watching the cloud of air slowly fade into the sky. "Should we go back for them?" He asked.

"I'm not sure." Kryn said. "Maybe they're just biding their time?"

"Or they're in trouble." Xeo said. "We can't leave them to die."

Kryn nodded. "Ya shire. I knew this was a horrible plan."

"Should have gone with mine." Xeo said.

"For once I'm going to say you're right." Kryn said. "It wasn't that bad going around."

"And now we have to go back." Xeo sighed.

"Yep."

"In the snow." Xeo said. "The deep snow."

"Yeah.

"And the freezing winds, making my face and hands numb."

"Yeah."

"I don't want to complain, but…" Xeo trailed off.

"But what? Afraid of getting cold?" Kryn laughed.

"Easy for you to say. You can't get cold." Xeo said.

Kryn smiled. "Yeah. It's pretty nice. When it was just Ziri and I she would stay in this bag while I would take us places if it was cold."

"Well…that sounds cozy." Xeo said.

"She appreciated it. Did all the cooking and cleaning in return. She's a good cook, too."

"Can I ask a favor?"

"You want in the bag?"

Xeo grinned. "If you're offering, I won't say no."

"Alright, but you're helping once we get to the fortress."

"No problem there. I'm not missing a battle. Especially if it's to prove my brother's plan was bad."

"A little bit of sibling rivalry going on?" Kryn laughed, opening the endless bag.

Xeo shrugged and disappeared into the bag before answering.

"Ah, Kryn. You're a saint." Kryn smiled to herself. She closed the bag and began walking back towards the Bruin Fortress. Not taking a circuitous route, she got there faster than she had expected. The wind howled, taking bits of snow along the way. Just from the wind itself one part of the road had nearly cleared, while on the other side it had towered over her. Although she couldn't feel the cold, the chilly wind and snow hitting her face was getting annoying. As her clothes grew wet and freezing in places she closed her eyes, letting the heat from within her radiate outwards. It wasn't long after this her clothes were dry again, only to repeat the process over and over.

The dim light of the Black Wall was fading, showing night was approaching. In the distance, she could see torches being lit on a massive structure. From so far away, it looked like the broken lower jaw of a giant beast. It was the Bruin Fortress she watched her friends voluntarily get captured in earlier that day.

"If I have to save everybody, none of them are letting it down." Kryn said. The bag jostled against her hip as a gust of wind blew from behind her. She let out a deep breath and watched as her puff of air slowly turned into miniature pieces of ice and fell to the ground.

Maybe she didn't need Xeo's help rescuing them? She didn't know Xeo or Tragi very well. All she knew is they had saved Rafik from dying in the Sarason Fortress two years ago and trained with them in a secret place. Before that, Xeo challenged the king to a duel. Depending who you ask, depends on who nearly won. Both were still living, so it obviously wasn't a finished fight. Yet. But he and Tragi both lost to Ziri when they ran into each other. Who knows how great of a fighter he really is?

Kryn glanced up, the light of stars pierced the Black Wall, though she didn't know the constellations like Rafik. They all just looked like dots of light poking through a cloth. And with the Black Wall being there, that was essentially what they were. Were the stars just on the other side of the wall? Or farther away? And where did they go when it was daytime? She had heard stories of some suddenly glimpsing what was beyond the wall. But it happened so fast, according to the witnesses, they could rarely describe what they saw.

She pondered these thoughts, trudging along through the snow towards the fortress. It wasn't much longer before she was screamed at from atop the wall, and she stood before its gate. "What? Oh. Already here." She laughed and craned her neck to see the soldiers leaning over the wall.

"Who are you? What are you doing out here so late?" The Kylix soldier shouted again.

The night was dark, nothing could be seen beyond the rings of light the torches provided. It was like they were all in their own world, separate of everything else. A plain, unimaginative world where the ground was pure white, and sky darkness with beads of light shining through in no discernible pattern. And in front of her was the only structure in this world. A fortress with teeth. "You have my friends." Kryn finally shouted after looking around at this world. "I want them back."

"Who are your friends?" The soldier asked.

"The children that arrived here earlier today." Kryn said. She wasn't sure if they gave fake names or not. "Give them to me, or I'll burn this place to the ground."

The Kylix soldiers laughed. "You? Burn this fortress down? Don't make threats you can't follow through on."

"I didn't." Kryn said.

The soldiers laughed again, dropping several buckets of snow on Kryn.

She allowed the snow to build up, and she felt every clump of it hit her. She stood tall as they buried her to her knees in the snow. She looked up, and one last bucket dropped, landing on her face. The soldiers laughed. Taunting and telling her to return home before they take her inside.

The teasing and laughter stopped as steam wafter through the mound of snow on her face. It melted and trickled off her. The snow encasing her lower half had melted, and small embers fluttered in the air around her. "You're testing my patience." Kryn said, any tone of hilarity now gone. Her lips were thin, pursed, and her brows furrowed. "Give me my friends."

"Listen, girly, we don't know how you did that, but you're not getting anything." One soldier said.

Kryn glared at the soldier. She threw her arms upward, hurling two fireballs toward them. They brightened the night sky, as they singed the tops of the fortress, and continued upward before finally fading from existence. As the soldiers tried composing themselves Kryn held her hands to the wooden poles making up the wall. The walls burned, turning black and billowing smoke before finally crumbling to ash beneath her feet. "Give me my friends."

A bell rang from above and soldiers screamed of being under attack. Kryn shot a wave of fire at the oncoming soldiers before diving to the side. She dashed up the stairs and pulled out her sword, fighting off the soldiers on the wall. Kylix soldiers came to her on each side. She kicked back one, fighting back another. The walkway was just wide enough for two men to walk shoulder to shoulder. Kryn ducked, pushing a soldier to the ledge. The soldier gasped and fell to the ground below. Kryn saw arrows protruding from his back. She whipped her head from side to side, trying to find the archer. Another arrow clinked on the floor near her feet.

Another moment and Kryn jumped off the wall, using her fire to slow down her fall. More soldiers were spilling out of the tower. There had to be at least 50 soldiers clamoring and shouting at her. Screams of saying 'she has talent' to 'kill her' echoed louder among the roars from the soldiers. They had to be in the tower, but where exactly, she wasn't sure. She dashed around the tower and jumped, shooting fire from her hands to propel herself to the wall. This part of the wall didn't have any soldiers, as everyone was behind her. She wouldn't have much time. She opened the bag and jumped in.

"I was thinking," Xeo said, tossing the firestone into the air. "Why don't I use the fire stone? You know, to help keep your cover."

"Um, sure. Go ahead." Kryn said between breaths.

"Wait. Why are you out of breath? Did you start without me? Are they already saved?"

Kryn shook her head. "No, they aren't saved yet. But I did start without you. Thought I could take them, but there's so many of them. Knock yourself out with the firestone. They already saw it come from me."

"Great. What's the plan? Or do I need to come up with that too?" Xeo asked.

"If you're such a great fighter, I need you to keep the Kylix distracted. Fight them. I'll go searching for everyone."

"I get to use the firestone, though, right?"

Kryn smirked. "Yes. Toss me a stone. Hurry, we don't have much time."

Xeo tossed Kryn the first stone he saw, the small yellow one. As she caught it a flash of light brightened the room. "Let's do this!"

There were shouts echoing throughout the fortress asking where she was. "Find the girl! She couldn't have just disappeared." So many said several times. Kryn crawled out of the bag, trying to stay as low to the ground as possible. Xeo was next.

Kryn snatched the bag the moment he was out and stood up. "Good luck. See you in a few." She said, jumping off the wall to the shouts of soldiers spotting her. She landed with a roll and squeezed the stone, blinding the soldiers. She weaved her way around them, making her way to the door. Now she just had to figure out which one they were in. She heard Xeo shouting in the background, blasting his surroundings with a ball of fire, and laughing.

"I know what that tattoo means." Tragi said. "But why do you have a gem in your hand sticking out like that?"

"Oh, the emerald?" Shallon said, raising his fist and looking at the gemstone. "Inheritance, you could say."

"Inheritance?" Rafik asked.

Shallon nodded. "I come from the hidden city of Emerald. Said to have been founded by King Emerald himself. And, obviously, named after him too. According to local legend, after his death he left an emerald to be guarded over by the leader of the city. Supposedly at the end of days he'll emerge from the emerald itself, restoring order to Alutopek."

"How did it get stuck in your hand?" Tragi asked.

"I was the last living male heir." Shallon explained. "I decided to go to Lynn, become a priest. My grandfather was unusually joyous. Got me drunk a few nights before I was to leave. When I woke up the emerald was stuck in my hand."

"And you never decided to take it out?" Ziri asked.

"No." Shallon shook his head. "I grew to like it. Felt like somebody was with me when I was down. Offered advice if I needed it."

"Makes sense if King Emerald was supposed to come out of that. There's a similar legend about a crystal in a statue in the town of Kristol." Tragi said.

"Yes. Supposedly each city founded by the Four Kings has a gem representing them." Shallon said.

The door creaked open above, and the four froze in their place. According to Shallon the Kylix shouldn't be back until morning. It didn't seem like that much time had passed. The room had grown cold, however, as the fire had died to little more than small bits of fire clinging to life in small chunks of wood. Light emanated from above, like a small sun. It didn't flicker like firelight, but was a constant, bright light.

"What's going on?" Rafik whispered.

Shallon shrugged. "This is new to me. Can't be good."

"Execution?" Ziri suggested.

"Late night interrogation?" Tragi guessed.

"No, I recognize the light, I think." Rafik said. He pushed himself up to his feet and leaned against the cage door, trying to peer farther down the corridor of cages. That bright light. There was only one time he saw something like that, and that was two years ago. When he was in the tunnels beneath Datz. "The lightstone."

The light got brighter, but still never flickered. Rafik wondered how many of the elemental stones were in existence. It would be foolish to think he had the only set. But they were so rare, most believed them to be fake. Something only in fairy tales. The mystery was soon solved as the figure holding the light came to view. It was just her silhouette at first, but Rafik recognized her instantly. Her hair reaching just passed her shoulders, the curves of her body, the bounce in her step.

"Kryn!" Ziri shouted. "Why aren't you using your fire?"

"Xeo is using the firestone. Thought I'd let him feel special." Kryn smirked. "Guessing the plan didn't work?" She tossed Rafik the lightstone, and everybody flinched as the room went bright, to dark, to bright again.

Rafik shook his head. "You could say that."

"Surprised seeing you here." Kryn said, noticing Shallon.

Shallon grunted. "You can chastise me after you've learned what's written in silver."

"I'm trying." Kryn snapped. "Would be nice if you gave me a hint."

"I already have." Shallon smiled. "The truth is written in silver."

"That doesn't help!" Kryn said.

"Will you just get us out of here?" Rafik asked.

Kryn nodded, held her palm to the lock and used her fire. The smell of melting metal permeated the room, and smoke billowed from beneath her hand. She yanked on the door, and it whipped open. "And done. Let's get out of here."

Tragi and Ziri ran up the stairs with Kryn. Shallon grabbed Rafik's shoulder, keeping him behind. "We'll catch up." He said to the others. "Rafik, I need to tell you about your father."

"You already have." Rafik snapped. "He's resting on the island in the Silent Sea. Dragon's Roost, right?"

Shallon sighed. "It's much more complicated than that. Your father…he was a hero. And don't be giving that island a name if you know what's good for you."

"That's why he is on that island and hasn't tried returning home." Rafik said. "Great hero."

"Take this letter." Shallon said, reaching deep into the sleeves of his shirt. "Been holding onto this for a while now. It may help you kids."

"How did you keep it hidden?" Rafik asked.

"The soldiers here aren't the most thorough." Shallon said. "Are you coming with us?"

"No." Shallon said. "You have your own path. If you and your friends solve what's written in silver maybe our paths will cross again. You are your father's son. You will figure it out."

"I don't know." Rafik smirked. "Anza was better at solving riddles than I am."

"I'm sure you'll figure it out." Shallon said again.

Without saying another word, the giant walked off, heading up the stairs and out to freedom. Rafik hurried after them, tucking the letter in his pocket. Maybe he and Kryn could figure it out together.

Xeo's laughter could be heard over the yells of the Kylix soldiers. Part of the fortress was in flames, and fire balls were scorching through the air. It was freezing in the dungeons below, but out here it was warm enough to be melting the snow and ice. As Kylix soldiers took a step towards Xeo he would shoot a wave of fire, pushing them back. It was clear he was enjoying playing with the firestone more than trying to fend off the enemy.

Though it had warmed up in and around the fortress because of Xeo, the unsettling fog with tinges of violet returned. At first it swirled around the ankles. Everyone the fog touched had shivers run down their spines. Their hearts beat faster and sweat trickled down their faces. Something was coming. Instead of focusing on the escaping prisoners the Kylix soldiers looked around, high and low, whipping their heads back and forth. Murmurings turned to whispers, and whispers turned to voices of worry and concern. Something was coming. As the fog grew higher, getting thicker and thicker, the sound of a heartbeat echoed within the fog.

"What is this?" Kryn asked. She spun around but couldn't see anything passed her nose. "Rafik!"

The fog muffled her yell, that just feet away Rafik didn't hear her. He held out his hands, making his way through the fog inch by inch. He walked into a Kylix soldier, they both screamed, punched, missed, and disappeared back into the fog. He squeezed the lightstone, the light pushing the fog away. Veins of violet grew darker in the fog, pressing against the light, pulsing like a heartbeat.

"Rafik!" Ziri said, dashing up to him. "What is this? I haven't seen anything like it."

"Me neither." Rafik said looking around. Even the soldiers in the ring of light were appearing confused. They didn't try to attack Rafik or Ziri, but reached out, touching the fog, and muttering to themselves in confusion.

"This is creepy." Ziri said.

Before Rafik could respond something pressed up against him. He jumped and spun around with fists clenched. Kryn was just doing the same thing. "Oh, it's you. You scared me."

"I scared you? Have you seen this fog?" Kryn asked.

"Give me the bag." Rafik said, holding out his hand.

"What for?" Kryn asked, slouching her shoulder, letting the bag slide off.

"We're going to get lost in this fog." Rafik explained. "Get in the bag. I'll get us out of here."

Ziri and Kryn nodded, disappearing within the bag. It wasn't much longer while wandering the fortress, the fog seemingly getting thicker, he came across Tragi and Xeo. Like Ziri and Kryn, they eagerly got into the bag. Rafik closed the bag, and ran forward, hoping he was going the right way. He shoved through Kylix soldiers, running in a straight line.

The light pushed away the fog. The pulsing purple veins shrank in size, getting lighter. He made his way to the wall and the fog had thinned. As the mysterious fog faded the Kylix soldiers returned to their wits and shouted after Rafik. Clanging of swords came from behind, but he didn't look back.

Then, Rafik heard it. The familiar voice returned. It was here. *'Kill!'* It shouted in his head. It felt off, though. Unlike last time where the voice was as loud as his own, it was now far away. Rafik shook his head, trying to clear his head. He had to find a way out of here. He made it to the wall, but the doorway leading in was still closed. In the distance was a charred opening he guessed Kryn created.

Blaridane's voice shouted once more. Rafik turned and saw the familiar dragon winged hilt of the sword being held in Shallon's hand. He had the sword now. His blood boiled, eyes narrowing to slits. That was *his* sword! How dare he use it! A Kylix soldier swung a sword down, nearly cleaving Rafik's arm off. Rafik side stepped and sprinted for the exit. Arrows whistled passed him, and a row of soldiers huddled around the opening. Without stopping Rafik squeezed the lightstone, blinding the soldiers, and jumped through the hole.

He rolled, springing to his feet, and ran into the night. He would have to find Shallon and take back his sword, but for now, he had to make sure his friends were safe.

Chapter 8: Crossing the Silent Sea

Silent Sea, Nyler Peninsula, Alutopek

Adrenaline pumped through Rafik for most of the night. They escaped the Kylix, yes. But he saw Blaridane. Knowing Anza was alive, possibly safe with their father, he allowed the thoughts of the sword to return to him. The longing for it. The itching in his hands, craving the touch. He needed the sword. And Shallon took it. Shallon. Who knew about his father all along. And Gorik did too. Why didn't anyone tell him? Why didn't he return home?

Maybe he was dead? If he were it didn't make sense for Gorik to take his body there. If possible, it was customary that the region you were born in, you would be buried in that necropolis. The Nyler Necropolis. Being 'lost at sea' Drane's body was never recovered. According to Shallon, though, he wasn't lost at sea. He was at that island. And Anza was somewhere called Dragon's Roost. It had to be the same place. Where else would Gorik take her? Where else could she be?

Lost in thought, he didn't notice his teeth clattering, or lips turning blue. He continued walking, stewing in his anger. He didn't even notice the light creeping ever so slowly across the Black Wall, stretching from behind him. What pulled him out of his hypnotic trance was the sudden shift of weight as the bag he was carrying bulged open. Rafik collapsed and Kryn crawled out, followed by everyone else.

"Ya shire, Rafik." Kryn cursed. "You could have told us you escaped."

"What?" Rafik asked, lifting his face out of the snow he fell into. "Oh, I didn't notice. After I escaped, I just kept running."

"Well, you made good progress. Can't even see the Bruin Fortress from here." Xeo said, looking back at the trail Rafik had made in the snow. "Probably even farther than Kryn and I made it waiting for you."

"Ziri told us what you found out." Kryn said, helping Rafik to his feet.

"That's great news!" Xeo said. "Do you think your sister is there? That place is Dragon's Roost."

"Don't name it!" Ziri snapped, a puff of pink air escaping her lips.

"Curses shmurses." Xeo laughed. "Everything has a name. I'm not afraid of any curse."

Rafik smiled, seeing Xeo's arrogant grin and puffed-up chest. For once his stuffy or snobbish attitude cheered him up. "Nothing gets you down, does it Xeo?"

Xeo shrugged. "We've made it this far. What's one more threat to our lives to overcome?"

Even Kryn laughed at that. "You know, eventually there will be something that kills you."

"But until then," Xeo smirked, "What doesn't kill you makes you stronger."

"Let me poison you, see how strong you are in a few days." Ziri laughed.

"Well, in most cases." Xeo said. "So, are we going to Dragon's Roost or not?"

"No." Rafik said.

"What?" The four said in unison.

"Rafik, your father is there." Kryn said.

"You told me you missed him. Now you can see him." Ziri said.

"If he wanted to see me, he would have come back." Rafik said haughtily. His hands itched for Blaridane. He didn't need to be attacked like this. From people he considered friends no less! "He probably started a new family there. Forgot about us."

"Don't say that." Ziri said. "You don't know that."

"If anything, do it for your sister." Tragi said.

"What do you mean?" Rafik asked.

"If your uncle sent her to Dragon's Roost, and that is the island in the Silent Sea, don't you think she would want to see you? She had no idea your father was there either. And you've been wanting to rescue her since the moment you found out she was still alive." Tragi explained.

"Ya shire." Rafik cursed. The darkness and rage swirling within him, with Blaridane at its center calmed for just a moment. A light within his mind shining through. Anza. She didn't know about their father either. She probably thought he was dead, like he did her. The light within him grew brighter, and Rafik's clenched fists and tightened jaw loosened. "You have a point. What about stopping Vanarzir?"

"A detour won't hurt." Xeo said. "It's a better plan than voluntarily getting caught and imprisoned in a Kylix fortress."

"Hey, it could have worked." Tragi snapped.

"Could have doesn't count when we almost died." Ziri said.

"Besides, I don't think we can do much until we find out what Shallon means about what's written in silver." Kryn added.

"He gave me this letter." Rafik said, suddenly remembering the letter he stashed away during the escape. "He said it should help."

"He gave you a letter to help but won't help me?" Kryn said, snatching the letter from Rafik's hands.

"He thought I would have already known how, since Gorik was my uncle." Rafik said. "Guess he took pity on me."

"Do you know how to get to the Silent Sea?" Kryn asked, turning from Xeo to Tragi to Ziri.

Xeo and Tragi nodded. "Just keep heading west from the Bruin Fortress until you get to water." Xeo said. "It can't be that hard."

"Here, take the bag." Kryn said, scooping it off the ground and handing it to Ziri. "Rafik and I will be in the bag trying to figure out the letter."

"What if we get to the Silent Sea?" Xeo asked.

"We'll find a boat." Tragi suggested.

Ziri shook her head. "No."

"Why? You have a better idea to reaching an island?" Tragi argued.

"I'm not listening to any plan of yours." Ziri said.

Xeo burst out laughing, hunching over.

"Hey, did we die?" Tragi said, his face turning red.

Rafik sat at the desk in the hidden room, reading the letter for the third time. It was the one Kryn and Ziri received two years ago. "Whoever wrote it is a good storyteller." He finally said, holding up the letter.

Kryn nodded. "Glad you don't understand it either."

The letter was written on a thick piece of paper. Seemingly made of linen more so than wood. It was thicker and didn't tear or stay permanently folded as easily. The ink still appeared wet, but to the touch it didn't smudge. And for being at least two years old, Rafik didn't expect it to. The letter, though, seemed to be a part of a much larger story about a dog seeking a treasure in the middle of a storm.

"This was supposed to mean something?"

Kryn shrugged. "According to Shallon. One of the last things Gorik said was to read what's written in silver. And what you said Shallon told you, there has to be something here."

"Did my uncle give you anything?"

"That's the strange part." Kryn said, getting up to one of the bookshelves. She grabbed a black stone and two vials of ink that rested beside the *Diary of Nekvaz* she had taken from the Hall of Records. The black stone clung to the outside of one of the bottles. Setting them on the desk, Rafik poked at the stone. It moved freely, but stuck to the bottle, as if by magic. "Any idea what that is?"

Rafik shook his head. He'd never seen a rock act like that. He pulled it away from the bottle easily but putting it close to the bottle of ink and it zoomed towards it, clattering against the glass as it touched. The other bottle was farther away and putting the rock near that one did nothing. It was only attracted to one. "That is strange."

"No, this is strange." Kryn said. She leaned over Rafik's shoulder, taking the stone, and dropping it on the paper.

It didn't bounce like he expected but stuck to the paper just like the bottle. "Whatever is enchanting the bottle is on the paper!" Rafik said.

Kryn nodded. "Yeah, that's as far as I've gotten. I don't see any silver. And I don't know how to read metal. Even if we had some."

"There has to be something hidden." Rafik said. He moved the smooth stone across the paper, but nothing changed. It was easy to move, but pulling it away from the paper, there was resistance. "This has to be some sort of magic. What about Shallon's letter?"

Kryn unfolded the letter and placed it next to hers. They were both made of the same thick, linen paper. Where Kryn's was a full story covering the whole page, Shallon's had random silver letters marked throughout the page. "That's weird. Why are the letters like that?"

Rafik shrugged. "And they're silver, not black."

"This is written in silver, then?" Kryn suggested, more to herself than to Rafik. She grabbed the smooth stone and placed it on Shallon's letter. It didn't stick to the page or act magical like it did on hers.

"It's like the magic is gone." Rafik said. He grabbed a different sheet of paper and quill and started writing down the letters. He rewrote them as he slowly deciphered the random letters. The letters didn't have to be rearranged to spell out the message, but it was easier to read once everything was combined.

"What does it say?" Kryn asked.

"Queen Kay is missing. King in Bomoku Mountains. Meet at Nassir River on spring equinox." Rafik read aloud.

"So...the queen is missing or dead?"

"And Vanarzir is in the Bomoku Mountains, already sweeping through."

"If they're stopping the Kylix at the Nassir River we're going the wrong way!" Kryn said. "How can we get there? It's still winter, but the spring is in four months! We won't make it just by walking."

"We'll have to sail." Rafik agreed. "I doubt we'll find someone to sail through the Silent Sea and around, but when we get to Lynn we can take the river that leads to the Vinsen Ocean, maybe find somebody to take us around?"

"That's a good idea."

"We need to hurry." Rafik said, rolling up the map.

"We still haven't figured out how to read what's written in silver, though." Kryn said. "How did this," gesturing to her letter, "become this?"

Rafik pointed from where one letter was on Shallon's message, to where it should be on their own. "The letters don't match." Rafik said. "We have a different message than him. I guess when we decipher it, the message should look like this?"

"Your guess is as good as mine." Kryn sighed. "Glad you didn't immediately figure it out. I've been trying to solve this for years now. And we still aren't any closer."

"We are." Rafik said. "We know whatever is written in silver, the message should look something like this. That's a start."

It was two more nights before they reached the shores of the Silent Sea. Every night they would do as they did before the Bruin Fortress, hanging the bag on a tree branch and everyone clamoring inside for rest. As the day grew dark wisps of smoke danced off the snow. It twirled and pulsed, and more than once they thought to see the pulsing violet veins, they saw back at the fortress. The smoke condensed, becoming a thick fog. Before much else could happen, they retreated into the bag. By morning, though, the fog was gone along with any sign of malice.

They hadn't gotten any further in solving the riddle of reading what's written in silver. Tragi and Xeo were convinced that from Shallon's letter Kay must have escaped. Once finding Rafik's father, they would have to hurry to get to the battle at the Nassir River.

On the third morning the group crawled out of the bag, snapping the branch the bag hung from. In front of them was the Silent Sea. They had made it without even realizing it because of the dark. The Silent Sea got its name from the tranquil waters here. Waves didn't lap against the shore, even in the strongest of storms.

It rested along the edge of a sandy beach like crystal. The water so clear, the bottom could be seen. On the horizon across from the Silent Sea is the island, a green spec poking out of crystal blue water and a dark, ebon sky.

"That water gives me the creeps." Xeo said. "Why isn't it moving?"

"According to some legends," Tragi said, walking closer to the sea, "this was where lost spirits, damned for eternity, were sent to Soboribor. The underworld for the cursed, evil, and unwanted."

"That's comforting." Kryn said. She leaned over and scooped up some cool water, watching it trickle through her fingers. It acted just like any other water. As it touched the surface of water it landed in droplets, slowly absorbing back into the water. Not a ripple had been made.

"That was weird." Ziri said. "Think we can walk on it?"

"Nope." Rafik said, putting his foot into the water and watching it sink beneath the surface.

"How are we going to get across?" Ziri asked.

The five craned their neck, turning to stare down one end of the shore, and to the other. There wasn't a sign of life anywhere, let alone an abandoned boat. "I guess spirits don't need a boat and can swim? Or walk on this weird water." Xeo said.

"Do you hear that?" Rafik asked.

The others paused, waiting to hear the noise. "I'm not hearing anything." Kryn said.

"Exactly." Rafik said. "Back home there were gulls and other birds flying around the shore and at sea. Here there's nothing. Just silence."

"Maybe that's why it's called the Silent Sea." Xeo said. "Not because of the water not moving, but no birds, or animals anywhere."

Rafik shrugged. "It doesn't make any sense. Even in the winter some form of life should still be around. Though I'm not even seeing fish swim around."

Ziri noticed it first and pointed. As the light grew across the Black Wall, lighting up the area, a ferry could be seen sailing towards them. The ferry wasn't impressive by any means, but the silhouette steering it was. It was tall even from so far away. As the ferry grew nearer, so did the silhouette. "I'm not imagining this, right?" Ziri asked.

Rafik nodded. "I see it too."

"Me too." Tragi said.

"Did your legends say who that was?" Kryn asked.

The ferry glided across the water, not making a noise or a ripple. Staring for too long sent shivers down their spines. Within moments the ferryman arrived, the small boat effortlessly making its way onto the sand. The silhouette of the ferryman was still just that. The figure was as tall as trees, clad all in black, and their face hidden beneath a hood. From the shadows hiding their face, Rafik could feel the piercing eyes from beneath the cloak bore into him.

"Can you take us to the island?" Rafik asked. "I believe my father is there."

The ferryman nodded, not saying a word. With creaking joints, they raised their arm, holding out their hand.

"I think we need to pay him." Tragi said. "How much to cross?"

The ferryman didn't answer. Nor did they move. A small breeze kicked up, though one couldn't tell by seeing the water. The outstretched hand of the ferryman had a long cloak, barely showing the thin bony fingers beneath. The wind rustled the cloak, though everything else remained still.

"I think this is creepier than the Sarason Fortress." Ziri said.

"We don't have any money." Rafik said' "But I need to see my father."

The ferryman didn't move or say a word.

"If you don't help us, I'll burn you and your boat to ash." Kryn threatened.

Even through threat, the ferryman didn't move or say a word.

"The ferryman needs payment." Tragi said.

"I would have never guessed!" Xeo groaned.

Tragi shot Xeo a glance.

"We should just go." Rafik suggested. "Find a different way to get there."

"When will you have a chance to find your father again?" Kryn asked.

"Kryn is right." Tragi said. "We need to find a way across. "I have this sword I don't use. Will you accept this as payment?" He placed the sword in the ferryman's hand. The next moment the ferryman gestured for them to climb aboard. The ferryman held up their hand, warning the five to stop. Only Tragi was allowed on.

The next few minutes were filled with the four scrambling, trying to find something to give the ferryman they didn't need and could use as money. Ziri dropped the enchanted locks into the ferryman's hands. The cloaked figure held it for a moment before dropping it, clattering on the rocky beach.

"Maybe we have to give him weapons?" Rafik suggested. He handed the ferryman his sword, something he noticed was much easier doing since it wasn't Blaridane, and the ferryman allowed him on board.

Kryn gave the ferryman throwing knives. Xeo gave his sword, and Ziri scrambled into the bag, crawling out with her own sword to give the ferryman. "Hopefully we won't need them." She said as she sat beside Xeo.

The ferryman dropped everything, and as if by magic, the blades turned, impaling themselves into the ground. The boat was long but narrow, only allowing each person to sit two to a seat. And even then, it was cramped. The ferryman stood on one end, not moving. Wind whistled, and for several moments they sat there. "Is this a good idea?" Tragi asked. He stared up into the shadows of the cloak of the ferryman. Something wasn't right. A chill ran down his spine and beads of sweat dripped down his brow. This figure just appears, and they immediately trusted him? He couldn't even tell if it was a man beneath the cloak.

As if reading his thoughts, the ferryman began to move. It lurched, and the cracking of bones echoed in the silence. Four long and smooth legs jutted out of the ferryman's back, tearing through

99

the cloak. Its movement was slow, as the four legs propped up the ferryman to stand well above the boat. Yet none of them could move. The five froze in place as this creature moved. Two legs rested inside the boat, while the other two pushed against the shore.

They were off, to the island in the Silent Sea. With the glow of the Black Wall reflecting atop the waters of the Silent Sea, it felt like they were in a void. A space between worlds. The spindly legs of the ferryman dug into the water, propelling them across the sea. Within minutes the island came into view. It was relatively flat, save for a single mountain in the center of the island. The shore appeared sooner than they expected, and with a lurch and crunch of pebbles, the ferry ran ashore.

The group scrambled out, and as Rafik turned to thank the ferryman, the boat and the monstrous figure was gone. "I didn't just dream or imagine that, right?" Rafik asked.

Tragi clapped him on the shoulder. "If you did, we all did. That thing was real."

"What was that thing?" Kryn asked.

"Who cares. We're here." Xeo said. "We'll worry about that when we need to leave. Now, let's find Rafik's father!"

Chapter 9: The Hound of Soboribor

Island on the Silent Sea, Silent Sea, Nyler Peninsula, Alutopek

Something felt off here. The moment they set foot on land everyone felt it. The feeling wasn't that of fear, like when witnessing the ferryman's extra appendages. It wasn't joy either. Everything was just...silent. Even the howling winds were softer here, blowing across the blades of grass. The leaves of the trees rustled, but quieter. As if the wind itself was whispering. It was freezing here, much like everywhere else in the Nyler Peninsula during winter, but a warmth grew in each of their hearts. It wasn't long before each of them shed their coats.

"This place is strange." Kryn said, spinning around. The mainland where they had come from couldn't be seen, but to the North and South massive mountain peaks jutted out of the water. She couldn't see where they started, nor where they ended. The mountains were like massive walls, keeping the water in.

"Shh!" Xeo said. "Why are you yelling?"

"I'm not." Kryn said in her regular voice. Sure enough, it was deafening.

"We need to be quiet here." Ziri said. Even her whisper sounded loud.

"This is a reverent place." Rafik whispered.

"Maybe once you're on the island you're not allowed to leave." Xeo suggested. "It just feels like one of those places."

Rafik shrugged. "I have no idea. My dad is a sailor, but I don't think he would be sailing on this sea for a living. We should head inward. Check out that mountain."

The group agreed, and they made their way deeper inland. Noises were never loud or deafening here. They found few deer who seemed uninterested in the group. There was a forest where the trees looked ancient and withered, but the foliage bright and full of life. Where they walked, the grass sprang back, not showing a sign of ever being stepped on.

The mountain grew closer, and closer. By midday they could see something surrounding the mountain. A wall. Not just any wall, though. This one looked meticulously built. It wasn't layered like usual brick or stone walls, where the above layer overlapped where the bottom layer's bricks touched. It was like corn still on the cob. Just slightly ajar from each layer, and so expertly placed not even a feather could fit between them. Designed into the stone walls were the outlines of spiders, and atop the wall, spaced out, were scarecrows.

"I recognize this place." Tragi said.

"What is it?" Ziri asked.

"A necropolis." Tragi said. "After I rescued Xeo from fighting the king, we fled and hid inside the Nyler Necropolis."

"The Silent Sea is part of the Nyler Peninsula." Rafik said. "Why would there be one here?"

Tragi shrugged. "As far as I know, there shouldn't be."

"Is it true?" Ziri asked. "Each necropolis is guarded by a monster?"

"I would say so." Kryn smirked. "Remember the ferryman. If he didn't want us here, he wouldn't have taken us."

"That's why he took our weapons." Ziri said.

"Most of our weapons." Xeo smirked and winked.

"Yes, it is true. And they're very territorial. I don't think the ferryman was the guardian." Tragi said.

"Reminds me of the Sarason Fortress." Rafik said. "I hate spiders. Hate them even more since then."

"The spider is to represent death." Tragi said. "Necromancers and dark magic users corrupted the symbol."

"No." Xeo said, shaking his head. "Spiders are just creepy."

The wall surrounding the mountain was even larger as they stood next to it. Each stone was twice as tall as them, and the wall spanned upwards for hundreds of feet. "The Nyler Necropolis wasn't this big." Tragi said.

"Maybe this is where dragons and other monsters are laid to rest?" Rafik suggested.

"Then why would your father be here?" Kryn asked.

There weren't any doors blocking off the inside, just one massive archway. This place was built for giants, and they felt puny just stepping foot near it. "Maybe he's in here?" Rafik said.

"A necropolis is a city for the dead." Tragi explained. "If your father is in there..." He didn't finish his thought. Rafik shot him a glare that sent ice down his spine.

"We'll find out. Together." Kryn said, stepping forward and holding Rafik's hand.

Rafik widened his eyes, brows raised, before his cheeks grew bright red and he squeezed her hand. "Together." The ground suddenly shook below them. It rumbled, with an echoing thud nearby. Then another. And another. Rafik craned his neck to glimpse inside. "What is that?"

"You'll see." Tragi smiled, taking a step back out of the entryway. "You may want to follow me."

Without hesitation the others followed suit, just in time as the source of the noise and shaking of the earth came into view. It was easily 20 feet tall, and still looked dwarfed in the entryway. The guardian had the body of a man, and the head of a fearsome bull. In his hands was a massive club. The tree it took to craft such a giant weapon had to have been one from the Timlin Forest.

"Who dares enters these sacred halls?" It yelled, causing the walls to shake. The minotaur glared at the children, billowing smoke out of its nostrils.

Tragi nudged Rafik. "I-I do." Rafik stuttered, stepping forward.

"Children? On this island?" He grumbled. "You are not dead. Come to bargain? What could you possibly have done to deserve a place in here?"

"I-I don't even know what this place is." Rafik said. "B-but I'm here t-to s-s-see m-my father."

"If your father is here there is nothing to say goodbye to." The minotaur said. "Turn back. Go home. You don't belong here."

"My-my uncle t-took my f-f-father here." Rafik said. "I was told he's here. I wish to see him."

The minotaur leaned on his club, scratching his hairy chin. "The last to come here was two years ago. What was your father's name?"

"D-drane of D-datz." Rafik said.

"The last hero." The minotaur said. "It was an awfully long time between Drane and the one before him arrived to be laid to rest here. I don't expect anymore, now that his friend is here."

"May I see him?" Rafik asked, biting his lip.

The minotaur nodded. "Family may see him."

Rafik turned, looking back at his friends. Kryn nodded, smiling. "We'll wait out here."

"Thank you." Rafik said. He took a step forward and the minotaur turned around. Rafik had to run just to keep up with the giant monster's slow strides.

"Welcome, child, to the Hall of Heroes." The minotaur said. "I am Grothel. The caretaker for this necropolis."

"I didn't even know this necropolis existed. Or that minotaurs were real!" Rafik said.

The minotaur let out a chuckle, causing loose debris nearby cascade off the walls. "That is the point. Minotaurs are guardians to sacred ground, proving ourselves a formidable foe to the Great Shepherds. As for this necropolis, it was meant to stay in secret, so heroes can be laid to rest without worry."

"The Great Shepherds are real?" Rafik asked. "I remember stories about them. Wrangling up monsters."

"Often fairy tales have a grain of truth to them. Even when I was a young calf." Grothel said. "It's how we hide stories too hard to bear."

The rest of the walk was in silence. The city built for dead heroes was massive. The streets were wide enough for five or six minotaurs to be able to stand shoulder to shoulder, and there would still be room. Each building was intricately carved in a tapestry telling of the hero's life. Above each door was a name of the person resting within. It was reading these names, seeing the dates just below them, that it hit him. His father may be here. But he wasn't alive.

The sudden realization caused Rafik's heart to drop into his stomach. He walked slower, and his eyes blurred from tears he fought back. For these last few days, he had been angry that his father was alive and forgot about him. And angry at Gorik for keeping it a secret. He should have known better.

"This isn't Dragon's Roost?" Rafik asked.

"Dragon's Roost?" Grothel boomed, laughing. "There hasn't been a dragon here for ages. Let alone a place for one to roost. This island doesn't have a name. To help protect the Hall of Heroes, there is a curse on the island, to not have a name."

"That's what I heard." Rafik said.

"Then why do you ask?"

"Hope." Rafik said. After learning Grothel's name he noticed he wasn't afraid of the minotaur anymore. "I'm trying to find my sister. I was told my father was here. Was secretly hoping they both would have been here."

Grothel nodded. "I hope you didn't name this island Dragon's Roost."

Rafik shook his head. "No." He lied. "Just wishful thinking."

"I've never heard of such a place." Grothel said. "In my time there were so many dragons, there would be too many roosts to call one just by that. Well, here we are."

Before Rafik could respond they had stopped at a peculiar building. Unlike the others around him, where momentous events were carved into the structure, this one was blank. A solid piece of white marble. A plaque resting atop the doorway was the only sign of anyone being inside. "Drane of Datz." Rafik read aloud.

"I'll be right here. But you go inside." Grothel said, nudging Rafik to take a step forward.

Light didn't enter the tomb. Even with an open doorway, and windows carved out high above, the darkness prevailed. Rafik was tempted to use the lightstone but thought Grothel may not be happy about it. So, he raised his hands and waded into the darkness. Within a few steps he was in the center of the building, a stone slab raised up from the ground. He reached forward and felt bones. An instant later Rafik yanked his hands back to his side as if he were struck by lightning.

It wasn't that he felt bones that startled him. He wasn't sure what to expect when entering the tomb, but he didn't expect his talent to kick in. He had mastered it while in Mahparry, but never tried it on bones before. "Hi Dad." Rafik said, biting his quivering lip. "It's me, Rafik. I…I don't know what to say. I never thought I'd be able to tell you goodbye. Now I don't think I can."

He let out a wail, pounding his fist onto the stone slab his father rested on. It was like losing him all over again. The knots in his stomach, the lurching of his heart, and the uncontrollable floodgate of tears bursting through. "I don't want you to be gone! I need you!" He finally said. "Please don't be gone. I don't know what to do. I tried keeping Anza safe, and she's missing. Mom is dead. I'm lost and just want you! Why can't you be here?" The words spilled out of him before he realized he was even saying them. Rafik reached out instinctively to grab his father's hand like he did when he was little. This time, as he touched the bones, he didn't let go.

"Dad!" Rafik shouted. He recognized his face instantly. His amber eyes matched Anza's, and Rafik had the same hair as his. A reddish brown that shined as the light hit in certain spots. Though his father's hair was longer, and he had a matching goatee. Aside from that, Drane appeared to be an older version of Rafik. Rafik dashed over to hug him and fell straight through like a ghost. These must be his father's final memories, he realized.

"We have a problem." Gorik shouted, rushing down the stairs. Rafik noticed he had both his legs, and they were in a sort of cavern or dungeon. One side appeared to be carved straight from a mountain. Jagged and rough edges across. On the other three sides there were stones placed by masons. There was a staircase on the far wall, and crates scattered around the room.

Rafik wandered the room, glancing in the open crates. Some had swords, others arrows and bows. Crates in the farthest part of the room, though, had jars of black powder he didn't recognize.

"What is it?" Drane asked. Hearing his voice brought back a flood of memories all at once. Rafik had nearly forgotten what it sounded like.

"The Kylix are coming." Gorik said. "I saw them myself. They'll be here within the hour."

"How could they know we're here?" Shallon asked, stepping forward and out of the shadows. "This was supposed to be a small operation. Few would know about it."

"There is only one person who knows that isn't here." Gorik said.

"Samron." Shallon hissed. "I knew we shouldn't have trusted someone so entrenched within the Kylix."

"Who it was doesn't matter until we get out of here alive." Drane said, his voice still calm.

"Brohl and Annorla are already packing up and leaving. We need to do the same." Gorik said. "We need to get out of here."

Drane shook his head. "I'm not leaving until everybody is safe."

"Then we aren't either." Gorik said. Shallon nodding, standing like a stoic giant behind him.

"At least make sure Brohl and Annorla leave safely. Once you do, meet me down here." Drane said.

Shallon and Gorik nodded, turning to go upstairs. Drane watched for a moment before turning to the jagged wall. He moved aside a couple crates, revealing an entryway. Rafik followed his father. There were so many things he wanted to say. If only his father could hear him. The dark tunnel only lasted a few feet before Drane turned the corner and arrived in a massive room. "What is it?" A man asked, coming to Drane.

Rafik recognized the voice. He still looked like the old man he saw in the desert, who traded him to pirates in Trinkit. The receding hair was slightly darker, but not by much. His stubby nose, and endless wrinkles jotted across his face telling of a hard and long-lived life. Paris Bantrita. The storyteller. "Traitor." Rafik muttered under his breath.

"The Kylix are coming. I don't know how they found us, but that's not important now. We need to get you, and everyone else, out of here." Drane said.

Rafik turned his attention from his father to the room. It wasn't just Paris here. At least a dozen old men and women crouching over cauldrons, the dancing lights flashing across their face. As he watched them, they appeared to age before him. Slowly, just ever so slowly, becoming more frail and decrepit. How old were these people really?

"We aren't done." Paris said. "We need more time."

"We don't have more time. Tell me what you have." Drane said.

Paris shook his head, rubbing his temples and letting out a sigh. "We don't have anything. I don't know who this man is, but he doesn't exist."

"What do you mean he doesn't exist? We know he does."

"I can't explain it." Paris said. "It's nothing nobody in our order has ever seen. The Bantrita go back for as far as history does, and we've never seen anything like it."

"How does he not exist? You can see him." Drane said.

"No." Paris said, shaking his head. "We can't. That's the problem. When we glimpse a moment that we know he's in he isn't there. People are talking to thin air. Not a murmur or whisper can be heard, or a shadow. Somehow, he's hiding from us."

"How do we fix this?" Drane asked, now ushering Paris to his cauldron.

"We aren't sure." Paris said. "We need more time."

"Sadly, that is something we don't have." Drane said. "Pack up what you can. You need to leave now."

Paris nodded and whistled a curious tune. The others jostled and shook, as if being yanked from a dream. They all glanced at Paris, their eyes narrowing as they nodded. One by one they kicked their cauldrons over, scooped up vials and stuffing them in their bags, before dashing to the other side of the room.

"Will you be safe?" Paris asked, slinging his bag over his shoulder.

Drane shrugged, not saying a word. As the storytellers disappeared, deeper into the cavern, Drane dashed to the other end, opening a cabinet revealing a suit of armor. The armor was unlike anything Rafik had seen before. The chain mail was layered, almost like scales, and the helmets were in the shape of a dragon's head. Soon after suiting up Shallon and Gorik appeared.

"What are you doing?" Gorik asked. "We need to get out of here."

"Yes, you do." Drane said. "But I'm not running."

"Drane, listen to me. You have a family. You have kids to go home to!" Gorik insisted. "Now's not the time to be the hero."

"They need more time." Drane said. "We can't let them think they were here. Just the Soniky. The rebels."

"Then I'm staying, too." Gorik said. "Brohl and Annorla have escaped. We can stay back."

Shallon nodded. "Three is better than one."

Drane smiled. "My friends. Suit up. We have a long battle ahead of us."

"Or a short one." Gorik grumbled.

Shallon jabbed him in the side as they went to their own respective wardrobe. As they suited up, they talked about how they could be betrayed. "The only other person who knew we were here was Samron." Shallon said.

"We will have to deal with that once we're out of here." Drane said. "If it is Samron, we may have a bigger fight once we escape. Let's just focus on the now."

The cavern echoed as shouts and banging reverberated off the walls, making it near deafening, from the tunnel Rafik had first come through. His head was spinning. Samron? He told the Kylix where they were. He was the reason his father died? No wonder he acted so strangely towards him.

Shallon noticed first, the Kylix soldiers pouring through. Their shouts and screams were like angry men, but their armor was made to appear as if the living dead were flooding the cavern.

Gorik, Drane, and Shallon yelled back, and charged forward. If they could keep them in the tunnel, they may stand a chance.

Rafik charged to join them, but just as any other vision, he fell right through his opponents. He was a ghost, visiting a memory. There was nothing he could do to change whatever happened. His heart raced, sweat streamed down his brow. If Drane didn't fall overboard, and be lost at sea, like he now knows was a lie, this had to be it. This had to be his father's last moments.

It wasn't long before the three were overpowered. Drane shouted for them to retreat the moment the Kylix started calling them Soniky. They turned and ran, heading towards where the Bantrita escaped. Randomly, one of the three would jump, or swerve out of the way of something that wasn't there. Moments later Rafik saw why. Bear traps sprang out from the dirt, ensnaring the Kylix soldier within its teeth. Others were whipped into the air and dangled from the ceiling as they stepped in chain traps. The three jumped together, and across the cavern, where the main entrance was, it collapsed in crashing thunder as the Kylix tripped over a wire they didn't see. A cloud of dust rushed through the tunnel, and Rafik watched as Shallon separated down one tunnel as Gorik and Drane took another.

The next moment Gorik screamed. Drane spun around to see his best friend dangling from a chain just above his knee. How the chain got that high he wasn't sure. "Go!" Gorik shouted. "Leave me be. I'll be fine."

"You told me to think about my family." Drane said. "I am."

"Do you recognize this one?" Gorik groaned, swaying softly, glaring at the chain. "Just my luck."

"I do." Drane smirked. "And if it was any other time, I would be telling you how ironic this was."

Before Gorik could respond the Kylix entered, coughing as they hacked at Drane. They didn't seem to notice Gorik dangling above them. Drane fought off six, seven Kylix soldiers. He moved with such speed Rafik just saw flashes of his sword. One by one the skeletal army was falling, never to get back up. Yet one by one they continued streaming into the tunnel, shouting, and screaming, roaring at Drane. Fatigue was setting in. Drane started moving slower. He didn't react to one blow or another. It wasn't long before he was surrounded by the Kylix, and on his knees, a blade to his throat. The Kylix soldier hovering over him reached and yanked off his helmet.

"This will be good." The soldier smirked, raising the blade.

Drane didn't flinch or even try to turn away. Rafik screamed for his father, but nobody could hear him. "Dad, no!"

From above a scream echoed louder and more painful than the rest. A moment later Gorik fell to the ground, bleeding all over. Rafik looked up to see his uncle's leg still stuck in the chain. The sudden crash landing startled the Kylix. Without skipping a beat Drane yanked Gorik and the two hobbled off deeper into the tunnel.

"What were you thinking?" Drane said.

"Saving you." Gorik replied. "Not my smartest move."

Drane shook his head. "You're a fool."

"You're alive." Gorik said. "Don't say I wouldn't do anything for you now. You owe me a leg."

Although he was joking, Rafik could see the pain in Gorik's eyes. He bit his cheeks hard enough blood dribbled out of his mouth. He wasn't the only one to notice. "If we don't do something, you're going to die." Drane said. He shoved his friend against a wall, and without warning, grabbed a nearby torch and stuck it to the open wound.

The screams Gorik made would haunt Rafik forever.

"At least you won't bleed to death." Drane said. "Once we're out of here we can get you properly looked at."

Gorik bit his tongue. His eyes changed from glaring to eyes wide in surprise and pain. He opened his mouth but not a word came out.

"Glad we can agree on it." Drane smiled. "Let's get you out of here."

The Kylix weren't far behind them. They hobbled through one tunnel, weaving in and out of another. The cave system they were in was like a labyrinth. But there, just up ahead, was a light. "Come on, Dad." Rafik shouted. "We can make it. We got to!"

The labyrinth was ending. The light growing closer. Kylix soldiers hollered from behind, and arrows whizzed past them. How they weren't getting hit was a miracle. Then Rafik saw an arrow fly through his chest, and remembered once again, he was only watching. They got to the light and jumped, Rafik joining them. They fell, straight down, into the calm, crystal-like waters of the Silent Sea. Gorik popped up first, Drane second. He seemed tired, and slow.

"We're almost there." Gorik said. "We'll swim to that island."

Within a few strokes Drane had stopped swimming, and Gorik clung to him, dragging him to the island. Once on the shore Drane coughed up water and blood. "T-t-take care of them." He sighed.

Rafik watched the light in his father's eyes fade. Arrows covered his back and neck. It was a miracle he had survived this far. As the vision ended, he and Gorik's cries were identical.

The island was quiet. They had all noticed it upon landing here, but wandering it was something else. The feeling of reverence was gone. Instead, it was unsettling. Like somebody had sucked all the air out of a room. Something horrible just occurred before your eyes, and you're waiting for something good to happen. The relief wasn't coming.

"I'm beginning to really hate this place." Xeo said, kicking up dirt on a game trail the four were following.

"Me too." Kryn said.

"I kind of like it." Ziri said. Her whispers were louder here. Nobody had to crane their necks in her direction to try and hear her. She spoke as loudly as everyone else. "You can hear me better, plus it's warmer."

They did notice that. It was winter here. In the Nyler Peninsula that meant freezing temperatures, countless snowstorms, and icy wind cutting through the thickest of coats. But here, it didn't seem nearly as cold. The skies above were dreary, but there wasn't snow. Even the winds were calmer.

"What do you think he's doing?" Xeo asked.

"Probably saying goodbye." Kryn replied. "You lost your father. How long would it take you to say goodbye if given the chance?"

"Good point." Xeo said. The four didn't talk much, as they wandered the island. They walked back to the shore, and then meandered into a nearby forest. Everywhere was calm. Even as night rolled in, and the light of the Black Wall faded, it was warm enough they stayed outside.

It was Ziri who noticed it first. Wisps of fog swirling around their feet. Thin, wiry veins of violet began to pulse within the fog, and the warmth plummeted. Suddenly their teeth clattered, bodies shook, and their breath could be seen once more. It was obviously still winter here at night. They donned their coats and began to head back to the necropolis. Maybe Grothel would let them enter and get warm? They could leave in the morning.

In the darkness, beneath a stone outcropping and between two large firs, the sound of stone scraping against stone grew louder. The fog billowed out of there, and the pulsing violet within the fog was thicker here. The four stopped to watch as a stone gate slowly inched and yanked out of the ground. One moment it would smoothly raise out of the ground like a knife going through butter. Other times time it would contort and twitch like pulling something heavy out of water.

"We need to get out of here." Tragi whispered. "We need to get out of here now."

"What is that?" Ziri asked.

A shiver ran down their spines as the gate came to full height, and creaked open. An unsettling roar echoed from within the gate. The wrought iron gate did show what was on the other side, but it was hidden behind violet fog, now gushing out. The growl grew louder and louder, and before anybody could react a shadow lunged from the gate, tackling Kryn.

Kryn blasted a fireball, startling the monster who instantly rolled off her, pressing Kryn deeper into the ground. Ziri and Tragi helped Kryn out of the ground as Xeo screamed. The monster stood upright, growling, making eye contact with Xeo. It was a hideous mashup of different animals. The body of a bear, the legs of a deer, ears like a wolf, and the head of a buffalo. It towered over all of them, and when it opened its mouth, it extended wider to even fit small children to be swallowed whole. Razor sharp teeth and burning orange eyes completed the monstrous visage.

"What is that?" Kryn asked. She threw another fireball at the monster, and it whipped around, glaring at her. The beast roared, lunging for Kryn once more. This time she dove out of the way, and the four ran for the necropolis.

Ziri looked back to see the monster charging after them on all fours and was gaining on them. She wasn't as fast as the others, she noticed. Turning forward again, she saw the others several steps ahead. Thinking she could poison it and save her friends, Ziri slowed down. She spun around, hands outstretched, waiting for the beast to attack her. The monster glanced at her but didn't stop. It continued after the other three, growling. "What is that thing?" She asked herself.

The group burst from the forest and into open land. Just ahead they could see the Hall of Heroes. It wasn't much farther. Each of them refused to look back swearing they could feel the monster's putrid breath on the backs of their necks. Kryn was first to trespass into the necropolis, followed by Xeo and Tragi. They turned the corner and stopped. They couldn't feel the monster's breath but could still hear its growls.

"Who dares enter my domain?" A voice echoed throughout the city of the dead. It was the voice they recognized as Grothel.

"So, we either die by minotaur or whatever that thing is." Xeo said, doubled over trying to catch his breath.

"Where's Ziri?" Kryn asked.

"I thought she was right behind us." Tragi said. He peeked around the corner and saw the monster feverishly pace back and forth of the entryway. Just behind it was Ziri. She slipped past the beast without it noticing and hurried towards them. "Are you alright?"

Ziri nodded. "I couldn't keep up, so I thought I'd poison it. Take it down with me."

"Did it work?" Xeo asked.

Tragi shook his head. "It's right there. How could it have worked?"

"Well, she's still alive, and there could be more than one." Xeo reasoned.

"No." Ziri said. "It didn't even stop for me. It just kept going."

"It's after one of us?" Kryn said, staring from Tragi to Xeo. "What did you do?"

"I didn't do anything this time!" Xeo said.

"That you know of." Tragi said. "This is just like back in Fogwood."

"You can remind me and scold me later about that." Xeo snapped.

The stomping grew louder, and Grothel turned a corner, coming into view. "How dare you enter!" He growled, raising his club. "I warned you!"

"No, wait!" Kryn said, as the four cowered beneath the giant minotaur. "We were forced in here. Look at what's at the gate!"

Grothel paused, took a step forward, and gasped. "What did you do?" He whispered. The beast and Grothel locked eyes, and for a moment, time stood still. The minotaur let out a piercing growl, and the four had to cover their ears from the noise. The monster's eyes widened before slinking back into the darkness and disappeared. The violet fog going with it.

"What is that thing?" Xeo asked.

"When your friend is done, I'll tell you the curse that is upon you." Grothel said. "Best you stay here for the night."

Rafik arrived soon after. His face was so pale it looked as if he had seen a ghost. Being in the city of the dead, it was entirely

115

possible, too. He didn't smile or say hi to his friends. He just showed up. Silent as the tomb they were in. There wasn't a smile on his face, and the light of his eyes seemed dimmer. Kryn hugged him once she noticed him, which partially shook him out of his trance.

"How long has that thing been chasing you?" Grothel asked.

"What thing?" Rafik asked.

"This was the first time we've seen it." Kryn said.

"And hopefully the last." Xeo said.

"What thing?" Rafik asked again, anger creeping into his voice.

"Have you seen any sign of it before? Sudden bursts of cold? Strange colored fog?" Grothel asked.

"Now that you mention it," Tragi said, scratching his chin. "Since we came back to Alutopek I have noticed it. As it would get dark, small traces of violet in the fog."

"I've only noticed it since the Bruin Fortress." Xeo said.

"What thing?" Rafik now shouted. "I'm right here. And I know you can hear me."

"Of course we can." Ziri said. "Are you alright?"

"I just watched my father die, and I couldn't do anything about it. Now my friends are ignoring me, talking about something chasing us?" Rafik said, clenching his fists.

"Oh, Rafik, I'm so sorry." Kryn said. She reached out to hug Rafik, but Grothel bellowed a growl, stopping her.

"There will be time for mourning later." Grothel said. "Right now, you have a bigger problem. Her name is Treshna."

"Treshna?" Rafik asked.

"It didn't look like a girl." Xeo said.

"According to the stories, it's a girl." Grothel said. "The Hound of Soboribor."

"Wait, that thing is from the underworld?" Xeo asked.

"What thing?" Rafik yelled again.

"While you were seeing your father," Ziri said. "Something attacked us."

"So, who or what is Treshna? Why is it after us?" Kryn asked.

"Long ago," Grothel began, stoking the fire they all stood around. "There was a woman named Treshna. Her husband had recently died, leaving her with a baby and two small children to protect. They were trying to find a better life and risked walking the Ohmrang Fields to do it. It was the dead of winter, and food was scarce. As the days rolled on with no hint of food, she watched her children starve. One froze, and not wanting the same fate for her other children, she killed them. Moments after doing this, with frozen corpses still in her arms, a group of men arrived, sent there to rescue her. They were so disgusted by her actions they bound her and threw her off a nearby mountain. Her restless and heartbroken soul was cursed to wander the world and collect the souls deserving to be taken."

"If she was human, how did she turn into that?" Xeo asked.

"The curse changed her. Contorted her into a monster everyone would fear. She now has immense strength, incredibly fast, and uses the gates of Soboribor to travel from place to place. Only hunting at night or the cover of darkness. Some say she can even change her appearance to help catch her prey." Grothel explained.

"One of us is cursed?" Kryn asked, looking from one to the other of her friends.

"It's not me." Ziri said. "It just ignored me."

"How have you made it here without it finding you?" Grothel asked.

"This bag." Rafik said, holding it up. "We all sleep in it. There's a room inside."

"Nighttime isn't your friend." The minotaur said. "Treshna can't enter sacred places, so you are safe here for the night. But use that bag. Don't enter caves or other dark dwellings. Otherwise, she will find you."

"You just had to name this island, didn't you?" Kryn said.

"Would naming this island curse us with the Hound of Soboribor?" Tragi asked.

117

Grothel shrugged. "I haven't met anyone who tried naming the island before you."

"How do we get rid of this curse?" Rafik asked.

"Find somebody powerful in magic. They may be able to lift the curse." Grothel said.

"Magic doesn't exist anymore." Rafik argued.

"Your friend summons fire, you witnessed your father's death, and there is a beast from the underworld after you." Grothel said. "Magic is still here. Now rest. You are leaving here at first light, when that infernal monster can't get you."

Chapter 10: Touched by the Moon

Dragon's Roost, Biodlay Desert, Alutopek

Anza sighed, closing yet another book. "How old do you think they are?" Anza asked.

"How old is who?" Izamar replied, not looking up from his own book. He licked his finger, turning the page.

"Rafik's grandchildren." Anza said. "Or do you think they've died of old age, too?"

Izamar laughed. "You think that much time has passed?"

"I don't know." Anza shrugged. "I can't tell. It feels like it. I should have gray hairs by now. Or be buried in the Nyler Necropolis. Or maybe Skage won and now the dead are roaming everywhere?"

"If Skage had won, I'm sure he would have come here." Izamar said. "Take comfort in knowing he hasn't arrived."

"But he could be on his way." Anza said. "And it's all my fault. I let him out. If he didn't trick me none of this would have happened. We would all still be safe."

"A single raindrop isn't to blame for the entire flood." Izamar said. "You didn't seem this irritable when learning about vampires in the last book you were reading."

"Because this one is boring!" Anza groaned, pushing the large tome away. "I can't even read half of it."

"What is it?"

"I don't know." Anza said. "'Squiggles and Chicken Scratches' by some old dead man is my guess."

"That's strange." Izamar smiled. "I don't remember owning a book called that."

"You tell me what it is." Anza said, holding up the heavy book. It was bound in leather, with ironwork along the spine and corners. Across the front were runes, some etched while others embroidered with a fine golden line. If any of it meant anything, the meaning was lost on her.

"That, my dear apprentice, is called 'Magic Most Marvelous" and is probably one of the oldest books in Alutopekan history. Also, written by an old dead woman. Not a man."

"Is that why I can't read the letters?" Anza said. "The language is extinct."

"Oh, the language isn't extinct. Just forgotten. I heard you mutter a phrase a time or two, even." Izamar said.

"That's impossible. I don't even know the language."

"You'd be surprised at what people say whether they realize it or not. The Bone Hunters were dying out when I was alive. The survivors of their race slowly integrated with others. In their language, the word for husband is 'forteek' and the word for prison is 'forteka.' Over the years the meanings were lost, and it wasn't long that in some areas, wives were calling their husbands prisons as a term of endearment. To most, it was a term of endearment. To a select few, an inside joke from an era now forgotten."

"Well, what am I saying?" Anza asked.

"Ya shire." Izamar replied. "You use it like a curse word when things don't go your way."

"I learned it from my uncle. He and my father would say it all the time." Anza said. "What does it mean?"

"Ya shire comes from that very book you're holding." Izamar said, pointing to it. "It's the beginning of a phrase, meaning 'I curse you.' You are trying to curse someone, without even knowing it."

"If that's true, why doesn't it do anything?" Anza asked.

"Two reasons. The most obvious being that you aren't aware of it being of the ancient language, or of its power. The second, you didn't complete the spell. Saying 'ya shire' doesn't work if you don't say what you're cursing. But you also need to be speaking in the ancient language. "For example, 'Ya shire turtles' means nothing, because you're using two different languages."

"This is getting confusing." Anza said, rubbing her head.

"The ancient language is confusing, and one of the many reasons it has become forgotten. The language is hard to pronounce, and there are dozens of runes and letters. Some more obscure than others."

"That sounds overly complicated." Anza groaned. "And people learned it?"

Izamar nodded. "Most remember maybe five runes at most. You see, writing the runes is the same as speaking it. But doing them together makes your spell twice as strong."

"Do you know all the runes?"

Izamar laughed. "I know more than five, but I doubt I know them all. That's why I have that book for reference. You should probably skip over that book for now. We can circle back to it when you're more advanced in the ways of magic."

Anza sat in silence, tracing her finger over the runes. They appeared ancient, even when compared to other old books in here. There was something strange about this book, as she stared at it. Knowing its history now, and how few remembered or even knew of it. "Could you teach me?"

"Why the sudden change in wanting to learn the runes and ancient language?"

"You didn't know very many." Anza said. "And Skage was your apprentice. So, he probably didn't know them all either."

Izamar stroked his beard, humming, his eyes staring at the ceiling. "I guess you would be right."

"So, if there is a loophole in getting out of here, it's probably in this book!" Anza said.

"That reminds me of another time when I was alive," Izamar started, a twisted grin growing from behind his gray beard. "There was a man who always proclaimed that today was the beginning of the end of the world. People believed him at first, but it didn't take long for most to consider him a fool. After three years of this proclamation, I sat down with the man, asking why he was doing this. Surely by now he would realize he was wrong."

"Because he was crazy." Anza interrupted.

Izamar smiled. "Most believed him to be. Myself included for a time. Yet every day he would climb the steps of the Junsharri Fountain and implore the end was coming. So, I asked the man. He smiled and told me that priests told him the gods would bring an end to the world when nobody expected it."

"So?"

"So, this man expected it. Every day. It was his belief that claiming the end of the world was today that kept the gods from bringing down their wrath." Izamar said. "To those who didn't understand, me included, he seemed like a man touched by the moon. Lunacy at its finest. But to him, it made perfect sense."

"A loophole." Anza said.

"Exactly." Izamar said, snapping his fingers, and smiling. "My dear young one, I think you may be right. If the answer is anywhere in this library, it would be here. How foolish of me not to think of this! I've been looking for a spell for escape from magical prisons, but I doubt the necromancer thought of the runes as a means of escape."

The smile grew on Anza's face. "If we find it, maybe I won't be too late for Rafik's great grandchild's birthday!"

"Go fetch some parchment and a quill. This is going to be a long lesson." Izamar said. "Truth be told, most magic users ignore this book, and the ancient language. There's much easier ways to do magic now. It will be something we can learn together."

Chapter 11: A Thief Among Ruins

Ruins of Kangor, Biodlay Desert, Alutopek

After seeing the Hound of Soboribor, the ferryman wasn't that unnerving of a character. His silence and spider-like legs were strange, but nothing to be afraid of. Grothel bid them farewell at the gates, not stepping foot out of the necropolis. Without wasting time, they marched to the shore, and the ferryman was there waiting. Once back on the mainland they gathered their weapons that had been left there and moved southward.

Nightmares of Treshna plagued their dreams. The burning orange eyes glaring into them, tearing them apart with its unnaturally extended jaw. Hearing of its description, Rafik was grateful he hadn't seen it. Though he had his own nightmares to contend with. He would often dream of witnessing Nayflin murdered by a ghost. But now it was watching his father die in Gorik's arms. He watched his father die, and there was nothing he could do. Every night since visiting the Hall of Heroes he watched it. Again. And again. And again. He remembered every moment of his father's last moments. Every little detail. Samron betrayed his father. Just the thought made Rafik's blood boil. After sharing what he had seen, the five agreed the trainer couldn't be trusted.

As the group traveled farther southward, the snow topped hills gave way to rain and slush. Not long after the dry grass turned to dirt, and from dirt, sand. They followed the shore and continued towards the Gateway Mountains where they walked the small foothills creeping into the desert. To the east was an ocean of sand. To the west were towering mountains, most of which they couldn't even see the tops of. Some mountains were sheer, offering no way to climb them. Others were more lenient but incredibly steep. It was no wonder nobody lived on this side of the desert. The mountains were like massive walls, but there wasn't a sign of water or life anywhere.

More than once they would come across a narrow crevice between two massive stones. According to their map, somewhere in there was the secret city of Anirats. The City of Secrets was said to house treasures and unimaginable wealth. Nobody who ever went searching for the city ever returned. To the five, it was just another story. Though Xeo, if they weren't already on a mission, would have loved to try and find it. Rafik and Tragi agreed to search for it with him once all of this was over.

The group traveled for weeks. Always during the day. As soon as it got remotely dark, they huddled inside the bag. One day they had lost track of time and noticed the fog swirling around their feet, hints of violet pulsing within. Just seeing that fog scared them enough they knew whatever they were doing could wait until morning.

In the mornings it would be freezing, just like in the Nyler Peninsula. By midday, it would be scorching hot. If it wasn't for the waterstone they would have dried up and became relics of the Biodlay Desert. The water kept them going, but their bellies growled for more. Xeo and Rafik would joke about hunting Treshna and cooking her. At least then their bellies would be full.

They had lost track of days. How long had it been since the Hall of Heroes? It couldn't have been much, but at the same time it felt like an eternity. They had to make it to the Nassir River by spring. Who knows what would happen after that?

On some nights, the group would try reading what was written in silver. So far, the answer to the mystery was just out of reach. Every time they tried working on solving it, it didn't take long for arguments to ensue. The answer was right there, they could feel it.

While not trying to solve the riddle, the group mostly kept to themselves. Tragi would meditate while Xeo slept. Rafik would exercise or use his talent repeatedly on the ruby that still sat on the shelf. Ziri would write, while Kryn read from her stolen book, 'The Diary of Nekvaz.'

It was around midday while wandering southward that they saw something. Jutting out of the mountainside was another fortress. Just like with the Hall of Heroes, the masonry of the walls was like that of corn on the cob. Not a feather could fit through

124

between the stones set askew from one another. Scarecrows still stood atop the walls, but where spiders were in the necropolis, hourglasses had replaced them.

"What is this place?" Rafik asked.

"Ancient ruins of some sort." Tragi said.

"Well duh." Xeo sighed. "I didn't think it was some extravagant spa or anything."

Tragi shot his brother a glare but didn't say anything. The five walked towards the ruins, the southern walls seemed to be more buried in sand than the rest. It was a large entryway, just like at the Hall of Heroes. About 20 steps into the ruins was a pedestal and a tablet resting on it. Most of the runes and letters were faded away, but Tragi managed to read some of it. "The Tomb of Kangor. All in need welcome." He finally said after studying it.

"Kangor?" Kryn asked.

"Yes." Tragi said. "According to Rhine-Pa, he was a god that protected mankind, but died."

"I didn't think gods could die." Kryn said.

"Obviously this one did." Xeo said.

"What's this?" Kryn asked. She was hunched over, brushing away something from the sand. Sand poured through the eye holes and a metal mask glimmered in the light.

"That looks like a Ravohka." Tragi said, eyes wide and jaw nearly on the floor.

"A what?" Xeo and Kryn asked.

"A mask." Tragi said. "Created by the Fohdorsha."

"I didn't know the dragonborn make masks." Kryn said, marveling at its craftsmanship. The metal mask was flawless, even after being half buried in the desert for all this time. She felt something course within it, pulse even, like a heartbeat. "Is it alive?"

"Most don't." Tragi said. "I only learned about them while doing my studies. The Fohdorsha wear these masks. It's part of their culture. They're sacred. They even have a band of warriors to retrieve fallen masks, so outsiders don't get them. I don't think it's alive. I've never heard of them being alive, at least. If this mask is out here, odds are the warriors who tried to retrieve it are beneath these sands as well."

"Feel it. There's something inside it." Kryn said, handing the mask to Tragi. The mask had a rounded head, two slits for eyes, and it slimmed downwards, giving the appearance of high cheek bones. The mouth had puckered like lips but was just a circle. Two fins, spanning the sides of the upper half of the mask fanned outwards, and four small spikes studded the mask from between the eyes to the top of the mask. It seemed both basic and advanced at the same time.

"It still works." Tragi said, holding the mask. "It's said that instead of talent, the Fohdorsha have these masks."

"What's it doing all the way out here?" The Fohdorsha are in the Bomoku Mountains, not in the desert." Rafik said.

Tragi shook his head. "They used to be all over Alutopek. In ancient times they were said to guard sacred or holy places. Guess that's further proof this is a tomb of a fallen god."

"Can I put it on?" Ziri asked, watching the mask with fascination in her eyes.

Tragi shrugged. "The original owner is long gone, and we're heading to the Bomoku Mountains to return it. I don't think outsiders are allowed to wear them."

"Oh, don't be a party pooper!" Xeo said. "Put it on, Ziri! Besides, it's not like they will know."

Tragi heaved a sigh. "Well, *she* probably shouldn't."

"Ignore him." Kryn said. "Put it on."

Ziri ran her hands across the smooth metallic surface. The mask's power pulsed at her fingertips, giving the semblance of life. She raised the mask to her face, and it clung to her like dried honey to fabric. The next moment she screamed and begged for it to be taken off. With all her might she pulled at the mask, and it finally ripped off with a 'pop' that echoed across the desert. "My head hurts."

"I thought that might happen." Tragi said. "It's said that if you have talent, you can't wear a Ravohka. It fights you on it."

"Fights? More like murders." Ziri sighed, rubbing her temples. "It felt like my head was going to split in half."

"But I can wear it?" Xeo asked, ignoring Ziri doubled over.

Tragi shrugged. "I guess."

"Try it on." Kryn urged.

With a wicked grin Xeo yanked the mask out of his brother's hands and put it on. The mask stretched, and the top of the mask wrapped to the top of Xeo's head. His face narrowed, contorting, and twisting to fit behind the narrowed jaw and high cheekbones. "How does it work?" He asked clearly, as if there wasn't something blocking his face. A moment later Xeo jettisoned into the sky. "Somebody get me down!" He stopped midair and began swooshing back and forth. He zig-zagged and shouted, laughing.

"Is he flying?" Kryn asked.

"He's doing something." Tragi laughed.

Xeo rushed towards them, coming to a sudden halt, kicking up sand beneath him, and hovered in place. "This is amazing! I can fly! Are there other masks? We need to collect these! Can you imagine having all sorts of masks from which you can change? Let's find the dragonborn and get more of these!"

"That's exactly why they keep them hidden." Tragi said. "Most people don't know how to react with just one power and want more. Take that off."

"I don't want to." Xeo said. "You know how amazing it is to fly?"

"You look creepy." Kryn said. "The mask changed your face."

Xeo shrugged. "I don't have to look at my face, so I don't care."

"Take it off." Tragi said again.

"No."

"Xeo." Kryn said, her hands roiling in flame. "Now."

Xeo lowered his head and touched the ground. He pulled the mask off, and his face returned to normal. He jumped in the air, only to land a moment later. "Guess it's not permanent." He sighed.

"No, it's not." Tragi said. "We'll put it in the bag and return it to the Fohdorsha."

"You take away all the fun." Xeo said. "Maybe us bringing it to them will make them kinder towards us, and they'll let us keep it."

Rafik took the mask and stowed it in the bag. "Should we be going?" He asked.

Tragi shrugged. "I kind of want to explore this place a little."

"That's a surprise, coming from somebody who didn't want anyone wearing a mask we found." Kryn laughed.

"I can explore without touching anything." Tragi said.

"Me too." Kryn said. "But...I probably will touch stuff. Come on, it'll be fun."

"Exploring a tomb is fun?" Ziri asked.

"We'll explore until night. Camp in the bag, and then leave in the morning." Rafik suggested. "We've been walking for who knows how long? We deserve a little break."

"I like that. See you all later!" Xeo said, dashing into the ruins of the tomb before anybody could protest.

Tragi shook his head. "Might as well let him have this at least. Wait up, Xeo!" He dashed after his brother, disappearing into the darkened corridors.

"Do you think Treshna will show up?" Rafik asked, eyeing the shadows with suspicion.

"No." Kryn said. "If this is a sacred place she can't enter."

"Good point." Rafik said. "Where should we start?"

The Ruins of Kangor were larger than Rafik expected. Seeing them from the outside, it was an impressive sight. A large, stone fortress in the shape of a horseshoe butted up against a mountain. Tunnels stretched and weaved about, creating a labyrinth within the mountain. Then again, having such an extravagant tomb for a fallen god, it made sense to make the

128

resting place hard to find. Some tunnels were built and had the familiar stone masonry so expertly crafted. Others it appeared more like somebody dug it out with an axe, cleaving at the earth.

Tunnels crisscrossed, and more than once Tragi and Xeo would come across Rafik, Ziri, and Kryn. The concern of getting lost in these hallowed grounds hadn't occurred to them. It was nice being out of the desert sun and being able to explore somewhere.

The continuous walking of their journey was getting to them. Rafik secretly hoped that the Fohdorsha would have steeds they could borrow to get to the Nassir River. Walking all that way just seemed exhausting.

"Can you read this?" Ziri asked. The three had come across a pedestal in the middle of a fork in the pathway. "I can't read it."

Rafik studied the tablet. The letters were worn and ancient. He didn't recognize half of the letters, but he understood most of it. "'Staff of Syrus ahead. Beware…' I don't know the rest." On the border of the tablets were silhouettes of Immortals.

"We should go check it out!" Kryn said.

"No." Rafik snapped. "No. Immortals are guarding it. I can't imagine they'd be happy with trespassers."

"Oh, come on. Where's your sense of adventure, Rafik?" Kryn asked.

"No." Rafik repeated. "Just trust me on this one. Immortals don't like trespassers."

"How do you know?" Ziri asked.

"I just do." Rafik said.

"Is that where you were for the last two years? Living with the Immortals?" Kryn accused, half in jest.

Rafik could tell by her tone it wasn't as light-hearted of a question as she tried making it to be. "Stories and legends." He finally said. "They must be true. We're in the tomb of a supposed fallen god. A hound from Soboribor is chasing us. Do you really want to risk having Immortals after us, too?"

Kryn glared at Rafik. She opened her mouth, just to close it a moment later. Smoke streamed from between her fingers. "Fine." Without saying another word, she turned, leaving Ziri and Rafik.

"Kryn, don't be like that." Rafik shouted.

"Guess she's upset." Ziri said, as Kryn didn't stop or turn back, but made an obscene gesture with her hands.

In the distance, far off from where Kryn could see, she heard the familiar laughter echoing through the tunnels of Xeo. She cursed under her breath and continued stamping away from everyone. Thinking of Rafik, living among mythical beings, enjoying life, while she spent two years looking for his sister and believing he had died infuriated her. He could have sent a message saying he was fine. Could have done something, at least. Now he shows back up, expecting everything to be normal, but when the Immortals get brought up, he would get shady and defensive. What was he hiding?

Wandering through the tunnels, she didn't notice the hall expanding outward until she was standing in the middle of a room. Light streamed down from several holes in the ceiling. Peering upward, she couldn't see the Black Wall, or anything else. Shadows crept out of the corners on the far side of the room. "Anything out there?" She asked, throwing a couple small fireballs into the darkness. The fire withered and dissipated, revealing nothing.

The room was barren, save for a small chest up against a wall. With how big the room was, the chest seemed out of place. Surely there was more in this room than this tiny box? Kryn inched over, carefully stepping to the ancient wooden chest. It opened with a creak, and inside, in the middle of the red velvet interior, was a round sapphire the size of a marble. It appeared similar to the ruby resting on the shelf in Rafik's bag. Just like with the ruby, as she touched it, a surge of energy coursed through her.

"Add to the collection, I guess." She said, pocketing the gem.

"That's mine." A voice said, stepping out of the shadows. The man's hair was white as snow that seemed to glow against his darker skin. Even his eyes were white like cotton. "You can either give it to me the easy way, or the hard way."

130

"You don't know who you're messing with." Kryn laughed.

"I don't really care." The man smirked. His nose was crooked, and he wore a thin, long coat with pockets sewn all over. "I'm not going to ask again."

"Good. Because I wouldn't have given it to you if you did." Kryn said. Not looking at the man she started walking away, head held high.

"Not so fast." The man said, putting his hand on her shoulder as she passed.

"Don't touch me, White Eyes." Kryn snapped.

"Or what?" He laughed. "Hand it over, girl."

Kryn shrugged, shirking off his hand, spinning, swiping her leg at him at the same time. The man jumped, kicking Kryn in the stomach. She doubled over, gasping for air. He yanked her hair, forcing her to stare up at him. Kryn's eyes burned, glaring at him. She opened her mouth, but she was still just gasping for air.

The man laughed. "You've got spunk. Now, give me the gem before I have to hurt you more."

Kryn regained her breath, and spit into his face. He cursed, raising his hand, and Kryn batted away his arm pulling her hair, her own fists igniting in flame. The man gasped, taking a step back, and Kryn swiped at him, punching him. He ducked and dodged every punch, slowly stepping backward. A few more steps and he was backed into a corner. With all her might, Kryn punched him in the gut. The man gasped and hunched over.

"You've got spunk. Now, leave me alone before I have to hurt you more." Kryn smirked. "Alutopek is a big place. Make sure I don't see you again, or I won't be so charitable." She shoved him and he fell to his side, still grasping at his stomach. Wisps of smoke billowed out from between his fingers.

"What are you?" He finally gasped as Kryn was in the doorway.

"The person who bested you, obviously."

Chapter 12: Written in Silver

Ruins of Kangor, Biodlay Desert, Alutopek

The secret room within the bag was a blessing. For instance, they could stow away their supplies without adding all that weight. Though, as it was called the Endless Bag, it was anything but. At night, as the five were tucked away with their supplies, hiding from Treshna, it was cramped. More than once, somebody would wake up with a kinked neck or from being kicked while they're sleeping. If they weren't exhausted from just walking all day, they were certain it would upset them much more than it did so far.

Being in an ancient burial ground of a fallen god, the group decided they could spend the night outside for once. Xeo eagerly setup tents in the courtyard where they first entered. Rafik and Tragi helped, as Ziri went to search for Kryn.

"Once she's here she can get a fire going." Xeo said, dusting off his hands and heaving a sigh.

"Have you forgotten how, or are you just lazy?" Rafik joked.

Tragi burst out laughing while Xeo's face soured. "No. We're a team. We setup camp. It's only fair."

Rafik shrugged. "Go ahead and start a fire. I don't think she'll mind if you do it this time."

Xeo opened his mouth to argue but didn't say a word. He nodded and got to shaving off flint on dried straw.

It was a chilly night, proof winter's grasp still reached this far into the desert. The towering mountains the tomb crept out from were like blotches of shadow as night came forth. Glowing light of the Black Wall faded, and few stars glimmered from beyond. Rafik noticed his favorite constellation, tracing it. It appeared to be in a different position this farther south than back in Datz. But it was nice to see the stars again. With being in Mahparry, Treshna after them, and taking shelter within the bag on freezing nights before that in the north, he didn't see the stars much. He heard his father's voice in his head, telling him stories about the stars. He heaved a sigh, watching his breath slowly fade into the darkness.

The crackling of the flames pulled Rafik from his thoughts. "Got it going." Xeo grumbled. "Think I could use that mask?"

"No." Rafik and Tragi both said at once.

"Nobody is using it." Rafik added. "Not until we get to the Fohdorsha. We already have Treshna after us. We don't want an entire people wanting us dead too."

"They don't need to know." Xeo urged.

"My father once told me a story," Rafik began, grabbing a stick and poking the fire. "About a boy. He avoided doing chores and helping others. When somebody asked for his help, he would make an excuse. These weren't simple excuses, but extravagant ones, like a death in the family or someone becoming seriously ill. One day, as he spun his lies, he later learned they were becoming true. If he lied that his house burned down, it would before the day was over. He claimed someone in his family passed, and they would soon perish. People grew afraid of this boy. When he started telling the truth, it was too late. His lies were unraveling, and everything he claimed to have happened, finally did. Until one day, all that was left was him."

"He got cursed." Xeo said. "Good for him."

"The story means your lies have a way of catching up to you." Tragi said, nodding to Rafik.

"Not to mention, if they ask if anyone wore it, I'm not going to lie." Rafik said.

"You would betray me?" Xeo gasped. "After everything we've been through."

Rafik nodded. "I'd tell the truth but stick by your side. I'm not lying."

"I'm not sure if I should be offended." Xeo said.

Before Rafik or Tragi could respond, Ziri and Kryn appeared. "Anyone notice that?" Kryn said, pointing towards the gate. The three boys jumped from their seats, not hearing the two girls approaching. They turned and saw the familiar eerie fog at the tomb's entrance. It billowed and climbed, wafting upward against an unseen wall. The violet pulsing within like a heartbeat grew more vibrant. It climbed over the ruins, trying to find a crack or crevice to worm its way into. The five watched the fog roll over them and jumped again as a roar echoed throughout the night.

The roar was deafening and made their blood run cold. Instead of watching the fog, they saw the silhouette of a monstrous figure at the gates. Kryn was the only one to notice the man with pure white hair sneak out from the tunnels, climb over a wall, and into the darkness. If Treshna noticed, she didn't pay him any attention. She wanted one of them.

"What does it want?" Rafik asked. Seeing the monster for the first time, he now understood what scared his friends so much. The body of a bear, the head of a buffalo, and legs of a deer. The spindly legs seemed too weak to hold up this monster, but Rafik imagined this thing running on all fours, being powered by those strong, skinny, hind legs.

"Not me." Ziri said. "It ran past me last time we saw it this close."

Treshna paced back and forth, pawing at the invisible wall keeping it from entering the sacred ground. She roared, her piercing orange eyes glaring at each of them. They were like miniature fires burning on the embodiment of nightmares. With every growl and roar their skin crawled and hair stood on end. The stench of death soon wafted around them.

"Even though we're safe here, I'm kind of thinking we should go in the bag." Kryn said, pinching her nose.

Ziri nodded. "I agree. I don't like this smell."

"Anyone who wants to stay out here, knock yourself out." Rafik said. "I'm with Kryn."

Kryn shot him a suspicious glance but didn't say a word. She crawled into the bag, Ziri not far from her. "I think I'm staying out here." Xeo said. "She can't get to us. We know it's a she, right?"

"According to Grothel." Tragi nodded. "I'll stay out here with my brother. Make sure he doesn't do anything stupid."

"I need to be babysat now?" Xeo joked.

"Knowing you, you'll find a different mask buried here, put it on and go fight Treshna. So, yes. You do." Tragi said.

Xeo sprang to his feet. "You're right! There could be more masks buried here. Rafik, do we have a shovel in there?"

"I think so." Rafik guessed.

"If there is one, toss it out." Xeo said, his grin growing from ear to ear.

"I found this." Kryn said, tossing Rafik the sapphire the moment he entered the room.

Rafik fell back against the ladder, catching the gem with both hands. Instantly flashes of history dashed across his mind. He recognized some of the people in the glimpses. He hurriedly pocketed the gem, not wanting to be torn away from such strong memories instantly. "Where was this?"

"In one of the rooms in the tomb." Kryn said. "Seemed similar to the ruby you have." She gestured to the one on the shelf beside the elemental stones.

"It is." Rafik nodded in agreement.

"What are they?" Ziri asked.

"You wouldn't believe me if I told you." Rafik sighed. He walked over to the shelf and placed the sapphire next to the ruby.

"Try us." Kryn said. "Unless of course it has to do with your new Immortal friends."

Rafik's eyes widened, but he didn't say a word for a moment. He investigated each of their eyes before finally swallowing air and speaking. "Alright. It has to do with the Four Kings."

"Are they heirlooms of them or something?" Kryn asked.

"Not quite." Rafik said. "According to legend, the Four Kings died defending Alutopek from some magical evil, uniting the land for the first time since the Kingdom of Rohz."

"It's not just legend, it's historical fact." Ziri said. "Everybody knows this."

"It's not true." Rafik said. "These gems are the eyes of the Four Kings. They were turned to stone, and their eyes turned to gems. Reuniting the gems with the statues will bring them back to life."

"How do you know?" Kryn asked.

"My talent." Rafik answered. "There should be eight of them. Two emeralds, two sapphires, two rubies, and two crystals. And they've been lost to history."

"And now we have two of them." Ziri said.

"Maybe we could wake the Four Kings and they could defeat Vanarzir?" Kryn suggested.

"I'm not sure if that's a good idea." Rafik said. "That might just be trading one evil for another. In my visions they weren't good people. Nothing like the legends say."

"How else are we going to beat Vanarzir?" Kryn asked.

Rafik paused. Ever since watching Nayflin's murder he didn't like using his talent. To view horrific things and be unable to do anything about it. Others not believing him. It was more of a hassle than it was worth. The only blessing his talent gave him so far was seeing his father one last time. Even if it was his last moments. "By finding out what's written in silver." He finally answered, turning his attention to the desk. Atop the desk were sheets of parchment, including the letter Kryn was given, and the deciphered one Shallon gave Rafik, *the diary of* Nekvaz, one jar of silver ink, and one of black ink, with a peculiar black stone clinging to it. "We need to find out what's written in silver before we get to the Nassir River."

"Why?" Ziri asked.

Rafik shrugged. "I just feel like we need to."

"Rafik is right." Kryn said. "We need to solve this."

"Shallon was disappointed we hadn't solved it yet." Rafik said. "It can't be too hard."

"That's reassuring." Kryn groaned. "Ziri and I tried solving it for almost a year before giving up. Then we tried decoding the last pages of the *Diary of Nekvaz* I took from the hall of records. It's strange. His whole life is documented until the creation of the

136

Black Wall, and then it's all in code. Honestly, if he was real, it seems like somebody else stole his diary to write this code. He's probably long dead by now. We can't figure that one out either."

"We aren't the best at cracking codes, I guess." Ziri said.

Kryn nodded. "We've tried for two years now to solve either one. I guess if it wasn't that hard, then we aren't that smart."

"What all have we done?" Rafik asked, reading over Shallon's letter.

"We've tried mixing the inks, writing them separately. Even tried smearing the ink with that magic rock." Ziri said. "Nothing works."

"We even thought maybe it could only be read in the moonlight." Kryn said. "That didn't do anything either."

Rafik glanced up at the trapdoor. "Maybe it has to be a certain night?"

"We tried almost every night for a month." Kryn said. "It didn't work. If reading what was written in silver means by moonlight, it didn't happen."

"Well, what happened to the other letters?" Rafik asked.

"This is the only letter we have." Kryn said. "Are you hiding one?"

"No, I mean on Shallon's note. His message." Rafik said, holding it up. "If it was by moonlight, the letters disappeared somehow on this one. Where did the rest of the message go?"

"That's a good question." Kryn said. "I didn't think about that before."

"So, the question is, how do we make the letters disappear in our note, to reveal the true message?" Rafik asked. He grabbed the message Gorik had given Kryn. He had read it so many times he could recite it by memory.

"Rafik, we need your help." Tragi shouted from the trapdoor, interrupting the investigation.

The three jumped, turning to the door. "What's wrong?" Rafik asked. Kryn was already dashing to the ladder.

The night still smelled like death, and Treshna paced back and forth at the gate. The monster, even though she couldn't get into the sacred ground, sent fear through all of them. It felt like just a matter of time before she broke through and ripped them all to shreds. Her growls pierced the air, and the fog swirled around the tomb with pulsing violet streaks lighting up the night. "Least she hasn't broken in." Kryn said.

"Where's Xeo?" Rafik asked.

"Over there." Tragi said.

In the distance, near the wall of the tomb, there was a shadow lumped on the ground. "A little help." Xeo shouted. The group hurried over to him, and atop him were three more masks.

Rafik laughed. "Don't tell me you're stuck under there."

"Alright, I won't." Xeo said. "Hey Kryn, will you tell Rafik I'm stuck under here."

Kryn, Rafik, and Ziri burst out laughing. "Three masks?" Kryn asked. "Xeo, I held one and they weren't that heavy."

"Then prove it. Pick up all three." Xeo challenged.

Kryn smirked and leaned over. The three masks on top of Xeo were different in shape than the one they found earlier. She tried scooping them up, and they shifted easily. As she tried raising herself upwards, the masks didn't budge. It was like they were bonded to the ground. She heaved a sigh and tried again. Once again, the masks didn't budge.

"Here, let me try." Rafik said. Kryn stepped to the side, and Rafik hunched over, grabbed all three. As he tried lifting them the masks didn't move. "I don't understand."

Tragi laughed. "I think I know what to do. Let me try." He leaned over, picked up each of the Ravohka one by one. With each mask he tossed to one of them. Ziri flinched, not even attempting to grab the mask, as it fell with a 'thwump' on the sand.

"How did you do that?" Ziri asked, eyeing the mask staring back up at her from the sand.

"It's protection from people like Xeo." Tragi said.

"Fun loving and eager for adventure?" Xeo asked.

"Greedy." Tragi laughed.

"I am not greedy!" Xeo gasped. "I am offended."

"I read how each Fohdorshan only has one mask." Tragi said. "But I think I know why now. Rafik, take the other masks."

Rafik nodded and grabbed each Ravohka from Kryn and Ziri. He grabbed Kryn's first. It seemed just as light as the one he held, but once he took it from her, both felt much heavier. As he took the one from Ziri the weight of the three caused him to collapse. The masks fell on top of Rafik's leg, and he couldn't wriggle it free. "What's going on?"

"The more masks you carry, the heavier they all become." Tragi said. "Some sort of magic."

"I can only have one mask, then?" Xeo groaned. He leaned over and picked up each mask off Rafik's leg separately, tossing them to the ground. "I don't even know what these ones do. Tragi wouldn't let me wear them."

"They aren't yours!" Tragi shouted. "The Fohdorsha kill to retrieve these masks. Who knows what they'll do when they find out you were wearing them."

"Ya shire." Xeo cursed. "Can't have any fun."

"Can we put them in the bag?" Rafik asked.

Tragi shrugged. "I don't see why not. The weight of everything else in there doesn't slow us down." Rafik, Kryn, and Tragi each grabbed one of the new masks, and put it into the bag beside the other one. "Try holding the bag."

Rafik scooped up the bag, and it moved just as freely as before. "Guess it works."

"Can't we just see what each mask does? They're different shapes, maybe they're different powers." Xeo said.

"No!" Everyone shouted at him.

"Oh no, the letter!" Ziri said, her alarming whisper of a voice seemed louder. She dashed to the fire, picking up a piece of parchment laying atop a stone.

"Is it ruined?" Rafik asked, dashing over. "I brought it out with me."

"I'm not sure." Ziri said.

139

Some of the ink on the letter began to bubble, and the edges of the parchment were singed. "I've never seen ink do that after it's dried on parchment."

"Me neither." Ziri said.

"Wait!" Rafik shouted. "Go get the stone. The one clinging to the bottle of ink."

Kryn dashed into the bag, and returned a moment later, tossing Rafik the smooth rock. From the underside of the paper Rafik moved the stone across the message. The bubbling and now liquid ink of the message swirled and moved with the stone. The group gasped in awe watching it. Rafik slid the stone to the bottom of the paper, and the hot, black liquid slid off the page.

"The letter is ruined." Xeo groaned. "Now we'll never know."

"I don't think so." Rafik said. "Look at the silver letters still on the page. We need to write it down, see what it says." The group eagerly retreated into the endless bag, leaving Treshna at the gate roaring and screaming.

'Rebel, find Jester in the Tomb of Tulang. The Soniky are waiting.'

"We did it!" Rafik shouted. "We solved it!"

Kryn laughed, jumping up and down with Rafik. "We know what's written in silver!"

"Who is Jester?" Xeo asked after rereading the message several times.

"We'll find out." Rafik said. "Where is the tomb?"

"And who is Tulang?" Ziri asked.

"What is Tulang?" Tragi asked. "I don't remember reading about it in my lessons."

The group rolled out their map of Alutopek, searching all over for it. Hoping they would get lucky, and it would be on there. "There it is!" Kryn shouted, pointing to the Akitung Jungle. "I thought people were buried in the region's necropolis?"

"They usually are." Tragi said. "Tulang must be pretty important to have a place all of his own."

"Like this one?" Rafik said. "Maybe he's another fallen god?"

Tragi shook his head. "If he is, I haven't heard of him."

"Looks like we'll reach the Nassir River first." Rafik said. "Maybe Shallon can help fill us in on who this Tulang person was."

The five stayed inside the endless bag for the rest of the night. They cheered and hollered, celebrating learning what was written in silver. It was like a weight being lifted from each of them. Xeo even mentioned if they missed the battle at the Nassir River, they could still join the Soniky thanks to this. With that realization, the group felt more at ease. They didn't need to rush or else they would miss it. Granted, they would miss the battle, which they didn't want, but the pressure of *needing* to be there was gone.

One by one they fell asleep, sitting against one of the walls. They didn't notice the fog fading, or Treshna retreating. By the time any of them had woken up, the Black Wall was glowing from the midday sun.

"I think that was a rest well deserved." Xeo said, stretching and yawning as he craned his neck in every direction, looking at the tomb. "Solved that riddle. Discovered more masks. I wonder how many more are out here."

"You're not wearing them." Tragi snapped. "Are we going to have to leave a guard near the Ravohka to keep you from stealing them?"

"No, I know none of you will let me have fun. But the Dragonborn might." Xeo argued. "If they're as important to them as you say they are, returning four masks should show them I'm worthy of one."

Tragi shook his head. "It doesn't work like that."

"How do you know?" Xeo asked.

"I was wondering that too." Kryn said. "If the Dragonborn don't talk to outsiders, how do you know so much?"

"During my studies," Tragi started, helping Rafik take down a tent none of them slept in. "The Immortals branched off of the Fohdorsha, so they shared a history. And they had several records of them even after. Long before the Four Kings there were the Dragon Wars. An entire tribe of the Fohdorsha were annihilated because of the destruction they caused. It was a fascinating read."

"How come we never heard of it?" Rafik asked.

Tragi shrugged. "Because the Four Jewels of Alutopek seem to be the most popular characters in history."

"What's this?" Rafik asked, holding out the tent. Across the side was a long slash in the fabric. "It wasn't torn when we put them up."

Xeo shook his head. "No, it wasn't." There was a second, smaller tent that was also slashed.

"Somebody was here?" Ziri asked.

"Or something." Rafik said. He dropped the tent and turned towards the gate. "Treshna couldn't have gotten in after we all went in the bag, right?"

Tragi shook his head. "Not that I know of."

"Who else would be here? Why didn't they take the bag?" Rafik asked.

"The bag appears to be pretty ordinary. If they just felt inside, they may not have felt anything and just left it there. Or didn't notice the bag." Kryn said.

"It had to be Treshna." Rafik argued. "What else is after us, or knows we're even out here?"

"If the Kylix are hunting us, we would know. There would be a sign or something, right?" Ziri asked.

"There was one man I ran into." Kryn said. "He tried taking that sapphire from me, but I beat him and left him in the tunnels."

"He could have been watching us all night." Rafik said, trying to keep his voice calm. Imagining a shady figure watching them, and then kidnapping them without anyone knowing flashed across his mind. "We could have died."

"If he watched us the whole time, he would have known we were in the bag." Kryn argued.

"Whoever it was, we need to get out of here." Rafik said, rolling up the tent and shoving it into the bag. "We can organize everything in the bag later."

Xeo trailed off from the group, examining the ground. He could follow their footprints. From the gate to the tunnel, and where he had discovered each of the masks. There was one pair along a far wall none of them had been. They came and went in the same footprints. To the tunnel, back to the wall, then to their camp, and back again. "Whoever it was knew Treshna was here. Climbed the wall to get out."

The group stared at the mountains and the ruins of the tomb. The unnerving feeling of being watched washed through them. "We need to leave." Ziri said.

Rafik nodded. "You can tell us more about this man as we're walking. It's already midday. We need to get going."

The group agreed, and without further discussion, left the Ruins of Kangor.

Soon after leaving the ruins, they each turned and gasped. The ruins were gone. "I didn't think we walked that far." Rafik said.

"We haven't." Tragi said. "We should still see it."

"Something is going on." Kryn said. "I don't like it."

"I don't either." Tragi said. "How much farther until Lynn?"

Rafik shrugged. "The Ruins of Kangor weren't on our map, so I'm not sure. Could be a few days, could be a few more weeks."

Ziri groaned. "I really hate the desert."

"I'm getting tired of walking." Kryn complained.

"We can't exactly stop now." Rafik said.

"If only one of us could fly ahead and see how far it is. Then come back." Xeo suggested.

"No!" Everyone else shouted.

"We'll get there when we get there." Rafik said. "Hopefully it is just a little longer, and that's why we can't see the ruins. We've just traveled that far." Even as he said it, he didn't believe those words.

The Gateway Mountains towered over them. Slowly, the sheer mountainsides gave way to slight inclines. As each day passed, the massive mountains separated and flattened, becoming large boulders and stones on foothills. It was the only indication the five were making any progress, as the desert sands swirled in the wind, but remained shapeless and indistinguishable from the days before. The air was still cold, and winds icy, cutting through the thickest of clothes.

By the sixth day the foothills were covered in lose stones, but strange larger ones stood proudly. There wasn't just one or two of these jutting out of the ground, but several dozen. At first, they seemed randomly placed, but Rafik noticed a pattern. "Look at these." He said, examining one closely. "I think this used to be a statue."

"They're just rocks, Rafik. Just like all the other ones out here." Xeo sighed. "I think the desert is making you go crazy."

"No, come see." Rafik said, gesturing for the others to come near. The stone did appear unusually smooth. In some places there were dings and marks of a chisel.

"I think you might be right." Ziri said. "Look at this one." She was examining one farther up the hill, in the middle of several stone outcroppings. A worn face could be seen, though most of its features were nearly nonexistent.

"What is this place?" Xeo asked.

"We must be getting close." Tragi said.

Shouting echoed in the distance. Yelling. Fighting. "Kylix?" Rafik asked, perking up his head and tilting it like a dog's.

"They should have already invaded Lynn if they did." Kryn said. "Remember his speech at the feast?"

Rafik nodded. "Then what's going on?"

The group slid down the scree, nearly tripping and falling on the loose rocks. They scrunched down, slowly inching forward towards the fighting. The last thing they needed was to walk blindly into the middle of the fight and be attacked by both sides. Slowly, just ever so slowly, they moved closer. Down the hill and around one more. In full view was a remarkable sight. Lynn. The City of the Gods.

Everyone gasped at the cityscape. Spires scraping the sky topped countless temples that glimmered in the light of the Black Wall like a small golden sun. What wasn't covered in gold was white marble and polished granite. Smoke billowing from the city streets below appeared out of place and peculiar in such prestige and glory.

"We're here." Tragi said.

"And I guess we're not the only ones. They're fighting somebody." Ziri whispered.

"We can't turn back." Rafik said. "Let's go. Maybe we can find out what's going on without being pulled in."

Xeo laughed. "We aren't that lucky."

As they cautiously stepped forward, the group noticed abandoned watchtowers. They weren't just recently abandoned but crumbling in ruin. "Reminds me of home." Rafik sighed.

"They have watchtowers but no wall?" Kryn asked. "That seems odd."

"Why would they need walls when they have gods to protect them." Xeo smirked.

"Yeah, look how well that's going for them." Kryn said.

From a distance the city was awe-inspiring. Up close, it seemed otherworldly. Every building rivaled the previous one in elegance and grandeur. The shouting was louder, echoing throughout the wide city streets. The shouting and chanting were coming from deeper in the city, but those out here were going about their lives like nothing was happening.

"What's going on?" Rafik asked one elderly woman who was sweeping the doorstep of her home. She brushed her long, curly gray hair out of her face as she turned toward them.

"Where did you come from?" She gasped. "I didn't notice anyone coming this way up the street."

"We just got here." Rafik said. "Travelled through the Biodlay."

The woman laughed. "Nobody does that. There's no food, protection, or anything that way."

"Well, we did." Rafik assured her. "Even took refuge in the Ruins of Kangor for a night."

"Now I know you're joking. That place doesn't exist."

"It's true. We even saw the field of weathered statues." Tragi said. "What are those for, anyway?"

The woman smiled. "An old hidden part of Lynn's history. You see, back before Lynn was dedicated to all the gods, it was home to carvers and builders. When somebody sought refuge here, artists would carve a statue of them, saying they would always have a home here. Not many know of the statues of the lost."

"Kind of hard to miss them." Xeo said.

"Not when nobody sees them. Nobody comes out this way. I'm guessing you're runaways? That's why you risked traveling such a dangerous path."

"What makes you say that?" Rafik asked.

"You seem to be of fighting age. Must be avoiding the Kylix. You'd have better luck hiding in the Lahmora Swamps."

"We are trying to get to the Nassir River, actually." Rafik said. "We were hoping we could take a boat there."

"Lynn ships aren't known for their seafaring prowess, but I'm sure we could get you there."

"Thank you so much!" Rafik smiled.

"For a price."

"What?" Kryn gasped. "I thought Lynn was full of priests and religious people. We can pay, but charging doesn't seem like the most...charitable thing to do."

"You want charity, talk to a priest. You want to ride in a ship, talk to a sailor." The woman snapped.

Xeo smiled. "I like her. What's your name?"

"Bahsha." The woman said.

A sudden echoing of shouts jolted them from the conversation, reminding them of the smoke in the nearby streets. "Nice meeting you. What's going on here, Bahsha?" Rafik asked.

"Protests. Riots. War." Bahsha sighed. "The city of Lynn is free from the king's influence. It's caused several to flee here in hopes of safety. People are fighting, if these refugees should be accepted, or sent away. If we should join Vanarzir or stay out of it. The whole city is erupting into chaos with this infighting."

"I didn't know Lynn was a free city." Ziri said.

"I'm sorry, dear, you'll have to speak up." Bahsha said, craning her neck, and holding her hand to her ear as if to scoop in the sound better.

"I didn't know Lynn was a free city." Ziri repeated.

Bahsha smiled. "It typically wasn't. King Vanarzir granted the city's freedom long ago. Before I was born, even. Rumor has it that he fears the gods. He never said if he believed in which ones, or any. But how he acted, it was apparent he feared for his soul. Not surprising, considering it's already doomed for Soboribor."

"Thank you for your time, Bahsha. Could you take us to the docks? Or at least point us in the right direction?" Rafik asked.

Bahsha gave a half chuckle. "I may be a lonely old bag of bones, but I insist you all stay the night. Get some rest, and I can make you a homecooked meal."

"We haven't had one of those in a while." Xeo said, holding his stomach and licking his lips.

"Taking the path you did, I can't imagine you've had much of anything to eat." Bahsha said. "You can enjoy a hot meal, get some rest, and I'll take you there in the morning."

"Is it safe?" Tragi asked.

"My cooking?" Bahsha laughed. "My children may have moved away, but it wasn't because of my cooking."

Rafik laughed. "I think he means, are the gods protecting us here? Is it sacred ground?"

Bahsha nodded. "If you are afraid of something creeping in the dark and snatching you, nothing can get you while you're in Lynn. I promise."

"Thank you." Rafik said, nodding to her. "And you don't care? That we aren't with the Kylix now?"

"Whether I do or not doesn't change the fact you're five children who showed up on my doorstep hungry and tired." Bahsha said. She turned to Kryn with a half-smile. "How's that for charitable?"

Kryn's cheeks flushed red, as the group laughed and walked inside her home.

Chapter 13: Stranger in the Night

Lynn, Biodlay Desert, Alutopek

The noise of the protests was nearly gone within Bahsha's home. A roiling fire emanated heat in the far corner of the main room. A cauldron hung over the fire, spilling over whatever was inside. As the liquid hissed, touching the burning coals, the smell of something savory and delicious filled the room. It was a cozy home, filled with trinkets and portraits of children. One large picture hung in the center of it all above the mantle of the fireplace. It was a much younger version of Bahsha and who they assumed to be her husband.

"It's nice having company again." Bahsha said, stirring the stew. She took a sniff, crinkled her nose, and tossed in more salt and herbs into the cauldron. "Been on my own since my husband died."

"Where's your children?" Xeo asked. "You said you have them. How come they don't come by?"

"Nice tact, this one." Bahsha said, shaking her head. "Most have passed, sadly. One is in Safsil, the others moved to the Akitung Jungle. They hated the desert and wanted far away from here. It's difficult to travel so far. We write often, though." She gestured to a stack of letters piled up on a nearby desk.

"Thank you again for taking us in." Rafik said, as they all took a seat at the table.

"My pleasure, my pleasure." Bahsha said. "Could you be a dear and help me?" She smiled and stared at Ziri fondly.

Ziri nodded. "Sure."

"You remind me of my granddaughter with that bright red hair of yours. And those vibrant blue eyes... Tell me, what's your name, child?"

"Ziri." She whispered, grabbing bowls from a cupboard, and helping ladle the stew.

"Ah. My grandbaby's name was Muirinda. She seemed sick since the day she was born. Didn't last long, sadly. Crushed my son's heart."

"I'm sorry for your loss." Rafik said, cutting into the silence that followed.

Bahsha smiled. "Thanks. It was years ago. The pain that's here has settled now."

As the night grew darker the cauldron grew emptier. Bellies were full, and laughter echoed throughout the home. The fire washing warmth over them. "I haven't eaten like this in a long time!" Xeo said, patting his belly. "That was delicious."

"Yes, thank you!" Kryn said.

"You are more than welcome." Bahsha smiled. "It's been much too long since this home has had laughter and smiles. I should be thanking you for showing up. My husband and I built this home nearly 60 years ago. You really did come from the north, didn't you?"

Rafik nodded. "It was quite the journey. You said the Ruins of Kangor don't exist?"

Bahsha nodded. "It's an old legend here in Lynn. The tomb of a fallen god. It's said to only show up when protection is needed. Several traveled along the Gateway Mountains to find it, but none have. Nobody even knows where it is."

"Protection was sure needed." Xeo sighed, imagining Treshna pacing at the gates. While he was searching for masks she growled and pounded on the unseen barrier keeping her away. More than once it made him jump nearly out of his skin.

"Oh, I am sure you do!" Bahsha said. "The infamous Xeo. Tales of you dueling the king even made it here. According to the Kylix you were captured and killed."

"Really?" Xeo asked.

"Yes, really." Bahsha smiled. "People began wondering how strong the king is. Some even wanted to join that rebellion and put you as king."

"Me? King?" Xeo laughed.

"That's why rumors of you dying spread so quickly. Whispers of rebellion soon died with you. At least in Lynn."

"Well, I'm still alive." Xeo said, puffing out his chest. "Never felt better."

"It makes sense they want you as king." Tragi laughed. "Our sister is queen after all."

"I didn't know Kristol had a queen?" Bahsha said, her lips pursing.

"It doesn't." Xeo said. "We still have no idea why, but our sister married the king. Valkayto."

Bahsha's face paled. "Oh, you poor dears, I'm so sorry."

"Sorry for what?" Xeo asked, his chest deflating. "I mean, yeah, I guess we are related to Vanarzir now. But we all have a family member we're ashamed of."

"I know being related to the king isn't something to brag about. But it is through marriage." Tragi said.

"No, not that." Bahsha said. "I guess you must not have heard if you have been traveling and avoiding people all this time."

"What?" Xeo and Tragi said at the same time.

"It wasn't long after their marriage a baby announcement came." Bahsha said.

"I'm an uncle?" Xeo asked.

"Yes, yes you are." Bahsha smiled. "But your sister…"

"What? What happened?" Tragi asked.

Bahsha's head lowered. "Your sister didn't make it."

The silence in the room was thick. Any feeling of joy or happiness evaporated out of the room faster than sparks striking off flint. "I'm so sorry." Kryn said. She reached across the table grabbing Tragi and Xeo's hands.

"I can't believe it." Xeo said, his voice hollow.

"I'm sorry to be the bearer of unwelcome news." Bahsha said. "Can I do anything for either of you?"

Tragi shook his head while Xeo stood still.

"It's his fault, isn't it?" Xeo finally said after several minutes. His voice deeper than usual, angry.

"Who, dear?" Bahsha asked.

151

"The king. Vanarzir." Xeo said.

"It's nobody's fault." Bahsha said. "Sometimes that happens during childbirth."

"That isn't fair! We were going to save her!" Xeo said, jumping from his seat, the chair flying backwards.

"She was queen of Alutopek." Bahsha said. "I don't think she needed saving."

Xeo shook his head. "No. She did. She hated him as much as we do." He darted towards the door and Tragi sprang to his feet.

"Where are you going?" Tragi asked.

"Anywhere but here." Xeo muttered. He reached for the door.

Tragi swatted his hand away. "You're not going anywhere right now. You'll end up doing something foolish."

"Get out of my way." Xeo barked.

"No." Tragi said, shaking his head. "She's my sister too. If you walk out that door, I don't want to be grieving the loss of both of you."

Xeo glared at his brother. "Ya shire."

"There's a bedroom just down the hall." Bahsha said, getting to her feet. "If you want to be alone, you're welcome to it."

"Thank you." Tragi nodded, shoving his brother away from the door. Xeo finally budged and turned toward the bedroom. Tragi followed, taking the bag resting on the back of Rafik's chair as they walked by.

"I guess we'll call it a night. I'm sorry it ended on a bad note." Bahsha sighed. "The company was nice, though. While it lasted."

"It's never a suitable time to share bad news." Rafik said. "I think I'll go help with Xeo."

Bahsha nodded and started collecting the dirty bowls from around the table. "I'll help." Ziri said. She took the bowls from Bahsha and finished collecting what was left.

Kryn stared down the hall, then to Ziri, talking to Bahsha in her usual soft whisper. The smile she had on her face reminded her of times she'd spend with her aunt and father. It was a peculiar day. Started out walking endlessly through the desert, ended with a delicious meal with a new friend, and now a cloud of loss hung over the place. She could feel it. Xeo and Tragi now mourning the loss of their sister, Rafik with his father, and Ziri her whole family she never knew. At least she still had her aunt. She just had to find her again. The feeling of loss was overpowering, and she felt the urge to leave.

She quietly excused herself from the table, tiptoed towards the door, and walked out.

The shouting and fighting echoing through the city during the day seemed calmer now. Off in the distance it was still there, but nowhere near as close. Like a moth to a flame, she started towards it, marveling at the city as she walked. Bahsha's home was built out of clay and sandstone, much like those in Haitu, but even her home was decorated with intricate designs. A blessing written over her door. As she walked deeper into the city the buildings became even more excessive.

Several homes were plated in gold or covered in white marble. Others had painted tapestries along the wall depicting myths from different religions. Every so often there would be a pitch-black building with silver etchings in it. Most of the glyphs and letters she couldn't read. The entire city felt foreign. Like she didn't belong.

In her childhood home of Syro, it was a massive arena. Their entire culture revolved around fighting and strength. She didn't learn to read until she was in Haitu, at the Sekolah Fortress. In Haitu the buildings weren't as elegantly decorated. The Kylix ruled there, and people feared them. In Datz, where she spent most of the last two years, it was a city of ruin, where it was a struggle to survive compared to the other cities she lived. But here? She had never seen such manufactured beauty.

Towers touched the sky, and homes here exuded wealth and prosperity. Smooth columns held up entryways to temples with ornate archways and tiered buildings. She never imagined something humankind made would be so beautiful. Walking in awe, she didn't notice as she weaved her way through the streets until she arrived at the chaos.

There were different kinds of soldiers here, pushing the rioters away, than what she was used to. They wore robes over thin chainmail and no helmet. As one turned to face her, she saw the tattoo of a crescent moon over their eye like Shallon's. One soldier spotted her and yelled for her to freeze. Kryn's eyes widened for a moment, shook her head, and ran down a nearby street. The soldier yelled, chasing after her. The guard was quick, catching up to her and cutting her off running through the maze of roads.

"Where do you think you're going?" The soldier asked, grabbing Kryn by the collar.

"Honestly, I don't even know." Kryn said. "I don't even know where I am."

The soldier looked her up and down before shoving her into a wall. "You're new here. What are you doing here?"

"Trying to find my way out." Kryn said. "I'm not part of the riots, or even know what's going on."

The soldier paused. "A likely story. You were probably recruited to help with the violence."

"I promise I wasn't." Kryn said, holding up her hands in surrender.

"There you are!" A voice said from the other end of the street. The man came running up to her, nodding to the soldier. "I was wondering what happened to you."

"You know her?" The soldier said.

The man with pure white hair and eyes nodded, eyeing Kryn with a look of malice. His sinister grin didn't help. "She's a friend of mine and came to visit me. Isn't that right?"

Kryn paused. Did she really want to deal with the thief from the ruins? Or take her chance with the soldier?

"Well?" The soldier asked.

"What?" Kryn asked, coming out of her thoughts. "Oh, yes. He's right. Sorry. Just a bit distracted and overwhelmed. Never seen such a city this beautiful."

"It would be better if these rabble rousers were out of here." The soldier snapped. "Take her home, before I lock both of you up."

"You got it, boss." The man said, putting his arm around Kryn's shoulders and leading her away. "Let's get home."

"Who are you?" Kryn asked, once out of earshot of the soldier. "And who are they? Never seen soldiers like that before."

"Those are Guardians of Lynn. They maintain peace in the City of the Gods. Usually, they're a lot more lenient and relaxed; easier to work with until these riots started. As for me, the name is Hurik."

"What are you doing here?" Kryn asked.

"I'm guessing the same as you. Just passing through." Hurik smiled. "Now I have questions for you. Firstly, what's your name?"

"Kryn."

Hurik paused before continuing as he ushered her through the back streets. "Short and sweet. I like it. Now, I know we didn't meet under the best of circumstances, but I must ask, where is my sapphire?"

"*My* sapphire, you mean." Kryn said. "Is somewhere safe, where you can't get it."

"Ah. One of your friends have it." Hurik said, nodding. "Where did you and your friends go?"

"What do you mean?"

"Don't play dumb with me." Hurik snapped. "With that monster at the gates of the ruins you couldn't escape. Which makes sense how you were able to summon the ruins with that thing after you. I tried searching for your camp, but you weren't there."

"You were the one who slashed our tents."

"Only out of frustration. I wouldn't have hurt you."

"I think I've proven I can hurt you better than you can me." Kryn laughed. "Don't fool yourself."

Hurik's smile soured, his eyes narrowed. "Indeed. And your friends, are they freaks like you?"

"Excuse you!" Kryn said, shoving Hurik and holding up her fists. Wisps of smoke slithering out between her fingers. "What did you call us?"

"Oh, come now. I meant no offense."

"By calling us freaks?" Kryn snapped. "I appreciate you helping back there with that guard, but if I see you again your face is going to be burned beyond recognition."

"No need to get violent." Hurik said. "I misspoke. A mistake, really."

"You don't mistake calling somebody a freak. You've been warned." Kryn said, shoving Hurik against a wall and turning to leave. After turning a few corners and arriving back on the main road, she noticed the guards rounding up the rioters, putting them in chains. Hurik was nowhere to be seen. Now to find her way back to Bahsha. She stared up at the Black Wall, hoping to find direction back to her. She had to be north of wherever she was. Finding the northern star, she started to beeline back home.

Kryn stuck to the back alleys and side roads until the shouting and the guards were a distant noise, rather than a deafening boom. Back on the main road, it was easy for her to find her way back to Bahsha's home. Some of the buildings were more familiar. She wondered if her friends would have noticed her absence. It would be alright if they didn't. Rafik was consoling Tragi and Xeo, and Ziri was spending time with Bahsha, who seemed to take a shining to her.

"I'm sorry." A voice shouted from behind Kryn.

Kryn spun around, fists lighting up in flame. "I told you what would happen if we ran into each other again."

"I misspoke." Hurik said, slowly stepping towards her. Inching forward, one careful step at a time, hands held high.

She noticed something in each of his hands. "What's in your hands? Drop it." Kryn shouted.

"A peace offering." Hurik said. "Two bottles of wine from one of the best taverns in Lynn. What do you say?"

"I say leave me alone." Kryn shouted, though her fiery fists returned to normal.

156

His cotton white hair blew on a stray gust of wind. He flashed a crooked smile. "One drink. And if you still aren't happy, you can burn me to ashes."

Kryn turned, staring back at the house her friends were in. "One drink."

"That's the spirit!" Hurik laughed. He lowered his hands, staring from one bottle to the other. They both seemed the same from what Kryn could tell. "Here you are."

Kryn pulled the cork out and sniffed the fruity aroma of mixed berries. "Thanks."

Hurik clinked the bottles together. "Cheers."

The two began speaking, but within moments Kryn's head began to spin. "I don't feel too good." She said, dropping the bottle and holding her head.

"Oh?" Hurik asked. "Losing your edge?"

"What did you do?" Kryn doubled over, eyes darting from the broken glass and purple liquid streaming down the gutter to Hurik. "Did you poison the wine?"

"Only yours, poor thing." Hurik said, yanking on Kryn's hair, pulling her head back and laughed. "Just proving I can hurt you more than you can me."

Kryn's eyes widened just before her world went dark.

Chapter 14: Booking Passage

Lynn, Biodlay Desert, Alutopek

Flashes of light flooded Kryn's mind. At first, they were blurs. Whites, yellows, reds, blues, and greens in no discernable pattern. The sudden blinking and speeding lights made her feel sick. Moments later her stomach was empty, and her vision began to come into focus. Where was she? What happened? It felt like the room was spinning. She stretched her arms and legs out, slowly feeling around. There was broken glass and pottery strewn about, parts of the ground were sticky, and it smelled like mold and filth. She tried to open her eyes, but the bright light made her sick again. A gust of wind bellowed down the alleyway, and Kryn shivered.

"What happened?" She asked herself, groaning. What was the last thing she could remember? Hurik. The thought of the thief brought flashes of something to the front of her mind. He was doing something, and she was struggling to fight him off. And…he was laughing. She finally managed to open her eyes without getting sick, and saw she was at the end of an alley. Near her was an empty bottle of wine. Seeing the bottle brought back more flashes of what happened. The pain. Hurik laughing. "Where's Rafik?" She asked herself, scrambling to her feet. The next moment she hobbled a few steps and fell over. Her body ached. Some parts searing in pain. Only flashes of what transpired were coming to her, but those were enough to know what happened.

Once again, she staggered to her feet and leaned against the wall, pushing herself to move forward. Her head was spinning, and every step shot pain through her body. She had to find her friends. Hopefully, they didn't leave her behind.

Hobbling out of the alley, freezing rain started to pour down on her. It wasn't long before she was soaked to the bone. She exhaled and saw her breath billow out. Her shivering intensified and teeth chattered. For the first time in her life, she felt cold.

It was a long night. There was a warm bed just steps away from Rafik. Instead, he slept leaning against a ladder in the room of the bottomless bag to prevent Xeo from escaping. In his rage and sorrow for losing his sister, he smashed the single chair and shattered the table. He and Tragi managed to calm him down before he destroyed everything else in the room. He turned, nearly falling from the ladder, jolting himself awake. He was surprised he even got sleep at all.

On the far side of the room was Xeo passed out in a pile of ruined supplies, and Tragi beside him. As he watched the twins sleeping, he reminisced about his first days in Mahparry. When he first learned Anza's life wasn't detected, anger consumed him. He believed she was dead, and he wanted nothing more than to avenge her death. Fueled by his rage and coupled with the lingering attachments of Blaridane, it took weeks to quell his thirst for blood. For endless hours Xeo and Tragi helped distract him. Allowed him to scream, roar, and eventually cry over her death. Now he was returning the favor.

The two of them were twins. Xeo the older of the two. The only similarity between them were the same honey-colored eyes. But as they slept, it was like the differences had washed away. He noticed the similarities in facial structure and nose shape. The way they both held themselves while they slept. He wondered how close they were with their sister. They didn't talk about her much while in Mahparry. Just that they were going to rescue her.

As he stood up, the floor creaked and Tragi sprang to his feet. Xeo continued snoring. "You're awake." Rafik said. "Were you even asleep?"

Tragi shrugged. "A little. Not really."

"How are you holding up?" Rafik asked.

"I feel numb." Tragi said. "Kay was always so energetic and lively. Even more than Xeo, but less of a troublemaker. She cared for us as much as our parents did. When she volunteered to leave Kristol and go with Vanarzir, it was to protect us. Xeo and I vowed to rescue her. Now we're too late. We let her down."

"You didn't let her down." Rafik said, putting his hand on his friend's shoulders. "These last two years you were training to save her. You didn't let her down."

"I know what you're saying is true." Tragi said, flashing a half-smile. "The trick is actually believing it."

"Easier said than done." Rafik said, returning the smile. "How do you think Xeo will be once he wakes up?"

Tragi shrugged. "I'm not sure. I've only seen him this upset once before. Once he was asleep like he is now, he was dreaming for nearly two days. When he woke up, he was like a zombie. Never reached that level of destruction again. I guess he's like a volcano. Once he erupts, it dies down.

"I hope you're right." Rafik sighed, scanning the room. So many broken and destroyed things. At least it was in here instead of in Bahsha's home.

"So, what's the plan?" Tragi yawned and stretched.

"We need to book passage to the Bomoku Mountains." Rafik said. "And replace as much as we can before leaving."

"I'm sorry he broke nearly everything." Tragi said. "He needs to learn to control his anger."

"At least these things are replaceable." Rafik said. He held up a small purse of coins and shook it. The clinging coins jingled but didn't sound like much. "I hope this will be enough."

"Only one way to find out." Tragi said. "If anything, all but one of us can stow away in the bag."

"That's a good idea." Rafik said. "I didn't think of that."

Tragi smiled. "Thanks. I have to redeem myself for that mistake of an idea back at the Bruin Fortress."

Rafik laughed. "Yeah, that wasn't your best idea. We all have bad ideas. Usually there's people there to stop you. It's our fault just as much as it is yours for that mess."

"Another clever idea is we should take the bag. If Xeo wakes up, that way he's with us."

"I like the way you think." Rafik said. "Let's go find us some breakfast first."

The two boys didn't have to travel far for breakfast. Once out of the bag they emerged in a quiet room, the smell of biscuits, bacon, and eggs, wafted in the air. Their mouths watered instantly from the aroma of all the food. Opening the door, it hit them even more.

"Good morning!" Bahsha beamed from behind the counter. Ziri beside her kneading dough. "This girl is a natural! Woke up early, and not only been helping me, but been able to keep up. I hope you boys are hungry."

Ziri smiled from ear to ear as Bahsha bragged about her. "Where is Kryn?"

Rafik shrugged. "She's not with us. I thought she was with you?"

Ziri shook her head. "Haven't seen her since last night."

"I'm sure she'll turn up." Bahsha said. "Once she smells what we're cooking. I'm sure the whole neighborhood will come by if we open the windows. Shame it's too cold for that."

"There's fresh juice on the table." Ziri said, pointing to the two flower vases now turned pitchers. "I made sure it's clean."

Tragi smelled both vases. One was orange, and the other apple. This brought him back to before going to Mahparry. Before Vanarzir came to collect children in their village of Kristol. Back when his family was whole. Suddenly the delicious smells soured. "I'll be right back." He said, excusing himself.

Before anything else could be said the front door opened. Kryn stood in the doorway, sopping wet.

"Kryn!" Rafik shouted, dashing over to her, grabbing her shoulders. "Where have you been? We were wondering where you were."

At first, she felt happy, seeing Rafik come towards her. The moment he touched her more memories of last night came to her. Without thinking she recoiled, stepping back. "Don't touch me." She snapped.

"Oh. Sorry." Rafik said, taking a step back as well. "I was worried about you is all."

"I don't need you touching me."

161

"I-I'm sorry."

Kryn shoved passed Rafik, staring at Bahsha and Ziri.

"Oh no." Bahsha said. "Go talk to your friend, dear. I'll finish here."

Ziri nodded and followed Kryn into another room.

"What's wrong with her?" Rafik asked.

"She'll tell you when she's ready." Bahsha said. "All you need to know is somebody hurt her. Just be there for her."

Breakfast didn't taste as good as it smelled after Kryn's return. After Tragi abruptly leaving, and Kryn pushing him away, everything just tasted mellow. The salty bacon, fluffy eggs, fresh fruit juice, and savory biscuits all tasted the same on his tongue. Worry and disappointment. Bahsha noticed this and tried to distract him.

He had told her his plans for the day, and she gave him more money to pay for the crossing into the Bomoku Mountains. When he tried to politely decline the gift, the elderly woman insisted, stating she wasn't going to be using it before she died anyway. With a gracious smile, Rafik accepted.

With his friends in the bag for one reason or another, he ended up showing Bahsha the bag before leaving. She was more astonished that five children, albeit older children, were in possession of such an object, than the bag itself. Rafik promised he would be back before nightfall and left to explore the city and find the passage they needed.

The streets were quiet as he left Bahsha's home. He marveled at the grandiose buildings decorated in golds, silvers, whites, and shimmering jewels. The streets were cobbled, not showing any sign of wear, yet still had the feeling of appearing ancient. He'd stare at a temple as he walked towards it, imagining the great structure to collapse and crumble, becoming a ruin like the ones that littered his home of Datz. Before the Black Wall did buildings there look just as majestic as they did here?

It wasn't long before he was lost in the maze of intricate structures, each distinct but complimenting the others beside it. A couple more streets and he saw a man shouting from the ledge of a fountain, proclaiming everyone to be cursed to Soboribor if they didn't repent. There was a woman screaming at those walking by that they were sinners. Most ignored these people, but slowly, some stopped to listen. If he wasn't set on finding a way to the Bomoku Mountains, he would have stopped once or twice to watch these interesting people spout and scream about their personal beliefs.

More people trickled onto the roads. Some shouting, demanding the end of King Vanarzir's recruitment of children. It was interesting to see people so opposed to the king shouting so in public, and not being killed for it. Anywhere else in Alutopek they would have been killed instantly. Watching a couple shouting, he wondered if any of these protestors were part of the Soniky. Would they stand up to him, be part of a rebellion, or was this as far as it went for them? Shouting into the wind and hope somebody who acts listens?

There was something about Lynn, he couldn't quite put it. He had been to Mahparry, grew up in Datz. Even spent time in Haitu and Trinkit. Nowhere made him think and wonder about so many things as it did here. It was more than just the City of the Gods; it was the city of learning. It was nice seeing more schools and churches, than fortresses and investigation stations.

Unlike in Trinkit where alcohol flooded the streets and air, paper and fruity wines filled the air here. In Haitu, a city on the other side of the Biodlay Desert, it felt lonely but busy. Like everyone were nothing more than skittering ants moving about aimlessly to onlookers. But here it felt like everyone had a purpose. A reason to be where they were in that moment. And when compared to his home in Datz, it was like night and day. There weren't ruins or decay. Just elegance and prosperity. Gawking at everything, Rafik realized at how intoxicating this new place was. It was a place he thought his father might like. A place where people didn't seem to struggle as bad to survive.

Rafik turned a corner and bumped into a woman, nearly falling over. They each apologized at the same time, which made the woman smile. "You seem lost." She said after Rafik helped pick up the scattered papers.

"I am." Rafik laughed. "Trying to find the docks."

"You're almost there." The woman said. "A few more streets over that way." She pointed towards the east.

"Thank you." Rafik said.

The woman nodded. "Just don't cross any bridges or you've gone too far. And take this, it might help if you're looking for guidance."

She handed Rafik one of the small pamphlets. They were all handwritten and showed a rough sketched map of the Lahmora Swamps. An arrow pointed towards one town on the edge of Opal Lake, but he noticed on other pamphlets it pointed to the other side. The pamphlets read 'Are you alone? Join the Haxama family.'

"I'm not alone." Rafik said, trying to return the pamphlet.

The woman smiled. "Of course not. Just in case." She refused the pamphlet and walked away, handing out the paper to others passing by.

Rafik tucked the pamphlet into the bag, realizing everyone else was in there. To everybody around him, he was alone. The thought unnerved him. For the last two years he was always with an Immortal, Xeo, or Tragi. But now, as his friends were tucked away, he felt the world around him pressing down from every angle. It was a peculiar feeling, like he was the deer being hunted. He shrugged off the feeling and hurried on his way.

The docks weren't as impressive as those in Datz. Even though this city was immaculate, and Datz was in ruins, he could tell they didn't focus on the docks and waterways as much. The temples and shrines had carvings of wind and water, a few for money. Even the smaller ones were ornately decorated.

It wasn't difficult to find the dockmaster. He was barking orders and cursing at sailors lugging materials to and from ships. "Looking for work, boy?" The dockmaster asked as Rafik approached. "Don't have too many boys working anymore since the Collection."

Rafik shrugged. "I'm trying to book passage to the Bomoku Mountains. I'm from Datz, so I know how to sail. I can pay, or I can work my way."

"A Datian?" The dockmaster said in surprise, eyes widened. He stroked his patchy beard before answering. "The less I know the better. You can work your way there. Sailors are normally allowed one small chest of personal effects. We will sail down the river, and to Safsil. From there you will stay on the ship, not get paid, and be taken to those cursed mountains. You'll be expected to work as any other sailor. And, since you're a Datian, I expect you to be just as good as some of the veteran sailors."

Rafik nodded. "Sounds easy enough. How long will it be until I arrive at the mountains?"

"A week. Maybe ten days if there's a storm." The dockmaster said. He spit a disgusting glob of muck from his mouth, wiping the dribble away with his bare hand. "Do we have an agreement, boy?"

"Aye, sir." Rafik said.

"And what's your name?"

"Rafik, sir."

The dockmaster paused before scribbling down Rafik's name. He stared at Rafik, head tilted, and eyebrows raised, before finally shaking his head and finishing his letter. "I've heard that name before." He muttered.

"I'm the only one I know of, sir." Rafik said.

"Course you are. Report to Captain Nehran. You'll be on the ship called the *Day Runner*. Tell him Dockmaster Yon sent you. Tell him the terms and give him this paper." Before Yon gave him the paper, he folded it and stamped it with a wax seal.

It was nice seeing the docks running smoothly and fully. He had never seen Datz like this, but Gorik and his father would share stories of older generations of Datians and how hectic the docks were. He never imagined it but seeing it in this smaller scale was proof. More than once, as he made his way to the *Day Runner*, he would stop and gawk at the hustle and bustle. There were sailors moving cargo on and off ships, and officers barking orders.

Sounds of rigging and the wind blowing, the smell of the river wafting across the docks. Nobody paid him any attention until he arrived at the ship.

"What are you doing here?" A man barked, marching up to Rafik.

"I was told to find Captain Nehran." Rafik said, holding up a letter.

The man was dressed in a well-tailored coat with tails and a tricorn hat that was common for captains of ships to wear. His square face was weathered, and eyes pits of ashy gray. "You found him. Give it to me, boy." Captain Nehran said, snatching the letter out of Rafik's hands. He glanced at the seal before ripping it open. "I assume you're Rafik?"

Rafik nodded. "I am, sir."

"Usually, I am the one who says who can and cannot be on *my* ship." The captain growled. "I already don't like you. And I suspect you're a sort of coward, fleeing enlistment from the Kylix. Another reason I don't like you. If you can tolerate that, you're welcome aboard."

"I'm not fleeing anything." Rafik said, clenching his fists. "King Vanarzir –"

Captain Nehran smacked Rafik, leaving a red mark on his face. "You claim to have sailing experience, but even the lowly cabin boys should know not to talk back to their captain. Is that clear?"

"Yes sir." Rafik said through clenched teeth, glaring at the captain.

"Good. We set sail tomorrow at high tide. Until then, get off *my* ship." Captain Nehran said, turning to scream out more orders to other sailors.

The rest of the day went smoothly for Rafik. He managed to visit different shops, all while marveling at the buildings of Lynn, collecting the much-needed supplies. By the time he was done, most of the money they had was gone. He opened his coin purse and saw only four gold coins, two silver, and five bronze. He opened the endless bag and tossed the coin purse down.

166

Throughout the day none of his friends came out of the bag. He wondered what was going on, what they were saying, but decided he could investigate after everything was said and done. Kryn wasn't acting herself, and he was positive Tragi and Xeo would still be upset. He felt guilty thinking it, but he was a little happy to have this alone time before delving back into helping his friends work through their problems.

Chapter 15: Terror in the Night

Lynn, Biodlay Desert, Alutopek

The city of Lynn was at the eastern end of the Gateway Mountains. It was situated at the beginning of the Oasis Trail, the only safe passage across the Biodlay Desert, and entrance to the western part of Alutopek. The edges of the Gateway Mountains were sheer, towering cliffs only allowing the canyon running through it the safest way through. Because of this, Lynn often had strange visitors from across the land. It being the home to most of the gods in most religions, and it was a place several wished to visit.

Rafik stood atop a bridge, watching a river run by beneath him. This river would lead up to the main river that ran through the canyon, and into the Vinsen Ocean. He imagined the *Day Runner* cutting through the river with ease before spilling out into the ocean. People in peculiar masks watching them from the trees, ready to strike. It was a vision he was positive he would see.

This bridge would have been the perfect spot to lose oneself in their thoughts if the growing protests and riots weren't surrounding him. The raucous they caused reminded him of seagulls squabbling over spilled fruit. Most of it was just noise. He stood on the bridge just a little longer, trying to burn the beauty of the city into his brain. Who knew if he would ever be able to return here again.

He had wanted to visit a few of the temples. Talk to some people with differing beliefs, but as he noticed the light of the Black Wall begin to dim, he started back to Bahsha's.

"How was your day? Did you get everything you needed?" Bahsha shouted as she stirred the pot hanging over the fire. Beside her was a brick oven with roiling flames, and he saw the bread baking within. The smell of herbs and freshly baked bread made him pause before he entered. This was a home. It wasn't his, but she sure made him feel welcome in it.

"I did. I only have a few coins left, but you can have them. I'll pay the rest back when I can." Rafik said.

"Oh, no." Bahsha laughed, holding up her hands and waving them. "Keep it. How are your friends?"

"Not sure." Rafik shrugged. "It was just me today. They're still in here." He patted the bag, setting it on the floor by the table.

"I'm not surprised. They're going through a lot right now." Bahsha said. "It's good of you and Ziri to be there for them. And you to do the chores while she comforted them. You five make a wonderful team."

"Thanks." Rafik smiled. "I feel lucky to have them."

Bahsha's eyes widened, nearly twinkling, as she smiled. "That's great, dear. Hope you're hungry, I made stew with fresh bread for dipping."

"It smells delicious." Rafik said. He opened the bag and shouted down that dinner was ready.

Xeo popped out of the bag first, followed by Ziri, Kryn and Tragi. From the looks on their faces, it seemed like they had a rough day as well. They all sat around the table as Rafik helped Bahsha set the food on the table. "I could get used to this cooking." Xeo said, licking his lips and eyeballing the stew. He took a deep whiff of the stew and sighed. His belly growled with approval.

"No need to stand on ceremony." Bahsha said, getting to her seat. "Dig in!"

The only person who didn't eat like ravenous wolves was Kryn. Ziri helped her fill a bowl, and she mostly just poked at it with a spoon.

"Are you alright?" Rafik asked during the middle of the meal.

Kryn nodded. "I'm not hungry."

"She'll be fine." Ziri whispered.

Kryn didn't respond, but nodded once more, and continued poking at her food.

"So, what's the plan?" Bahsha asked as dinner was beginning to end.

"We leave tomorrow." Rafik said. "I used your idea, and so I'm working for passage. Everyone else will be in the bag."

"We have to be in the bag? The whole time?" Xeo asked. "You know how cramped it gets down there? How long will we be stuck down there for?"

"A week to ten days." Rafik said. "But I'll be sure to let you out when the coast is clear. And at least you don't have to work the whole time."

"And tomorrow?" Xeo asked. "We didn't get to see the city!"

"You should have come along." Rafik said.

"I was busy." Xeo said.

"Throwing a tantrum?" Kryn asked.

Xeo sprang up from his seat, knife raised. "You're one to talk, you've just been crying in the corner all day. You want to fight?"

"Actually, I do." Kryn said, getting to her feet.

"Enough!" Rafik yelled. "We've all had rough days. No need to take it out on each other. Xeo, put the knife down. "Kryn, sit down." The two glared at each other before finally relenting. Both sitting back down.

"Rafik is right." Bahsha said, smiling at Rafik with an air of pride. "You five are on this journey together. And sure, you may want to rip each other's throats out at times, but you need to remember who the enemy is. And it isn't each other. You all have a long trip ahead of you. Go to bed. Not in the bag. In real beds. "I'll clean up."

It didn't take long for everyone to fall asleep. The moment their heads touched the pillows and being in a warm bed, they were out like a light. Darkness enveloped them, and the chilly night air of the Biodlay Desert wafted through the home. It settled into every nook and cranny, causing everyone to wrap themselves in thicker blankets. The fire began to die in the main room of Bahsha's home, which didn't help keeping the cold at bay.

A wind howled and a fog slithered into the streets of Lynn. It was common for fog to settle on the streets, being at the base of the Gateway Mountains, but this fog felt different. Colder. Thicker. Shadows danced and darted among the gloom, smothering the torchlight. As the last of the lights were snuffed, tendrils of violet pulsed within the fog. At first it was faint, but slowly, just ever so slowly, it became brighter. More vibrant like purple lightning wriggling through the wisp.

The few guards standing at the gates cowered as a howl echoed through the night. Spears and shouts were aimed at the hound of Soboribor. Treshna swatted them away with ease and ran into the city. For the first time in ages, evil prowled the streets.

Rafik sprang from his bed, grabbing the knife off the nightstand. He heard the echoes of that familiar growl. Peering out the window he could see the fog swirling around. "We've got a problem!" He shouted, banging on the walls, and stamping on the floor.

Xeo, Tragi, Kryn, and Ziri appeared from their beds, alert and disheveled. "Can I just get one full night's sleep in a comfortable bed?" Xeo snapped.

"Not while Treshna is here." Rafik said.

"Treshna?" Bahsha asked. "That's just a myth. Besides, she shouldn't be allowed to enter the city."

Xeo shrugged. "You should probably tell her that." He darted back into the room, coming back moments later strapping on armor and holding a sword.

"I'm sorry." Ziri said. "It's after us."

Bahsha shook her head. "Even so, she can't be here. Evil isn't allowed in."

"Yeah, right." Kryn scoffed. "Evil is definitely here."

"It doesn't matter how she got in." Rafik said. "We know what she's after. We need to get out of here. We can lure it away from here."

The stomping and smashing were getting closer. Before anyone could say anything else they heard the sniffing at the door. Banging and pounding, followed by a roar. Treshna was here. The group raised their weapons and braced for the battle. Shouts from the Lynn guards came next. Treshna roared, and the guards screamed.

A moment later the monster exploded through the door. The door flew off its hinges straight towards Bahsha. Tragi and Ziri dove in the way, blocking her. Xeo, Rafik, and Kryn charged forward at the beast. With thick claws it deflected each blow, swatting them away like they were flies.

"Use your fire!" Xeo shouted.

"Ya shire!" Kryn cursed, glaring at Xeo. "If I could you would already see her in flames!" She ducked, stabbing at the massive paw that swung at her.

"You can't use your fire? Since when?" Xeo asked. He charged forward, seeing an opening. Treshna gnashed her teeth at him, hitting him with the side of her mouth.

"Now isn't the time!" Rafik shouted. "Keep her distracted. I have an idea."

Rafik noticed her skinny deer-like legs. They appeared disproportionate compared to the rest of her hulking frame. If he could attack her legs, maybe he could stop her. As Treshna focused on Xeo, growling, and raising herself to full stature, Rafik charged at her, sliding on his knees with his sword held to slash at her. As he got close enough, he swiped and the legs buckled, one of them severing. An instant later she collapsed on top of Rafik, squirming to get up.

"Rafik!" Kryn shouted. She made her way towards Treshna. The monster noticed and swatted her with both hands. Kryn dodged one hand as the other came down on top of her.

"It's just you and me." Xeo glared. He raised his sword and pointed it at Treshna. She growled and screamed. Her tongue flickered in and out of her mouth like a snake, and orange eyes glowed with fiery intensity. Violet fog swirled around her legs, and she raised herself once more. As the fog vanished, he saw Rafik beneath her, not moving. More surprising were Treshna's legs. Instead of two deer-like legs, there were eight long spider legs, propping her up. "Ya shire."

Treshna roared and Xeo screamed, diving into the back of the house. The Hound of Soboribor tried snatching at Xeo and missed. She scuttled after him, tearing apart the home as she went. Xeo jumped through a window and escaped into the night. Treshna followed, leaving ruin behind.

Ziri was the first to wake up. The house was in pieces and strewn around the wreckage were the bodies of her friends. Glancing further out, onto the streets, were a dozen guards. Some weren't moving while others stayed still. Screams from those within Lynn echoed and mixed with the roars of Treshna. She was still loose somewhere in the city.

She glanced over and saw Tragi closest to her. Just beside him was Bahsha. "Wake up." She said, shaking the two of them. Her body ached as she hobbled to her feet. "Please wake up."

Bahsha coughed up dust and rolled on her side. "What happened?"

"You're alive!" Ziri smiled, hugging the old woman.

"I'm too stubborn to die." Bahsha smiled. "But it's tempting. I feel like a mountain fell on me."

"Not quite." Ziri said.

Bahsha nodded. "Just my home." She said looking around. Tears welled up in her eyes as she glanced at the wall that held the portraits of her family. It was now gone, shreds of debris on the ground, but no sign of any memories frozen in time. "It's all gone."

"I'm so sorry." Ziri said. "This is our fault."

Bahsha cried, not saying a word.

Tragi gasped, springing to his feet. "What happened? We missed the fight?"

"Missed, but you and Ziri saved Bahsha." Kryn said, rubbing her head. "That thing is strong. Where is it?"

Tragi shrugged. "My guess is wherever that screaming is coming from. She's left us alone. Finally."

"That means it got what it wanted." Kryn said. She hobbled to her feet, wobbling and holding her head as she balanced herself. "Where's Rafik?"

"Where's Xeo?" Tragi asked.

They shouted for their friends, but there wasn't a response. "This isn't good." Ziri said in her whisper of a voice.

"What did she want with either of them?" Bahsha asked. Her voice was like Ziri's, barely above a whisper. Her breathing came in heavy wheezes, and a trickle of blood ran down the side of her face.

"Rafik!" Kryn yelled, ignoring Bahsha. She scrambled over the rubble, noticing Rafik half buried in it. "Please be alive" She cradled Rafik's head in her arms, holding him.

"If Rafik is here..." Ziri said, turning towards the chaos rampaging through Lynn.

"Xeo is out there. Either captured or running." Tragi said.

"We need to help him." Ziri said.

"You go on. I'm staying here with Rafik." Kryn said.

"It's alright child." Bahsha said. "I can watch over him." She got to her feet, collapsing a moment later.

Xeo ran out northward into the desert. If he was fast enough, maybe he could make it to the Ruins of Kangor before Treshna caught him. He lunged over a rock and Treshna swatted at his feet, causing him to fall and roll into the sand. Without stopping he launched himself back to his feet, spun around, and stared at the beast.

Treshna towered over him. The body of a bear, the head of a buffalo, and mouth like a wolf's, it was already a fearsome sight to behold. But now, instead of two skinny legs, it stood on eight spider-like legs. Each one was smooth and glimmered like the edge of a blade. Her orange eyes burned into Xeo, drips of saliva sizzling as it hit the sand.

If she was just after him, maybe he could lose her in the city? There was no way he could outrun her in the openness of the desert. The trick was running past her. "What do you want with me?"

Treshna leaned over, getting eye level to Xeo, before screaming at him. The urge to flinch, cower, or run away from the roar almost overcame him. But he wasn't going to allow this mythical monster to know he was scared. He shoved his sword forward. Treshna pulled upwards, scooping up her hands as she did, getting sand in Xeo's eyes. He dropped his sword, pawing at his eyes.

"You cheated!" He shouted, taking steps back.

The monster inched forward, her growl turning from frustration to victory. Xeo knew what was about to happen. Either she was going to kill him or snatch him and take him back to Soboribor with her. Either way, he was as good as dead. He suddenly jumped, just slightly, raising both his legs to his chest, and plopping into the sand just as Treshna tried grabbing him. She screamed and stamped the ground in frustration. In the cloud of sand, Xeo managed to roll and crawl around her and retreated into town. Moments later the monster followed.

Dodging Treshna in town was much easier. He weaved through the streets, taking alleys, and circling back. More than once Treshna growled and clamored over or around buildings as she couldn't fit through the narrower roadways. Some of the guard tried to help, but as she ignored them, they just watched as Xeo tried evading her.

He finally made it to the greatest of temples in all of Lynn. The one in the center of town. It scraped the sky with spires topped in gold and had white granite walls. Running along the base were lines of red and silver. Carved into the massive oak doors was an hourglass showing who this temple was for. Barely inside the threshold and Treshna lunged at him.

Just like at the Ruins of Kangor, Treshna was stopped by an unseen wall. Xeo rolled onto his back, propping himself up, and gasped for breath. "Take that!" He panted.

The priests coming to his aid made a mark of protection with their hands as they saw the hellish beast. The oldest of the priests stared at Xeo in disbelief. "What did you do?"

Chapter 16: The Imposter

Lynn, Biodlay Desert, Alutopek

"What did you do?" The priest repeated, his voice beginning to waver. His wrinkled, leathery skin was shaking, causing his elegant silk robes to dance in the moonlight streaming in from the open front doors. His eyes widened as he glanced back at Treshna. He made a silent prayer, moving his hand for the sign of protection. "That...that thing! Must have come from the depths of Soboribor."

"As a matter of fact, she is." Xeo said, brushing himself off and getting to his feet.

"She?" The priest gasped.

Xeo nodded. "Treshna. The Hound of Soboribor."

"That's just a myth." The priest said.

"Try telling that to her. Pretty sure she's real." Xeo said.

Treshna paced back and forth, scuttling around on her new spider legs. They glimmered in the moonlight, giving it an unearthly sheen. Her furry bear-like body and head of a bison appeared even more out of place and monstrous. She pounded on the invisible wall, roaring. A moment later she spun around, an arrow protruded from her back.

She lunged for the guard, swatting him like a fly. Two more guards stepped forward holding spears but didn't move. Treshna growled at them and turned around, glaring at Xeo.

"What does it want?" The priest asked.

"I'm guessing me." Xeo said. "I don't know why."

"You are in sacred ground now. It can't hurt you." The priest said.

"I thought this whole city was supposed to be protected by the gods?" Xeo asked.

The priest shrugged. His ancient and hollow voice didn't even echo across the massive room like Xeo's as he answered. "Just because it's supposed to be, doesn't mean it is. Wickedness can slither into the hearts of even the most righteous of men."

"I guess so. Mind if I stay here until she's gone?" Xeo asked.

The priest chuckled. "If I said no, that would be a death sentence for you. Can't exactly say no when that is the outcome if I do."

"Thank you." Xeo leaned against a pillar, sliding down until he finally plopped onto the floor. The temple entryway was large, with six columns spanning the entryway The top and bottom of each column was covered in gold with silver writing running through it. The silver resembled wisps of sand across a desert. On the walls were statues and tapestries of the god this temple was dedicated to. He was positive Tragi would know who it was, but Xeo never paid attention when the Immortals tried teaching him.

"Tell me, child, have you considered serving the gods?" The priest asked.

"No. Why would I do that?"

The priest shrugged. "You've seemed to have been able to run away and hide from King Vanarzir and his collection of children. And you have a monster from the underworld chasing you. Seems like you could use a little help. And the gods will help those who help them."

Xeo shook his head. "I'll leave that to my brother. He's a peacekeeper."

"Oh, is he now? That's fascinating. Who is he?"

"Tragi of Kristol." Xeo said.

The priest scratched his chin, narrowing his eyes and tilting his head. "Tragi of Kristol? I've never heard of such a name. Strange. If he is, I would know him. All peacekeepers come to Lynn to study. And I help teach them."

"He learned somewhere else." Xeo said.

"Then he isn't a peacekeeper." The priest snapped. "Maybe that's why Treshna is after you? You two are practicing in wickedness."

Treshna roared and pawed at the invisible barrier, startling them both. She kicked at it with her spider legs and disappeared into the night. Fog with pulsing violet veins filled the area before finally disappearing. The sudden disturbing imagery distracted Xeo. He didn't answer the priest and by the time he got his wits about him the priest was gone. Through a high window he could see the light on the Black Wall begin to glow.

Xeo dusted himself off and started back to Basha's. He hoped everyone would still be safe there.

The protests that ran through the city since they had arrived were absent. People whispered about the monster that ravaged the city instead. Elders stood on corners and ledges, proclaiming the end of the world. That Treshna was a sign for the end of times.

"Repent!" One priest shouted at Xeo. "Repent or spend eternity in the depths with monsters like that. Each one more horrifying and crueler than the last."

Xeo ignored the man, as he shouted and pointed, claiming he was now damned for eternity. Three more times it happened, before he saw Tragi wandering the streets. "What are you doing out here?"

"Trying to find you." Tragi said. "Glad I did."

"Is everyone alright?"

Tragi shook his head. "Rafik is hurt. And Bahsha didn't make it."

"Bahsha!" Xeo gasped. He clenched his fists, lowering his head. When he finally spoke it was cold, and just above a whisper. "It's my fault."

"What did you say?" Tragi asked.

"It's my fault!" Xeo shouted. "Treshna is after me. I don't know why. But she chased after me."

"Maybe she's after all of us, and she was just trying to bring you back to the rest of us?" Tragi suggested.

"No." Xeo said, shaking his head. "No, she came after me when she could have taken the rest of you. This monster wants me."

"Well, she can't have you. We'll all die trying to protect you before she gets you."

Xeo smiled. "No. Maybe that's where my journey ends, Tragi. I stay behind, luring Treshna into the desert while the rest of you go on."

"I don't believe that for a second." Tragi said. "We'll get through this together. All of us or none of us."

"You're my brother. You're supposed to say that."

Tragi shrugged. "Maybe. But I'm sure they'll all say the same thing when we get back."

Bahsha's home was in ruin. The early morning light reflecting off the Black Wall streamed down onto the wreckage. Only the chimney remained standing. Everything else scattered about the ground. In the middle of it was Ziri crying and holding Bahsha, and Kryn holding Rafik.

Neighbors had slowly inched out of their homes and began huddling around the rubble. Some homes nearest to Bahsha's showed signs of being in a war, but most of it was centralized to her home. Murmurs spread among them, wondering what the old woman was up to.

"You need to leave." One older man said, throwing a rock at Ziri. "Get away from her!"

"You have a problem?" Kryn asked, getting to her feet. She clamped her fists, jutting them downward. Without the flames erupting around her it just appeared as if she was on the verge of throwing a tantrum.

"Yes, we do." The man said. "She kept to herself. And then you came along."

"Shouldn't you be in Haitu?" A woman asked, stepping forward to stand beside the man. Both had a pompous air about them. "Maybe that's what King Vanarzir is collecting you little brats for. Some of you are cursed, and he's trying to protect us."

"She was kind enough to open her home to us." Kryn snapped. "We didn't do anything."

"Then maybe you should have done something, and she would still be alive." The man replied.

180

"You need to leave." The woman said, and the crowd nodded, grumbling in agreement.

"No." Ziri said. "I'm not leaving her."

"What?" The man said, putting his hand to his ear. "You'll have to speak up." The crowd snickered at his comment.

Ziri looked down at Bahsha, as she cradled her head in her lap. "I'm so sorry we couldn't protect you." She gently moved her to the side and got to her feet. Her veins popped and glowed red, her icy blue eyes grew dull, and her lips more vibrant. "I'll make you feel how I feel right now."

The crowd took a step back, some of them called for the Lynn guards.

"They're not worth it." Kryn said. "We need to go."

Ziri shook her head. "I'm not leaving her."

"Ziri, we need to." Kryn said.

Ziri turned to Kryn and saw the light in her eyes. It didn't have the usual fire or spark in them. And for the first time that Ziri could remember, she looked scared. Her veins stopped glowing, and light returned to her eyes. "Alright." She spoke.

Kryn dug around in the rubble for a moment and pulled out the familiar endless bag. The two carried Rafik awkwardly down the road.

"Take care of her please." Ziri said to the crowd as they walked by.

Rafik jolted awake, springing to his feet and gasping for air. Instinctively he reached for his sword. A moment later he groaned, grabbing his head. "What happened." He grumbled, collapsing back onto the bed.

"Relax." Kryn said, dashing to Rafik's side. She sat on the edge of the bed holding his hand, in the other the *Diary of Nekvaz*. "You're safe."

"What happened?" Rafik asked. He opened his eyes and saw the room spin and blur from double vision. Slowly it came into focus. He recognized the brick walls and ladder on the far side of the room. There was never a bed down here, though. "How did a bed get down here?"

"A little bit of remodeling." Tragi said, putting pots and pans on the shelf now tucked away in the corner. "Welcome back to the world of the living."

"How long have I been out for?" Rafik asked.

Tragi shrugged. "Couldn't be more than a day. Surprised it wasn't longer with Treshna falling on you."

"What were you thinking?" Kryn asked.

"Her legs." Rafik said, closing his eyes and rubbing his temples. "They were her weak spot. Must have worked if we're alive and she's not here."

"Not anymore." Ziri said.

"What do you mean? I know I cut them off." Rafik said.

Kryn shared the rest of what happened. Describing how Treshna now had spider legs and tearing down the rest of the house. Tragi shared how Xeo managed to run to a temple and was safe there until morning. Ziri finished by explaining the aftermath of the attack. Bahsha's home was destroyed. They dug through the rubble to find the bag while being scolded at the crowd.

"She just didn't wake up." Ziri whispered, fighting back tears. "She was so sweet. And we killed her."

"We didn't kill her." Tragi said.

"If we weren't there Treshna wouldn't be either." Ziri argued. "It's our fault."

"I'm so sorry, Ziri." Rafik said. "You two seemed really close."

Ziri nodded. "She felt like family."

"Where's Xeo?" Rafik finally asked after a long stretch of silence.

"He's pretending to be you." Tragi laughed. "After we all met back up, we put you in the bag, and found some looters from where Treshna had attacked."

"We joined the looters, packing the bag with a bed and a few other things, along with you. Then we made our way to the docks. We agreed Xeo would pretend to be you, in hopes it wasn't too late." Kryn said. "Apparently she caused a big enough delay that if we hurried, we could make it."

"He's pretending to be me?" Rafik laughed.

"You wouldn't wake up. So, Xeo said he would pretend to be you." Kryn said.

"Did it work?" Rafik asked.

The three shrugged. "We haven't been discovered or kicked off yet." Kryn said.

"I guess Treshna is hunting Xeo?" Rafik guessed.

"We think so." Tragi said. "Now we're trying to figure out what he did."

Rafik's head felt like it was going to split. If he moved too fast, or there was a sudden noise his stomach turned. As time went on the pain numbed and became more of an ache.

In a flash the trapdoor opened and Xeo jumped in. "You're awake." He grumbled, collapsing on the bed. "You can go up there. Why did you have to tell him you're a sailor?"

"Because I am." Rafik laughed. "My dad and Uncle Gorik taught me. Remember? I've told you that several times."

"Yeah, but I'm not a sailor." Xeo said. "I think the captain is starting to suspect I'm not you."

"He didn't before?" Rafik asked.

Xeo shrugged. "He said he thought I looked different. His first mate suggested to hold off the alcohol."

Rafik laughed. "I'm sure you're doing fine."

"I don't think he can trade places with you anyway." Tragi said. "I think the captain would notice that for sure."

"Ya shire." Xeo cursed.

"Do you know how much longer we'll be stuck down here?" Kryn asked.

Xeo shrugged. "A few days, I think. I'm trying not to think about that."

"Oh, come on. It can't be that bad." Rafik said.

"Treshna attacked everywhere trying to find me. A lot of people got hurt and couldn't sail. So, we're all being pushed extra hard." Xeo explained. "Pretty sure Captain Nehran would be trying to conscript children if there were any for him to snatch."

"And Treshna hasn't returned?" Rafik asked.

"Not yet." Xeo said. "When it gets dark I come straight down here."

"And they haven't noticed?"

"Not yet. But it's just the second night so far." Xeo said.

Before Xeo could say anything more he was out like a light. Rafik and Kryn nudged him, but he didn't make a sound, let alone move. "He must be exhausted." Kryn said.

"Sailing isn't easy work." Rafik said.

"He can enjoy relaxing once we get to the mountains." Ziri said. "We agreed once we're there he will stay in here until we can get the curse lifted."

"That'll drive him crazy." Rafik laughed.

"That'll save lives." Ziri said, the scowl on her face seemed to be a permanent fixture now.

As Xeo snored, and Tragi and Ziri drifted off to sleep on piles of blankets, Rafik reached for Kryn's hand as she still sat by his side. "How are you?" He asked.

Kryn shrugged. "I'm cold."

"You've never been cold." Rafik said, wriggling a blanket out from under Xeo and wrapping it around Kryn. "Does this have to do with you not able to use your fire?"

Kryn nodded, not saying a word.

"What happened?"

"I don't know." Kryn lied, as flashes of what happened came and went as quick as lightning within her mind. They were like parts of a bad dream. She could see it vividly in her mind, but she couldn't find the words to describe it.

"You know I'm here for you, though, right?" Rafik asked.

"I know." Kryn said, squeezing the blanket tight around her. She leaned over as Rafik scooted over closer to Xeo, giving her room on the bed.

Not saying a word Rafik wrapped his arm around her, and the two fell asleep.

"You said you were from Datz?" Captain Nehran barked, marching up to Xeo.

Xeo nodded. "Ugh, yes sir."

"Datz is known for their sailors." Captain Nehran said. "The best across all Alutopek."

"I'm sure that's an exaggeration." Xeo said.

"Clearly. I would think any sailor worth his salt would know the difference between a half hitch knot and a square knot." Captain Nehran said, holding up the rope Xeo was just tying down.

"Is that not it?" Xeo asked.

"The fact you can't tell is embarrassing." Captain Nehran said. "It's clear you lied to me. You're either not from Datz, or you're not a sailor. Or both. My crew doesn't have time to train you. Give me one good reason I shouldn't have them throw you overboard."

"I have a charming personality?" Xeo suggested.

"Excuse me, Captain!" A voice hollered as the captain was about to place a hand on Xeo.

The captain turned, a man with pure white hair and cotton-colored eyes stood on the deck. "What do you want? You know passengers aren't allowed on deck."

"I know, and I apologize for breaking the rules. This was a prank that got out of hand."

"Excuse me?" The captain asked.

"I challenged my friend here to try and get a free ride. I bet him 30 silver coins he could trick you and the crew. I will gladly give you the money if you allow him to live."

"Make it 60." Captain Nehran snapped.

"40." The man countered.

"60 and I won't get rid of you either."

"Captain, you have yourself a deal." The white-haired man smiled, shaking hands with the captain, and giving him a small purse of coins.

"I better not see either of you up here for the rest of the voyage."

"We promise, Captain." He replied.

The white-haired man led Xeo down to the hull of the ship where the rest of the passengers were staying. "Thank you." Xeo said. "I owe you one. My name is Xeo, by the way."

"Not a problem, friend." He smiled. "The name is Hurik. Pleasure to meet you."

Chapter 17: Maelstrom

Vinsen Ocean, Alutopek

Hurik's laugh echoed throughout the belly of the ship. The smell of potatoes and fish cooking over a fire in the galley wasn't far, making their stomachs rumble. Captain Nehran didn't feed his crew much. Apparently, he fed his passengers even less. Among Hurik were three other passengers, and Xeo made the fifth. "You are a hoot, Xeo." He roared, slapping his knee. "I'm glad I rescued you."

"Me too. Don't quite like being fish food." Xeo said.

Again, Hurik erupted in laughter. "I can't imagine most would. Or monster food like back in Lynn. So many are trying to flee that place. Like rats skittering from a burning building."

Xeo nodded. "I thought there would have been more on this ship."

"I know Captain Nehran." Hurik said. "He doesn't like carrying people on his ships, unless they're working for him."

"Are you from Lynn?"

"Me?" Hurik laughed. "No. Far from. Where did you say you were from again?"

"I don't think I did." Xeo said. "I'm from Kristol."

"Wow. All the way up north. Are you running from something?"

"Why does everyone think that?"

"Because nobody travels that far." Hurik explained. "And you appear to be young enough that you should be in the Kylix."

"I'm not running from that old bag of bones or his army." Xeo snapped. "I'd fight him right here and now if I could."

"That's mighty big talk." Hurik said. "Most fear the king."

"I don't." Xeo said. "Never have. Never will."

The other passengers started looking intently at the wooden hull. They continued fumbling with their hands and shuffling their feet. Hurik watched each of them before finally responding. "You must have a trick up your sleeve."

Xeo shook his head. "Nope. Just confident in myself."

"I see." Hurik said, scratching his chin. He brushed his cotton hair out of his eyes. "Surely there must be something. A souvenir, maybe, that you've come across."

"What do you mean?" Xeo asked.

"You can't make it from Kristol to here without seeing a few things. Exploring places. Maybe finding something." Hurik said.

"There is nothing between here and Kristol." Xeo said. "Most of it is desert."

"The ocean of sand still has secrets." Hurik said. "There is so much hiding beneath that sand, Xeo. Treasures lost to time. Even…burial grounds."

"What are you getting at?" Xeo asked, his voice shaking slightly, eyes narrowed.

"Have you ever heard of Syrus?" Hurik asked.

Xeo paused. "An old legend." He finally answered. "A hero in the Rhine-Pa religion."

"Indeed." Hurik said. "A legend some believe."

"Do you?"

"I do." Hurik said. "You see, I come from the Sampra Tribe. Before the Fohdorsha came together, it was the Pearl Tribe. Home to some of the greatest guardians known to Alutopek, maybe even all of Amlima."

"Was Syrus part of the Sampra Tribe?" Xeo asked.

Hurik's thin lips curled into an unnatural smile. "No. Syrus wasn't even Fohdorshan."

"Oh." Xeo said matter-of-factly as if his response answered all the questions.

"Syrus was much older than most peoples. You see, the Fohdorsha were coming out of the Dragon Wars. The Dragon Riders were extinct. The last of the Dragon Lords defeated. And former soldiers were looking for work. The Sampra Tribe became guardians to sacred sites." Hurik said. "The era of dragons was closing, but through the elegance of the Sampra Tribe, there seemed to be hope to our return to grace."

"I'm guessing something happened?" Xeo asked.

"Yes." Hurik said. "The Sampra Tribe started a network, to help travelers get to places safely. People trusted them with their treasures, and their lives. And then someone started attacking us. One by one the great guardians fell or disappeared. We found a pattern to the attacks and met the enemy in the Biodlay Desert. A battle ensued so great it's said the mountains that dotted the desert crumbled to bits of sand from the fighting. And when the dust settled, there was only a single soul left standing."

"Who was it?" Xeo asked.

"His name was forgotten to history." Hurik said. "For the rest of his days this forgotten one searched the labyrinth for the greatest treasure."

"He never found it?"

Hurik smirked. "If he did, we wouldn't be alive today." He died searching for it.

"What was the treasure?"

"It's called the Staff of Syrus." Hurik said. "According to Fohdorshan legend, it's hidden in a labyrinth within the Ruins of Kangor. The man lost to time cursed the ruins, so only those in need would find it. That way he could search the ruins in peace. He left the bodies of the conquered where they died."

"Sounds like an interesting legend. I think you could take a couple storytelling tips from my friend, Rafik." Xeo said. "You should hear him tell the story about the constellation of Quellor."

"I want to find those ruins."

"They say that place only appears to those who need it. And I'd imagine you need to be in front of it first. Not just anywhere in the desert." Xeo said.

"Which you were." Hurik said.

"What makes you say that?"

"I saw you."

Xeo's eyes widened as he stood up straight. "Who are you?"

"Not much of a poker face, eh, Xeo? I already told you who I am." Hurik said.

"What do you want, Hurik?" Xeo asked.

Hurik's eyes darted to the three others. They were eagerly talking amongst each other in low whispers, their eyes flickering towards Xeo and him. "I'm...I'm a treasure hunter." Hurik finally answered. "You see, those guardians never got a proper burial. Their bodies are still lost in the sands of the Biodlay. Their masks never found. And the ruins were lost forever. A common punishment within the Sampra Tribe is that a person isn't allowed back home unless you bring back a mask of one of our fallen brothers from those ruins."

"If I come across them, I'll be happy to share." Xeo said. "I think I'm going to explore the rest of the ship." He got to his feet, but two of the other passengers scrambled to theirs and blocked the door.

"Where is it, Xeo?" Hurik asked.

"I don't know what you're talking about." Xeo said, turning to Hurik.

"I saw you use the mask." Hurik said. "And I know you can't carry more than one at a time. Your fiery friend didn't have it. So now I'm asking you. Or maybe your friend Rafik has it? Or one of your other two companions?"

"What did you do to Kryn?"

"Nothing she didn't deserve." Hurik laughed. "And oh, did it feel good."

Xeo lunged for Hurik, and the two fell backwards, knocking over the chair he was sitting on. Hurik jabbed at Xeo's throat, rolled on top of him, and started punching. Xeo pulled a knife from his side and plunged it into Hurik's stomach. The Fohdorshan grabbed at his side, taking steps back, allowing Xeo to scramble to his feet. The three passengers yelled, charging after Xeo as Hurik shouted for them to capture him. It wouldn't be long until the crew would be down here and lock them up, or worse. He turned his head, glared at Hurik, and darted into the darkness of the ship.

Hiding in the shadows, Xeo evaded the crew and attackers and made his way back to the bag. He slinked from shadow to shadow, pausing as sailors shouted for him. Hurik claimed Xeo attacked him unprovoked, which the three other passengers confirmed as he stood menacingly near them. He tucked the bag behind two barrels. Once he was happy the bag couldn't be noticed within the darkness, he climbed in.

"What's wrong?" Kryn asked the moment she saw Xeo.

"Hurik is here." Xeo said.

"Who?" Tragi and Rafik asked.

Kryn clenched her fists. "You met him."

Xeo nodded. "Piece of work, he is. From what I gathered, he's after the Ravohka we found to redeem himself."

"Redeem himself?" Kryn asked. "There's no redeeming someone like him."

"What's going on?" Rafik asked.

Xeo explained to his friends what Hurik said. "So, returning these masks allows those in exile to return. It might work for us, too."

"That'll be our plan." Rafik said, nodding in agreement.

"See, and you wanted me to leave them there." Xeo smiled.

"A happy accident doesn't make you less of a fool." Tragi said. "We can celebrate your luck if we all get out of this alive."

"We don't have enough masks, though." Ziri said.

"But we can take them to the rest if they need us to." Rafik said. "I think they might be willing to help us."

"It's worth a shot." Kryn said. "In the meantime, I'm going up there and finding him."

"No." Tragi said. "It's bad enough we're stowaways. If they find us now, though, it could be even worse. We'll have to sneak around. Not bring more attention to us by hunting him down."

"The last time we listened to you I had to save you, if you remember that?" Kryn snapped.

"Besides, if we're stuck down here, how will we know where we're going?" Ziri asked.

Rafik frowned. "We'll think of something. You're both right. We can't stay down here, but we can't go chasing after Hurik when the entire crew is looking for Xeo, and anybody who shouldn't be there."

Kryn shook her head. "I don't want to just sit and wait down here. I want to find Hurik."

"We will." Rafik assure her. "He said he saw you use the mask?"

Xeo nodded. "I only used the first one." He gestured to the Ravohka now hanging on the wall like the head of a trophy from a hunt.

"Alright. Here's the plan. Xeo said he hid the bag in the darkness of the ship. We can sneak out one by one. Stick to the shadows. Except Xeo. He will have the mask and call for Hurik. If anybody else shows up, we can knock them out. Don't kill them."

"What about Hurik?" Kryn asked, examining one of her knives. "I'm not knocking him out if I have the choice."

Tragi frowned. "We aren't murderers."

"I agree. We aren't." Xeo said. "Everyone we've killed has been Kylix trying to kill us. We've just been defending ourselves. Hurik isn't any different."

The frown on Tragi's face grew deeper, and his brow creased. Finally, he shook his head. "I don't know what to say."

"Don't worry. You're a peacekeeper." Xeo said. "You do your thing, and we'll do ours."

"Just stay out of our way." Kryn said, walking passed Tragi, shoving him with her shoulder to the side.

It was Rafik that left the bag first. He insisted since it was his plan after all. He inched out of the bag, squeezing himself upward, shimmying upwards between the barrels and a wall. "I didn't think I was *that* fat." Rafik groaned, sucking in as the barrel widened.

The creaking of the ship was like a familiar voice to Rafik. He put his hand on the ship wall and closed his eyes. Memories from when he was a child, sailing with Gorik and his father flooded him. The smile on their faces was bigger than he remembered. A tear trickled down his face. He doubted those good times would ever happen again. His memories swirled like mixing paints together before darkness overtook them. A moment later the ship's memories came to him. He watched the *Day Runner* pierce through the waves, making port and sailors filling it with cargo. Then he saw Captain Nehran arrive, and the ship grew dark. It was like happiness left the ship. People in chains were bound to the hull. Whipped. Beaten. The cruel laughter of Captain Nehran echoed throughout the darkened halls.

Rafik pulled his hand away and his face soured. He signaled for the rest to come out.

"You couldn't have picked a narrower spot?" Kryn asked. "I'm not a stick like you."

"I was just trying to find a safe place to hide." Xeo said, glancing down at her chest.

"Don't stare!" She snapped. "I might not be able to use my fire right now, but I can still poke your eyes out."

"Oh, uh, sorry." Xeo said, quickly turning away, his face turning pink.

"Tragi isn't coming." Ziri said. "Said he's going to protect the bag."

Xeo rolled his eyes and sighed. "What good is a pacifist if we can't use him as bait?"

"You're the bait." Rafik said. "Remember?"

"We're twins!" Xeo shouted, and the group shooshed him all at once. "We're twins." He repeated in a whisper.

"Yes. Except he has long hair, and you don't." Rafik argued.

"Do you think Hurik is that perceptive?" Xeo asked.

It was Rafik and Kryn who rolled their eyes this time. "Listen, we don't have time for this. Everyone hides except Xeo. I'll be right back."

"Where are you going?" Kryn asked, a slight look of panic on her face.

"I'm going to talk to Tragi. Stick to the plan." Rafik said, climbing over the barrels and falling back into the bag.

"You can't change my mind." Tragi said as he noticed Rafik return. "I'm not going to be a part of this."

"I'm not here for that." Rafik said, shaking his head. "I need your help."

"With what?"

"I want to take this ship."

"Are you serious?" Tragi gasped. "I mean, Rafik you're my friend. Like another brother to me, really. I'll help you so long as there isn't killing. I trust you."

"This is a slave ship." Rafik said. "I used my talent and saw the history of it. It's Captain Nehran. Before him, the *Day Runner* wasn't one. We need to stop this. He's a slaver."

Tragi's face went grim. He nodded, heading towards the ladder. "Do the others know?"

"No." Rafik shook his head. "I figured they can get Hurik. We can take the ship."

Kryn, Ziri, and Xeo weren't anywhere near them as the two left the bag. "Doesn't sound like they've found him yet." Tragi said.

Rafik held his hand to the wall of the ship, eyes closed. "No, it doesn't. This way."

"Did you just find out where Nehran is?" Tragi asked, his eyes wide. "Your talent is getting so powerful!"

"No." Rafik said. "I watched the *Day Runner's* memories and learned the layout of the ship. The captain's quarters, and the deck are both this way."

"Oh." Tragi laughed. "That makes more sense."

"Follow me." Rafik said. He bent over the barrel, scooped up the bag, and led the way towards the captain's quarters. The ship rocked, creaking in the familiar way Rafik felt comfort in. It was like the ship was speaking to him. Pleading with him to redeem its soul. Thunder echoed from above. The familiar smell of the food cooking mixed with the salty sea. They had made it to the Vinsen Ocean.

Tragi teetered back and forth with the ship as Rafik walked smoothly. "I think I'm going to be sick." He said, his face turning green.

"Don't have your sea legs yet?" Rafik laughed.

"Sea legs?" Tragi asked, looking down at his and then Rafik's.

"It's an expression." Rafik said.

Echoes came from below them as they found the stairs leading to the deck. The pelting of rain made the stairs slippery, and both held onto the rail. The quartermaster could barely be heard barking orders over the howling of the wind and roaring thunder. Lightning struck nearby, lighting the sky for the briefest of moments. The only other light came from lanterns hanging from the mast. Sailors were trying to fight the storm as the ship turned, a wave crashing into it.

"Uh...Rafik." Tragi shouted. "We have a problem."

"What's that?" Rafik asked. He was staring up at the helm where the quartermaster was. It didn't appear the captain was there. Which meant he was in his quarters.

"Look." Tragi pointed. Faint purple wisps swirled in the air, pulsing.

"Where's Xeo?" Rafik asked. His face paled, imagining what Treshna could do in such a confined space.

As if on cue something burst out of the ship, flying into the air. Ziri climbed out of the hole, followed by Hurik. Kryn was next, cursing like a sailor and throwing one of her knives at Hurik. "Get down here!" Rafik yelled.

Xeo floated in midair, his face hidden behind the mask. Some of the sailors noticed and watched in awe. "Listen to your friend, boy!" Hurik shouted, fending off an attack from Kryn.

Hurik ran to the rigging and started climbing. Halfway up Xeo plummeted towards the ship. He skidded to a stop. Nearly crashing into Tragi. "Here." Xeo said, handing the mask to Rafik. "We need to help Kryn, she's gone crazy."

Rafik dropped the mask into the bag, nodded, and handed it to Tragi. Hurik and Kryn were fighting, nearly getting tangled in the rigging. "Xeo, get in the bag."

"Why?"

"Look!" Tragi shouted.

The purple veins within the fog were getting thicker, pulsing now like a heartbeat. "How can she get out here? We're on the ocean?" Xeo asked.

"Hold on!" The quartermaster yelled. "Hold on before the sea takes you!"

The group looked up and saw a massive wave hurdling towards them. It was twice the size of the ship and curled, like a gaping mouth eagerly stretching outward to swallow the *Day Runner* whole.

"Ya shire." Rafik cursed. He wrapped his arm around the railing and knelt towards the floor. Kryn's eyes widened and her face paled, twisting her legs and arms around the rigging, Hurik doing the same. The wave crashed into the *Day Runner*, tipping the ship on its side. Tragi fell over, losing the bag. As the ship righted itself, Hurik dropped from the rigging and snatched the bag.

"Help me!" Kryn shouted, dangling from one of her legs, tangled in the rigging.

Rafik looked from the bag to Kryn. He couldn't let Hurik discover not just the bag, but everything that was in it. But he also couldn't let Kryn fall. Blaridane's voice echoed from the recesses of his mind, urging to forget her and go after Hurik. He shook his head and started climbing.

"Help me!" Kryn repeated, not noticing Rafik. She had lost her knives from the wave and couldn't free herself.

"Maelstrom!" The quartermaster shouted. He darted to the wheel and began steering the ship away from it. The whirlpool grew bigger, twice, thrice, four times bigger than what it was when he first announced its presence. The maelstrom pulled at the ship and water, taking everything into the abyss of the sea.

Tragi glanced over the edge and saw two bright white lights towards the bottom of the maelstrom. Looking into them his body

196

froze in fear. His thoughts turned to nightmares of being devoured by the sea, like a minnow to a shark. A splash of saltwater getting into his eyes was the only thing to pull him away from those thoughts.

"Stop Hurik!" Rafik shouted, nearly to Kryn now.

Xeo and Ziri turned, looking every which way, but didn't notice the cotton haired fiend. Suddenly, the bag bulged, and a mask came out. Then another. And another. "We need to get them!"

Ziri nodded, and Tragi soon followed. The familiar roar of Treshna echoed with the thunder, and the deck exploded behind them. She roared, turning and spotting Xeo, she screamed again and gave chase. By this time, most sailors abandoned their posts. The maelstrom was even bigger now, and slowly the *Day Runner* was circling the funnel, getting closer and closer to the bottom with the two glowing white lights. The quartermaster shot an arrow at Treshna, distracting her for the briefest of moments, allowing the three to grab the masks.

"I got the bag." Tragi said. "Is he in there?"

Xeo nodded.

The bag bulged once more, and Tragi fell over from the sudden weight. "Give me the masks." Hurik ordered, kicking the bag away from Tragi and into the air. He seized the bag and pulled out a sword as Tragi reached for it.

"How about a trade?" Xeo said. "A mask for the bag?"

Before Hurik could respond Treshna roared. Half of the quartermaster slumped near the wheel, the other half in Treshna's clawed hand. She took a bite of him, throwing the rest out to the sea. Rafik and Kryn dropped from the rigging. If everyone wasn't staring down the Hound of Soboribor, most would have been startled by their sudden appearance.

"I think it's too late to get in the bag." Xeo said.

The ship creaked and groaned. Thunder boomed, followed by an earsplitting *CRACK*. The mast fell, being swallowed by the sea. "We're not getting out of this alive." Hurik said, making the sign of protection from the Rhine-Pa religion.

Treshna glared at Xeo and roared. Her spindly spider legs started towards him as the group screamed and separated. "I have an idea." Xeo said. He had grabbed the mask of flight and put it on once more. Immediately he shot out passed the ship and into the center of the maelstrom. Treshna roared and scuttled toward the edge of the ship. She banged her claws, roaring more.

Thunder boomed, and the ship began to crack. The maelstrom had won, and the *Day Runner* was being torn apart like it was nothing but toothpicks.

"We're going down!" Rafik shouted. He turned to Kryn, the fear he felt echoing in her eyes. He wrapped his arms around her, and they both closed their eyes.

Xeo rocketed towards his friends, grabbed Tragi and Ziri, but wasn't fast enough. The maelstrom disappeared as quickly as it started, leaving the storming seas behind. Not a trace of the *Day Runner*, the crew, passengers, or even Treshna remained.

Chapter 18: Deep in the Trees

Amsahvi Tribe, Bomoku Mountains, Alutopek

The salty air and cool breeze brushed against Kryn's face. Was she dead? The last thing she remembered was seeing those bright white lights. They say when you die you see a bright light. But two? Maybe one was for the good souls, and one for the bad? Which one did she end up going to? It felt like it took all her strength, but slowly she opened her eyes. The brilliant light blinded her, and she blinked several times before the light slowly turned to shapes, and then to actual things. Not far from her was Ziri. She smiled. That had to mean she wasn't damned to Soboribor after all.

She groaned, slowly pushing herself up off the sand. She turned her head and saw Xeo. '*Never mind.*' She thought. She was cursed to the realm of despair. At least they were all together, she noticed. Getting to her feet she fell immediately into the sand, catching herself at the last moment. A moment later she heard it. Some labored breathing. Leaves rustling. Somebody was nearby.

Kryn got to her feet, this time managing to stay up. Ahead of her, towards the rustling noise, were the Bomoku Mountains. She recognized them instantly from stories. Crimson peaks stretching into the sky like serrated teeth. And at the bottom was a thick forest, she doubted any sort of large game could even fit through. She squinted her eyes and saw flashes of white bobbing up and down just inside the tree line of the forest.

"Hurik." She hissed, hurrying, and stumbling toward him. About halfway towards him Hurik noticed. His face paled and he darted into the forest. Kryn gave chase, tripping a moment later. He had the four masks they found at the ruins. Since only one could be held, she noticed they were each farther away than the last. He had been tossing them one by one, playing a sort of game of leapfrog with them. Before continuing the chase, she threw the masks back to her friends, and then disappeared into the forest.

Hurik weaved in and out of trees like a rabbit evading capture from a fox. Kryn chased after him like a bull.

Straightforward and without stopping. As he would duck and dodge between branches, Kryn crashed through them, barreling through brambles and branches. She had screamed at first, but now she hunted in silence. Hurik glanced over his shoulder, but every time he did, she was getting closer. Suddenly he lunged to the side, tucking, and rolling down a small hill. He sprang to his feet and continued onward.

The sudden change caused Kryn to stumble as she tried making the turn. By the time she got to her feet he was gone. "Ya shire." She cursed to herself. She brushed herself off and spun around, trying to find where she was. The trees towered into the sky, even blocking the red mountains from view. She could see the small hill she fell from, but everywhere else appeared the same.

Pine permeated through the air as a soft wind whistled between the trees. A faint voice echoed. She spun around, unable to tell where it was coming from. A figure fell to the forest floor behind her, causing her to scream.

Kryn turned, balling her fist. The figure caught her fist in midair, and she gasped, taking a step back. The figure appeared human. But the face wasn't. The face was nearly a perfect oval, with narrow, crescent shaped eyes. Tusks jutted upwards, out like an animal's, at the edge of the mouth. There wasn't a nose, but thick vertical lines. At first she thought them to be a sort of wrinkle, but realized they're more akin to slits of a nose from a snake.

"No need to fear-scream." The high-pitched voice chuckled, taking off their mask. "There's no danger-harm here." Behind the mask was just another regular face. Bluish-green eyes and dark chestnut hair with a tint of emerald as the light glowing from the Black Wall touched it. "I'm friend-safe."

"You startled me." Kryn said. "I wasn't expecting to see your Ravohka."

The woman's face lit up. "I thought you were an outsider."

"I am." Kryn said.

"But you know the proper name of the masks." The woman said, her face crinkling in confusion.

Kryn nodded. "It's a long story."

"We love stories." The woman said, clapping and bouncing on her toes.

"We?"

The woman nodded. "I need to escort-take you before the others get you."

"What others?"

"Ghosts."

Kryn's jaw dropped, her face paled. "Ghosts?"

"Not dead-spooky-ghosts, but hunter-ghosts." The woman said, as if this answer cleared up any sort of confusion. "Come on. I'll take you to my village-home."

"What's your name? I'm Kryn."

"Junla." She responded. "Pleasant-greeting you."

Kryn smiled. "Likewise, Junla. I like the way you speak."

"Thank you." Junla smiled even bigger. "Most open-landers don't."

"Open lander?" Kryn asked.

"Yeah." Junla confirmed, nodding. "People who live on the ground."

"Wait, you live in the sky?"

"You're clown-funny, Kryn. I like you." Junla said. "Hold on." She put the mask to her face and watched it contort to that unnatural shape. Though this one did seem more natural than the one Xeo enjoyed wearing.

Massive eagle wings sprouted from her back. Before Kryn could respond she jumped into the air and took flight. Kryn clung onto her arm, squeezing harder the higher they got. "What is going on?" She finally asked.

"Hang on, friend-Kryn." Junla said. "I'm taking you to the village-home now."

"I think I really am dead." Kryn whispered. She glanced at the ground, now being shrouded in branches. They were still within the trees, and the ground appeared too far away for comfort.

The Black Wall and Bomoku Mountains grew closer and bigger as the trees thinned. Just before breaking free from the grasp of the trees, Junla slowed her flying. A platform spanned a handful of treetops, but there wasn't any sign of much else. Junla gently landed Kryn on the platform before her wings disappeared and she landed with a thud. She took a deep breath of the cold, pine filled air. It was crisp, chilling the lungs and sent a spark of energy starting from her lungs. "Air-fresh up this high."

"Where did your wings go?" Kryn asked, walking around Junla, examining her. "Do all dragonborn have that?"

Junla shook her head, frowning slightly. "Guess you are an outsider. No, it's from my Ravohka. It's the mask of affinity."

"Affinity?" Kryn asked, her head tilted.

"If I see an animal then I can mimic their abilities." Junla said. "I enjoy-love coming up here and bird watch. Eagles, especially."

"What about a dragon? You come from dragons, right?" Kryn asked.

Junla laughed. "The great dragons of ancient-old times are gone. All that's left are little ones. Like frosted tangles, savage husks, or sand dragons."

"I saw a big dragon." Kryn said.

Junla laughed. "Sure you did, friend-Kryn. And I saw what's beyond-far the Black Wall."

"I did!" Kryn snapped. "In the Biodlay Desert two years ago. It was a big black one."

"That's not funny." Junla said, her smile wiped from her face.

"I swear I did." Kryn said.

"Rathsa lives." Junla whispered.

"Who?"

"I guess we both have stories to share-tell." Junla said. "Come-follow. We're almost there."

"Where?" Kryn asked. She spun around, squinting her eyes. The view from so high was beautiful. The tops of trees just barely out of reach, and the red rock of the Bomoku Mountains appeared even bigger as they towered over her. Nowhere in this breathtaking view was there a sign of a home, let alone a village.

Junla made her way to the center of the platform. The tallest of the handful of trees built in and around the platform protruded out. She grabbed on the bark and pulled, revealing a massive hole. "This way, friend-Kryn." A moment later she ducked into the hole, a jovial echo followed.

Kryn glanced over the edge. "Ya shire." She muttered and followed her new friend. The darkness enveloped her, and the floor vanished. Below her she could hear Junla's squeals of delight, flashes of her eyes blinded her as she looked up to check on her. Kryn's heart beat faster as she slid down the tunnel. Her stomach lurched and more than once it felt like her insides were trying to escape through her mouth. Even with the unsettling feeling, she started to smile. The air brushing against her faster than wind, it felt almost like she was flying. The chute started curving, twisting more, and her body slowed. Finally, as she stopped, her organs returned to where they were originally, and the feeling of being sick slowly left.

"Where am I?" Kryn asked.

Small lanterns hung from the ceiling, and all around her it smelled like wood. Pines, cedar, aspens, and others she didn't recognize. The light showed wood surrounding her. Along the walls of the narrow corridor, the floor she sat on, and the ceiling that held the lanterns. Upon closer examination, she could even see the familiar rings a tree has on the walls.

"This is my village-home." Junla said, smiling. "My people-kin live here."

"We're in the tree?" Kryn asked.

Junla laughed. "The deep-roots to be exact."

"Why hide away in here?" Kryn asked.

"The other tribes…" Junla said before trailing off. She scratched her chin and scrunched her eyebrows together. "They hate-despise us. We're safe-free in here."

"And they don't know you're in here?"

"Most don't." Junla smiled. "Though some of us are try-making a small village-home in the middle of the forest."

"Wait, why don't they like you."

"Follow me, friend-Kryn. I'll take you to the elders. But allow me to welcome-greet you to the Amsahvi Tribe."

"Amsahvi?" Kryn said. "I've never heard that word."

Junla nodded. "Yes, since the others believe us to be extinct-dead, our tribe isn't on map-drawings anymore. We're the descendants-children of the great Cavernous Lazywings. We're the Earth Tribe." As she said this her chest puffed and her chin held high.

"I don't know my dragons." Kryn said. "But I come from the Akitung Jungle, in a city called Sysinal. It's a place of warriors, and I was one of them."

"But you're so young!" Junla gasped. "The great dragons must have blessed-gifted you with mighty strength."

Kryn smiled. Junla's voice was rhythmic, almost whimsical. And how she spoke gave an air of innocence and light. She could listen to her speak all day, and not get bored. "I have talent."

"You were blessed-gifted!" Junla smiled. "What talent were you given?"

"I could control fire."

Junla's face scrunched and her eyes narrowed. "Nobody has that talent. That belongs to dragons. And us Fohdorsha don't even have that. Are you joke-lying?"

"No, I promise!" Kryn said, raising her hands in surrender. "One time I was even able to shoot fire out of the bottom of my feet and zoom across the ocean."

"Now you really are joke-lying." Junla laughed. "I like your stories. If you do have power-talent of fire, prove it."

Kryn's head lowered in defeat. She clenched her fists. There was an emptiness there. As if part of her was missing. A cold washed through her as she tried searching for that warmth. That spark. "I-I can't." She finally said. "Something happened to me."

"Did you partake in the ritual?" Junla asked.

"What ritual? No. At least I don't think so. A man...attacked me. When I woke up it was gone." Kryn said. She

204

paused as images from that event flashed in her mind. It was coming in pieces, and she wasn't sure if she wanted to remember the full thing.

"Poor-sad thing." Junla sighed, wrapping her arms around Kryn. "I know the feeling. Of both wicked-bad men like that and losing talent."

"You do?" Kryn asked.

"Every Fohdorshan is born with talent. When we come of age it is ripped-taken from us, and we must earn-win it back. If we do, we get a Ravohka." Junla explained.

Kryn stared at the mask she held in her hands. To think that power was once inside her. How was that even possible? "Could I have a mask?" She finally asked. The cold and emptiness in her felt like it was consuming her. Even the warmth of the sun felt colder. And most peculiarly, she felt distant. Like a link had been severed from her and everybody else.

"Outsiders usually don't get Ravohka." Junla said. "But most outsiders don't have power-talent of fire like dragons. We can ask the elder-priest. Follow me, friend-Kryn."

For being inside trees and their roots, Kryn was surprised at how open and spacious everything was. After mentioning this, Junla pointed out where one root ended, and another began. Between them they had built bridges that mimicked the look of the root. It was hard to notice at first, but she could tell the more open areas were all built to mimic the roots. The walls on these didn't have the intricate ring design and had things more than lanterns hung on them.

There were people all around her similar in appearance to Junla. Most of them were fairly short, however. Junla mentioned the shorter people with dark hair and chestnut-colored eyes were the Amsahvi who hadn't intermingled with other tribes. Kryn noticed her bluish-green eyes. Between that and her height, she was different. As if reading her mind Junla chimed in. "My great-grandad was from-born the Lepal Tribe. Water Tribe. I'm not ashamed."

"You should be." One person said, spitting at her feet. "You ruin-shame our home. And bringing an outsider! Kolinda don't belong here." He was an older man. If he ever had hair on his head, it had long since disappeared. His skin was rough like bark, and wrinkled, making him appear like he was turning into stone. His hands trembled and teeth clattered when we wasn't speaking. Kryn hid a smile as she noticed his earlobes were long and stretched that reminded her of melting wax.

"Ignore-shun him." Junla said, grabbing Kryn's arm and pulling her along. "Hateful-wrong people aren't worth your time-life."

The old man yelled at the two in their own language Kryn couldn't understand. Junla shook her head and continued making her way through the village. Finally, they had made it. Each hut was a dome covered in mud. It was a major difference to the intricate temples carved out of stone back in Lynn. This dome they stood in front of was larger than the rest, and light poured out of the windows. Shadows danced in the light as somebody was walking around inside.

Junla knocked and entered without waiting for permission. "Elder-priest Teller, I have a friend. Her name is Kryn."

"Welcome Kryn." Elder-priest Teller said, turning from the fire that was in the center of the dome. He was hunched over and hobbled towards them using a staff. A gemstone rested on the top, bound to the staff by cord. Over his common clothes was a robe draped over his shoulders woven with yellow and purple patterns. His hands were leathery, and his face hid behind a mask like the one Xeo had found that allowed him to fly. The fins on either side of his face, and spikes running along the top. Even the puckered mouth was the same. "My appearance doesn't scare-frighten?"

Kryn shook her head. "One of my friends found a mask like the one you're wearing. I've seen it before."

It perplexed Kryn how even though it was a mask, it conveyed such emotion. Teller's eyes narrowed, and the puckered lips drooped like a frown. "So you are with them?"

"Them?" Kryn asked.

"Invader-killers." Teller said. He pointed his staff at Kryn, and his shakiness was now gone. "The bone-hunters."

"Bone hunters?" Kryn gasped. "Elder-priest Teller, Bone Hunters are extinct."

Teller shook his head. "No. They arrived-came months ago. With the one claiming to be king."

"Oh, the Kylix!" Kryn gasped. "The Kylix. Their uniforms are like Bone Hunters according to legends, yes."

Teller scratched the chin of his mask. "We've been live-dwelling in darkness for so long. Lepal Tribe asked for help."

"They knew you were here?" Kryn asked.

Teller nodded. "Us elder-priests stay in touch. I thought it was a joke-trap."

"Why?"

Teller sighed, turning back to the fire. He muttered some words Kryn couldn't understand and tossed bright powder into the flames. The fires reached the top of the dome and flickered in unusual colors. Finally, images started to appear. "Back when ancient times were still in the future, three Tribes went against the rest. For this, we were banished or killed-hunted. Our ancestors hid in the roots of trees and remained here. Run-fleeing that persecution and violence. Only recently have we revealed ourselves."

"Was it that bad to deserve such cruelty?" Kryn asked, watching the images of genocide, her heart breaking.

Teller nodded. "The great dragons are no more because of us."

"There's at least one." Kryn said. "I saw it."

"She tell-speaks of Rathsa." Junla interrupted. "In the desert."

"The last Obsidian Dragon." Teller said, glancing up. The images flickered and then turned to a woman with hair darker than night, barreling through the forest, and climbing the red mountain peaks. She was carrying an unusually smooth stone that was easily a quarter of her size. Men chased her to the edge of a cliff. She skidded to a halt, dropping the stone over the ledge. "Legends tell of this tale-story. And we heard it finally hatched, becoming Rathsa. The rider that the egg hatched for traded it to King Vanarzir. With the new power the king created the Black Wall, and enslaved Rathsa."

"Maybe there's more dragons?" Kryn suggested.

"I'm afraid not." Teller sighed, shaking his head. He whispered into the flames, and they disappeared. "Our people have searched high and low for the great dragons. When we first went into exile, we tried finding any trace-sign of them. Rathsa, if he is real, is the only one."

"What do you mean if he's real? I saw him. Don't your flames show him?" Kryn asked.

"After the Black Wall was created, we lost him. Most believe he was a trick-joke all along." Teller said.

Kryn opened her mouth to speak, but Junla cut her off. "We didn't come-greet to talk about the great dragons, Elder-priest. Kryn needs our help-aid."

"Oh?" Teller said, cocking his head. His leathery skin cracked as he smirked. "Not many have come-sought to the Amsahvi for help. Even before we were exile-shunned. What is it, child?"

"I-I was hoping I could have a mask." Kryn stammered, lowering her eyes to the floor.

"Ravohka are sacred-treasures." Teller said, his voice calm yet sounded scolding. Like a parent teaching a toddler what they had just done was wrong. "Only the Fohdorsha are allowed one."

"Oh. I...I understand." Kryn said.

"Her talent was stolen-taken." Junla interrupted. "She feels the cold-loneliness."

Teller shook his head. "I'm sorry, Junla and Kryn. This is one rule-law we cannot break. Maybe another tribe might, but I won't risk-peril our tribe in breaking this rule."

"My friends and I found Ravohka in the Ruins of Kangor." Kryn said. "I left the three we brought with them back on the shore. If I return one, could I then be accepted as Fohdorsha and have one?"

"Returning a lost Ravohka does allow exceptions," Teller said scratching his chin. She saw flecks of dirt and dried mud fly off as he scratched. Even with the cleaner skin, it still looked crusty and leathery. "But you don't have it with you. Tell me, did this attacker give you anything to drink?"

Kryn thought long and hard before answering. That whole night was fuzzy. And the images she saw weren't ones she wanted to remember. "Yes. Yes, he did!" She finally answered.

"I see." Teller said. "Did this drink smell different, or act strangely?"

"No. It was just a drink. He offered me one."

"And what talent is missing-gone?"

"Fire."

"Fire?" Teller scoffed. "No man, Fohdorsha or Nomad has that talent."

"I do." Kryn snapped. "I did, I guess."

"Are you a half breed?" Teller asked.

"A what?"

"Oh, sorry-regret if that term offends you. Was one of your parents Nomad and the other Immortal?" Teller corrected himself.

Kryn shook her head. "No."

"Impossible." Teller said, muttering and turning back to the flames. Without looking he grabbed a mask off the nearby shelf. "Here. Wear-put this on."

Junla opened her mouth to interrupt but Teller shushed her. Kryn reached for the mask. She felt the warmth it was giving off in her hands just like when she had fire. "Thank you." She slowly inched it to her face, feeling the power pulsing, hearing a slight hum as it got closer to her face. The moment she put it on she screamed. Her head felt like it was being split, and a ringing in her ears was deafening. She fell to her knees, ripping the mask off and instinctively throwing it as far away as she could from her. Junla dove, snatching the mask and rolled to a stop.

"*If* you do have talent of fire, it's still within you." Teller said, taking the mask from Junla. "But you do have talent, regardless."

Kryn shook her head. "Then how come I can't use it?"

"Fear." Teller said calmly. "You are afraid-scared."

"I'm afraid of nothing." Kryn snapped.

If you want your talent-power back, find the one who hurt-harmed you."

"Do you think he has it? Did he steal it?" Kryn asked.

Teller smiled. "Long ago, back when this old-ancient man was a boy, I had a friend who lost their talent. Their talent-power couldn't save him when he needed it. He had to find himself again. Reconnect with it."

"And finding this man will do it?" Kryn asked.

Teller shrugged. "It's a suitable place to start. You need to reconnect-find your talent. It's still in you. Just lost."

"Thank you." Kryn said, nodding. "I'll try to find him. Do I have your permission to leave and search for him through the forest?"

Teller laughed. "Permission? Not only do you have permission, but we'll also give-gift you a sword, too."

"I'm going with her!" Junla snapped.

"Of course you are." Teller laughed. "Since you found-discovered wings, it seems like all you want to do is adventure-leave."

Junla laughed, putting on her mask. Wings instantly sprouted from her back and a smile grew from behind the tusks. "So grateful-happy for my mask."

"You earned it." Teller smiled. "Take-guide Kryn to get supplies. Then you can be off-leave."

Chapter 19: New Allies

Lepal Tribe, Bomoku Mountains, Alutopek

Rafik had heard stories of shipwrecks before. Ships being taken by the sea from a storm, running aground, some even crashing against mountains of ice jutting out of the water. Very few survived. He tried recalling the stories of maelstroms with two bright white lights at the bottom. Nobody mentioned that little detail before. If it wasn't for the shipwreck, Treshna would have gotten them. It was a bittersweet moment, realizing they were doomed either way. He balled his fists, scooping up sand and opened his eyes.

The cool gentle breeze brushed against him sending a shiver down his spine. The Tahlbiru Ocean constantly had freezing waters. He heard the Vinsen Ocean was warmer, but it didn't seem by much. Then again, it was still winter. He slowly pushed himself up, noting all his clothes were in tatters. He had scrapes and scratches on his arms and legs, and his head hurt. But he was alive.

Slowly, he inched towards Tragi, then to Xeo, then Ziri who was farthest away. They were all alive too. But where was Kryn? Last he remembered he was holding her. She couldn't have gotten that far if he were here. By the time he reached Ziri he was walking again. He noticed the three masks scattered around the beach, and footsteps leading into the forest. They had to be Kryn's. He was sure of it.

Ziri was next to wake up. Followed by Xeo and then Tragi. "Where's Kryn?" She asked.

"She went this way." Rafik said. "We need to find her."

"Why didn't she wait for us?" Tragi asked. "Thought we were a team?"

"We are." Xeo said. "Someone or something must have made her leave."

"What would do that?" Rafik asked.

"I'll give you one guess." Xeo said, pointing to another pair of footprints not far from them.

211

"Hurik." Rafik said.

Xeo nodded. "I think so."

"Where's the bag?" Rafik asked, scrambling across the sand. He scanned the beach as waves rushed in.

Everybody shrugged. "I think it went down with the ship." Tragi said. "I'm sorry."

That was one treasure Rafik didn't want to lose. The bag not only offered them shelter and protection, but the treasures inside. The elemental stones, the jewels of the Four Kings they had somehow collected. Even their cache of weapons and food. All gone. Most importantly, it was the one connection he had left to Anza. They had found that bag together. Used it. He tried fighting back tears, but they broke through, and he collapsed to his knees. It was like losing her all over again.

"We'll find the bag." Ziri said, putting her hand on his shoulder. "Maybe Kryn has it."

"If she did, she would have put the masks in." Rafik reasoned.

"Maybe Hurik has it." Tragi suggested. "Maybe he has it, and Kryn stopped him from getting the masks, chasing after him."

It wasn't likely, but it's possible. Rafik nodded, regaining his composure, and turned towards the Bomoku Mountains. "We'll find her. We'll find the bag. Stop Hurik. And stop Vanarzir."

"That's the spirit!" Xeo said, clapping Rafik on the back.

"This is weird, though. Is it not?" Tragi asked, holding his hand to his brow, scanning the beach.

"What is?" Rafik asked.

"Here. The beach." Tragi said. "If we got washed up, shouldn't there be wreckage from the ship too?"

Rafik was surprised he hadn't noticed it before. But he was right. Not a splinter of the ship had made it to shore. Not a piece of cargo, or even other sailors. How did they get so lucky?

"Maybe it was Treshna. Wanted to continue the hunt." Xeo laughed.

"She only wants you. The rest of us would have died." Rafik said. "Something else had to have happened."

"Maybe those bright lights weren't lights after all. Maybe they were portals, and it took us to the nearest shore for safety?" Ziri suggested.

"Then there would be a lot more here, I'd imagine." Xeo said.

"We can't dwell on the past too much. Come on, let's find Kryn." Rafik said, leading the way into the forest.

None of them carried a weapon, so one by one they each found weighty sticks. "A club is better than nothing." Xeo reasoned, being the first to find one. He had suggested to wear the mask for extra help, but the three others vehemently refused. Tragi, Ziri, and Rafik each carried one, not trusting Xeo.

The forest was thick along the tree line next to the beach. The deeper they trekked into it, the thinner it got. Though some trees were so thick around they couldn't see around it. And walking around the tree felt like they were going off course completely. Traveling deeper into the forest, snow started falling from branches, becoming the only noise. Even the steady wind rustling the branches seemed quieter. Rafik raised his hand and froze. The others stopped midstride.

"What's going on?" Xeo whispered.

Rafik turned to Xeo and nudged his head. All three tilted their heads in confusion like dogs. He repeated nudging his head, but nobody noticed. Finally, he rolled his eyes and shouted, "There's something there." He pointed to just a few steps ahead of him, there was a trail of footsteps in mud and snow that stopped right in front of them. At the same time, he ducked and dived to the side. The invisible footsteps charged towards the group.

Xeo swung his branch, but something grabbed his arm mid-swing. He screamed, kicking the invisible figure in the shins. The figure groaned, and a moment later he doubled over as if being punched in the gut. Tragi had fallen to his knees and had his hands bound behind his back. Ziri was throwing punches in midair as vomit erupted from nowhere around her. Rafik tried throwing punches but was quickly subdued and tied down like Tragi. After a small skirmish Ziri was knocked over, and her hands bound.

"Thief." An invisible voice said. "You stole these masks."

"We found them and are returning them." Rafik said. "We aren't thieves."

"A likely story."

"If we were, wouldn't we have tried using them?" Tragi tried reasoning.

The air was silent for a long moment before the voice responded. "Where did you find them."

"The Ruins of Kangor." Rafik said.

"Liar!" The voice shouted.

"He isn't lying." Tragi said. "We found it because we were being chased and needed refuge. The ruins revealed themselves to us."

"Are you Kylix?"

Rafik shook his head. "We want to stop Vanarzir."

The four were suddenly hoisted into the air, bringing them up to their feet. "You may be able to keep your life after all." The voice said. He removed a mask from his face and turned before anyone could see him. "Follow me."

They marched through the trees, feeling points of spears and swords at their backs that couldn't be seen. Slowly, they climbed the hills hidden beneath the blanket of trees. It was hours later as they shivered in the cold, that they finally arrived at a village.

"Where are we?" Xeo asked.

The village had clearly seen signs of war. Buildings had been damaged or burned. Repairs were being made, but the hollow look in everyone's eyes were telling. "Lepal Tribe." The man said. "Let's hope our leaders believe you. At least for your sake."

Marching through town, hands bound behind their backs, the people of the Lepal Tribe glared at the four newcomers. Some wore peculiar and intimidating masks, making it seem like man and monster were staring them down. Several buildings were in ruin, and Rafik noticed there weren't any children here. "King Vanarzir was here, wasn't he?"

214

The soldiers nodded in response. The one leading them finally spoke up. "As winter first started. It's been a nightmare ever since." He led them through town, winding along the stone road.

Towards the end of the road Rafik noticed the large building. Arches holding up the structure appeared to be bone. Lanterns dangled from the tips by chain that swayed in the wind. Snow wisped along the road from gusts of wind, along with the smell of the sea. The familiar scent comforted Rafik, even if there wasn't as much snow as his home would get. Grasses poked through the thin white sheet, giving it an otherworldly feel. Two guards stood on either end of the arched entrance, both wearing a different kind of mask. They nodded to the soldiers, allowing them entry into the great hall.

It was one massive room, with three separate rooms branching off on either side. Long tables spanned the room, with a great table running perpendicular to the rest on the far end. The entire setup reminded Rafik of the feast back at the Sekolah Fortress in Haitu. Sitting in the center of the table on the opposite side of the room was an elderly man speaking with five others.

The old man looked up from his conversation and frowned, staring at the four prisoners. His icy blue eyes sent cold shivers down Rafik's spine as they made eye contact. "Kylix deserters?" He growled in a harsh voice.

"We thought so. Though we found them near the beach where they first arrived." The soldier said. "They claim otherwise."

"Of course, they would. After what they did. Even deserters aren't allowed. And they should know that." The old man snapped.

"We also found them carrying these." The soldiers each revealed a mask being pulled on a sled.

"Where did you find them?"

"They claim –"

"I was talking to them." The old man cut off the soldier. "Can they speak?"

"Yes, sir, we can." Rafik said, stepping forward. "I promise we aren't Kylix. We've come a long way in hopes to find Vanarzir and stop him."

"Where did you find the masks? Ravohka are forbidden to outsiders."

Rafik nodded. "That's what my friend, Tragi, has told us. So, we tried taking care of them the best we could. We found them in the Ruins of Kangor."

A sudden gasp and murmurs echoed throughout the hall. The old man's face scrunched together. "The ruins are a myth."

"We're starting to learn that every myth has a grain of truth." Tragi said.

"Step forward, you four. Tell me your story, and I will judge your fate." The old man reached for a mask resting on the table in front of him. His face contorted as he put it on. It was a long oval, with a spike for a chin. A mane of horns surrounded the rim of the mask, and there was a triangular indentation for a nose. A thin lip was all there was for a mouth, and the eyes were just as narrow. Almost like they were judging Rafik. "And I'll know when you're lying."

Rafik recounted leaving Datz, the fiasco at the Bruin Fortress, and even his discovery of his father's tomb on the island in the Silent Sea. He hadn't originally planned on being so detailed, but as he spoke the words just spilled out of him. His eyes never stopped staring at the old man's eyes, and it felt like he was bound to it. Whispers in his head urged him to tell this man everything. He was grateful he decided to start his story there, rather than back in Mahparry. Through it all, he managed to keep two secrets from the story. The first being the endless bag that was now lost to the sea, and Xeo using the mask.

Finally, he finished. The man stared at Xeo, Tragi, and Ziri asking if it was true. Each of them nodded, confirming the story. "You said two lights?"

Rafik nodded. "Yes, sir. At the bottom of the maelstrom."

"It can't be." The man turned to each of the others at the table, silently nodded. "And this Kryn. She's...missing?"

216

"Yes, sir." Rafik confirmed. "Xeo noticed tracks and believed them to be hers."

"Very interesting." The old man said. "Well, Rafik. You know a bit about Ravohka, let me tell you about mine. This one is called the Ravohka Perjong. In common tongue it translates to the mask of truth. So long as you're making eye contact with me, I'll know if you're lying."

"What happens if they're blind?" Xeo asked, interrupting the elderly man.

The soldier nearest him smacked him on the back of the head. "Don't interrupt him!"

"I'll still know." The old man said, his tone harsher. "A blind man still has eyes. Now, as I was saying, since I've confirmed you're all telling the truth, allow me to introduce myself. I am Lortimo. Village elder of the Lepal Tribe. We do have customs here. Traditions. Laws, as you might say."

"We understand." Rafik said as Lortimo didn't continue his speech. "We had hoped returning these Ravohka would allow us safe passage through your lands. After we beat Vanarzir we can show you to the ruins and find the rest."

The village elder shook his head. "That criminal, Hurik, was right. Finding a mask that's been lost does grant you back into the good graces of the Fohdorsha. We can only allow it one per mask. No exceptions."

"What does that mean?" Rafik asked. "We can travel safely?"

"I suppose it depends on who you talk to. As those rules are only meant for fallen Fohdorsha. Not Kolinda. Outsiders." Lortimo explained. "There is another. These are trying times for the Fohdorsha. If you become one of us, we will let you pass. However, if any of you have talent, you must, regardless of returning priceless heirlooms you are returning."

"What's that?" Ziri asked in her usual tone of nothing higher than a whisper.

"Each Fohdorshan is born with talent." Lortimo started. "A gift from our ancestors. But we are a tribe. A people. United. We

217

are one. And as such, keeping your talent is selfish. It tells us you don't care about your fellow man. When you come of age, you're given a choice. To give up your talent and become part of the Fohdorsha or leave these lands forever."

"Are you saying we would need to give up our talent?" Rafik asked. He remembered when he first discovered his psychometry back with Anza. He used it to help them escape the Kylix. Discover the truth about his father. He gained allies like Paris Bantrita and made enemies like King Vanarzir or Krista. He remembered wanting to trade with Kryn when he first met her. But now, to give it up? It felt like it would be ripping part of his very soul out.

"I am." Lortimo confirmed. "In return, you will take part in a ritual. A trial of sorts. Depending how you do, you will receive a Ravohka. It could be the same power you had before, or something completely different. I know outsiders aren't aware of our customs, and you weren't expecting to make a decision like this. So, I will allow you one day to decide."

"What if we don't want to?" Rafik asked, imagining him losing this talent and never being able to find Anza or Dragon's Roost.

"Then you can stay at the beach you came from. If you need to get to the other side of Alutopek you can sail around." Lortimo snapped. He glared at Rafik through the mask. "You do have an interesting talent. Not many have that one. A Ravohka of that power would be quite uncommon."

"Can those who don't have talent try the ritual?" Xeo asked.

Lortimo smiled. "As I said, these are trying times. Usually no. But I am making an exception. If you do decide to, the masks you've returned to us are still ours to keep."

"I understand." Xeo said, beaming. "Count me in, chief! I'll do the ritual."

"So it shall be." Lortimo nodded. "The rest have one day to decide. One of my men will take you to a home to stay in."

"Will we be safe here?" Rafik asked before turning to leave.

"What do you mean? Are you worried my men might harm you? Do you not trust my hospitality?"

"No." Rafik said. "Treshna. The Hound of Soboribor."

"She is lost to the sea." Lortimo said. "Fearing her now would be like fearing the sunsetting in the middle of the night."

"Thank you." Rafik said, nodding. As they were marching out Rafik heard more orders. He was sending the soldiers who found them to find Kryn, and to investigate the maelstrom.

The buildings of the Lepal Tribe that weren't in ruin were something to marvel at. Some were made from mud, but most of those had collapsed from the Kylix. Those still standing, though, Rafik was in awe. The walls were carved out of the red sandstone rock like the nearby mountains were and topped with clay cobalt shingles. Even some of the lesser prominent buildings had a tint of blue in the thatch. As they were being guided to wherever they were going to be staying, he even noticed a handful of the buildings covered in leathery scales. Turning the corner, they arrived at a home with a massive tree in front of it. A woman knelt at the trunk with a candle, praying. Unlike the rest of the trees this one was still green and had leaves on it. Though, some branches were bare.

"Kaliboon." The guard escorting them said.

"Bless you." Xeo said.

Rafik and Tragi both sighed, hitting their foreheads, and rolling their eyes.

The woman turned from the tree, revealing a tear-streaked face. "Yes?" She wiped them away and stood up straight. Her grayish blue eyes welled with tears, and her body appeared frail. Her matted hair and bags under her eyes showed how exhausted she was. She stared at the four strangers. "More prisoners?"

The guard laughed. "The opposite. They've come to help stop Vanarzir."

"It's too late." She said, turning and putting her hand on the tree. "He can't come back."

"It's not too late." The guard said. "Let me introduce you to Rafik, Ziri, Tragi, and Xeo."

"Xeo?" Kaliboon asked, perking up. She squinted at Xeo, looking him up and down. "I heard you were dead."

"I don't think I am." Xeo laughed. "Then again…that shipwreck."

"And you're here to stop Vanarzir?"

Xeo nodded. "We all are. If we pass the trials, that is."

"I heard about your fight with that wicked man."

The smile on Xeo's face stretched from ear to ear and his eyes widened. "I didn't know my reputation spread this far."

"Oh, calm down. If it wasn't for me, you would have died." Tragi said.

"Only because he cheated." Xeo said, glancing at Kaliboon with guilt-stricken eyes. "It won't happen again. I promise."

"Were these two with you when you fought him?"

"No, ma'am." Xeo said. "Picked up these strays along the way." He smiled at Rafik and Ziri. "With their help we can't lose."

"Yes. We were strays, lost to wander." Ziri whispered.

"Then this great man found us and saved us." Rafik added. Ziri, Rafik, and Tragi burst into laughter and Xeo glared at them.

"Maybe there is hope." Kaliboon said. "How can I help?"

"They need a place to stay until the trial." The guard said. "Lortimo decided they could stay with you."

"Absolutely!" Kaliboon said. She brushed herself off and began hobbling towards the door. A gust of wind blew through, and she nearly toppled over because of her frail frame.

Rafik and Ziri reached to grab her. "We got you." Rafik said, patting her back and grabbing her shoulder.

"Thank you." Kaliboon smiled. "Believe it or not, I used to not be so weak. If my ancestors could see me now."

"Oh?" Rafik asked, as they entered her home. There was patchwork to an interior wall crudely done. Her fireplace only held dying embers, and a thick layer of dust covered everything. "Did you get sick?"

"You could say that." Kaliboon said. She leaned on the furniture as she made her way through her home, finally relaxing into a worn leathery chair with a sigh.

"I'll get the fire going." Ziri said. She knelt by the fire, breaking sticks, and adding logs into it, slowly poking at the embers.

Tragi nodded and went to the pantry to find food, while Xeo sat across from Kaliboon on a wicker sofa. The cushions that were on it were all piled on the floor. Rafik made his way to the far end of the home where a small well was made. The bricks were worn and aged, and the rope frayed, but it still worked. He filled a pot of water just as Tragi finished gathering vegetables.

"So, what happened?" Xeo asked.

"King Vanarzir." Kaliboon said. "He came at the end of autumn. Took the children. Most of our Ravohka."

"He has the Ravohka?" Tragi asked, turning to face her as he stopped cutting potatoes. "Outsiders aren't allowed to have them."

"My people are trying to stop him. We weren't expecting an army to arrive." Kaliboon said. "We tried to defend ourselves, but they were like a swarm of locusts. They just kept coming and coming."

"I know what that's like." Rafik said. "They did the same thing back at my home of Datz."

"He's a monster." Kaliboon said. "I refused to give up my son. With that twisted smile, he let me. The next morning my baby, Dahsho, was gone. I called for him, but it was just quiet. It wasn't like him to wander off, and I doubted he would have now; considering the violence that just happened. I ripped open the door, expecting to see Dahsho being taken by the Kylix. Instead, I saw that tree. Fully grown, covered in vibrant green leaves. Being the end of autumn, it was more than out of place. A shiver ran down my spine, and when I got closer, I saw it. My boy had turned into the tree. I screamed, and Vanarzir showed up. He told me if I told

221

him everything about my people and the masks, he'd turn Dahsho back. But he didn't. And once the last leaf falls, he's stuck like that forever."

"That's horrible!" Ziri said, kindling the growing fire. "Did you tell him everything?"

Kaliboon nodded and she brushed her auburn hair out of her face. "I'd do anything for my boy. After I told him everything they left, planning to raid every village, trying to find every cache of Ravohka."

"We'll find a way." Ziri said, putting her hand on Kaliboon's knee. "But you need to eat."

"I agree." Rafik said. "You won't be any help to Dahsho if the wind sweeps you away."

"I suppose you're right." Kaliboon feigned a smile. "That smells delicious."

After chopping the vegetables Tragi placed them in the pot and hung it over the fire. Between Ziri and him, they made quite a tasty stew.

Only when the light of the Black Wall began to fade and darkness enveloped the Lepal Tribe, did the group breathe a sigh of relief. Treshna wasn't here. Maybe she was taken by the sea? Tragi warned that maybe she was just recovering, to which everyone told him to stay positive. Even Kaliboon joined in on the teasing and joking. For the first time in months, she finally had a real smile on her face.

Though he wore a smile, Rafik's thoughts were being pulled elsewhere. He stared at his hands, remembering all the times he used his talent. All what he's discovered. He couldn't just give it up. But it felt like he had to. Maybe he could go around? Maybe he could convince Lortimo to keep his talent? Lost in thought, he hadn't noticed the room growing quiet, or him crawling into bed. It was as if one moment he was talking and joking with friends, and the next suddenly in bed, staring up into the ceiling. The familiar snores of his friends pulled him from his concern. So long as he had them, he'd be alright. He just wished Kryn was here too.

Rafik tossed and turned throughout the night. When he could sleep, he was plagued with dreams of dragons swirling around and landing on a massive beam within an even bigger birdcage. At the bottom was Anza, cowering from the dragons and calling for help. He'd try to find her, but as he placed his hands on objects to find any hint of being near Anza nothing happened. Strange-shaped faces would float in the air laughing at him, and as he turned to run, Vanarzir was waiting for him. After jostling about beneath blankets and lurching awake from bad dreams, he finally gave up and crawled out of bed.

He wasn't the only one awake, he noticed, as he made his way back to the fire. It wasn't as large as when Ziri tended to it, but it was still bright and warmed the room. "Couldn't sleep?" Kaliboon asked, poking a stick at the fire.

"No." Rafik shook his head. "I have a lot on my mind."

"I heard some of it, talking in your sleep." Kaliboon said.

"I'm sorry. I hope that I didn't keep you up."

Kaliboon shook her head. "I don't sleep much nowadays. You want to talk about it?"

Rafik made himself some tea and sat beside Kaliboon on the wicker sofa. "I have to make a decision, but I feel like the decision has already been made for me."

"And what decision is that?"

"To get to Vanarzir I must go through the trials. Give up my talent. I'm not sure if I can do that. If I keep it, I can find my sister, but the training I went through to defeat the king would be in vain."

Kaliboon nodded. "I have an older brother, Jessux. While growing up we would tease each other. I was born with the talent of night vision and used it to scare Jessux every chance I could get. In my defense, he would try to scare me during the day constantly. It was kind of a game for us. I didn't want to lose my talent, and my edge, so it was hard for me to decide."

"What made you choose?"

"Family." Kaliboon said. "Keeping my talent makes me lose my family. And, as a family, we could borrow each other's masks."

"But you didn't get to choose your mask, right?"

"Correct." Kaliboon nodded. "How you react to the trials determines the mask. But there were shops before Vanarzir that allowed trades as well. Though they did put limits and laws on that."

"I could get my power back then?" Rafik asked, a twinge of hope in his voice.

"Maybe. After this war, things could change."

"Thanks." Rafik said.

"Your sister is lost?"

Rafik nodded. "My uncle took her to Dragon's Roost for her to be safe. He died, and nobody knows where Dragon's Roost is. Have you heard of a place?"

"Dragon's Roost?" Kaliboon asked. Her eyes rolled upwards as if trying to search her memories as she thought. "Now that you mention it, I don't think there's ever been a place called Dragon's Roost in the Bomoku Mountains. For people descended from dragons, that seems like a lost opportunity. I'm sorry."

"It's ok. I'll find her." Rafik said.

He and Kaliboon sat in silence, watching the flames dance and eat at the sticks. Snow silently drifted outside, gently falling to the ground. The bitter cold nipped at the edges of the room, and the two huddled beneath a blanket together. Neither spoke, just enjoying not being alone. Rafik imagined Anza with him, while Kaliboon imagined Dahsho. It wasn't long before they were both finally asleep.

Chapter 20: Torturous Decision

Lepal Tribe, Bomoku Mountains, Alutopek

Rafik sat atop a watchtower at the edge of the village. Much like in Datz, there was a large field between the village and the tree line. The dense forest shrouded the floor in shadow, and the red mountains jutted up in most directions. The watchtower didn't offer much of a vantage point, with the surrounding mountains and thick trees. He had told his friends he'd keep a lookout for Kryn, hoping she'd show up. But as he sat up there his attention turned inward.

Giving up his talent. There had to be another solution. Was he being selfish for not giving up his talent? How did they even remove his talent? Would it hurt? Could he arrive in time for the battle if he didn't give up his talent? He heaved a sigh and threw a pebble into the clearing.

"Thought you could use some company." Ziri said, opening the door to the stairs below.

"Are you doing the trial?" Rafik asked.

Ziri leaned over the ledge. "I never knew my family. My earliest memories were being used to poison people. People feared me. Using poison feels like fire flowing through me every time I use it. I don't like it. I'm tired of it, and if there's an opportunity to stop it, I'll take it. I know you feel differently with your talent, though. It doesn't hurt you."

"Not like that, at least." Rafik said, envisioning the memories he got of his father's last moments. "It can hurt in other ways."

"It's because of Anza, isn't it?" Ziri said. "Why you aren't sure of doing the trials."

Rafik nodded. "What if the only way to find her is through some artifact?"

"Your uncle, Gorik, found Dragon's Roost without talent." Ziri said. "I think you can too. It's not like you've been searching for her for the last two years like Kryn and I."

"I thought she was dead." Rafik snapped.

"I know. I'm not saying you refused to, or you're a horrible brother. I'm just saying I'm sure if you were here and tried searching, she would have been found within the week." Ziri explained. "You won't let anything stop you from finding her."

"Aren't you afraid that losing your talent means you're losing a part of you?" Rafik asked.

"For me, I see it as losing the part of me that causes me pain." Ziri said. "I'm willing to make that sacrifice and not have a mask in return. You weren't born with it like I was. Do you remember how it was before you had talent?"

Rafik nodded. "Barely. Seemed like a simpler time, you know, with no war going on."

"You escaped Datz without talent while an army was after you." Ziri reminded him. "You sailed with your uncle and dad, took care of your family. The talent you have doesn't define you."

"Thanks." Rafik said, smiling.

Ziri returned the smile, grabbing his upper arm. "If you're ever feeling down, come to me. I'll remind you how great you are."

Rafik closed his eyes for a moment, when he opened them Ziri's face was bright red with a slight smile. She noticed Rafik staring and suddenly stopped, turning away, and heading for the door. "Where are you going?"

"If you're keeping an eye out for Kryn, somebody needs to look out for Xeo. We all know Tragi can't manage him all the time."

"True." Rafik laughed. "Plus, I think he's afraid of you since you can poison him."

"I've threatened him a couple times." Ziri laughed. "I'm sure he'll be happy if I get anything other than a poison mask."

"Sounds like one of us needs to so we can keep him in line." Rafik said. He watched Ziri leave, craning his neck to see her make her way back, deep into the village.

From this vantage point it did look like the Lepal Tribe was built a particular way, but Rafik couldn't quite put it. He scanned the area, noting on the other end of the village was another watchtower atop a hill. This western side was closer to the beach where he had hoped Kryn would be coming from. He didn't want to leave her behind but couldn't wait either.

As the stars began to peer through the Black Wall Rafik traced the constellations in the sky. Being this far south he didn't recognize some, but he found Quellor slightly closer to the horizon than usual. Seeing the warrior reminded him of his father. On calm and clear nights, he would sit in his father's lap as he pointed out the stars and the stories behind them. As Rafik got a little older his father taught him how to navigate with the stars. Something much easier than navigating during the day with the sun because of the Black Wall.

Climbing down the watchtower a guard was waiting for him. "It's time."

Rafik nodded. He lowered his head, barely noticing his feet. The last time he felt like this was back in Haitu as he was being marched to his death. He was fairly certain the Fohdorsha wouldn't try to kill him, but with every step forward his feet grew heavier.

It wasn't long that he arrived at the great long house he first met Lortimo in. Sure enough, in the same place he was one night ago, the chieftain sat. His fingers were tented, and he was already wearing his mask. A simmering cauldron now stood in the center of the room with three masked and robed figures tending to it. "Welcome back, Rafik." He spoke. His voice was more intimidating than the last time they spoke. "Your friends have made their decisions. Now it's your turn."

"Can you tell me what they chose?" Rafik asked.

Lortimo shook his head. "No. You, and you alone, must decide."

"I understand." Rafik said. He stared from the door to the cauldron, spilling over with a reddish smoke. Whatever it was, it had a peculiar mixture of a smell, like rain dampened earth and rotting wood.

227

"I can tell this hasn't been an easy decision for you. I find surprising. I thought you would understand our customs." Lortimo said.

"I do." Rafik said. "That doesn't mean I have to agree or follow along with it."

"Yes, you are an outsider. You do have the choice to refuse. If you do, I grant you permission to travel our lands, since we do have a common enemy. But you aren't to receive help from any of the Fohdorsha." Lortimo explained. "I had hoped my people could help you, though. And they'd be more apt to help if you were one of us. What say you, Rafik of Datz. Are you going to take part in the trials, and become one of the few outsiders to be honored as a Fohdorsha? Or are you leaving here, divided from the people you're trying to help?"

Rafik looked from Lortimo to the cauldron. He knew if he said yes, he would have to interact with it. He had made up his mind just before entering, but now, he wasn't sure. Not because Lortimo offered him passage still, but with everything the chief had said. It felt like he was trying to guilt him into doing it, and he didn't appreciate that. He opened his mouth, just to close it a moment later. "There's no guarantee of me getting this talent back?"

"No." Lortimo said coldly. "It depends how you do in the trials."

"What if I make a deal with you?" Rafik asked.

"A deal?" Lortimo scoffed. "This isn't a time for making a deal, and you're now making a mockery of our own customs and rituals offering one."

"I know where the Ruins of Kangor are." Rafik said, ignoring Lortimo's protest. "I know there are several other Ravohka there. And I know you want them. Let me keep my talent, and I'll help you find the ruins."

Lortimo's eyes creased. It was eerie how the mask could do that. "Our customs go back millennia. No exceptions. And I won't tolerate you making a mockery out of it. Especially when you're an outsider in the first place. I won't stand for anymore of this nonsense. Either you're doing this, or you're not." His voice was ice cold, and strong like the sea crashing upon rocks.

"I understand." Rafik said. He didn't turn away from Lortimo as he raised his voice but continued making eye contact. "About a month after my dad died my little sister had gone missing. I found her in a cave near the shore. She was scared, since the water had been rising and closed off where she got in. I promised her then I'd do anything for her. Today that includes giving up my talent. I have to believe it'll work out. I'm going through with it."

Lortimo smiled. "Great choice, boy. Take a drink of this potion. When you wake up, the trial will begin."

The three robed figures circled the cauldron, now beckoning for Rafik to step forward. Their faces were hidden behind their own Ravohka. They were a dark bluish tint with a narrow, rectangular chin, rounded head, and eyes in the shape of X's. What the power of that mask was, he wasn't sure. As he stepped closer, though, the figures seemed larger, and the masks more menacing. One of them lifted the lid with an iron hook, and liquid sloshed out with smoke billowing into the air. The smell of damp earth started growing stronger.

"Does it hurt?" Rafik asked, staring into the X shaped eyes of the guardians of the cauldron.

The guards stood motionless. "Extremely." Lortimo said, removing his mask and taking a drink from a mug Rafik hadn't noticed earlier.

Once Rafik was close enough to touch the cauldron two of the guards moved behind him. Each of them grabbed his shoulders while the third produced a ladle from their robes and poured Rafik a drink. "Bottoms up." Rafik said with a half-smile. He held the cup to his lips, took a deep breath, and swallowed it all in one go.

The moment the liquid touched his mouth it felt like swallowing fire. His body pulsed from extreme heat to extreme cold in less than a second. One eye zoomed in at what he was staring at while the other zoomed out. His breathing became frazzled, nearly hyperventilating and his insides writhed in agony.

He tried hunching over, but the guards held him in place. He let out a scream, his body shivering. His heart beat faster and faster, and something within him felt like he was being torn apart from the inside out. The heat was fading, replacing with a cold he had never experienced before. For a moment, he even forgot what warmth even felt like. The touch of the sun, and the love from family and friends. He was hollow, and the world now appeared bleaker than ever before.

The guard that offered him the drink held a vial to his face, and glimmering golden tears trickled down from his eyes. They were collected, corked, and pocketed before Rafik realized what was going on. His world was going dark, and the cold was over taking him. *'So, this is what death feels like.'* Was his final thought as he closed his eyes.

Chapter 21: Day of Trials

Lepal Tribe, Bomoku Mountains, Alutopek

It felt like one moment Rafik was freezing, wasting away from the inside out. The next, he was warm. The emptiness in his stomach was still there, the sounds of the world more distant. His eyes were still heavy, making it hard to open. He stretched, feeling his body from head to toe once more. Finally, after several moments, he opened his eyes. The room slowly came into focus as the dancing lights swirled into shapes. He was alone in an empty room. A bedside table and the bed were the only pieces of furniture in the room. The nearby window streamed the morning light in.

Rafik reached for the table and closed his eyes. Nothing. Not a spark of the table's past. The cold pit in his stomach felt bigger, and the sudden loneliness was consuming. What had he done? Now he was talentless. He sat up, cupping his head in his hands as he weighed his decision. Was it the right one? How could he just give up his talent? One that has saved him, Anza, and his friends so many times. It felt like he had traded his soul and was now just as empty as one of Skage's minions the necromancer summoned two years ago.

His thoughts began to turn elsewhere as he remembered what Lortimo had said. From the moment he woke up his trial would begin. There would be time for self-pity later. He sprang to his feet, dashed to the door, and tripped a moment later. "Ya shire." He cursed, wondering what would be at his door. "Ziri!" He scrambled over to her, shaking her awake.

Ziri was trembling. She was paler than he had ever seen her and had cuts all over her arms. "Rafik." She whispered in her familiar weak voice. Her lips weren't the bright pink like they usually were. "Rafik."

"What happened Ziri?" Rafik gasped, propping her up and holding her.

"I...I got rid of my talent." She answered.

"I did too, but I'm not beat up like that. Come on, let's get you into bed." Rafik said.

Ziri shook her head. "I did this."

"You?" Rafik looked her up and down. "Why would you do this to yourself?" He scooped her up and carried her to his bed.

"That…that drink. It's poison." Ziri said. "I kept curing myself. I started cutting myself so I would pass out from the pain. If I'm passed out, I couldn't keep curing myself."

"You know there's easier ways to do that than continuously cutting yourself, right?"

Ziri ignored his comment. Her eyes darted every which way before growing heavy once more. "I'm tired."

"Do you need anything?"

Ziri shook her head. "Let me rest. Go complete the trial."

"Are you sure?" Rafik asked. He draped the blanket over her, tucking in her feet.

"Positive. Go get your talent back." Ziri smiled. Her eyes fluttered, and a moment later she was fast asleep.

Rafik brushed her hair out of her face. "Wish me luck." He stepped out of the room, gently closing the door behind him.

"Are you excited for the trial?" Kaliboon asked, tending the fire. She didn't look up as Rafik entered. How she even knew he was there, he wasn't sure. "Remember, everything you do today is part of the trial."

"So, if I just stay inside, it still counts?"

Kaliboon nodded. "Some of the lazier people have done that. I don't think you'd like the results."

"What do I do? I was kind of expecting somebody to tell me I need to be somewhere."

"Xeo and Tragi thought the same thing. Explore the tribe and surrounding area. Some of the village elders usually setup tests. Some can be pretty challenging. The farther you go from the tribe the harder they get. You can find each challenge by a torch that's burning blue."

"They're already gone?" Rafik gasped.

232

Kaliboon nodded. "Not too long ago. If you hurry, you may be able to catch them. Xeo said he's going to the farthest challenge."

"Thanks." Rafik said. He snatched an apple from the basket near the table and dashed out the door.

Throughout the village he could see bright blue lights glowing, with faint traces of smoke wafting into the air. "Good luck!" One person shouted to Rafik as they walked by. "After Vanarzir we didn't expect to have another trial so soon."

"Thanks." Rafik said. He scanned the horizon and noted blue smoke coming from within the woods. The next moment he was off, running through the town, and zigzagging around obstacles. It wasn't far, though, before an elderly woman hobbled in front of him.

"Oh, thank goodness I found you young man." She spoke. "I need your help."

Rafik turned his head from one side to the other. There wasn't anybody else around him. "Me?" He finally asked. "I have the trial today, ma'am." He noticed the first blue torch was just two houses away from him. He didn't even get to the first challenge before being stopped! How was he going to catch up to Xeo?

The older woman nodded. "I need your help. I'm much frailer than I used to. Can't even use my Ravohka anymore. Hangs on my wall next to my husband's. You see, he died several years ago, but I still miss him. And now my grandchildren are mostly gone."

"Mostly?" Rafik asked, cutting her off.

"I managed to hide two of my grandsons in the cellar. But the Kylix are sniffing around. I need your help. Can you distract them?"

"The Kylix are here?" Rafik gasped. "Where?" He took three steps forward and was already ahead of the woman. With her cane she slowly stepped forward, shaking and wobbling as she went. "Where are they? Maybe I can run on ahead?"

"No need to run into danger, sweetie. We'll get there soon enough." She replied. With every step Rafik made, it took her three to catch up. They were going away from the blue torches. At this rate, he would be lucky to get to the first challenge.

Slowly, just ever so slowly, she led Rafik away from the village, and near the foothills of the red mountains. Hidden behind a swath of trees was a black hole. A small cave that appeared to be cleaved away from the mountain by an axe. The jagged walls and entry were different from the rest of the mountain's smooth surface.

"In there?" Rafik asked.

The old woman smiled and nodded. "Yes. They're stuck in there."

"Stuck?" Rafik gave the woman a quizzical look. "I thought you said your grandsons were in your cellar, and the Kylix were near?"

"Oh, forgive me in my old age." The woman laughed, turning away from Rafik's gaze. "My grandchildren are in there. The Kylix weren't far from here." She leaned on her cane and peered around a few trees. "Now's our chance to save them."

Something didn't seem right. Rafik watched the old woman. She licked her lips, and her eyes were fierce, staring at Rafik. The old and frail frame shivered from the wind, but her gaze never lingered. "Are you coming with me?"

"Ooh, child!" The old woman laughed. "I would just get in your way. I will watch over the cave, and make sure you're safe."

It didn't feel right, but he couldn't back out now. Rafik nodded and made his way to the cave. The darkness reminded him of the tunnels in Mahparry, as it just consumed everything. He stuck his hand in the cave and could no longer see it. Seeing the end of his arm without a hand made his skin crawl. He turned back to the old woman who was eagerly smiling and nodding, gesturing with one of her hands to continue.

"Ya shire." Rafik cursed and stepped into the cave.

The cold darkness devoured him. He heard a cackling from behind him and spun around, but the light of the world was gone. The entrance had vanished, and all that was behind him was a solid rock wall. He instinctively reached for the endless bag, hoping for the lightstone, only to again realize it was missing. Again, he cursed.

Rafik stretched out his arms and began walking. No point in staying here when the entrance to the cave was gone. He aimlessly wandered the darkness, inching deeper into the cave. Minutes later he found another wall. Rafik placed both of his hands on the wall, chose a direction, and started walking. Whether he was walking in circles, he couldn't tell. He closed his eyes and imagined a cave full of treasures and forgotten and cherished items, secreted away to never see the light of day again. It comforted him imagining that more than being stuck a tunnel of eternal darkness.

A frigid wind brushed against Rafik. In the far distance was a light. Like a torch on the other side of a field. Rafik clung to the wall as he made his way towards the light. It got brighter as he got closer, and halfway there he had to start using one of his hands to block the light. The light didn't give any warmth but started to flicker like torches and campfire light. Once at the wall of light Rafik turned around and saw the ever-consuming darkness. He nodded and stepped into the light.

His sense of smell was the first to detect something. This new room smelled of sweat and decay. There was a warmth here, and he could hear a crackling fire just in front of him. Finally, his eyes adjusted, and he could see the round room. In the center of the room was a fire nearly stretching halfway up the room. On the ceiling were dark burn marks, clearly showing the flame had been bigger. Across from him, on the other side of the fire, was a tunnel. Chains rustled next to him, and Rafik jumped, raising his sword. The prisoners chained to the wall were just as surprised to see him, as he was them.

"What are you doing here?" Rafik asked. It had taken a moment to recognize them. They were much skinnier now. Emaciated, even. Their clothes were nothing but rags, and every bone could be seen. Their faces were like empty husks of what they once were.

235

Bound to the wall were three people he thought he'd never see again, let alone in some dark and mysterious cave in the Bomoku Mountains. "Hey…Rafik was it?" The one in the middle said. His voice was weak, and he spoke slowly, like every word he had to concentrate on saying.

Rafik nodded. "Hello Haloro. Guess you weren't fast enough to escape this?"

Haloro glared at Rafik before frowning and looking down. "He doesn't know."

"I don't know what?" Rafik asked.

"What happened." Krista said, who was closest to Rafik. She was the feistiest of the three, jostling her chains as she spoke. Blood trickled from a wound on her head, and her arms were covered in bruises. On the other side of Haloro was Taygin. "You have to help us, Rafik."

"Why? You're the Kylika. The elite Kylix soldiers." Rafik said. "Last I checked, at least two of you wanted me dead." He nodded to Taygin who returned a half-smile.

"We aren't part of the Kylix anymore." Haloro said.

"They're monsters." The old lady spat.

Rafik jumped and spun around, feeling relieved. "Oh, it's just you."

"Yes…just me." The woman said. "Now, child, should we do this the easy way or the hard way?"

"Do what?" Rafik asked. "I think you tricked me."

"It's not hard to trick young men with delusions of grandeur." The woman cackled, poking her cane into the flames. "You must choose. Kill them or join them."

"Is this part of the trial?" Rafik asked.

The woman shook her head. "If you kill them, yes. If you don't, you can join them, chained to the wall."

Rafik turned to the three of them. They all looked beaten and exhausted. Haloro and Krista weren't ever kind to him. Taygin was, but only when it suited him. "Ya shire." He muttered to himself before turning back to the old woman. "I can't let you hurt them."

236

"So be it." The woman glared. Her entire face flashed bright like lightning. The next moment, when Rafik could see again, the woman was gone. In her place was a snarling red dragon. Its eyes were the same as the woman's but everything else was like the reptilian monster. Scales, sharp fangs and claws, a long tail, and leathery wings. The dragon was half the size of the room. It lunged forward, over the flames. Rafik dived out of the way.

The dragon spun around, gnashing their teeth, and charging at Rafik. It chased Rafik around the fire, nipping at his legs. Rafik raised his sword, spun around, and swung it at the dragon. The blade struck the dragon's face, and it sounded like metal hitting metal. The dragon's head turned, and the entire body flickered from existence. Something fell from the dragon's face, and the body disappeared. A metallic mask skidded to a stop just before falling into the large fire. The dragon was gone, as well as the old woman. A much younger woman with bluish brown eyes glared at Rafik, slowly getting to her feet.

"A shapeshifter?" Rafik asked, staring from the woman to the mask reflecting the flickering flames. The face of the mask appeared more menacing and monstrous than the others he had seen so far.

"Congratulations." The woman said. "Not many have been able to knock off my mask."

"It wasn't that difficult. Wait, this was a test?" Rafik asked. He spun around, expecting to see a barren wall where the three were chained, but they were still there.

"Oh no." The woman laughed. "Just thought I'd congratulate you before killing you. You can die proud."

Rafik raised his sword. "You aren't even armed."

The woman lowered her head and raised her arms. She wore thick, bronze bangles with purple jewels lining the end near the elbow. She raised her hands as if in surrender, and small knives shot out from the bottom of her wrists. The bangles on her arms had a hidden blade within it. She got to her feet and pointed one knife at the three chained, the other at Rafik. "All of you are outsiders. Kolinda. Invaders. Murderers. We were happy before you arrived. We don't want you here. Now you're participating in the trial is complete blasphemy. A mockery to our ancestors."

"I'm trying to help you." Rafik said. "I want to stop Vanarzir."

"We can take care of ourselves." The woman snapped. She turned, facing the three that were chained, and shoved her arm forward at Haloro.

Haloro, Krista, and Taygin screamed, closing their eyes and wincing.

"No!" Rafik yelled. He jumped, tackling the woman. "I can't let you hurt them." He got to his feet, raising his arms to protect the three of them behind him.

"You don't even like them." The woman yelled.

"They're chained to a wall, defenseless." Rafik argued. "I can't let you hurt them."

The woman got to her feet. One of the knives had snapped and broken from hitting the ground. The other she held up, ready to use. "You are a fool."

"But at least I'm not a monster."

Her icy glare narrowed, and she screamed, lunging for Rafik. It wasn't difficult dodging her attack. Rafik side stepped, grabbed her arm, and pushed down, forcing her back on her knees. She screamed, trying to tear herself free before Rafik applied more pressure to her joint. "Let me go!"

Rafik released her and she fell forward, barely catching herself before her face hitting the sand. "Where are the keys? I'm freeing them and leaving you here."

"They're my prisoners!" She snapped. "Mine! One of them killed my husband. My babies were taken. These three were left behind, and I'm going to make them pay."

"You're starving them to death." Rafik said. "Look at them. I knew them before they came to the mountains, and they didn't look like this."

"They wanted to look like skeletons, I'm just making it so they don't have to play dress up in their fancy armor to do so." The woman said.

Krista opened her mouth, and the woman shot her a glance, and she fell silent. Rafik shook his head. "I'm sorry for your loss. Truly. What Vanarzir is doing is horrible. Believe me, I know. I still can't let you do this, though."

"You're going to have to kill me!" The woman said, suddenly springing to her feet.

Once again Rafik sidestepped her. "Where are the keys? I'm freeing them."

The woman began sobbing, whispering into the fire. "It's in the other room." Taygin finally said from behind Rafik. "Where she came from."

Rafik nodded and headed for the door, taking the mask still laying on the ground with him. He felt the familiar warmth from when he had talent just by touching the mask. The feeling, like he was part of something, and wanted, was intoxicating. He stared at the mask, frozen in place. He could just leave now. Take the mask and run. Nobody would find him.

"Rafik?" Krista asked jolting Rafik out of his hypnotic temptations.

"Oh, sorry. I'll be right back." Rafik said. He went through the darkened doorway the woman had used and found himself in the back of a small workshop. A roaring fire was next to him, and a bookshelf on his other side. He looked down and saw the familiar marks of it being dragged. The room she was keeping them in was hidden. He scanned the room for the keys, finally finding them hanging next to the door above a shelf.

He could hear Blaridane's voice in his head, tempting him. *'Take it.'* It hissed repeatedly. *'You don't owe them anything.'*

"I can't leave them." Rafik whispered.

'Then tell somebody as you leave with the mask. Come find me, Rafik. Come find me.'

His fists tightened on the mask, remembering Shallon at the Bruin Fortress. He had Blaridane. It was his sword. Even after two years he longed for it. The cravings never really went away. But with this mask he could sneak out and find the sword. Reclaim what was his! Between the mask and the sword, he could be unstoppable. Rafik's hands shook, his eyes were closed, listening to the whisperings of a cursed sword still plaguing his mind. Finally, he opened his eyes and put the mask on the shelf. He grabbed the keys and returned to the secret room. The woman was gone, and the three arguing over if Rafik would return.

"I knew you'd come back!" Taygin said, noticing him first.

"Thank you." Haloro said, nodding to Rafik. "We owe you."

"Yeah, you do." Rafik said. "Krista, you can use your talent now. I'm guessing you stopped using it, so she'd stop torturing you?"

Krista and Haloro both turned their heads, looking downward. "They can't." Taygin said. "It was taken?"

"Taken?" Rafik asked. "How? What happened?"

The three were silent.

"Tell me, or I'll leave you here for somebody from the Lepal Tribe to find you." Rafik said.

"We were in the Pokoto Tribe." Taygin said. "King Vanarzir learned how to take away people's talent. He wanted to experiment on one of the Kylika. Haloro was forced to. Things started going sideways. The people of the Pokoto Tribe were expecting us and lured us into a trap. The things Vanarzir did…they make nightmares seem good. Krista and I tried stopping him. For that, we were exiled, and Krista's talent removed as well. We were trying to make our way back to the shore we came from, when that woman tricked us and captured us. Been here ever since."

"Does Lortimo know?"

Krista shook her head. "I don't think so."

"Maybe he can give you your talent back." Rafik said, unlocking them. "Follow me. I'll protect you."

"Thank you." The three of them said once free. They each grabbed at their wrists and ankles where the chains had been. More

240

bruises and blisters covered them than Rafik first noticed. They limped behind Rafik as he led them out of the shop.

The four of them made their way through the village. Rafik had explained why he was in the tribe, and of the trial. The three of them, although weak, insisted on participating as well. He wasn't sure if they were allowed, but couldn't find anybody to ask, either. Some of the Lepal Tribe offered them food, which the three former soldiers wolfed so fast a few villagers warned them not to eat their own hands. Rafik watched them complete a few trials around the village, helping others.

One trial was finding a missing cat, while another was collecting chickens. They were all simple tasks. After a fifth one Rafik imagined all any of them would get at this point would be a mask to catch chickens faster or to detect missing things. Admittedly, the detecting power would be interesting, but he hoped for his original talent. He had a feeling that wouldn't happen, as he watched the light on the Black Wall slowly fade. The day was ending. He couldn't find Xeo or Tragi. Although he got stuck helping three people he barely knew, he enjoyed watching them come to life as they ate more, accomplished tasks, and were thanked and appreciated. He wondered how often they were shown heartfelt gratitude rather than fear.

Rafik did take part in some of the tasks. There was one he particularly enjoyed, which was sparring against a man. The fighting got intense enough two others joined in, and a crowd formed, cheering each other on.

Finally, as the light was nearing its end on the Black Wall, they made it to the village edge where Xeo and Tragi were returning, beaming with excitement. The village gates closing behind them. "Where were you?" Xeo asked.

"I told you we should have waited." Tragi said. "I'm sorry, Rafik. Did you get lost?"

"No, I had to help these three." Rafik said.

"Well, while you were making new friends, Tragi and I went hunting. We rowed a boat in the ocean, caught some fish.

Even had a small swordfight on the beach. Oh! Have you ever heard of the Lonesome Abyss?"

"The what?" Rafik asked.

"We have." Krista said. "One of the dragon deities in the Lepal Tribe."

"That's what we were told!" Xeo gasped. "This dragon creates giant whirlpools sucking in everything to eat while sitting at the bottom of the ocean."

"That's fascinating." Rafik said, imagining a dragon on the sea floor being the cause for all the sailors' problems across the world.

"You haven't heard the best part." Xeo said. "It has two glowing white eyes that can be seen while being sucked in."

Rafik opened his mouth, then paused. "Wait-"

"That's what I said!" Xeo said. "They thought I was just making up stories until Tragi backed me up."

"If that's true, how did we not get eaten?" Rafik asked.

Xeo shrugged. "Maybe we taste funny? Anyway, who are your friends?"

"This is Taygin, Haloro, and Krista." Rafik said.

"Kylix!" Xeo gasped. The guards near them turned to face them, spears at the ready.

Rafik shook his head. "Former. We'll have to talk about it with Lortimo."

"Good, because that's where we're going." Xeo said.

"The trials are over." Tragi said. "Where's Ziri?"

"Resting. She was hurt losing her talent." Rafik said.

"*She's* here too." Krista spat. "I thought she was dead."

Rafik glared at her. "I was hoping your attitude would have changed."

Krista made a face and followed the others back towards the heart of the tribe. "Don't tell me that fire spitter is alive too? Where's Kryn?"

"We're not sure." Rafik said. "But last we checked, she's alive too."

Chapter 22: City of Gold

Tahmlo Tribe, Bomoku Mountains, Alutopek

"I've never been this far-gone away from home." Junla said, freezing in place.

"How can you tell? Kryn asked. "This looks like the same spot as it did ten minutes ago. And it'll probably look the same as where we'll be in ten minutes. Unless we've been going in circles."

"We haven't been adventure-walking in circles." Junla laughed. "I would know. Sometimes you just know. I've wander-explored these woods since I could escape those roots."

"Escape?" Kryn asked. "I didn't know you were a prisoner."

Junla nodded. "The Amsahvi were banish-exiled because of our ancestors. Hunted like animals. We moved-hid to the roots. When the Black Wall was made, we came out of hiding. Most still didn't want us, so the elder-priests forbid anyone from leaving. Only the elder-priests could leave. And that was with protection-guards."

"I can't imagine spending most of my life stuck inside a tree." Kryn said. "I would go crazy."

"Thank the Cavernous Lazywing I didn't." Junla said. "One day I saved Teller, and he award-gifted me with a new Ravohka. Soon after, Teller select-chose me to guard-protect him. I was so amazed with the outside world. Then I saw-found an eagle. I used my mask to grow wings of my own. Now they can't stop-keep me inside the village."

"Can your mask do other things?" Kryn asked.

Junla nodded, grinning exposing the tusks on her mask more. It was eerie how the masks contorted for the user's facial expressions. "If I see an animal, I can mimic it. But only one power at time. If I change-swap the power, I lose my wings."

"Well, you're free now." Kryn said. "After we find Hurik you can join my friends and me. We're going to stop King Vanarzir."

"I'd enjoy-love that." Junla said. "We can explore the Wild Lands. Maybe even find the Great Dragons! It's said-rumored the Great Dragons will return at the final age of man. They'll save-rescue the worthy."

"As much as I would love to see dragons flying over Alutopek, I don't want the end of the world to happen." Kryn laughed.

"I want-crave for it. Then my people-family don't have to live in tree roots." Junla said.

"I understand." Kryn said. "Maybe after we beat Vanarzir your people will be accepted before the end of the world happens."

"Maybe." Junla sighed, her breath danced in the night sky before disappearing. She turned upwards, marveling at the twinkling stars, shining through the Black Wall. "I heard before the Black Wall there were more stars."

Kryn nodded. "So, they say. I'm starting to think that's a rumor. There's nothing beyond the Black Wall."

Junla frowned. "That's a sad thought." She shivered and pointed to a cave nearby. "We can rest-sleep there."

Kryn looked over her shoulder before agreeing. She didn't expect to see Treshna hunting her, but she wanted to be able to run just in case she was. She silently wondered if Treshna had gone down with the ship, or somehow miraculously survived like she and her friends did. Could a mythical beast from Soboribor actually die? Or would she just return after being sent back to where she came from? The thoughts puzzled her, and she didn't notice her body moving on autopilot as she helped Junla set up camp within the cave. "How did you see the cave?" She finally asked after pulling herself away from her thoughts.

"I'm Fohdorsha." Junla smiled, puffing out her chest. "The Amsahvi are descendants of the Cavernous Lazywings. We have excellent night vision."

The air was cold and stagnant. Not a breeze had touched them while traveling so close to the mountainside but still within the dense forest. Being in the cave it wasn't any warmer, and the air felt colder. Denser, even. The two hurriedly started a fire. The stale stench in the air of the cave changed to the cooking of meat and a strong tea Junla had brought from home.

"What was it like to control fire?" Junla asked, sipping her tea.

"I wasn't cold." Kryn laughed, tightening a blanket around her shoulders.

Junla smiled. "It's so cold-freezing here than back home."

"Where are we going, anyway?" Kryn asked after chewing on some of the cooked meat. "I haven't noticed any tracks of a person, so I don't think we're following Hurik."

"No." Junla said. "Not yet. We are going to the Tahmlo Tribe. People there should be able to help us find-hunt him."

"Will they let an outsider and somebody from the Amsahvi Tribe in? Let alone help us?" Kryn asked. The last thing she wanted was to walk into a village filled with people who wanted her dead.

Junla paused, scrunching her brow, and stared into the fire for a minute before answering. "I think so."

The two finished their scant meal and watched the night from the mouth of the cave. It wasn't snowy here like in other parts of the forest. Just cold. The tall pines blocked most of the stars. "Well, Night Eyes, you can take first watch." Kryn yawned.

With a frog in her throat, Junla smiled and said, "I've never had a nickname before. Does this mean we're friends?"

"Yes it does." Kryn said, already closing her eyes and nestling in for the night beside the fire. Within a matter of moments sleep had taken her.

Junla wiped her face from a tear trickling down and sat facing the opening of the cave. Her jaw was clenched, eyes narrow, as she was determined to not let anyone in.

By morning, the fire had burnt out. Junla stayed on watch the rest of the night and didn't complain about being tired. There even seemed to be a skip in her step. She led Kryn through the forest, deeper and higher into the mountains. More than once she would spring into the air, fly ahead, and return moments later, telling Kryn how much farther they had. It was just after midday that she returned from one of these flights with a smile on her face.

"We're almost-near there." Junla said.

"That's what you said last time." Kryn said. "We'll get there when we get there."

"No, the tribe is just ahead." Junla pointed up into the sky. Small wisps of smoke wafted towards them.

Kryn nodded. "Tell me again about the Tahmlo."

"Before the tribes intermingled like they do now, they were the Fire Tribe. Their Great Dragon was the Crimson Shroud, the most feared dragon. An abomination-curse to the world. And the people of the Tahmlo Tribe were just as frightening-scary. They were great warriors. But now, they're just stubborn." Junla explained.

"And you've been here before?" Kryn asked. She was beginning to regret not getting any of this information sooner. It was bad enough being in a foreign land, but not knowing anything about the villages one would visit just seemed foolish. Before meeting Junla she believed all the Fohdorsha were some sort of half dragon creatures with monstrous faces. Now she knew better. They were people, just like her, but with magical masks.

"Once." Junla said. "They were surprised to see someone from the Amsahvi, let alone two. I was with Elder-priest Teller."

Before the conversation could continue two figures dropped from the trees in front of Kryn and Junla. Their swords already raised. "Before pulling out your sword, know that there are three archers in the trees."

Kryn glared at the man who stood much taller than her. He had fiery red hair and eyes. His face hidden behind another mask she didn't recognize. This one had a long face and nose, giving their entire head a long and narrow appearance. The eyes were

246

almond shaped, and mouth outlined in thick lips. What first looked like whiskers were thin, long vents along the sides of the mask. She noted where Junla's mask was a dull brown color, his appeared metallic with a tint of red. Almost like a thin layer of fire shimmered within it. "I can tell you're friendly." She said, raising her hands away from her sword. If she still had talent, she was positive she could have beaten them.

"You brought an outsider?" The man growled, turning to Junla. "One would have thought the Amsahvi wouldn't associate with creatures that made them seem even more inferior."

Junla bowed her head. "She's a friend. Elder-priest Teller approves."

"Your chieftain doesn't speak for us." The man said. "What are you doing out of your hole?"

"We're hunting for somebody." Kryn said.

"Hunting?" The man asked, eyes widening. "That's an interesting word choice."

"What else would you call it?" Kryn asked. "When I find him, I'm going to kill him."

The man lowered his sword, and the other guard did the same. "I like you." He smiled. "What's your name?"

"Kryn of Sysinal." Kryn said, puffing her chest. It wasn't often she got to introduce herself.

"You're a long way from home. If you haven't caught your hunt by now, you never will." The man said. "Best you go home."

"She's been search-looking for him just recently." Junla interrupted. "She would have caught him, too, if I didn't crash into her."

"Which explains why you're with her." The man said. "I assume since Vanarzir has come through the Fohdorsha are allowing all outsiders in now?" He glared at Kryn, eyeing her up and down. "You might have a fiery spirit, but you're still Kolinda. An outsider."

"I want to stop Vanarzir more than anyone." Kryn said. "But this man took something from me. And I plan to take it back, even if it kills me."

247

"Who is it you hunt?" The man asked.

"Hurik of…the something tribe." Kryn said, trailing off. "Xeo told us before our ship sank. Snack? Sample? Sarah? He has white hair. Guessing that means something."

"Sampra." The man said flatly.

Kryn snapped her fingers, shouting "That's the one! Hurik of the Sampra Tribe. White hair and eyes. A little taller than me. Skinny."

The man frowned, making the lips of the mask contort that almost made Kryn laugh. "We know of him. He has no allies here. Just like across the Bomoku Mountains, he isn't allowed in the Tahmlo Tribe."

"Have you seen-spotted him?" Junla asked. "We lost his trail-scent."

"If we spotted him, he would be dead."

"I was worried about that." Kryn frowned. "He has to be here somewhere."

"Why don't you use your mask?" The man suggested. "Get the skill of a hound. Sniff him out."

"That could work." Junla said. "But then I can't scout-look ahead." She jumped into the air, spouting wings and flew between the trees.

"You flying around like that is what helped us spot you. Besides, you can always just spot another eagle." The man said.

"If she wants to keep her wings, I'm not going to stop her." Kryn snapped, noticing how hurt Junla was as she quietly skidded to a halt beside her.

"Then wander the mountains until the Great Dragons return." The man said, turning to leave. "Leave us out of it."

"We aren't allowed into the Tahmlo Tribe?" Kryn asked.

"There is nothing for you there." The man said.

"I could go for a soft bed. Maybe some good cooking." Kryn said. "How about you?"

"Bacon pie sounds yummy-delicious." Junla said, rubbing her stomach.

"Bacon pie?" Kryn asked.

248

"Oh, Kryn. You haven't lived happily until you've eaten-tried bacon pie." Junla smiled.

The man glared at the two young women. "Fine. Don't touch anything." The three archers fell from the trees, surrounding them. "Keep up."

The five surrounded Junla and Kryn and hurriedly started marching deeper into the woods. The second man who had stayed quiet started talking. "Don't mind the guards, Junla." He said, constantly looking back at her and smiling. "Just a formality since Vanarzir is here."

"Did he attack the Tahmlo Tribe?" Kryn asked.

The guard shook his head. "Not yet. Scouts tried searching this way, but we made sure they didn't find anything." He had the same mask as the first man. Though his hair wasn't as vibrant of red, and his eyes were a dark grayish red.

"What do those masks do?" Kryn asked.

"It's the mask of mirages." The guard said. "Allow me to introduce everybody. The bottle of happiness here is Captain Hushrin. He leads the guard for the Tahmlo Tribe. And I'm Palok."

Kryn stopped paying attention as they turned a corner, and the village came into view. "Wow." She said, jaw agape. Even the most basic of buildings were covered in gold. The light glowing from the Black Wall danced and shimmered across the golden surface. Each building was topped with crimson shingles, layered that reminded Kryn of dragon scales. The streets were all built of the red rock of the sandstone mountains that surrounded them in varying sizes.

Most of the people here had red hair. There were some with blue, gray, green, and golden hair as well. Even a couple white. Kryn thought Ziri would fit in here with hers more than back at the Amsahvi Tribe. She was beginning to realize that depending on their tribe lineage it showed in their hair, eyes, and colorful tint to their masks.

"This is the second largest of the tribe settlements." Palok said. "Also, the oldest. Unlike the Lepal Tribe that use invisibility in their guard, we use mirages to keep our tribe safe."

Kryn thought she had seen everything, being from Sysinal, spending time in Haitu, Datz, and lastly Lynn. But this village rivaled the temples and shrines in the City of the Gods. There were statues of dragons she had only heard about. There was a shop selling Ravohka, and another ancient texts, written in the Fohdorshan language. On some golden edifices black ink swirled and turned in gorgeous intricate artwork. "I could spend eternity here." Kryn said.

Palok laughed. "A lot do."

"Take them to the Savage Tavern." Captain Hushrin ordered. "Meet back at the tower."

Kryn scanned the horizon. "What tower?" She couldn't see much, with how tall some of the buildings were, but she didn't notice a tower.

Captain Hushrin scoffed. "Kolinda aren't privy to that information." He and the archers marched off, leaving Palok to take them to the tavern.

"A lot of our defenses are hidden behind a mirage." Palok said. "It's said you can explore the entire tribe, and just when you think you've seen it all a mirage fades and a new avenue opens."

"Couldn't you just hide the whole village?" Kryn asked.

"You try making the entire city disappear." Palok laughed. "Easier said than done."

The Savage Tavern was just a couple of streets over from where they were. It looked like most other buildings, but this one had a sign hanging above the door of a wiry red dragon drinking from a large sphere. "That's an interesting name." Kryn said, pushing open the door.

Inside smelled of sweet drinks, savory meats, and applewood burning in a fireplace on the far side of the room. Palok mentioned something to the barkeep and then called the girls over. "He'll take care of you from here." He said. He nodded to the two and left without saying another word.

"What'll you have?" The barkeep asked. "Palok says you need a room?"

Kryn nodded. "Yes, one room. We need some food too. Bacon pie, I guess."

Junla smiled, nodded, and licked her lips. "Two pies. And two honey-rums."

"Honey-rum?" Kryn asked.

"Trust me. It's good-tasty." Junla said.

Within minutes the two were served salty bacon ends in a thick stew with a pie crust over it, and a spiced rum with a touch of honey. Before long, their bellies were full, and the room was slightly spinning. Others were laughing and hooting and hollering behind them, when Kryn heard something that sobered her up immediately.

"Aye, he's a lucky one."

"Survived a shipwreck by the skin of his teeth. What's next?"

"Not lucky enough. Still doesn't have a Ravohka."

"Claims he found one, though."

"Still doesn't have one. Hope the guard doesn't find him."

"I wonder what his next score will be?"

"Any bets on how long he'll last before he gets caught?"

"Hurik? He'll die before he gets caught."

Kryn spun around and saw a group of people boisterously drinking. They didn't appear to be upstanding citizens, and their clothes was more filth than fabric. "Excuse me," she said, hopping down from the bar. "Did you say Hurik?"

"What's it to you, little lady?" One man asked, burping, and picking his nose.

"I'm trying to find him." Kryn said. "I survived the shipwreck, too."

"You?" The man laughed.

"He said he was the only survivor." Another said, hiccupping.

"No, I survived too." Kryn said. "Barely. I met him at Lynn where he found someone with Ravohka."

The group fell silent, looking from one to the other. Finally, one of the women spoke up. "If you were there, what caused the shipwreck."

"A maelstrom." Kryn said, staring off into the distance. She could see it again just as clearly as if she was back there in the Vinsen Ocean. "It was a strange one. Had two lights at the bottom."

"A Lonesome Abyss." The man said.

"A what?" Kryn asked.

"You're a kolinda." Another man gasped. "Here? Are you one of those bone soldiers?"

Kryn shook her head. "Nope. Fellow treasure hunter like Hurik."

The first man spoke up. "Alright, we'll take you to him. But you need to do something for us."

"What's your price?"

With a devilish grin he sneered at Kryn. "I want your room."

Kryn nodded, not saying a word, and returned to Junla at the bar. "I think I found him. But we're not sleeping in comfortable beds tonight."

Junla frowned. "Maybe next time."

"Excuse me, barkeep." Kryn said. "We're giving our room to that group behind us."

The barkeep frowned. "Are you sure?"

Kryn nodded, and the barkeep shook his head. "Alright."

"You got a room." Kryn said, giving them the details.

"Let's go!" The man said, snatching and yanking on Kryn's arm.

Kryn pulled her arm free faster than a startled deer fleeing a hunter. "You get the room, but I never agreed to be in it with you."

The man frowned while the others laughed. "I can see why Hurik likes you." He finally said.

Chapter 23: Chasing the Sunrise

Lepal Tribe, Bomoku Mountains, Alutopek

"Where did you find them?" Lortimo growled. They were in the great hall where they had been first taken to. Behind Lortimo's throne was a wall covered in masks of different shapes and sizes. Hooded figures stood on either end holding spears. What Rafik could only assume were nobles sat on either side of Lortimo. The chief glared at Taygin, Krista, and Haloro.

"A cave. I think a witch had them." Rafik said.

"You said you weren't part of the Kylix." Lortimo said. "You even tricked my Ravohka!"

Rafik raised his hands and shook his head. "I didn't! I didn't know they were there. I thought it was part of the trials."

"And you didn't leave them there for punishment?" Lortimo asked.

"No, sir." Rafik said. "There's punishment and then there's torture. I couldn't in good conscience leave them there."

Lortimo nodded, scratching his chin atop the mask. "I sense the truth in you, boy. You have a good heart. But those three helped invade our lands. Killed several. Taken our children! They need to be punished. And *you* expect them to not just take part in the trials, but to earn a Ravohka? To be accepted and be part of the Fohdorsha?"

Rafik hadn't thought about that. He assumed that after freeing them if they participated in the trials they could be accepted. He stared at Lortimo, blank faced, thinking. These were soldiers, even if they tried to abandon the Kylix. How foolish was he to think all would be forgiven? "I...I just wanted to save them."

"Not everybody is worth saving." Lortimo barked. "Let alone these Bone Hunter pretenders who committed such atrocities. Did they bring back our children? The masks that were stolen?"

"No." Rafik said. He finally bowed his head, slumping his shoulders.

"If I may?" Tragi asked, raising his hand.

Lortimo shifted in his seat and glowered at Tragi from head to toe. "You really want to throw your lot in with him? Think that wise?"

"I think going up against you in any fashion would be unwise." Tragi said, stepping forward and putting his hand on Rafik's shoulder. "But Rafik is my friend. Since I've met him, he's always tried helping others. Even if it cost him dearly."

"The boy's a fool." Lortimo said.

Tragi gave a half-smile. "No. He has a heart. Before even starting the trial, he made sure Ziri was going to be alright. He then tried helping an elderly woman who ended up tricking him and found himself in a sort of dungeon with three others already in chains. Was this a prison that your excellency had put together?"

"No." Lortimo said, shaking his head.

"If Rafik hadn't found them, these three would have still been in there. Prisoners to that witch and receiving her justice. Not yours. Shouldn't that count for something? That he brought you three Kylix soldiers to be punished under your law, not a vigilante?" Tragi explained.

Lortimo sat silently, scratching his chin, looking from Rafik, to the three former Kylika soldiers. He stood up, banging his staff on the floor three times. "I have decided, Rafik of Datz, that you are not Kylix. You are still welcome in this tribe."

"Thank you." Rafik said, bowing to Lortimo before stepping back in line with the others. He flashed a smile to Tragi, mouthing 'thank you' to him.

"As for you three." Lortimo said, glaring at them. "You are to be imprisoned until I decide what to do with you. Tonight is a night of celebrating. One which none of you are deserving of, let alone welcome. The honorable deeds you may have done today do not make up for the atrocities you have committed."

Krista opened her mouth to speak, but guards appeared out of nowhere and yanked her so hard she just gasped instead. They were being dragged away, as those of the Lepal Tribe turned their backs on them. Fighting the guards, Krista kicked the door, and a fog seeped into the room.

"It's cold." Ziri said, shivering. She was closest to the door out of the four of them, bundled in a blanket and still appearing as sickly as when Rafik last saw her.

Rafik put his arm around her, rubbing her shoulder. "We'll get you by the fire in no time."

Ziri smiled up at him and leaned in closer to him.

Lortimo stayed standing, not saying a word, staring from Ziri to Rafik, to Tragi, and then Xeo. "You have completed the trials. Congratulations. Each of you showed how helpful you are to the tribe in your own way. You will see behind me four different rows of Ravohka. Each row was specially chosen for each of you. With how you performed – or didn't perform –" he eyed Ziri longer when saying this. "The Lepal Elders and I chose six masks that would suit you well on your journey. And, more importantly, how you would best help your fellow Fohdorshan. For those of you who had talent, your former power is among them as well. Since you don't know what any of these mask powers are, there won't be a need to blindfold you as you choose."

Xeo's eyes lit up as he saw the familiar shape of the mask of flight. That was the one he was after. But the other five? What could those be? Could there be something better than flight up there?

Tragi stared at the wall, not giving any sign of emotion. He wasn't sure how often he would be using his mask. He made it this far without needing one. What were the odds that he would need it now? Especially if his brother stayed by his side. He noticed the row with the mask of flight and knew which one Xeo would be after.

Rafik searched the four rows of six, wondering which row was his. Which mask was that of psychometry? His fingers were itching, ready to take a mask, but his heart beat even faster. What if he chose wrong? What if he got a different mask?

Ziri's eyes were locked on one mask. Even without knowing what power each mask had, she saw her old talent hanging on the wall. It was a metallic gray, just like the others, but in her mind, it oozed with poison. The eyes were glaring back at her, with four small spikes jutting back like a sort of mohawk. From each corner of the mask what appeared to be a bone stuck out. It wasn't hard to imagine the skull and cross bones on this mask. If it wasn't a mask of poison, it was definitely one of death that she didn't want any part of.

The fog swirled around their feet, slowly growing thicker, and drawing any warmth from the room. The torches flickered, no longer giving off heat, and small colorless wisps pulsed within the fog. As Lortimo announced for Xeo to step forward and claim his mask, the wisps grew darker, changing to that of violet. The walls became enveloped in shadows, like the entire room was suddenly engulfed in gloom.

Xeo was directed to his row of masks. He inspected each one, wondering what it was before grabbing the mask of flight. The smile on his face rivaled that of any child's on their birthday. He put it on and sprang into the air. His whooping and hollering echoed throughout the freezing room, flying from one end to the other, before finally landing next to Tragi.

"You're next." Lortimo said, pointing at Rafik. "I believe you've earned this more than most. Helping others, regardless of your own safety or standing. A very admirable quality. I believe any mask you choose will suit you well."

"Which one has my talent?" Rafik asked.

Lortimo laughed. "I cannot tell you. Let your heart decide."

One of the hooded guards turned a wheel, making the rows of masks shift, so his row was just at eye level. It had gotten darker in here, but he could still just make out his reflection on the masks. Each one appeared intimidating. None of them called out to him like he hoped. He closed his eyes. "Help me, Dad." He whispered. "I want to see you again." He paced back and forth, hovering his hand over each mask, as if in doing so it would speak to him.

There was a roar outside. Those in attendance for the ceremony spun around to face the door, murmuring of a dragon. There were some screams, but Rafik recognized the noise. His face paled as his blood ran cold. It couldn't be. There was another roar, this time much closer, and a few more screams. He turned to Xeo, Tragi, and Ziri, who all had the same petrified look on their faces.

"We need to get out of here." Rafik whispered.

"Nonsense." Lortimo said, feigning a smile. "Go on, pick your mask. Probably a wild boar made its way into the tribe. Not the first, shan't be the last."

"No." Rafik said. "This is different. We need to get out of here. Now!"

The fog had grown heavier, the violet pulsing ribbons now thicker, growing with every flicker. The color seemed darker than when he last saw it back on the Vinsen Ocean. Now more than ever he wished he still had the endless bag. Rafik pulled out his sword and ran to Xeo.

"Think if I fly away it'll follow?" Xeo asked.

Rafik shook his head. "It survived a shipwreck fighting us. I'm guessing it wants all of us now."

"Who?" Lortimo asked. "Guards, defend your chieftain!"

The doors burst open, followed by the entire wall exploding towards them. They all crouched, taking cover as the Hound of Soboribor roared in triumph. She had changed again. She still had her eight spider-like legs jutting out the base of the body of a bear. Her arms were bulkier now. Long, muscular, and ending in sharp claws with webbing between the fingers. Treshna was permanently staying upright, making what wasn't covered in fur appear more like a dragon. Scales glimmered in the faint light on the insides of her arms. Her head had changed the most now. It was still that of a bison with a maw that could swallow a man whole, but the fur was gone, replaced with more ebon scales. Behind the wolf ears were slits that opened and closed with every breath.

"I didn't think she could get more hideous." Xeo shouted, donning his mask. "I'll lure her out of here."

"Save the Ravohka!" Lortimo shouted. Invisible hands each took the masks and disappeared.

Rafik watched them, wondering which one was his. It was too late to ponder, though. Treshna spotted them, growled, and lunged forward. Rafik shoved Ziri, protecting her from one of the sharp claws and Tragi dove out of the way on the other side. Rafik stood up, pointing his sword at Treshna. He didn't have a talent, though it didn't help much in the middle of a battle, and he didn't have Blaridane. But he wasn't going to let the Hound of Soboribor win.

The monster glared at Rafik with her burning orange eyes and swiped at him. He jumped out of the way, slicing his sword at the same time giving a glancing blow off her scales. At this point Treshna noticed Xeo fly off. She spat at the three of them. The ground sizzled where her saliva had touched. She raised her head and tried snatching at Xeo who got out of the way at the last moment.

"Come on! I thought you were faster than that." He taunted.

Treshna growled, thrusting her arms about, clearing a path, and snapping her jaw at Xeo. Every time she was just inches away from Xeo. His laughter enraged her more. She forgot about the others, and went after Xeo, nipping at him like when a puppy goes after a butterfly. To the others, any sign of intimidation was gone, watching her reach and slightly jump, just to fall short. After a dozen tries, Treshna roared and spit more of her acidic saliva. Xeo dodged the attack but hurtled back to the ground where she then swatted him. Rafik and a Lepal guard rushed over to Xeo, dragging him away from the fight. Several guards raised their spears, and a few appeared out of nowhere, rocketing towards her. Treshna howled, swiping at the guards she could see, and screamed from invisible attacks.

"Get out of here!" Lortimo shouted. "We'll take care of this monster."

Rafik nodded, and the guard near him rushed to help in the fight. There was a strange whinny of a roar coming from his side.

"Out of the way!" Kaliboon shouted, waving her arms driving a carriage. It wasn't horses pulling it, though. Four strange serpent-like lizards weaved over and under each other before untangling themselves. The green scales running along their backs appeared more like vines than dragon scales. The rest of their

258

bodies were covered in white scales that shimmered in and out of existence among the thick fog and limited light.

"Are those dragons?" Xeo asked, gawking at them. He shook his head and sprang to his feet. As the carriage skidded to a halt in front of them wings sprang out from their shoulders and the front two fluttered in the air. Even while stopped the four weaved around each other, snapping at one another. "I've never seen or even heard of these ones before."

Kaliboon nodded. "We can marvel at them later. Get in."

Xeo, Tragi, and Ziri climbed into the carriage while Rafik sat beside her. "I'll help." He said.

"If you have good aim, then thank you. Otherwise, get in the back." Kaliboon said, handing Rafik a bow and a quiver of arrows. "Where are we going?"

"East." Rafik said. "We can't stay here. We need to keep moving."

Kaliboon cracked the reigns alerting the four horse-size dragons to start moving. They snarled before hurtling forward. Watching the green stripes slither and dance was hypnotic. Treshna's roar echoed behind them as she gave chase but couldn't keep up with the carriage. "I can't make them go this fast forever." Kaliboon finally said.

"I know." Rafik said. "We just need to make it to sunrise."

Treshna didn't let up until light started to glow off the eastern side of the Black Wall. She gave one more roar and disappeared into the shrinking shadows. Kaliboon slowed the carriage. The dragons continued to slither around each other but didn't pull as hard. "What are those things?" Rafik asked.

"Frosted Tangles." Kaliboon said. "They're pretty common in the Bomoku Mountains. Originally from the Sampra Tribe. Most just raise them to pull carriages or heavy carts."

"Can you ride one?" Rafik asked, mesmerized by the way they moved about. It was obvious how they got their names. With the white scales and green stripe, and them constantly moving around each other, it was like a living knot.

259

"Only if you have a death wish." Kaliboon scoffed. "If that thing is going to be chasing us at night we'll need to rest during the day."

"That's fine." Rafik said. "Are we stopping in any villages or tribes to get supplies?"

"No." Kaliboon said flatly. "They'll ask too many questions. Can't imagine many being kind to any kolinda. Plus, if we overstay our welcome that monster will be back."

"A what?"

"A stranger or outsider." Kaliboon said.

"Where are we going then?"

"You wanted to make it to the Nassir River. We'll try to go there. Maybe give Vanarzir a surprise."

The carriage slowly came to a stop, pulling over on a well-worn road. Trees from either side stretched, making a sort of tunnel of trees, and the overgrowth kept most of what was out there out of sight. It was so dense they couldn't even see any of the Bomoku Mountains. "Where are we?"

"We cut through a forest surrounding Mt. Korban. Probably halfway to the Pokoto Tribe, I reckon." Kaliboon said. She hopped off the carriage and banged on the side. Several voices stirred inside.

The door burst open, and Krista emerged from the carriage. Xeo was next, followed by Taygin, Ziri, Haloro, and Tragi. "What are they doing here?" Rafik asked.

"During the attack I offered to take them." Kaliboon said. "Thought they might come in handy."

"We are pretty strong." Taygin said, smiling. "We won't let you down."

Xeo laughed. "The three of you look so weak I doubt you could even fight a broom."

Kaliboon glared at Taygin. "That's not what I meant. If that thing is chasing us, I won't hesitate for a second to trip you so the rest of us can get away."

"That's rude." Krista said. "What did we do?"

"I remember you." Kaliboon said. "I remember all of you. Invading our home. Stealing our children. And what you did to my baby boy!"

"We didn't do that!" Krista shouted.

"You didn't stop it."

"Well, we're going to try now." Krista said. "Aren't we?" Taygin and Haloro nodded.

"I wouldn't trust them, Rafik." Kaliboon said. "If you have any plans, I wouldn't share it with them until they need to know. They're probably spies."

"We aren't spies." Taygin said.

"That's what a spy would say." Xeo said.

Tragi rolled his eyes. "Whether we can trust them or not doesn't matter. We have a common enemy. Treshna. And until she's captured, killed, or whatever curse is on us is broken, it's coming for us. So, save the backstabbing for after the Hound of Soboribor isn't a problem. Deal?"

Each of them eyed the other with suspicion. "Deal." Rafik finally said. The others soon followed. "Do you think we can capture it?"

Tragi shrugged. "I've never heard of someone doing so."

"Just that nobody has succeeded in doing that yet." Krista said.

"Or nobody has even tried." Xeo argued.

"I was thinking the same thing." Tragi said. "If we can come up with a plan to trap her, maybe we can stop her."

"Tragi," Xeo said. "What kind of trap can hold her? She sank in that maelstrom, only to come back."

Tragi nodded. "Yes. And when Rafik cut off her legs she got spider ones."

"I see where you're going with this." Rafik said. "We need to trap her. But not in a way that makes her be able to change."

"Exactly!" Tragi said. "Every time she changed, she was hurt or about to die. If we just put her in a strong enough cage, she may be stuck there."

"That might work." Kaliboon said. "My daddy used to always say before he died that the simplest trap is the best trap."

"My dad said never and always are two works you always want to remember never to use." Rafik smirked.

"Smart man." Tragi smiled. "Both of them."

"In the meantime, let's get some rest." Rafik said. "Until we find a way to stop her, we need to travel at night, rest during the day. Once night falls, we'll be running until sunrise."

Xeo nodded. "While you're all resting, I'm using my mask to find us some food. Maybe scout ahead."

"That's not a bad idea." Rafik said. "Just be careful."

"What Ravohka did you get?" Xeo asked. "I got distracted with Treshna. Didn't notice your choice."

Rafik lowered his head. "I didn't get one. Treshna showed up before I could."

"No good deed goes unpunished." Kaliboon sighed. "I'm sorry."

"What do you mean?" Rafik asked.

"You saved those three. If they weren't there you probably could have chosen sooner." Kaliboon explained.

Rafik shrugged. "Only one who got a Ravohka was Xeo. Now I'm weaker than when we first got here."

"I left my Ravohka at home." Kaliboon said. "Sitting there beside the tree. Just because you don't have one, doesn't make you useless."

"I know." Rafik said. "Do you think I could get one at the Pokoto Tribe?"

"It doesn't work like that." Kaliboon said. "The tribe that allows you to be part of the Fohdorshan is the tribe that gives you your mask. Nobody else can. Plus, you're still kolinda. That's also why I'm here, to vouch that you completed the trials at least. Who knows what they might do to you otherwise? Especially with Vanarzir and his Kylix soldiers running around. Not to mention, we aren't stopping there, remember?"

Rafik nodded and turned back from where they came. His talent was back there. He wasn't sure if he would ever get it back. With Treshna now chasing them he regretted doing the trials.

"I know you want your talent back." Ziri said. Her voice wasn't a whisper anymore, and her lips weren't as pink. "After all this is over, we'll go back and get it."

Rafik feigned a smile. "Thanks. I hope so."

"I can't imagine choosing to give up your talent." Krista chimed in. "That is one of the dumbest things you could do."

"I can't imagine choosing to kidnap children and murder innocent people." Xeo countered, putting his hand on Rafik's shoulder, preemptively restraining him. "That has to be one of the worst things you could ever do."

Krista glared at them but didn't say a word. Taygin and Haloro stood by her side, though their heads were cast downwards.

"This is going to be a fun trip." Kaliboon grumbled.

"Enough fighting!" Tragi said. "We have a monster chasing us, in a land we aren't familiar with. We all want the same thing. So, stop fighting. We need to work together, not tear each other apart."

"He's right." Rafik said. "Let's make camp before it gets too late in the day and get some rest. "How long until we get to the Nassir River?"

Kaliboon shrugged. "I don't rightly know but shouldn't take too long going as fast as we are."

"Do those tangly things need food?" Xeo asked, watching them. They had finally stopped moving and were now resting atop one another.

"Frosted Tangles." Kaliboon said. "If you're going to be an honorary Fohdorshan, you may want to start calling things properly. But yes, they do."

Xeo nodded. "Tragi and I will go hunting if the rest of you want to setup camp?"

"Sounds like a plan to me." Rafik nodded.

Before anyone else could object Xeo launched into the sky. "Hunting from above like a bird, let's go Tragi!"

Rafik noticed the trees here were different than back home in Datz. Trees here had large leaves jutting out of thick branches, and the bark was smooth, making them slick when wet. Everything was wet here as well. Freezing rain drizzled constantly, and he could see his breath as he exhaled. Kaliboon assured him this was how winter was for most places south of the Bomoku Mountains and into the Wild Lands.

He wandered out of the damp forest, and into the open field lands. To the south, east, and west he could see nothing but grasslands and the occasional tree. To the north was the forest they were gathering wood from, but if he craned his neck higher, he could see a lone mountain sticking straight up into the sky, nearly scraping the Black Wall. Unlike the red color the Bomoku Mountains were known for, this was ebon. Like darkness had taken a physical form. It reminded Rafik of a scar, as it stood out from the rest of the landscape.

"That's Mt. Korban." Kaliboon said, noticing his gaze. "It's a sacred place for our people."

"Why is it black? It looks…unnatural." Rafik said.

"It wasn't always like that." Kaliboon said. "That was the birthplace of the Dragon Riders, the first being Korban, who the mountain is named after. Magic spilled from those peaks, gifting us with that power. After the fall of an ancient kingdom people turned to the Dragon Riders for guidance. It didn't take long for some riders to take advantage of that and become kings over everyone. Other riders didn't agree, believing they would hold too much power. The Dragon Wars started. Dragon Riders against the new Dragon Lords. It was horrible, and it finally ended with the Dragon Riders winning. The victors banished or killed everyone from those tribes who became Dragon Lords. So many innocent lives were taken Mt. Korban turned black with sorrow and closed itself off from all Fohdorsha. It's said the dragon who slaughtered an entire tribe is locked away in there. If he breaks free, all Alutopek will crumble."

"We never learned of the Dragon Wars." Rafik said.

"I'm not surprised." Kaliboon smirked. "Most are obsessed with what came after. Alutopek was so torn apart, that warlords came and went within a matter of days. Until the Four Kings came along. One of them took something from Mt. Korban and was able to conquer everything and unite Alutopek once more."

"What did they take?" Rafik asked.

Kaliboon shrugged. "Nobody alive knows."

They finished collecting wood, grass, and leaves for the camp in silence. Rafik kept stealing glances at the obsidian mountain that peaked through small holes from the treetops above. Maybe he could go there and find something to defeat Vanarzir?

A crude lean-to style hut was made beside a fire. Xeo and Tragi returned with rabbits which they roasted over the fire. They mentioned Kryn, who Krista was surprised to learn was also still alive.

"Around here was where we deserted the Kylix." Krista said. She held one of the large leaves over her as rain drizzled down. The campfire flickered in and out, being overpowered by the rain.

"You weren't that far from the Lepal Tribe." Kaliboon said.

"King Vanarzir wanted to explore Mt. Korban. In the Pokoto Tribe was where we all lost our talent. He forced us." Krista said.

"Now the Kylika is just whoever has those masks." Haloro said. "And King Vanarzir didn't think we deserved what was rightfully ours."

The camp grew quiet at the news. Maybe they could catch up to the Kylix before the Nassir River? Rafik felt a weight lift off his shoulders. If the king was exploring, he might still not know the plan. The Soniky were going to battle the Kylix at the Nassir River on the spring equinox. But if the Kylix weren't there yet, the rebels would be waiting, and he could still get there in time.

Chapter 24: Shadow Raiders

Bomoku Mountains, Alutopek

Kryn groaned, rolling over in the musky barn. Thunder roared outside, pulling her from her dreams. She rubbed her eyes and saw Junla already awake sitting against the doorway, watching the storm. "How long have you been up?"

Junla shrugged. "I'm not sure-certain." She said. "Isn't it beautiful, watching the rain?"

The two slept in a vacant barn near the Savage Tavern. The group they gave their warm beds to the night before had agreed to come at daybreak to take them to Hurik. Kryn didn't trust them, but she didn't have much of a choice, either. The rain poured down in sheets, pelting the brick laden streets like miniature missiles. The crimson rooftops were still vibrant within the storm. Memories of back out at sea flashed across Kryn's mind. The maelstrom was bad enough. But Treshna there, too. She was grateful that monster had went down with the ship. "That's one less monster in this world." She whispered.

"Something's happening." Junla said, sitting up straight. "They're escape-leaving."

Kryn stretched and hobbled to her feet. Sure enough, the group of people they saw last night were stumbling out of the Savage Tavern. The barkeep shouting at them, fist raised and waving at them, as they did. "Come on." She said, stepping into the rain.

"Are you ready to take-escort us?" Junla asked as they got into earshot.

The man closest to them, leading the group of recovering drunks, squinted. "I don't know you."

"We met last night." Kryn said. "You said you'd take us to Hurik in exchange for the room."

"I did?" The man asked, turning back to the Savage Tavern, a quizzical expression on his face. "Was wondering how we ended up there. Most don't like us sleeping in their beds."

'I wonder why.' Kryn thought to herself. They were covered in dirt and grime, and even in the rain she could smell them. It was like they hadn't washed, let alone even attempted to change their clothes, in months. The grimy clothes clung to them and was so stiff their sleeves stayed firm even when moving. Pools of dirty water soon collected at their feet as they stood there. "A deal is a deal." She said.

"A deal wasn't even made. Right?" He turned to his friends who all grumbled and nodded their heads in agreement. He turned and smirked.

"Take me to Hurik." Kryn demanded. "I'm not going to be playing this game. Take me to him now."

The man shook his head. "If Hurik wanted you he would get you himself."

"Yeah, and we don't know any Huriks." A woman chimed in. The group once again grumbling in approval.

"You were talking about him last night!" Kryn shouted. She bit the inside of her cheek, wanting to scream at them more. "Fine. We'll get the guard."

"The guard doesn't care about kolinda." The man laughed. "Go ahead."

"Fine. We will." Kryn said. "Come on Junla." She stamped off, walking the length of a building and turning down an alley.

"Where are we going?" Junla asked as Kryn crouched down behind a barrel.

"Just stay quiet and stay hidden." Kryn said. A moment later the group shuffled by the entrance to the alley. She gestured for Junla to follow and sneaked back. Peering around the corner, she saw the group hustling away, glancing over their shoulders.

"You think they're going to him?" Junla asked.

Kryn nodded. "They don't seem the brightest."

Sure enough, they didn't stop as others yelled at them or tried getting their attention. Some tried berating them, while others called for them to stay away. It was clear they weren't the most welcome of people within Tahmlo Tribe. After another man hollered at the group, and chased after them, they began to run away.

Kryn hurried after them, trying to keep her distance while Junla leapt into the skies. They ran out of the tribe and into the wilderness, weaving in and around trees. Kryn had a sense of déjà vu chasing after them. They moved the same way as Hurik as she chased him. Though this group was clumsier. The group ran deep into the woods, coming to a clearing that separated into five different directions. They each took a separate path. Kryn cursed and followed one. She hoped Junla could follow another but couldn't see if she were still flying.

The path took them up and down hills, across a gully and slipping down scree. There were less and less trees to hide behind as they ascended the red mountains. Kryn glanced back, hearing the loose rock slip and shift behind her. A moment later she dove behind a boulder. Another of the group was running up the mountainside. A shadow moved over her, and she saw Junla tailing them. Before she could get up the rest of the group reunited and started up the mountain.

Turning a sharp corner and squeezing between two boulders, Kryn finally made it to their meeting place. She crouched down, scooting across the ground as quiet as could be. There were dozens of Fohdorsha messing about. Some with blue or green hair, others with white or red. But most of them had varying shades of silver and gray.

"Where are we?" Kryn whispered to herself.

The leader of the group doubled over panting, asking for Hurik. A moment later Hurik shoved his way through the crowd. His white hair shined like a beacon among the sea of gray on the red mountains and stormy skies.

"You're drunk." Hurik hissed.

The man shook his head. "I was drunk. But we hurried here as fast we could."

"Why?"

"There's a girl asking for you. Kolinda." The man said. "She asked for you by name."

"What did she look like?" Hurik asked.

"Dirty blond hair, green eyes. Fair skin."

"Ya shire." Hurik cursed. "Where is she now?"

The man shrugged. "She was fetching the Tahmlo Guard when we left."

"And you came straight here?" Hurik asked.

"Yes." The man nodded. "We weren't sure what else to do."

"You fool!" Hurik shouted, shoving the man to the ground. Others in the crowd began to murmur, almost panic. "If we're lucky it's just her who probably followed you. Or we could have the Tahmlo Guard here any moment."

"Oh." The man said. "Didn't think about that."

"The Menjua Tribe was gracious enough to allow people like us to live among them. And you bring our mutual enemies here because you couldn't manage an outsider?" Hurik shouted. "I knew you were stupid when I allowed you to work for me, but I didn't think you were this dumb."

The man tried to speak but Hurik slapped him across the face. A larger crowd was forming and watching the two. Some whispered and pointed at the man Hurik was chastising, while others glanced in Kryn's direction, fear etched into their faces. Hurik's face suddenly shifted from anger to worry. He turned his head from side to side, before slowly backing out of the circle.

Kryn watched him duck, hiding in the crowd, and disappear. Kryn tried to move but noticed another standing right next to her. If he even just glanced down at her she would be seen.

A scream echoed in the air, people in the crowd started claiming the Tahmlo were here and scattered like roaches exposed to sudden light. Junla held up her hands in surrender as she landed, taking off her Ravohka. "I'm not Tahmlo!" She shouted just as others were noting her chestnut hair and bluish eyes.

"How did you find us?" One asked.

"I follow-hunted them." Junla said, gesturing to the man and his friends.

"We thought your kind was extinct." Another in the crowd said.

Kryn noticed the way Junla spoke in the common tongue compared to those in the Menjua Tribe. The ones here, their accent harsher as they over emphasized certain syllables or letters. It was proof of their isolation. She guessed with the majority having gray hair and eyes like Junla had brown, they were part of a different tribe.

"We thought you were dead-gone, too." Junla said. "A lot has changed since our exile-banishment. Come here, Kryn." She spun around, holding her hand above her eyes, trying to search for her.

Kryn slowly got to her feet as people gasped and jumped out of her way. She noticed none of them had masks like the other tribes. "Hello." She said, waving a hand and hurrying to Junla's side.

"Kolinda aren't allowed." One said, stepping forward. Her silvery hair was in thick braids that flowed down her shoulders and back like liquid metal, and her eyes were as bright as any newly forged blade. Wrinkles, however, covered her face showing her true age. "I'm the chief of the Menjua."

"I've never heard of the Menjua." Kryn said, bowing to the chief. "I'm honored to meet you."

The chief spat at her feet. "Wish I could say the same, outsider."

"Kryn doesn't mean-want any harm." Junla said. "She's a brave warrior who is after a thief. She's been hunt-finding him since the Ruins of Kangor. And I'm help-aiding her."

"But the Tahmlo are coming." The chief said, glaring at Kryn. "And you brought them here."

Kryn shook her head. "No, it was a bluff, so they would lead me to Hurik. I didn't know he was living among you."

"All who are banished by the Fohdorshan Tribes are welcome among us. Our very existence isn't allowed by them. Shame since we used to be the greatest of all tribes." The chief said.

Junla nodded and turned to Kryn. "The Ashen Tribe had the most Dragon Riders. They used to bring peace-safety to Alutopek."

"What happened?" Kryn asked.

"Our ancestors were on the wrong end of a war." The chief said. "And for generations since we have had to pay for it."

"I hope I'm not out of line for speaking," Kryn said. "But for a tribe full of misfits and exiles, I'm surprised outsiders aren't accepted."

"Kolinda taint everything they touch." The chief said. "We aren't interested in that poison touching our wells."

"Will you allow me to leave?"

The chief shook her head. "You said much has changed. Let us catch up before I decide your fate."

"I'm after Hurik." Kryn said. "I can't let him get away."

"I can't allow you to leave yet." The chief said. She turned and started walking away, relying heavily on her decorated staff topped with a skull of a ram. Junla nudged Kryn to follow her, and the two went in step behind her. "Hurik is like a sparrow. Easily skittish, but always returns if there's a meal."

The chief's hut was a small dome with semicircle windows around the top. From the outside it was a rough, gray, textured clay covering it, but on the inside it was smooth. A fire crackled in the center, with smoke streaming out of the windows. Junla did most of the talking, as she explained the Amsahvi slowly coming out of hiding.

"It's been ages since we Menjua have been accepted. Occasionally one or two leave the tribe never to return. We've accepted the Fohdorshan exiles, even if most are criminals. Maybe it is time for us to reveal ourselves once more and return to our ancestral home."

"You don't live here?" Kryn asked.

The chief shook her head. "We do now. Before I became chief, we didn't have a home. We wandered the Bomoku Mountains. Anyone who saw us were either forced to join us or killed in fear of the rest of us being discovered. Before we became

271

shadow raiders, as we've been called in the common tongue, we lived in the Wild Lands with our dragons. Now, we're just legends. Stories to tell around a campfire to not go wandering into the mountains. Shadow Raiders will find you."

Junla nodded. "I hope you can return-go home again."

"You don't wear masks." Kryn noted, as the chief gave Junla a smile. "Nobody does here."

"No. The art was lost when we were exiled." The chief said. "We have the talent we were born with."

There was a pause in conversation as the three stared into the fire. They could hear the bustling of the tribe just outside the hut. Junla thought how amazing it was to find another lost tribe of the Fohdorsha, while the chief imagined bringing her people out of hiding. Kryn stared into the fire, yearning to feel the roiling flame inside her again. The warmth it gave her, and confidence to do anything. The longer she went without, the more she felt like an abandoned furnace, forgotten, and growing cold. Finally, Kryn cleared her throat and spoke. "Will we be allowed to leave?"

The chief didn't answer right away. She poked at the fire with her staff, letting it crackle and more smoke billow out. "You have seen two tribes now, Junla?" She asked.

Junla nodded. "Tahmlo and Lepal."

"Fire and water tribes." The chief muttered. "You didn't mention much of the Tahmlo Tribe."

"No." Junla shook her head. "They're as prideful-stubborn as ever."

"My people will not be seeking acceptance from either tribe. We will remain Shadow Raiders until I believe it fit to reveal ourselves. It may even be for our best interest, considering the war that is spreading." The chief said.

"I thought-believed the Menjua were noble warriors who weren't afraid-scared of a fight." Junla said. "I heard so many story-legends of Ashen Champions flying into battle with the Menjua. Even Korban himself came from the Menjua."

"We are." The chief said. "But this isn't our fight. You two may leave to find Hurik. I never really cared for him. He's more of a snake than a man. I knew his misdeeds would catch up to him. But if any other outsiders find us, we will hunt you down."

"I swear we won't tell a soul." Kryn said.

Junla got to her feet and bowed. "As you wish-want."

The two were guided out of the hut and to the far end of the tribe. "Hurik is like a squirrel." One guard said. "He'll be hard to find, and even harder to catch. Be careful."

The two nodded and left, hoping to gain on his trail quickly. Junla walked beside Kryn as they turned a corner, and the tribe was gone. The wilderness consumed them once more as trees and brush now covered the mountainside.

"Ever heard the phrase of finding a needle in a haystack?" Kryn asked.

Junla shook her head. "What does it mean?"

"It means this is going to be next to impossible." Kryn sighed.

"Oh! We say like finding a pebble in a pool of mud." Junla said. "Yours sounds silly-strange."

Kryn smirked, staring at her friend with the darkest of mahogany hair she had seen, and eyes bright as teal-colored sapphires. There was a peculiar mixture of innocence and ferocity that just made Kryn want to protect her. "I'm glad you found me. It's been a fun adventure with you."

Junla smiled, her cheeks growing pink, as she held her mask at her side. "It's nice having a friend-pal."

Chapter 25: The Obsidian Orphan

Morvar Tribe Ruins, Bomoku Mountains, Alutopek

Kryn and Junla followed a trail they thought was from Hurik. More than once they doubled back. He was like a ghost and disappeared into the shadows. Not long after losing his trail they wandered out of the mountains and onto the meadows and flatlands between the northern Bomoku Mountains and Mt. Korban. Junla mentioned every time she caught Kryn glancing at the jagged, black bluff how it was a sacred site to every Fohdorshan.

While on the flatlands they made great time, as Junla held Kryn and the two flew, scanning wherever Hurik might be. It didn't take long to be arriving on the eastern rim of the Bomoku Mountains. *'I could get used to flying.'* Kryn thought, noting how much faster they were than just by walking.

"The problem-trouble with flying," Junla said as they made camp on the foothills of the mountains. "Are the bugs."

"At least you have a mask to shield your face." Kryn laughed. "I've been trying not to complain, but I hate them hitting my face."

"At least that's a sign-symbol of spring." Junla said.

"Spring?" Kryn asked, poking her head up like a prairie dog sensing danger. "Already?"

Junla nodded. "I'm no timekeeper, but spring can't be more than a week away by now. The bugs bothering us are called-named messenger flies. They are only alive for the first week or two of spring. It's a sign of no more wintry weather."

"We've spent all this time searching for him?" Kryn asked, suddenly pacing back and forth, glancing towards the east. "I lost track of time and now I won't be there."

"Be there for what?" Junla asked.

"We need to hurry." Kryn said, the smile gone from her face. "I need to meet up with my friends."

"I'm your friend-pal." Junla said.

274

"Yes, you are." Kryn said. "But my other friends. They need me. We're supposed to stop Vanarzir at the beginning of spring. And I'm not going to make it. We got split up."

"Destiny has a strange-weird way of working." Junla said.

"You call this destiny?"

"Of course!" Junla gasped. "How else can you explain this world? Coincidence is only for those too stubborn-thick to see the bigger picture."

"And what's the bigger picture?" Kryn asked. "I'm roaming the Bomoku Mountains hunting a man that took my talent instead of going up against the king who had me forced in his army for seven years."

Junla shrugged. She opened her mouth to speak as they rounded a corner, only to close it the next moment with a slight gasp. In front of them were long forgotten ruins. Only the foundations and a crumbling wall was left. In most places vines and weeds had reclaimed the ruins. The pathways worn into the mountain itself were filled with dirt and debris, but still visible.

"Where are we?" Kryn asked.

"We got to go-leave." Junla said. "Now." She made a mark of protection and slowly stepped backwards.

Kryn held up her arm, barring her exit. "Where are we?" She repeated in a sterner tone.

"Morvar Ruins." Junla answered. "A cursed place."

"Cursed? Why?"

"At the end of the Dragon Wars there was one Dragon Rider so angry-furious, all he could see was blood. He rode on the , Crimson Shroud, largest and fiercest of all dragons. Breath wrong, and they'll destroy-vanquish you where you stand. The rider fed-absorbed off that anger, and after the war was won, swore-promised it would never happen again. He and his fellow riders came here, to the Obsidian, or Morvar, Tribe. They slaughter-killed everyone. Legend says one Obsidian Dragon egg was spared, lost-gone during the final hours. Those who survived-lived were accepted into other tribes, but never forgiven for the war."

"The last Obsidian Dragon." Kryn whispered. "That sounds familiar. I think I've heard that legend before." As Junla told her the story she vaguely remembered the images seen in Teller's fire back at the Amsahvi Tribe. There was something else about the story as well. Like she had read it from a book, but couldn't place a finger on it.

Junla nodded. "It's a common-accepted one, I think. A dragon still hide-lurking out there. Waiting to return. You mention-say you even saw it in the Biodlay Desert."

"That massacre, though…I can't imagine." Kryn said, now looking at the ruins in a new light. She imagined having Rafik's talent and witnessing the violence. The heartache, as she watched their home destroyed and loved ones fall. "I…I can't imagine that."

"That's why Mt. Korban turned black-dark. In remembrance-honor of the Morvar Tribe. Elder-priest Lortimo said-told that when the Kylix arrived, it was like what happened here. A surge-wave of death that couldn't be stopped." Junla said.

"Nobody comes here?" Kryn asked.

Junla shook her head. "It's removed-gone from most maps. Maybe not on smaller ones. Best not disturb-wake the dead, after suffering in such a way in their final-last moments."

"If nobody is here, I bet you it would make a good hiding spot." Kryn reasoned. "Nobody would come searching for you."

"I'm not going-searching in there." Junla said.

Kryn nodded. "Use your mask and fly over everything. Would that be disrespectful?"

Junla didn't say anything. She tilted her head, grasping her chin, and hummed. "I…I guess not."

"Then it's settled. Fly over the ruins and see if you can spot anything. I'll wait here." Kryn turned away from Junla, only feeling her gone from the sudden 'whoosh' of air as she took off. There was something strange about this place. She couldn't put her finger on it. The vines and weeds crept around all the ruins, some even growing between the bricks. It was something magical and eerie, watching nature reclaim what man had taken.

276

She pressed her hand against a gray stone. What seemed like scorch marks were burned into the brick. The creeping vine that was ensnaring this part of the wall had been singed as well. It was faint, but she could feel warmth from the mark. This was fresh.

"There's nothing here." Junla said, landing beside Kryn. "Can we go-leave now?"

"Look at this." Kryn said, pointing to the burn.

"Remnant-pieces of war from long ago." Junla sighed. "So much heartache in one place-spot."

"Touch it." Kryn demanded. "It's still warm."

"Because this place is cursed." Junla explained, whipping her hand back the moment her finger brushed against it. "We shouldn't be here."

"How long ago was that massacre?" Kryn asked.

Junla shrugged. "Ages ago. Millennia."

"Before the Four Kings, right?"

"Yes." Junla nodded.

"Shouldn't this place be more overrun by nature than just weeds and a few vines?" Kryn asked.

"No." Junla said, shaking her head. "It's a mark-sign. Just like Mt. Korban."

"I don't think so." Kryn said. "Somebody is here, and I'm going in."

Junla hollered for Kryn, but she ignored her, stepping into the ruins. It didn't feel any different than before she arrived. A cool gust of wind whistled through the ruins, giving her chills. Yet, she didn't stop. She closed her eyes, brushing her hand against the ruins. These stones were warmer, but it felt like the ones in Datz. The sudden and jagged end to a wall; the dips, craters, and divots in the brick. She imagined being back in the City of Ruins, turning the corner and disappearing from Junla. A sudden slight shifting of small pebbles alerted Kryn. She opened her eyes, spun around, and saw a shadowy figure dart deeper into the ruins. Without hesitation Kryn charged after them.

"It's Hurik!" She shouted.

"There's something here." Junla shouted, flying overhead.

"I thought you checked." Kryn yelled, swerving out of the way of fallen boulders while the shadow quickly climbed and hurtled over them.

"He was sneak-hiding!" Junla yelled. She surged forward and dived down, trying to cut off the shadow. The figure tripped, nearly falling, but Junla continued flying onward, chasing something else. It hobbled forward, arms outstretched, and pushed against a wall. The figure spun around in one swift motion, hurtling into the air, and kicking Kryn who was coming up behind them.

Kryn had enough time to raise an arm to block most of the blow, but she fell to the ground, skidding to a halt just before hitting one of the crumbling walls. She growled, jumped to her feet, and charged at the shadow.

It was difficult fighting the shadow. One moment it appeared to just be a blot of darkness upon the ruins, the next, a shadowy embodiment of a man with four horns protruding from its head. Kryn tried slicing at the shadow with her sword, but to no avail. It couldn't be touched, but the figure landed several punches on Kryn.

"I need your help!" Kryn shouted.

"It's the guardian-protector of the ruins!" Junla replied, hovering in place above the fighting duo. "We need to leave."

Kryn shook her head. She hadn't run from a fight yet. She didn't want to start now. Even if it was against shadows. The shadow lunged forward and Kryn darted out of the way, but she fell backwards, as if being yanked by her hair. It wasn't her hair, though, but her entire body that was being wrenched. The shadow wasn't anywhere near her. She spun around and noticed the shadowy menace standing on her own shadow. Kryn tried stepping to the side but couldn't pull away. "I'm trapped." Kryn yelled. "Make it move!"

"Make what move?" Junla asked. From where she was watching, it appeared only that Kryn was just standing still, pretending not to move like a mime. She hadn't seen Kryn attack

278

anything, but she did see her getting thrown to the ground at the beginning. "It's the ghosts of this place. Apologize-beg and maybe it'll let you leave."

"She can't see me." The shadow spoke in an old and raspy voice. "Maybe hear me if she's close enough."

"But...but I can? How?" Kryn asked.

"You can see my shadow. Which is all that is left of me." The shadow said. "Because you know me."

"I don't know you." Kryn said, shaking her head. She tried imagining all the people she had met. Nobody had that raspy and venomous of a voice. It was like a bear's roar mixed with the hissing of a snake.

"I know of you, but I didn't think it would be you who was the thief. The one who ruined everything!" The shadow said. "But you see me, so you do know me. You must be the thief."

"Thief?" Kryn asked. "I'm no thief."

"What's happening-going on?" Junla asked. She floated down to stand beside Kryn but refused to touch the ground. "I can't see you, but my friend-pal isn't a thief-burglar."

"There is only one way you could see me." The shadow said. "You read my book. My journal. You're the one that ruined everything!"

Kryn's eyes widened in sudden realization. "Nekvaz!" She shouted. "How did I ruin everything?"

The shadow nodded. "For starters, you weren't supposed to steal that book. Second, you shouldn't have read it. And third, I know who you are, Kryn of Sysinal. I've seen you with the Kylix. You were one of Vanarzir's first pets."

"Excuse you! I'm nobody's pet." Kryn snapped, her blood instantly boiling and her fists clenching. Deep within her she felt a tinge of heat. Like a dying ember from kindling that wouldn't take light.

"Who?" Junla asked.

"You're Kylika. Said to be dead from the Battle at the Golden Gate two years ago." Nekvaz said. "But that is neither here nor there. The fact remains, you stole my book. You weren't supposed to read it."

"I'm sorry." Kryn said, still unsure of what else to say. She couldn't move, and his tone didn't feel threatening.

"You don't even know what you did unless you're this pathetic at apologies." Nekvaz snapped.

Kryn glared at the shadow. "I don't need to be insulted by some ghost who's been dead for over two hundred years."

"Who?" Junla asked again, her tone getting angrier.

The shadow laughed. "I'm not dead, though I wish I were. I knew you hadn't decoded the rest, or you would know what happened."

"Well, do you mind filling us in?" Kryn asked. "Can't exactly go anywhere." She tried tugging away, but her shadow was still trapped beneath Nekvaz.

"Who are you talk-speaking to?" Junla snapped.

"Junla, the man you can't see is Nekvaz. According to him, the last of the Morvar Tribe. A Fohdorshan banished from the Bomoku Mountains." Kryn said.

"Banished?" Junla asked. "Why?"

"According to his journal," Kryn said. "He didn't want to give up his talent. Claimed to have found the last Obsidian Dragon, too. That's where I heard that legend. From his diary."

"We shouldn't be talk-engaging him. He's banish-exiled." Junla said, glaring where Kryn was looking. She still couldn't see him.

"Junla, we just made it through an entire tribe of banished Fohdorsha. One more won't hurt." Kryn said. "Before you explain to me why I shouldn't have taken your book from the Hall of Records, is it alright if my friend here steps on the ground?"

Nekvaz shrugged.

"She can't see you." Kryn said.

"It's fine. The land is cursed to those who killed the people on it. You don't appear to be the fiery type from Tahmlo." Nekvaz said.

Junla shook her head. "Amsahvi Tribe." She said proudly, puffing out her chest as she landed on the ground. "Earth Tribe, born and raised."

"Now, how did I ruin everything?"

"Might as well tell you. The plan is ruined anyhow." Nekvaz said. "I saw the creation of the Black Wall. Rathsa and I flew to Alutopek to see how I could help, believing Alutopek was under attack. At the time, I was falling into the good graces of King Arzir. His son, Vanarzir, was on the throne when I arrived. Gone for several years, and now king. He was different than I remembered, but I couldn't tell how. I just felt it. So, I started spying on him. He discovered me, and cursed me to this shadowy form, and enslaved Rathsa. I'm now his slave and forced to do his bidding."

"And Rathsa?" Junla asked.

"My dragon is still in the king's possession. I don't know how to free him. I can't fight against King Vanarzir directly." Nekvaz said. "I met Queen Valkayto on her way to her coronation to become queen. She shared with me things she learned, and together we devised a plan to stop Vanarzir. I wrote it in the final pages of my diary. Kay took it to the Hall of Records where a man named Paris Bantrita was to find it and deliver it to the Soniky. Without that information they can't win."

"What did you learn?" Kryn asked.

Nekvaz shuddered. "Vanarzir's weakness. Because of the curse he put on me I can't share it. That's why I needed Kay's help. Together we were able to write it down. Where is the diary now?"

Kryn paused. Last she saw it the book was within the endless bag that Rafik always carried. But was he carrying it at the time of the shipwreck? Or was it lost to the sea? She finally shrugged. "I think my friend has it."

"You think?" Nekvaz scoffed.

"Why are you here?" Junla asked.

"Hiding. And searching." Nekvaz said. "I managed to disobey Vanarzir and turned into this shadow because of it. Before

281

I was just invisible. Now I'm even less than that. Vanarzir said if I disobey one more time my soul will be his for all eternity, and I will cease to exist. I'm too weak to even try to. But...I managed to run away. Go into hiding and find a way to stop him. I'm looking for something. A treasure that can stop Vanarzir that hasn't been seen in ages."

"Can you at least share that?" Kryn asked.

"It's called the Iospa Diamond. The jewel of loyalty. Legends say it had been created by the first dragons to bring dominion over the monsters that roamed this land. If I find it, I can force Vanarzir to relinquish his power." Nekvaz said. "Maybe then I can be redeemed for what I've done."

"Rafik saw you." Kryn gasped.

"Who?" Nekvaz asked.

"One of my friends. The one who has your diary now." Kryn said. "He saw a boy get murdered in the Sekolah Fortress. That was you."

Nekvaz sighed. "By command of Vanarzir. Though it doesn't make my hands any less bloody."

"I read your diary." Kryn said. "You've been heartless and ruthless since before meeting Rathsa. What changed?"

"Queen Kay." Nekvaz said, his voice choking up as Kryn assumed the shadow was attempting to cry. "Aside from Rathsa, my only friend. She allowed me to call her Kay like her friends and family. She even refused to allow Vanarzir call her that."

Kryn nodded, thinking of everything she had learned. "You were to hurt her. That's why you escaped."

"What?" Nekvaz asked. "Hurt who?"

"Queen Valkayto. The king demanded you hurt her." Kryn said.

"Why?" Junla asked.

"She gave birth to a monster. Everyone in the room was immediately killed by Vanarzir's hand. Through the chaos Kay managed to escape with the baby, and I was sent to kill her. Save the child. I found them. But I couldn't do it. It hurt disobeying. Like a raging fire eating at the inside of me. I allowed her to

282

escape, and I returned the baby. It wasn't like any human I had seen."

"She escaped?" Kryn asked.

Nekvaz laughed. "You don't escape King Vanarzir. He found her. The fear in her eyes…" He trailed off, now on his knees, sobbing. "I used that moment to escape. I ran as far and fast as I could, leaving Rathsa and Kay behind. I'm positive Kay didn't survive the night. Her screams still haunt me. And I'm sure Rathsa was punished cruelly for my absence. If he believes you to be alive, he'll find you. There's no doubt about that."

"He hasn't found you." Kryn said.

"I'm hoping he's believed me gone and dead." Nekvaz said. "But I'm not yet. Just mostly."

As Junla cried, hearing his story she began to see the shadow of Nekvaz and gasped. "I see you."

It was a somber night in the Morvar Ruins. The three each shared their stories of trauma. Kryn shared battling in the Sysinal Arena as a child until King Vanarzir showed up and snatched her, killing her father in the process. She wanted to mention Hurik, but with the memories being fuzzy or non-existent, she wasn't sure if that counted. Junla told of being shunned and mocked for being part of the Amsahvi tribe and how she spoke, along with having an ancestor from the Lepal Tribe. Nekvaz divulged his whole life story. It was one catastrophe after another. It wasn't a surprise he ended up as nothing more than a shadow with how he used to live.

A fire roared in a hearth that hadn't seen warmth in ages. Kryn glanced behind her and saw hers and Junla's shadows flickering in the light. Nekvaz, who sat between them, didn't have a shadow. His black form was like a void of darkness, even in the firelight.

"I spent time with the Menjua Tribe before I met Vanarzir." Nekvaz said. "Mostly good people, but wanting to be accepted by the other Fohdorsha Tribes, they've allowed scum to live among them. At one time, I was part of that ilk. I've grown and changed since then."

"Did you ever know Hurik?"

Nekvaz laughed. "Hurik isn't much older than you. He was after my time."

"Any idea where he is?"

"No." Nekvaz said. "He sounds like someone I knew once. Always slinking in the shadows and only showing up when there is a prize worth having. He'll show himself eventually. Until then, you need to continue living your life."

"But he took my talent." Kryn argued.

"In my long life, I've never met somebody who had that ability to take talent. Except for King Vanarzir. I doubt Hurik did. He hurt you. And you're trying to accept that. Until then, your talent is just out of reach." Nekvaz said.

Kryn growled. "I hate that you're right."

Nekvaz flashed a smile nobody could see. "I've been there. It'll come back. Just give it time."

"Unless" Junla started. "Unless he gave-gifted you a drink."

"Why?" Kryn asked. She remembered him handing her a drink before everything got fuzzy.

"The way you remove somebody's talent is through a poison." Nekvaz explained. "A potion."

"But Teller said I still have my talent. Remember?" Kryn said.

"Maybe you didn't drink-swallow it all." Junla suggested.

"Or he didn't know how to extract your talent." Nekvaz said.

"Is it painful?" Kryn asked.

Junla nodded. "Like getting a piece of you ripped-taken out of you."

"Maybe that's why I don't remember? He didn't drug me, but poisoned me, trying to steal my talent." Kryn said. "And my mind is trying to block it out?"

Nekvaz nodded. "I wouldn't put it past him if he's anything like you've described. Maybe he wanted your talent for himself. Create his own mask."

"I don't like this man." Junla said. "He's evil."

"Maybe we can lure him out." Kryn said.

"Are we supposed to meet-greet your friends?" Junla asked. "We should hurry-run to them while there's still time."

Kryn shook her head. "We won't make it. Might as well make us not being there be worth it."

"How do you know-think we won't make it?" Junla asked.

"You said it yourself how close spring is." Kryn said. "I needed to be at the Nassir River by the spring equinox."

"You could make it while flying on a dragon." Nekvaz said.

"Yeah, let me just jump on one really quick." Kryn said. "If you hadn't noticed, we don't have one."

"No…" Nekvaz said, trailing off. He sat frozen for a moment before getting to his feet. "You two get some rest." He walked away without saying another word, disappearing into the darkness.

"Look what you did!" Junla said. "Watch your mouth-words."

"I didn't mean to upset him." Kryn said. "I should apologize."

"Good luck finding him in this dark-night." Junla said.

Kryn glanced over her shoulder. It was pitch black everywhere the firelight wasn't touching. It was impossible to see where he had disappeared to.

Chapter 26: Then There Were Seven

Bomoku Mountains, Alutopek

Within a couple days a routine had been established. As soon as the sun began to set, and light fade from the Black Wall, the Frosted Tangles would already be saddled. When the fog rolled in, and the violet streaks pulsed, they charged off eastward. Not long after the roars and growls of Treshna would come behind them. She seemed to be getting faster, and more than once Rafik believed he felt her breath on the back of his neck. Every night they would flee as fast they could, and every night just narrowly escape.

During the day they would unsaddle the Frosted Tangles, and setup camp. Rafik and Kaliboon would rest while the others foraged for food or created a quick shelter. Xeo practiced with his Ravohka while Tragi and Ziri examined plants.

As each day passed Ziri's body changed. Her hair and lips were less pink, and color returned to her skin. By the end of the week, one wouldn't recognize her anymore as the girl she once was. Her voice was still soft, though getting louder. Most notably her laughter.

At first, Krista, Haloro, and Taygin, eagerly helped where they could. Their frail frames didn't let them accomplish as much as the others. Trying to prove their worth, they breached being too helpful at times. Especially towards Kaliboon who constantly glared and scowled at them. As the days went on, and they slowly found their place within the group, the suspicions dwindled. Krista was great at tending to the Frosted Tangles while Haloro kept the campfires alive and helped prepare and cook their food. Taygin would flutter like a butterfly from one chore to the next. He didn't quite fit in because of this, but he wasn't an outcast either, though Xeo teased him often.

The only role nobody else did was the nighttime driving and escaping. Rafik would sit beside Kaliboon as she guided the Frosted Tangles where to go. Rafik watched and warned if Treshna was getting close. At least once a night he would use a bow to shoot an arrow to make Treshna swerve.

On one night he did this, and she crashed into a tree. She collapsed and swayed back and forth after getting to her feet, much to Rafik's enjoyment. A couple of nights later and when he tried it again, she burst through the tree without stopping. She was getting stronger.

The Bomoku Mountains were distant hills now in the north and south. Kaliboon assured them that even though they appeared like foothills, it was only because of how tall the mountains were and how far away they were. It took Xeo flying into the air to check for himself before he believed it. The farther east they went the less trees they found. Tragi believed they were in the Wildlands now, but those were still farther south.

Winter was losing its grasp here. The mornings were still freezing, and air crisp, but the days were getting longer, and warmer. Rafik enjoyed making camp out in the fresh air, rather than inside the endless bag. He often thought about and dreamed of the treasures that they had collected, but it was nice not having to worry about it constantly. The only problem was Treshna.

The Hound of Soboribor was relentless, and the Frosted Tangles getting tired. They couldn't keep doing this. "We need to stop her." Rafik said after resting during the morning. "These little guys can't keep this up." He reached over and scratched the closest one's chin. "It's wearing on them."

"Rafik is right." Kaliboon said. "They need rest and more food than we can give them."

"I'm doing my best hunting." Xeo said. "Tragi and I aren't finding much game. It's not our fault."

"I'm not saying it is." Kaliboon said. "It takes a lot to feed a dragon. Let alone four. And these are some of the smaller ones."

"There's bigger ones?" Xeo asked.

"Of course there were!" Kaliboon laughed. "Two kinds from most tribes. Frosted Tangles were one of the smaller ones. But that's a lesson for a different day. We need to come up with a plan. What are her weaknesses?"

"We need to stop her without defeating her." Tragi said. "Every time we have, she's come back stronger."

"Or get the curse lifted. Whatever curse that is." Xeo said.

"Is there a way of lifting the curse?" Krista asked.

"Not without knowing how they're cursed, or what they did." Kaliboon said, rolling her eyes.

"So…don't try to kill her. Just capture her?" Rafik asked.

Tragi nodded. "We don't know any of her weaknesses. Except sunlight. She disappears before light even hits the Black Wall."

"If we can get her locked in a cage where she can't escape, then the sun can finish the job." Rafik said. "How are we going to lure her into it? And what can keep her in?"

"She had crashed, torn, and broken her way through everything so far. We need something strong." Ziri said.

"I don't think we'll find anything like that along the road." Kaliboon sighed.

"Do you remember our last hunt in Kristol?" Xeo asked, turning to Tragi.

"How could I? You nearly killed me." Tragi said, pinching the bridge of his nose between his eyes and taking a deep breath.

"*Nearly.*" Xeo emphasized. "You're still in one piece. I have an idea."

"If it's using me as bait then I'm not interested." Tragi said.

Xeo shook his head. "As much as I'd prefer to use you as bait, it won't work. I need to be the bait."

"What are you talking about?" Krista asked.

"Back in Kristol we would hunt in Fogwood." Tragi said, nudging his head to the north. "Xeo and I were the best hunters there. Our secret was using one of us, mostly me, as bait."

"We would track something huge. Usually something that wanted to eat us. I would be hiding in brush, or in a tree, and Tragi would lure it into a clearing acting wounded or bleeding. Then I'd ambush it, and together we would take it out." Xeo explained.

"You really trusted your brother." Haloro laughed, clapping Tragi on the back. "I don't even think I could trust my former

Kylika soldiers like that." As he mentioned his past within the Kylix, he quickly glanced to Kaliboon and slunk back.

"Probably why you're here then. You had a conscience." Kaliboon said, not staring up from the stick she was fiddling with.

"We just need to lure it somewhere?" Krista asked.

"Somewhere she can't escape from." Rafik said.

"We could build a cage." Taygin suggested. "Lure her to a certain spot and drop it on her."

"I don't think there's enough steel around here to make a cage." Xeo said.

"If we can't drop a cage on her," Rafik said, lighting up with his idea, "Why don't we let her drop into one?"

"What do you mean?" Krista asked. "Why does anything have to drop? Just surround her and kill her."

"That won't work. We tried that back at Lynn." Rafik said. "But, if we dig a big enough pit, maybe she couldn't get out."

"That might work." Tragi said.

Ziri, who had been quiet this whole time, finally spoke up. "If we dig a pit, and Xeo were the bait, he could lure her into it. Dig it by trees so he can climb the tree. Treshna could fall into the pit instead."

"I like this idea." Tragi smiled. "Good luck." He laughed at Xeo, who was now regretting suggesting himself to be the bait.

"One of you were supposed to say *'no, Xeo, you're too important. We can't take that risk.'* And then we would come up with something else."

Tragi shrugged. "This plan works."

Xeo frowned, half scowling.

"All in favor?" Rafik asked, raising his hand.

Everyone, including Xeo, raised their hand. "I wasn't expecting that." Krista laughed.

"Great job caving into peer pressure." Tragi smiled. "Don't worry, Xeo, I'll protect you."

Xeo laughed, shaking his head. "Oh, I don't give into peer pressure. I just do what they say the first time before any pressure is given."

"That isn't any better!" Kaliboon snapped while the others laughed.

The rest of the day was spent moving camp from the open field they were in and trekking back towards the foothills of the Bomoku Mountains. There were more trees, several of which were like mushrooms, with large foliage almost creating a bit of a dome around them. Kaliboon called them *mirage trees* as they appeared like dense walls of vines. Brushing them aside, though, and you'd find a wide clearing between the drooping leaves and vines of the tree, and the trunk. They made excellent hiding spaces from foreigners and some of the dumber carnivorous monsters that roamed these mountains.

There were only two shovels in the small pack of supplies stored atop the carriage. Kaliboon was surprised there were even two, as she had just taken the nearest carriage when Treshna attacked. The group took turns digging. Two would dig while others would slowly trim away the vines to let light into the area. The soil was loose and soft, and switching often allowed them to make progress quicker than anyone expected.

It wasn't quick enough, though. The group was so distracted digging and preparing the trap for Treshna, they didn't notice the light dwindle and fade. The glowing light of the Black Wall was gone, and the eerie fog rolled in.

Rafik was the first to notice as he wiped his brow while pausing from digging. "We have a problem." He said, climbing out of the large hole.

"What's wrong?" Tragi asked.

"Did you find treasure?" Xeo asked, scrambling towards him.

"No." Rafik said. "It's night. Are the Frosted Tangles ready?"

Kaliboon shook her head. "I was completely distracted." For the last several hours those who weren't digging were using the vines they had cute to weave a sort of platform to camouflage the hole.

"What are we going to do?" Krista asked.

290

"We don't have time to saddle them." Kaliboon said.

"We run." Rafik said. "We can't let her discover this hole. We need to get out of here. Run, and circle back in the morning."

"Do we split up?" Krista asked.

"I'm not leaving my friends." Ziri said, standing proudly beside Rafik.

Rafik flashed a smile at Ziri. "I don't know if Treshna is after any of you, but she is after us." He gestured to Xeo, Tragi, Ziri, and himself.

"Take the Frosted Tangles." Kaliboon said. "It'll be uncomfortable riding them, but it might work. Just promise to come back."

"We promise." Xeo groaned. "I can use my mask and just fly away."

"No." Rafik snapped. "What if she adapts to that and gets wings? Then this hole will be useless."

Xeo nodded.

The fog was getting thicker, and stocky streaks of violet began to appear. It pulsed like a heartbeat. Not far from where they are they heard a strange sound of stone scraping against stone, and ominous purple light glowing from within one of the domes of a mirage tree. Creaking of iron was next, and a loud roar echoed through the valley. The four hurried to the Frosted Tangles.

"Hurry. Be careful!" Kaliboon yelled.

"How do I ride this thing?" Xeo asked, jumping onto its wiry back. The next moment the Frosted Tangle lurched forward, and he squeezed the sides of the dragon to hold on. Its scales were smooth, and he was unsure where he could grab with his hands. A moment later it was decided for him as the dragon Rafik was riding lunged over his own. Xeo crouched lower to its body, wrapping his arms around the sides. The next moment Tragi's jumped from the other side. Ziri's was next, leap frogging Xeo's. Her dragon veered to the right as Tragi's took the center position. He watched Ziri's jump, then Rafik's, and then his own hurtling over Tragi's. It was so hypnotic watching the dragons weave in and around each other that for a moment he had forgotten Treshna was chasing them.

The dragons seemed faster now that they weren't pulling a carriage. Treshna snarled and growled, once even swiping at them. Rafik noticed the dragons were running in a circle around the tree they were digging their trap at. Out of the corner of his eye he could see the slight fire, glowing faintly through the fog with glowing violet veins.

Treshna howled, her feet tearing into the ground with every step. Her mouth hung wide open, ready to swallow any of them whole if she could just catch up. Just as she was about to the dragon would jump over the others. It was a constant game of cat and mouse. She also noticed the circle, though, and slowly faded back into the fog.

The dragons skidded to a halt as the four turned both directions, trying to find her. "Where is she?" Xeo asked.

"She couldn't have given up." Tragi said.

"If she were to give up, she would have before she sunk in the middle of the Vinsen Ocean." Ziri said. "She's hunting us."

It was hard to see through the fog. Even the light of the campfire was diminishing. The violet light was getting stronger. Bolder. As it pulsed Treshna leapt out from the fog, tackling the Frosted Tangle in the front of the pack, which had Ziri on it. Ziri rolled out of the way and Treshna clamped down on her prey, tearing it apart with her strong jaws. The other Frosted Tangles reared up on their hind legs like horses, causing the other three to fall to the ground. The dragons ran into the fog, disappearing into the night.

"I thought dragons were supposed to be brave and fearless monsters." Xeo said, grabbing his left shoulder he had fallen on.

"Maybe the bigger ones are." Rafik said.

The four backed away slowly, not taking their eyes off Treshna. She finished tearing apart the Frosted Tangle like paper, before glancing up and noticing them. Her orange eyes glowed with a fierce intensity. Like a burning furnace eagerly devouring a new piece of wood. Her jaw dripped with blood and drool, taking a step at a time towards the four. Rafik could tell she was savoring this. She had been hunting them for almost as long as he'd been back in Alutopek. They brandished their swords, no longer retreating.

"Fly away." Rafik said. "Leave, Xeo."

"I can't leave you." Xeo said. "Besides, she wanted me originally."

Treshna was now upon them. She stood on her rear legs, staring down at them and licking her lips. The grotesque monster smashed her feet down, just in front of the four. The ground shook and the four nearly lost their balance. Rafik lunged forward, swiping his sword at her. Treshna raised her thick arm, swatting at Rafik. Ziri mimicked Rafik's move, but Treshna was prepared and tried to swat her as well, but Tragi threw his sword, stabbing the Hound of Soboribor in the hand. She screamed in pain and yanked out the sword, turning her attention to Tragi. With his mask power, Xeo flew up into the air and landed on her back. He tried plunging his sword into her spine, but the sword snapped, not even penetrating her skin.

With a ferocious shake, coupled with an intense roar, Xeo slid and flew off her back. He crashed into the ground, but a moment later was back into the air. Shouting echoed through the fog, and the remaining four joined the battle. Kaliboon wielded a club and was the first to make it to Treshna. She swung her club hard, hitting Treshna's side.

She was surrounded now. The eight of them just pestering her, as her skin was thick. As she would lunge to attack one of them, the one behind her would agitate her enough just to force her to spin around. They continued doing this, and all she could do was stop them long enough to get another to start. Not much longer and she started feeling lightheaded. She would stumble as she would spin around to stop one of them, and soon the world around her began to spin. Treshna roared but collapsed soon after.

"Is…is she dead?" Rafik asked, poking her side with his sword.

"I don't think so." Ziri said, putting her hand in front of her nostrils. "Still breathing. And we didn't even break the skin. Stop poking her! Probably making her angrier."

"Did we win?" Xeo asked.

"We aren't that lucky." Tragi grumbled. "Probably just upset her even more."

The eight didn't move. They each shared ideas on what to do next, or how to try to kill her. She had fallen on her belly, which seemed to be the softest part of skin that could be punctured. For now, she was safe. Xeo poked her side while Ziri swatted at him, scolding him to stop.

Without warning, Treshna sprang forward, gnashing her teeth. She snarled and bit down on the first person she plowed through. Haloro screamed, banging his fists on her face as he begged for help. The Hound of Soboribor skidded to a stop, turned, and glared at the remaining seven with her burning oranges eyes. She clamped her jaw, and Haloro screamed again, before both halves of his body fell to the ground. He let out one last cry and fell silent. Everyone in the group screamed, and Rafik and Xeo took a step forward.

"You won't hurt anyone else." Rafik ordered.

Treshna stood on her hind legs and howled. Her extra legs and arms flailed in the air frantically. She crashed into the ground, and the surrounding area shook. Fog swirled around them, but light was creeping onto the Black Wall once more. She noticed this, glared at them once more, and hurried off, slinking into the shadows.

"We made it." Taygin said, breathing a sigh of relief.

"Not all of us." Rafik said, kneeling beside Haloro. "We need to finish that trap. This can't happen again."

There was a debate on what to do with Haloro's body. Kaliboon mentioned in ancient times most took their dead to a necropolis in the region they were born in. It was said not doing so, their spirit would roam Alutopek for all eternity. Though that wasn't the custom now, it brought back memories of Skage, and the unending horde of dead sweeping across the Nyler Peninsula. Rafik realized he must have gotten most of his legion from there.

When asked what the Fohdorsha do with their dead, Kaliboon explained most would be burned on a large funeral pyre. Though if they were lost at sea, there would be a small boat they would send adrift and burn. They finally agreed on burying Haloro at the bottom of the pit they were already digging.

By midday, they had a makeshift ladder to help climb out of the pit. If they hadn't seen her standing on her hind legs the night before, they believed it would have been deep enough then. But now, they all agreed it had to go deeper.

One of the shovels broke, and a constant rain threatened to flood the pit, yet they continued digging. There was a sense of urgency and vengeance for what happened to Haloro. Ziri blamed herself, as she stood nearest him when Treshna made her attack. Maybe she was going for her? Even Krista worked harder, weaving the vines that was to cover the pit.

As evening crawled the pit was complete. Rafik sighed, leaning on the shovel as he stared at the massive hole. It amazed him how much they did in just two days. At the very bottom was the fresh grave of Haloro. He didn't know him very well. Back at the Sekolah Fortress he was a sort of bully towards him, but these last few weeks running and escaping Treshna they had gotten closer. Enough to call him a friend, at least. He vowed he wouldn't die in vain, and tonight he would prove it.

"The cover is ready." Ziri said. "How are you?"

"Tired. Ready for this to be over." Rafik sighed. Returning to Alutopek wasn't anything like he had hoped. He expected to find the rebellion, fight Vanarzir, and tear down the Black Wall. Instead, he'd been chased across Alutopek, survived a shipwreck, gave up his talent, and now digging massive holes to trap what was hunting them.

Tragi climbed out of the pit, dragging the ladder out after. The sides were steep, and there wouldn't be a way of getting out without it. They pulled the cover slowly, hoping the weaves would hold, as it dragged along the edges and drooped into the pit. Once it was finally covered, they each hammered stakes into the ground to hold it into place.

"What's the plan?" Krista asked, brushing her hands, and putting them on her hips.

"We know she wants me most." Xeo said. "I'm going to use my mask to be hovering just above the platform. If we're lucky, Treshna will come after me and fall into the pit."

"And if we're not lucky?" Taygin asked.

"The rest of us will be hiding in the tree." Rafik said, pointing to the one they had made a camp around. Hopefully, she won't notice us."

"And if she does?" Taygin asked.

"Then we run." Tragi said. "And pray she doesn't catch us."

"I don't like this plan." Taygin said. "Too risky. Shouldn't we just leave Xeo behind?"

"Hey!" Xeo snapped. "I'd love to say I'd return the favor and leave you behind if you ever get a curse on you, but we all know you're too big of a coward to even achieve that."

"Enough!" Rafik snapped. Taygin had been creeping onto everyone's nerves as his pessimistic views were held at bay. After Haloro's death, they rang truer and more foreboding than anyone cared to admit. "We don't have time to bicker."

"On the bright side, Taygin," Xeo laughed, stepping away from the group and jumping into the air. "Our grave is already dug."

Taygin made a face, turning to climb the tree. Kaliboon released the Frosted Tangles who they had wrangled in a nearby grove, and they hurried westward. "I hope this works." She whispered. The carriage couldn't be pulled by the three without tiring them out too quickly. From here on out, they would have to walk on foot. Rafik cursed, knowing how close the spring equinox was. They had to stop Treshna now, though. Enough was enough.

One by one they each climbed the tree and Xeo hovered in the center of the platform, just high enough that it appeared like he was standing on it. Night came minutes later, and so did the ominous fog. The violet veins pulsed, giving off their eerie glow, and the strange sound of stone scraping stone and the creaking of a gate. The bloodthirsty and angry howl echoed in the night. Treshna was on the prowl.

It didn't take long for her to arrive. She stood at the edge and glanced at the cover. Another howl, and Xeo laughed. "I'm not afraid of you." Xeo said, brandishing his sword. He dropped the sheath, and it landed on the cover. Several hushed gasps came from the tree, but the platform held. If Treshna noticed the slight divot the sheath made, she didn't show it. "After what you did last night, this ends now. One way or the other."

Treshna roared and took a step towards Xeo. The cover held. One more step, and there was a slight sag. Treshna stared at the ground and Xeo roared, acting like he was charging towards her on ground. The Hound of Soboribor charged forward. The next moment, as Xeo swatted away a clawed paw with his sword, the monster shrieked and fell. The cover wrapped around her as she tried to get to her feet.

She tore at the woven leaves, ripping them to shreds, and glared up at Xeo, laughing and hovering above her. She jumped but couldn't reach him. She ran at the sides but couldn't climb up. The others dropped from the tree and surrounded the pit. If she even got close, they swatted her away with their own weapons.

"This...this was anticlimactic." Xeo said, watching the monster circle her prison. She glared at them with such ferocity he knew she was wishing them dead with her very being. "Now what?"

"Now we wait." Rafik said.

The fog grew thicker as Treshna stayed in her hole, but no matter what she tried, it was in failure. She was stuck down there. Occasionally with a jump her claws gripped the ledge, only to be kicked or stabbed at by one of them.

Her howls grew from anger and murderous, to fearful and desperate. As light began to come onto the eastern edge of the Black Wall, the familiar scraping of stone could be heard at the bottom of the pit. With the fog so thick, it was hard to see what it was. They believed it had to be something for Treshna. How she disappeared at the end of the night.

Rafik lit a torch and tossed it into the pit. The scraping sound continued but disappeared a few seconds later. Treshna cried and stamped at the torch. As soon as it was extinguished the sound returned. Xeo tossed another torch in. Then Tragi as the monster extinguished his brother's. They each took a turn tossing a torch as that sound started. With every light Treshna's growls grew more and more frantic. Light was now hitting the brim of the pit, and the fog was dissipating. It wouldn't be long now until Treshna was defeated for good.

The thick fog remained at the bottom of the pit, but Treshna's final howl echoed in the morning light. It sounded weaker. And her movements stopped. The monster collapsed, and her silhouette could be seen through the thinning clouds. Even the pulsing violet disappeared. The silhouette changed, and Treshna screamed in agony. Her claws, legs, and head contorted, and body shrank. Her legs and arms changed, and soon enough, at the bottom of the pit was the silhouette of a woman.

"Think you can protect us from a dead witch?" Xeo laughed, clapping Taygin on the back.

"Stop teasing him." Kaliboon said.

Taygin glared at the silhouette. Xeo's taunts were getting to him. He could do anything they did. He was positive of it. And he was going to prove it. But how? Then, he saw his chance. The figure in the bottom of the pit began to move. Without hesitation, Taygin slid down the side of the pit, holding a knife, and ran towards the figure. The six others screamed for Taygin to stop, but he didn't listen. There was a slight wrestle for the knife, but Taygin overpowered her, and plunged his knife into her chest. There was one last garbled scream from the figure who was once Treshna.

Moments later Taygin let out his own scream. The fog began to clear, and in his arms, was Valkayto, Queen of Alutopek, dead.

Chapter 27: Anza's Escape

Dragon's Roost, Biodlay Desert, Alutopek

"I think I'm ready." Anza said, closing another large and dusty tome. The runes on the dingy cover were engraved into the leather and glowed an emerald green. This one was written entirely from the ancient language. It taught how to write, not just in the language, but to make it powered as well. It was a combination of writing the runes perfectly, along with saying an incantation precisely. Any accident, including writing the runes a different way than what was instructed, and it wouldn't work. There were 56 individual runes, or letters, and over a 100 that were symbols that was specific to something. It was a miracle she could remember half of them, let alone all of them.

"Are you sure?" Izamar asked, peeking up from his own book. He was sitting on the far end of the table among his own stack of books. One particular stack teetered back and forth. He muttered something under his breath and the books realigned, straightening up and stopped wobbling.

Anza nodded. "Only one way to find out. I think I found the loophole."

"And what's that?" Izamar asked, curious. He had nearly given up trying to find one. Skage was meticulous with his spells, even if they weren't as strong as others, they were hard to break free from.

"This place is unnatural." Anza said. "I'm not dead, but technically not living. Just…somewhere in between. If I say this spell correctly, it should yank me back to the world of the living, or the afterlife."

The gray wizard stroked his beard, nodding. "And you found the right words, I'm guessing?"

Anza stared at the large book for a moment before answering, nodding. "I need to write the words 'travel safely' while saying the spell aloud. Just like Skage made me say a spell while performing a ritual."

"Yes," Izamar said. "If you don't say the spell, your written word or ritual won't have as strong, or even any, effect. Are you sure this will work?"

"If I do it right, yes. I'll be sent back to the Sarason Fortress where I last was in the world of the living."

"Just make sure you go back that way, and not the world of the dead." Izamar said. "You still have a long life ahead of you."

"Yeah, what could go wrong?" Anza sighed, imagining all the unusual ways it could end horribly. Half the books she had been reading about rune-magic was how it ended in disaster.

"Did you not read the book?" Izamar gasped. "Everything. Magic isn't something to fool around with."

"I was being sarcastic." Anza smiled. "But I think so. I've memorized all the runes, and you've helped me how to pronounce the words in the ancient language."

"Before you try, Anza," Izamar said, clearing a spot on his table. "I need you to etch something on the table."

"What's that?"

"The symbols for anchor and home." Izamar said. "If you do manage to escape the mirror, doing that here will allow you to return to the mirror."

"Why would I want to return to this prison?"

"It's just in case you get stuck and need a way out. And, to make it even safer, spell your name atop the runes, so only you can use it." Izamar said.

Anza nodded, and with a dull knife she had found on one of the shelves, she etched the symbol for 'home.' As she carved out the last line it glowed a dark green for a fleeting moment, before fading back to the old, wooded color of the table. On top of the 'home' rune she started on the 'anchor' symbol. It flashed green just as the earlier rune did. She then wrote her name out of runes on top of the two. This time they didn't glow, but she felt a tug in her heart. Like a sudden memory of a tragic event, she now couldn't pull away from. The feeling faded, but she could still feel the tether. "Am I supposed to feel this way?"

"Yes, yes." Izamar said, patting Anza on the back. "You bound yourself to this table. Not in the way of you confining your soul to this spot for all eternity, but that you laid claim to this land. Only you can use those runes beneath your name."

"Could I place these runes everywhere I go, and magically pop up wherever I want?" Anza asked.

"You certainly could." Izamar smiled. "And you wouldn't be the first to think or want to try that. But that feeling you have, the tugging of the heartstrings, will come with each one you create. If you make too many, your heart will be too heavy, and you will perish. Best you do not try that."

"Now I'm ready." Anza said. She grabbed a loose piece of parchment resting on the table and began writing the runes.

Izamar stood over her, watching and reading it as she finished. "If this works, and you find your way out of here,"

"I won't forget you, Izamar." Anza said, turning and beaming up at him. "I promise. And I'll be back."

"I would hope you do come back." Izamar smiled. "Dragon's Roost is now yours. What I was going to say, though, is go to Fang-Elsea Island to continue your training."

Anza froze. She wasn't sure if she heard him correctly, and if she had, which to respond to first. "How can I continue my training there if I'm the only witch?" She finally asked.

"When there is a stormy night, and the moon can't be seen, does it no longer exist?"

"No." Anza said, shaking her head. "It's still there."

"Exactly." Izamar said. "This...Vanarzir that you've told me stole magic. He is the storm. He cannot take away all magic. It just can't be seen right now. Head to Fang-Elsea Island."

"Thank you." She paused before continuing. She stared into his gray eyes. By now she had lost track of any sense of time and wasn't sure how long she had spent with him. Days, years, centuries. No matter the length, she knew she would never forget him. Memories of her father had faded or became distorted as she remembered her uncle, Gorik, where her father once was. She

301

knew that wouldn't happen with this ancient wizard. "I'll never forget you."

Izamar smiled and wrapped her in his arms. "Nor I, child. When I created the Mentor's Mirror it was a somewhat selfish way of staying among my things and helping the next generation of magic users between my studies. I didn't expect to care for you."

"Is that why you're giving me Dragon's Roost?" Anza asked, pulling away from Izamar with a mischievous smile.

"Partly." Izamar nodded. "If you are the last witch of Alutopek, it feels only right to give this gift to you. My life's collection of knowledge, secretly stowed away here."

"If Gorik could find it in the middle of the desert, then I guess I can too. That way I won't be stuck in a mirror next time either." Anza smiled.

Izamar laughed. "He only found it because I helped him. There is much more to the roost than this library, that I think you will enjoy it all."

Anza stared at the runes she etched in the table. "Do you think you could come with me?"

"Me?" Izamar asked. He stroked his beard, humming, as his eyes narrowed. "I sincerely doubt that child. You came from the portrait that Skage bewitched. Through my magic I allowed you into the Mentor's Mirror, and by extension, my enchanted library. I am only here because of the Mentor's Mirror. Do you remember what I said when you first found me? Only a spirit who you have interacted with, and has interacted with the mirror, can be summoned. My spirit is confined here."

"If I leave, will you disappear too?" Anza asked.

"Since I am now in my library, I don't believe so. But, if I do, worse things have happened. Being a ghost within a magical mirror isn't horrible."

"Rafik and I saw a ghost in Datz once." Anza said. "That's why we always slept together in front of the fire."

Izamar smiled at the thought. "Many children are afraid of the dark. Ghosts may haunt a place if they have unfinished business. But, as the last of those who remember them or could help have moved on, they will as well."

A pang tore through her, thinking of the ghost. Perhaps it was her father trying to say goodbye? And they cowered in fear of it. Maybe she shouldn't be so quick to cower from what she doesn't understand.

"I hope this works." She repeated, clutching the parchment tight. "My first attempt at magic and it could kill me. And you don't even know if it works."

"Oh, Anza," Izamar said in his tired, gruff voice. "What's the point of living if you aren't willing to take risks?"

"I like my risks to be a little less...risky."

Izamar boomed with laughter, the library echoing from his laughter. "Have confidence in yourself. If you don't believe you can, you've already set yourself up to fail."

"I hope this works." Anza said again.

"Enough dawdling." Izamar smiled. "This is the moment. This is your moment. You can do this, Anza."

Anza nodded, closed her eyes, and started taking deep breaths. The parchment with the words 'travel safety' was held between her hands. Technically she could just use the spell. But, holding onto these runes, it should allow her to get there in one piece. She imagined the great room at the top of the Sarason Fortress. Spiders decorated the walls, while one dangled from the ceiling. A massive statue of one stood in the center facing spider-shaped doors. The stone floor was worn and dusty, and in the corners and along the pillars holding up the ceiling, were thick cobwebs. Like white yarn strewn about. The air there was stale, but also mixed with the saltiness of the ocean. Lost in thought, she muttered the words "*Ako tinda bisini. Ako basana Sarason Fortress.*" *I'm not here. I'm there, at the Sarason Fortress.*

Before she could recite the runes etched on her paper her stomach lurched. She felt her insides twist and shrink while her body twisted and contorted. It felt like she was continuously being folded into smaller pieces. It wouldn't be long until there was nothing left of her. *'And then I'll be dead.'* She thought to herself. *'I failed.'*

The excruciating pain felt like an eternity, but also, in an instant. One moment she was being yanked, bent, pushed, and pulled in every direction. The next, she was whole again. An icy dagger plunged into her chest as she gasped. It was like thousands of tiny needles poking at her now and going down her throat. She couldn't breathe. Her lungs filled with frozen water. Her body flailed about, but there was some resistance. Not wind, but...water.

With that realization Anza's eyes burst open as she silently screamed. She couldn't even say a spell to return to the mirror. This was her end. Trying to return to the Sarason Fortress, but instead ending up at the bottom of whatever body of water she was in. It was freezing like the Tahlbiru Ocean. She looked around and saw light shimmering above. Her lungs burned and begged for breath. With every stroke trying to swim to the surface she felt her body getting weaker. It was hopeless. She stretched out her hand, praying for a miracle, when her world went black.

Anza rolled on her side, coughing up sea water. The gravelly sand beneath her was rough, but she didn't care. She was alive. Thank the gods she was still alive! The last thing she remembered was darkness, and freezing water enveloping her. It couldn't have been a dream. She was soaked to the bone, after all. The wind howled and she shivered.

"Hold on, hold on." A strange, garbled voice said from nearby.

Anza spun around, coughing up more sea water as she did so. She couldn't recognize whoever it was. The closest thing she could think of were stories Gorik used to tell her of an ancient race of sea people. The figure's pale-green skin was the least of her concerns. Fins ran along his forearms and head. He turned to face her, and she let out a gasp, seeing his mouthful of serrated teeth and lidless, pitch-black eyes.

"Oh, come now. I'm not that hideous. Had a wife who didn't think so, at least." The man said, smiling. "Can you help me?"

Anza tilted her head in confusion. This couldn't be real. "Um…what?"

"Can you help me?" He asked again. "I'm not used to making fires on dry land like you folk. Want to get you warm. Maybe even dry before the others get here."

"Others?" Anza asked. She scanned her surroundings, but nothing appeared familiar. On the far side, westward and across the sea, were ruins she thought looked like Datz. That had to be impossible, though, since the Sarason Fortress wasn't anywhere in sight. "What's going on?"

"I wanted to ask you the same thing." The man said. Although his voice sounded like a logger speaking underwater, there was a sort of charm to it. She could imagine him singing and her just being hypnotized by his voice. "There I was, swimming and scouting ahead, when you just land on me. You weren't there a moment before. I'm not that blind, you know."

"I'm…"Anza paused. Should she use her real name? Could he be trusted? Finally, she decided he could be. If he wanted her dead, he could have left her in the ocean. "I'm Anza. I was trying to get somewhere and got lost."

The man laughed. "Clearly. One doesn't just end up in the depths of the Tahlbiru. What were you doing?"

"Trying to get to the Sarason Fortress." Anza answered.

The man's face soured, and any hint of happiness gone. His serrated teeth seemed more menacing as he glared at Anza. "What makes you think it's down there? And why would you want to go to such a place?"

"I don't." Anza said, turning her head from one side to the other. "It's a long story."

"We have time." The man said. "Are you going to make the fire?"

Anza nodded and crawled towards the pile of sticks. Her legs and arms still felt weak. The wood was damp, and there wasn't anything there to even get a spark. She fumbled with the sticks before drawing a rune in the sand beneath the pile. It glowed a dark green like the last ones she etched in Dragon's Roost before fading. If her rescuer noticed, he didn't mention it. Satisfied, she whispered *"Omurahi." Wild fire.* From her breath a miniature flame appeared, taking the shape of a horse. It charged into the rune, and flames began to grow. The fire bit at the wood, and a moment later it was a crackling flame anyone would be proud of. She held out her hands and embraced the warmth.

"Well?" The man said.

"Well, what?" Anza asked. She wasn't trying to be difficult she had genuinely forgotten what he wanted. She had created fire! Not just that, she was out of the mirror! Her smile grew on her face, and she quickly frowned, stifling her excitement.

"Why are you searching for the Sarason Fortress?"

"Before I tell my story, can I learn your name?" Anza asked. "I'd like to properly thank my rescuer, at least."

The man smiled, his pale-green cheeks turning a slight pinkish color. "The name is Inakus. Exiled member of the Taktor."

"Exiled?" Anza asked.

Inakus laughed. "I find it funny you're more surprised about me being exiled than being a Taktor. Most Nomads are the opposite."

"My uncle told me stories when I was younger about Taktors. Never really believed him." Anza said.

"When you were younger? You still look like a child."

"Why were you exiled?" Anza asked.

"Sounds like we both have stories to share. I asked first. And, of course, ladies first. Tell me your story, and I'll tell you mine." Inakus said.

"I'm going to be honest with you." Anza said. "But it is going to sound fake."

Inakus nodded.

"I didn't know the fortress was down there. I've been trapped in a portrait for I don't know how long, and I finally found a way to escape. I had to return to where I last was. So, I tried it.

Next thing I know I'm choking on water, about to die, and no idea where I am. I woke up, and now I'm talking to you."

"A portrait?" Inakus asked, not even hiding the skepticism in his voice. "And I thought my lies were horrible."

"I'm not lying." Anza said. "I learned magic. That's how I was able to get the fire going. Did you not see how wet the wood was? Did you bring them here across the ocean?"

"Yes." Inakus said, matter-of-factly. "Do you see any wood here?"

Anza glanced from one end of the island to the other. It was more of a glorified sandbar than it was an actual island. "Oh. Thank you. And thank you for saving me."

Inakus nodded. "A portrait? Isn't that…isn't that those things you hang on the wall that's been painted?"

"It is." Anza said. "Do they have portraits where you're from?"

Inakus shrugged. "We have art. If you came from the portrait, you aren't real, then?"

"No, I am real. "I just got trapped there. It was an accident."

"Magic users are weird." Inakus sighed, shaking his head. "What are you, a wizard? Warlock? Mage?"

"A witch." Anza said, smiling and puffing out her chest.

"A witch." Inakus repeated, stroking his chin with his webbed hand. "I was under the impression magic was gone. I guess anything is possible nowadays."

"I told you my story." Anza said, holding her hands to the campfire. It was warming her up, but not nearly as fast as she would like. "Your turn."

"A deal's a deal." Inakus nodded. "Let's see…it started two years ago. During the Battle of Trinkit I teamed up with a Nomad boy to defeat the evil in the Sarason Fortress. If I were to take him to the fortress, he would help me find food for my people. Sadly, he died during battle. My people believed me to be a traitor, as I left my command and men behind, and didn't have proof of the promise. They exiled me."

Anza paused, absorbing what she had just learned. "You're telling me that Skage...Skage is defeated?"

Inakus nodded. "You aren't from around here, are you? The battle has been all most have wanted to talk about around the fire for the last two years."

"I'm from Datz." Anza said. "But I told you. I was trapped in a portrait. Wait, so the Sarson Fortress..." She trailed off, spinning around. Taking long and quick strides she hurried to the shore and tried peering into the ocean's depths. "It's down there now?"

"Yes." Inakus nodded. "As the necromancer fell, so too did his tower."

"How long was I stuck for?" Anza whispered. She sat there, letting the freezing water grasp her as it lapped onto shore. It could have been days, weeks, years, or much longer. Her home was behind her. With no torchlight glowing as the night grew darker, she knew it was abandoned. Everything was gone. Tears streamed down her face, realizing she was too late. Even if it had only been days or weeks since she was stuck there was no telling where her brother was. Or even Gorik. Though, from what Inakus just said, it was at least two years. That part slowly registered with her.

"Anza, come back to the fire." Inakus shouted. "It's still much too cold and you're much too wet to spend time on the freezing shores of the Tahlbiru."

She didn't recall moving. One moment she was at the shore, letting the icy water bite at her. The next she was wrapped in a mesh-like blanket huddled around the fire. Her eyes burned from the smoke and tears. Everything was hitting her now. What Izamar had said, about the world being different when she returned to it. Maybe she should have stayed in the portrait.

Inakus splashed a bucket of water on himself and then nudged Anza. "Did you hear me?"

"What? No, sorry. Lost in thought." Anza said.

"Well, least you aren't crying anymore. That's a good sign." Inakus said.

"I don't think I can cry anymore." Anza said. "My family is gone, and I don't even know if they're dead or just gone somewhere else."

"When I was first exiled it hurt that I would never see my family again." Inakus said.

"They didn't come with you?"

Inakus shook his head. "No, I wouldn't let them. I didn't know where I would end up. I wanted them to be safe. I had a wife and two girls. Leaving them felt like my heart shattered into a million pieces."

"At least you know where they are." Anza argued, noting she hadn't meant for it to sound as cold as it came out to be.

"I do. But what is worse, knowing where your loved ones are and never being able to see them again, or knowing they're out there and you just need to find them?"

"Both of our situations aren't the best." Anza finally said. She had paused for at least a minute before answering. Even as she spoke, she could hear Izamar's voice speak through her in that moment.

The laugh that came out of Inakus was a peculiar one. It sounded like a child's giggle mixed with the chiming of a dolphin in a low pitch. It made Anza smile hearing it. "Not one bit." He finally said, nodding. "When the others get here maybe we can help find them? You're from Datz, shouldn't be too hard to find a lost Datian."

Anza shrugged. "I don't know how long I was stuck in the portrait. They could be dead."

"They could be alive." Inakus said. "We have this saying back where I'm from. It goes, 'if all you see are sharks you will always be afraid of the ocean.' It means if you keep focusing on negative things, all you will find is the negative in everything."

"So, save the crying for after I know they're dead." Anza said.

Inakus frowned. "In a way, yes. What are their names, anyway? Maybe I have heard of them? I have been roaming these waters and shores for two years now."

"My uncle's name is Gorik. He was a sailor." Anza said.

Inakus nodded, lowering his head, and scratching his chin. That name sounded familiar, but a face wasn't coming to mind. Where had he heard it before? "The name sounds familiar."

"Really?" Anza asked in a hopeful tone.

"It does." Inakus said. "I know I've heard it, but at the moment I can't recall. The expression you use is on the tip of my tongue. Who else are you looking for in your family?"

"My brother." Anza said. "His name is Rafik."

Inakus paused. His eyes widened. Tentatively, he raised his head and stared at Anza in a different light. Her hair was much darker than his. Where hers was a deep brown like the bark of a tree's, Rafik's had a tint of red in it, like rust. But the shape of their face and eyes were similar. He remembered Gorik's name now. He froze. How could he tell her that her family was dead when he just told her to be hopeful? "Anyone else?" He asked.

Anza shook her head. "No. My dad was lost at sea a long time ago. And my mom died protecting Rafik and me when the Kylix invaded Datz. Is Vanarzir still king?"

"Yes." Inakus said. "Though a rebellion is growing in the east. You've been gone for two years, Anza."

"How do you know?"

"As the Sarason Fortress collapsed and fell into the ocean, the brave warriors inside managed to escape. One of them had fallen. His name was Gorik. Gorik of Datz. According to his friends, he was a great sailor. Had a peg leg that didn't stop him from adventuring."

"Gorik!" Anza shouted. "He's gone?" She sprang to her feet. "This was where he last stood. I'm two years too late! I could have saved him!"

"He gave his life to protect Alutopek from another evil ruler." Inakus said. "The dead rising from their graves, attacking the living. They were a mindless hoard that swept across the Nyler Peninsula. If it wasn't for Gorik…and the other brave soldiers, it's likely I wouldn't be here today to save you."

"Was Rafik in battle?" Anza asked. "He helped lead us Datians to safety. Then I got stuck in a portrait at the Sarason Fortress and didn't see him again. I saw Gorik, though. He was going to find Rafik and tell him I was safe."

"I don't know if Gorik was able to relay that message." Inakus said after pausing for a moment. He was choosing his words carefully now. He stared at the small girl. Her family was gone, and all he could envision was one of his daughters sitting there, discovering her own family had perished. He wrapped his arm around Anza. "I'm so sorry."

"I need to find Rafik." Anza said. "He must be out there somewhere. And if Gorik didn't get to tell him I'm safe, he's probably still searching for me."

Inakus didn't respond. He poked at the fire with a stick and stretched. "I'm sure the others will be here in the morning. Get some rest."

"What others?"

"After being exiled I joined a crew from Trinkit I met during the battle. You'll meet them in the morning."

Anza nodded. Fatigue was taking her as Inakus mentioned rest. Who knows how long she had been crying. And now to learn Gorik was gone. Her heart was broken, and she wasn't sure how much more heartache she could take. But Rafik could still be alive. She had to cling to that thought. He had to be out there. She curled up beside the fire, beneath the mesh-like blanket, and closed her eyes. Her last thought being this was the first time she would be sleeping in two years! Realizing this both impressed and alarmed her. No wonder she was suddenly tired.

As she dozed off Inakus stared at the young girl. He now saw Rafik more than ever in her calm, dreaming face. How he hadn't noticed before puzzled him. It was only a matter of time before she learned the truth. At least for now, she was asleep and full of hope.

Chapter 28: No Time to Mourn

Sampra Tribe, Bomoku Mountains, Alutopek

While Taygin screamed, and everyone else stood aghast, Tragi skidded down the side of the hole. Xeo, who was smirking just moments before, was now frozen in place. He saw his sister, knife sticking out of her chest, lying on the ground. Taygin standing above her. He watched Tragi hurry to their sister, and he scooped her up in his arms. Was that his sister? She looked like it, but she was now more emaciated. Even more than Taygin, Krista, or Haloro were when Rafik found them. But her beauty radiated through even now. "Kay…is that really you?" He muttered.

Nobody answered.

Xeo hurried to his brother's side, shoving Taygin back into the ground as he tried climbing up the wall. Tragi looked up at his brother and nodded. "It's Kay."

"No." Xeo shook his head. "No, it can't be."

"I'm so sorry." Ziri whispered, choking back tears. She didn't know Queen Valkayto personally, but traveling with Xeo and Tragi she had heard stories. And seeing their hearts break right in front of her was breaking her own.

"Rafik!" Xeo screamed. "Rafik! Get down here and use your talent. Find out what happened like you did your father."

"I can't." Rafik said. "Remember? It's gone."

"How did she turn into that? What happened, Kay? You shouldn't be dead! We should have saved you!" Xeo cried. He spun around and glared at Taygin. "You!"

"Me?" Taygin squealed. "It's not my fault. I didn't know it was her."

"You killed her." Xeo said, his voice cold, making Taygin's hair stand on end. If looks could kill, he would have been dead in a flash.

"Because you called me a coward!" Taygin argued, backing up and hitting the wall. "S-so this is your fault."

"My fault?" Xeo yelled. "I didn't murder my sister!"

312

"If I knew, there's no way I would have done it." Taygin said, raising his hands. "I swear."

"Of course not." Xeo said, now just inches away from his face. "Do you know why?" In his hand he held a knife now pointing at Taygin's belly.

"Xeo stop!" Rafik shouted. "Stop right now."

"Xeo, stop. You don't want to do this." Ziri shouted.

"I'm going down there." Rafik said, grabbing the ledge of the hole and sliding down.

"Because you're a coward. Aren't you?" Xeo said.

Taygin nodded.

"Say it!" Xeo yelled, spittle covering Taygin's face.

"I-I-I'm a coward." Taygin said, sobbing.

Xeo raised the knife and shoved it towards Taygin as everybody screamed for him not to. The knife stuck into the wall just next to Taygin's ear, and Xeo screamed. "She's gone."

Rafik got to Xeo and pulled him away, holding him close. He whispered something into Xeo's ear, and he collapsed in his arms, sobbing. Rafik caught him and gently leaned back against the wall and slid downwards. Xeo cried, screaming, and pounding his fists into the ground as the tears streamed down his face like a broken dam.

"I don't understand." Tragi whispered. "How did she turn into that? Why? And why was she trying to kill us?" He stared at the lifeless face of his sister. All their life she would protect them, only for now be the one trying to hunt and kill them. "It doesn't make sense." He repeated.

Xeo hobbled to his feet, wiping his tears, and donning his mask. "It does make sense, and I'll give you one guess who is behind this."

"Vanarzir." Kaliboon said, a shiver running through her as she remembered her own experience with him. Her son now encased in a tree forever.

"Don't go." Tragi said, pulling on Xeo's arm.

Xeo shrugged it off. "Not now, Tragi. If you didn't pull me away two years ago then I could have beat Vanarzir and he wouldn't have done this to our sister."

"He shoved you into a fire! You wouldn't have survived." Tragi argued.

"I don't care. He's not getting away with it this time." Xeo snapped. He lunged into the air and Rafik tried grabbing at him, but he was too quick. He flew eastward as fast as he could.

"Where's he going?" Taygin asked.

"To his death." Tragi whispered. He gently laid Valkayto's body on the ground. "We need to stop him before he does something reckless. Do we know how far away Vanarzir is?"

Rafik shook his head. "We were so worried about Treshna we never scouted ahead. Could be days."

"I lost one sibling today." Tragi said, glancing back at his sister. "I can't lose another. We need to stop him."

"How?" The Frosted Tangles are gone. Running isn't nearly as fast as flying." Taygin said.

"You shouldn't be speaking right now!" Tragi snapped. "I'm not as quick tempered as my brother, but I'm just as angry with you." It was the first time since knowing him that Rafik ever heard him raise his voice. It was more intimidating than Xeo's quick bursts of anger.

"I'll find a way." Rafik said.

Tragi shook his head. "No, I need to go."

"No." Rafik said, putting his hand on Tragi's chest as he tried stepping forward. "You're upset too, and you could do something…irrational."

"I need to stop him." Tragi said. "He's going to kill himself trying to get revenge."

"Remember, blood of the covenant." Rafik said. "He's my brother too. Let me go after him. You take care of your sister. We'll meet up after I bring Xeo back, unharmed."

"Do you really think that wise, us splitting up?" Tragi asked.

Rafik shook his head. "No, but we don't have time to argue. At least Treshna isn't after us anymore. Who is staying with Tragi?"

"I will." Krista said, volunteering. "Don't really want to be captured as a deserter."

"Smart." Kaliboon laughed. "I'll go with you, Rafik."

"I will too." Ziri said.

"I'm staying behind." Taygin said.

"I don't want you here." Tragi said. "You're going."

"Best hope they don't catch you for deserting." Kaliboon said. "Come on."

She helped Rafik up out of the hole, and together they moved their makeshift ladder they had used back into the pit. "We'll meet back here." Rafik said.

Tragi nodded, and the four ran eastward in the direction Xeo had been flying.

"How are we going to catch up to him?" Ziri asked after they had been continually running and stopped to catch their breath. Behind them, the tree Tragi was under was out of sight. But ahead, it was still just a vast expanse of field with mountains sandwiching them in from the north and south.

"I-I don't know." Rafik panted. "I was hoping a plan would come to me by now. Kaliboon, do you have any ideas?"

Kaliboon shook her head. "Fohdorsha don't usually travel by foot unless they're in exile. We have carriages and Frosted Tangles for traveling."

"Any horses?" Ziri asked.

"Maybe in the Wild Lands." Kaliboon said, shaking her head.

"We need to keep going." Rafik said. Without looking if the others were following, he continued eastward, running as fast as his body could allow.

Another hour later and smoke was swirling into the air. "You see that too?" Ziri asked.

315

"It's a camp." Kaliboon said. "There shouldn't be any fires there otherwise."

"We're almost there!" Rafik shouted. His heart was pounding out of his chest and lungs begging for air. Even his legs were beginning to quiver with every step. "We can't stop now."

Suddenly Rafik fell backwards, groaning. Before Ziri could stop she also fell over, flat on her back. As the two gasped for air, struggling to get up, Kaliboon skidded, tackling an unseen object. The invisible figure groaned, falling on top of Rafik. The familiar sound of armor moving, and footsteps coming towards her gave them away. She dived between them, pulling a knife out at the last second and stabbing into the air. Blood started trickling out of thin air, and the man collapsed.

A moment later Kaliboon was hit in her stomach with a blunt, invisible, object, and she doubled over. She leaned forward, rolling and springing to her feet, spun around and threw a knife. The next moment she lunged at the invisible soldier, tackling him. She wrestled their sword free, it suddenly becoming visible as she took it, and stabbed him in the gut. As he died, she ripped off the mask, and put it on.

The invisible world was hazy. Colors washed together like an untrained artist with watercolors. She saw the one she had stabbed and tore off his mask. Those also invisible were sharper, more prominent, and detailed. The moment the mask was gone he became a blurry blackish puddle on the ground oozing red from the middle. The final soldier had gotten up and the two circled each other.

It was the Kylix soldier who attacked first, slashing haphazardly at Kaliboon. She easily dodged his attack, swatted his hand with the flat of his sword making him drop it, and kicked him in the side. The soldier fell backwards, and Kaliboon didn't waste time in slicing at the soldier. He fell a moment later. Kaliboon tore off his mask and returned to her friends.

"That was amazing." Rafik said.

"Even though it just looked like you were fighting imaginary monsters." Ziri laughed.

"Wow." Was all Taygin could say. Instead of fighting or trying to help, he had just stood there and watched in puzzlement.

Kaliboon shrugged. "You don't grow up in the Lepal Tribe without learning how to fight the invisible warriors. These ones weren't well trained either, so that made it easier."

"I guess we're closer than we thought." Rafik said, taking one of the masks he was given. "And we have our way in."

"Yes." Kaliboon said. "We will still need to keep an eye out for anyone else who is wearing one of these Ravohka, but we should be ok, the closer we get to the camp."

"And we need to hurry. If we're already here, Xeo is too." Rafik said.

"I guess just follow where the commotion is." Ziri asked. "Sounds easy enough."

"Wait, what about me?" Taygin asked.

"What about you?" Kaliboon said. She had given Ziri and Rafik a mask and kept one for herself.

"I need a mask." Taygin said.

"You can go find one." Kaliboon said.

"If you're that worried, you can stay behind." Rafik said.

Taygin glanced from Rafik and Ziri, to westward back from where they came. He nodded. "I'll stay right here and wait for you. I'm not feeling good anyway. Feels like I'm going to be sick. And my head hurts. My body is starting to ache."

Kaliboon and Ziri rolled their eyes. "Of course." Ziri said under her breath.

"Do you know where we are?" Rafik asked.

Kaliboon nodded. "Just outside of the Sampra Tribe. They're the Pearl Tribe."

"Do they have special masks like you with the invisible ones?" Ziri asked.

"Not as elegant, but yes." Kaliboon said. "Each tribe really excels at one Ravohka power to help with their duty. Samprans pride themselves in being the greatest warriors and guards. They aren't stealthy like the Lepal Tribe. They use brute force and specialize with the mask of strength. That's probably why the Kylix are here instead of at the Nassir River."

"I guess we got lucky." Rafik said. "Alright, let's do this."

It took a moment to get used to the invisible world. Ziri even was sick two times as they made their way closer to the Kylix camp. It was disorienting, as the colors were a vibrant mixture that felt static, but also shifted and vibrated as things that weren't invisible moved. They went unnoticed, as most others who were using the mask were scanning the horizon lazily. It was clear they weren't expecting an attack from this direction. When one turned their way, they quickly huddled together and collapsed to the ground, taking off their masks, making them appear to be a muddled splotch of ground.

Once inside the camp Rafik and Ziri took off their masks. They weren't sure if they could ever get used to viewing the world in such a mess. Kaliboon kept her mask on, agreed to scout around, and help if needed. The Sampra Tribe was to the south, so most forces were pointed in that direction. It wasn't hard to see the tribe, even from here.

Where the Lepal Tribe was made of small huts and appeared rustic, the Sampra Tribe was elegance. Atop one of the foothills at the end of the Bomoku Mountain Range were tall white spires atop grand towers. It was like each tower competed with the other to be the tallest. It glistened in the Black Wall's glowing light, and shouts from within those walls echoed even down here, though indistinguishable.

"You two go on." Kaliboon whispered. "I'll stick to beneath the Ravohka."

Rafik nodded. "Good idea."

"Any idea where Xeo would be?" Ziri asked.

Rafik shook his head. "Wherever Vanarzir is."

"I have an idea." Ziri said.

"Don't do anything stupid." Rafik said.

She hurried over to a soldier sitting at a makeshift table playing cards with a few others. They hadn't noticed their

318

approach. Ziri began panting and hunched over. "Please. Where's the King? He must be warned?"

"Can't you see we're in the middle of a game?" A soldier said, not looking up from his card.

"Do you really want to receive the king's wrath just because you're too busy gambling?" Ziri asked.

The soldier turned away from his cards, looked at Ziri from head to toe, and then returned to his cards. "I'm not too worried. Where's your armor, anyway? You a deserter?"

"No." Ziri snapped, tossing the Ravohka onto the table with the coins. "I was on guard duty and got ambushed. These dragonborn, they're…they're something else. I barely escaped. More are heading this way."

With that, one of the soldiers watching the game scrambled to his feet. "I'll take them." He spoke.

"Thank you." Ziri said, turning and following behind him. Rafik hurried after her but stayed a couple steps behind while near the gamblers.

The other soldiers chuckled, laughing that of course it was that soldier who would take them. Rafik thought it was odd until they had turned the corner, well out of ear shot from the others, and started speaking. "Are there really more coming? How many?"

"Thinking of deserting, too?" Ziri asked, noticing his fidgeting, sweating, and constant glancing over his shoulder.

"What? Me? No. Of course not. I don't want to die. I didn't sign up for this, though." The soldier sputtered out faster and faster with a shaky voice.

Ziri nodded. "Head west, just beyond where our guards are. Then immediately north. You'll be safe there."

"How do I know I can trust you?" The man asked, eyeing her suspiciously. "You said they're coming from the west. That will get me killed!"

"Stay here or go, makes no different to me." Ziri said.

They stopped in front of a tent guarded by one soldier. She glanced at them and rolled her eyes. The tent wasn't fancy, like they had expected, but just slightly bigger than the others. "He's busy." She said in an even, unimpressed tone.

"It's important." The soldier said. "Dragonborn are coming from the west. Took out some of our guards." He gestured to Rafik and Ziri holding the Ravohka.

"This doesn't look like the king's tent." Rafik muttered.

"It's the next best thing." The soldier said. "I promise. And if your information is good enough, maybe you'll see the king."

He opened the flap of the tent and gestured for Rafik and Ziri to enter. The soldier, instead of entering with them, hurried off towards the west. The man at the desk hadn't noticed them enter. He appeared familiar, but older. The hair atop his head was gone, and just had the graying rim just above his ears. He wore a goatee now, with black and gray splotches. It was strange seeing him in armor rather than cloth. Finally, he glanced up. His skin turned pale, and eyes widened as if he had just seen a ghost.

"I thought you were dead." He finally said, regaining his composure.

"Hello Samron." Ziri said, taking a seat across from the table.

"Ziri." Samron nodded. "You look the most different. Not surprised, being in hiding for two years. And Rafik. Everyone thought you were gone. They've even written songs about you. Though the Kylix and King Vanarzir hate you."

"Did you even try looking for me?" Rafik asked, still standing. There was something different about him now. Memories of seeing his father get killed while escaping the Kylix kept flashing in his mind.

"Of course I did!" Samron said. "Your Taktor friend claimed he couldn't find you. I guess he was lying. Is that where you were?"

Rafik shook his head. "That's not important. We need to find Xeo."

Samron frowned. "Xeo? He's not here. Why would he be?"

320

"That's a long story, and we don't have time for it." Rafik snapped. "If you're really on our side, you'll get us to Vanarzir. Xeo wants to kill him right now."

"Isn't that what you want?" Samron asked. "For the king to be dead."

"Isn't that what you want? Or are you showing your true colors now?" Rafik asked.

Samron tilted his head and gave a nervous laugh. "My allegiance hasn't changed since we last spoke, Rafik. But committing regicide isn't how it should happen. That would cause war to break out across Alutopek."

"We're already at war!" Rafik yelled, taking a step closer to Samron. "I found out what happened to my father. Saw it happen. They wondered how the Kylix would know they were there."

"Oh." Samron said. He placed one of his hands in his lap and pushed himself away from the table. "And you believe I betrayed them?"

"They sure did. And I do too." Rafik said bluntly. "I'll deal with you later, though. Right now, we need to find our friend."

"I'd love to help. Truly I would. But I haven't heard of anything yet." Samron said.

"Samron!" A familiar, squeaky voice hollered from the door. Jinuk appeared a moment later, catching his breath and pushing up his glasses. He gasped, seeing Rafik. "How did he get in here?"

"I take it you remember Rafik?" Samron asked.

"Of course I do." Jinuk said. "You should have died. Now we can have two executions. Maybe three. Who is this?" He pointed at Ziri.

"Another survivor of the Battle at the Golden Gate." Samron said, getting to his feet and placing the knife that was in his lap on top of the table. "I'll take them to the king."

"I'll tell him you were meeting them in private." Jinuk said. "Another sign you're a traitor."

Samron rolled his eyes. "We were just heading there ourselves, but sure, tag along."

Rafik's eyes darted towards Ziri. Jinuk had said two executions, but only recognized Rafik. That had to mean only one thing. Xeo had been captured.

The group made their way farther south, and deeper into the Kylix camp. There was a grand, black tent, guarded by four soldiers. The black tent was easily four times bigger than any other and had thick poles in either corner holding it up. The stitching on the tent glistened in gold. One flap was pinned open showing a goldish-yellow interior. Beside the grand tent was a basic one like any other soldier would have. King Vanarzir crawled out of that one, brushing himself off, and laughing.

"It's a ruse." Samron explained in a whisper so Jinuk couldn't hear. "He's grown paranoid after several former Kylix deserted him and uses his old royal tent to trap would-be assassins. I'm guessing that's how Xeo was captured.

"Ya shire." Rafik cursed.

King Vanarzir smiled at Samron and then noticed Rafik. "I remember you. That honest boy." His voice was as strong as ever. "Shall we string up a new noose for you?"

Rafik glared at the king, clenching his fists. "I'm not a liar and didn't deserve to be executed then."

"And what about now?" The king asked.

Before answering Rafik stole a glance to the inside of the royal tent. Bound and gagged in the middle of it was Xeo. He winked at him, then turned back to the king, and nodded. "Probably."

"Once again I admire your honesty." Vanarzir smirked. "I can confirm now what I suspected then, though. It's stupidity. Naivety of a child. You're just an idiot. It's decided! You can be hanged like you were supposed to along with that *boy* in there."

"I actually came for him." Rafik said, nudging his head in the direction of Xeo. "He's one of my best friends, and I came to stop him from doing something foolish. Do you really think I wouldn't come here without a backup plan?"

322

King Vanarzir's eyes narrowed. "I'm not interested in your games. You were supposed to be dead two years ago, and you won't be getting away a second time. There's no necromancer this time."

Rafik flicked his eyes to the side towards the tent just briefly. Xeo was no longer bound, and he guessed Kaliboon was slowly untying the rope. He had to keep stalling. "What about my friend?" He asked, gesturing to Ziri.

Ziri's eyes widened and gave a side glance towards Rafik. "What about her?" Spat the king.

"I thought since she was my friend that would be enough." Rafik said with a tone of disappointment.

"She'll be sent to the front lines without any armor or weapons. See how long she can last." Vanarzir said. "Makes no difference to me."

A large crack echoed through the air, louder than any thunder. Everyone jumped where they stood and turned towards the south where the noise had come from. Off in the distance, one of the great white towers of the Sampra Tribe began to topple. A massive crack inched and wormed its way up the side, and where a marvelous tower once stood, it was now nothing more than rubble and a cloud of dust engulfing the area. At the same time as the dust cloud came forward, raucous roars of rioting erupted. The sound of metal clanging against metal echoed, signifying the battle had just begun.

Xeo burst from the tent, flying the moment he put his mask back on. He swooped down, scooped up Ziri as Kaliboon helped guide Rafik away from the sudden chaos. Vanarzir cursed, screaming at the Kylix soldiers to attack while simultaneously demanding the capture of Xeo and Rafik.

In the commotion, more screaming and yelling rumbled through the valley. "It's a different army." Xeo said, landing next to his friends who were now far away from the center of camp or the frontlines. "I don't think they're more Kylix. It's coming from the north."

"Could be more Fohdorshan." Kaliboon suggested, taking off her mask and revealing where she was standing. "No matter what, Fohdorshan always stick together against kolinda."

Xeo shrugged. "I have no idea, but Vanarzir is about to be stuck between two armies.

"Let's stop this once and for all." Rafik said. "Are you with me?"

The smile on Xeo's face was like a child's on their birthday. It stretched from ear to ear as he found a sword leaning against a vacant tent. "Did you really have to ask?"

"Count me in." Ziri said.

"Me too." Kaliboon nodded. "Let's stop this monster."

Chapter 29: The Spring Equinox

Sampra Tribe, Bomoku Mountains, Alutopek

It was simple to see who the enemy was. The Kylix still wore the familiar bone armor that made them look like the walking dead, but the Sampra wore armor much more elegant. White armor with flecks of gold, it was like ice and snow had been touched by starlight. They surged down the foothills and onto the field, shrouded in dust from the collapse of one of their towers. By the time the dust had settled the Samprans were already on the Kylix camp and attacking anything dressed as a Kylix soldier.

The Kylix scrambled to retaliate, taken completely off guard. They were quick to respond, though, and fought back the Pearl Fohdorshans. It wasn't long before each side was entangled with one another, where bows became useless in fear of hitting one of their own. Spears whistled through the air at nearby attackers, and swords clashed. But as the Kylix were beating back the Sampra Tribe, retaking the camps, a rumble came from the north.

Dressed in black, wearing a helmet with a bright red mohawk running down the center like solid fire, the soldiers clashed against the Kylix. One soldier stood taller than most, with a halfmoon tattooed over his eye, and an emerald embedded into the top of his right hand. It was Shallon, leading the Soniky into battle. He swatted the Kylix soldiers away like flies with a massive club. Resting on his hip was an opulent sword with a dragon head jutting out of each side for the guard. The hilt covered in small forest green and yellow jewels. The small bit of blade that poked through at the top of the sheath was like shimmering shadow. It was Blaridane.

Rafik felt a jolt, not physically, but in his heart. Like something calling to him in the dead of night. He froze, turning to the north, and there he saw it. The moment his eyes laid upon the blade the familiar voice slithered into his mind, calling for him. *'See how he doesn't use me?'* It said in the most venomous voice he'd heard. He didn't think it was this bad last he heard it two years ago. *'I need a true warrior. Come claim me!'*

"Shallon!" Rafik shouted, waving, and running towards him. He tossed his sword to the side, appearing defenseless. "Shallon!"

The giant turned and his eyes widened. "I wasn't expecting to see you here."

"You're not at the Nassir River." Rafik said.

"No." Shallon said. "Our scouts discovered they were laying siege to the Sampra Tribe. We coordinated with the chief for this attack." All while talking Shallon swatted away soldiers who tried charging at him. His reach was so great most of their swords barely reached Shallon before they were taken down. One spear zoomed through the air, and Shallon narrowly dodged the attack. He growled, glaring at the soldier who nearly killed him. He raised his club and pounded it into the ground, sending up dust. In the cloud Shallon charged ahead, grabbed the Kylix soldier without him realizing what happened and shoved him into the ground, his club falling atop him.

"You like that club, don't you?" Rafik said in awe at his friend's fury.

"After leaving the Bruin Fortress I had to use one for a time. Kind of grew to liking it." Shallon laughed.

"Since you're not using it, can I use your sword?" Rafik asked.

Shallon's demeanor changed. He narrowed his eyes at Rafik and stared at him for several seconds before answering. "No." He said, shaking his head. "This sword is evil. I can barely control it thanks to this." He raised his hand, showing the emerald embedded in his hand. "I'll tell you what, after this battle, I'll tell you all about it."

"Ya shire." Rafik cursed under his breath.

'Kill him!' Blaridane screamed inside Rafik's head.

Rafik shook his head. "I-I understand. I'll fight on ahead." Before Shallon could respond he turned and hurried away in hopes of finding his friends. Blaridane screamed obscenities in his head, though faded the farther away he got from the sword. Now that his talent was gone, he wanted it now more than ever. There had to be a way to get Blaridane. But now wasn't the time. Not when surrounded by enemies. He squeezed between two tents and came face to face with King Vanarzir who just finished defeating three Sampran Warriors.

The king's face was hidden behind a skull helmet topped with a crown. Where everybody else's armor had white bone, his was gold. "I see you returned for execution." He said. "Nice ruse to distract us so your friends could get in position. Shame it was for nothing." He slashed his sword at Rafik, and he dove out of the way, quickly snatching one of the fallen soldier's swords.

Rafik parried the next attack and Vanarzir swung even harder. It took all his strength to hold onto the blade that he fell to one knee. Rafik tried pushing back, but the king was too strong. As a killing blow swept across where his head was, Rafik ducked, rolled, and sprang to safety. He didn't turn around to face the king. Instead, he darted between some of the tents, hoping to circle back and surprise him.

As he jumped out the king was ready, deflecting another blow with ease. "For someone who supposedly defeated Skage, I expected more from you."

"Well, being dead for two years kind of takes the strength out of you." Rafik replied, dodging another blow. How was the king, this old man, this strong and powerful?

"No, you have the stench on you. The World Beneath the World. No matter how long it's been, you can't get rid of the smell." Vanarzir snarled.

Rafik's eyes widened for the briefest of moments and his head tilted in confusion

The king laughed. "Yes, I know of that realm all too well. Tell me, did you try searching for something to stop me? Or did those pathetic birds want to train you to defeat me?" Another blow came crashing down on Rafik, this time breaking the sword. Rafik lunged forward with his broken blade, and Vanarzir sidestepped.

He shoved Rafik forward, causing him to lose balance and topple over into a tent that collapsed upon impact.

"You killed my sister!" Xeo shouted, suddenly appearing on the far end of the row of tents.

King Vanarzir laughed. "I can promise you I didn't."

"You turned her into that monster." Xeo yelled. "You're going to pay for what you did to her!"

"So that's why she didn't come home. I suspected as much. Though I had hoped she had actually succeeded in her duties in the process. Guess she really was utterly useless after all. Nothing to cry over. I wonder who has the curse now?"

Xeo's lip flared, and his knuckles turned white from gripping the sword too tight. "Enough talk. Let's finish this." He charged forward, screaming. Just as Xeo was about to hit the king he fell to the floor as if something invisible tackled him. He scrambled to his feet, fighting off an unseen enemy. During the grappling, a mask was torn off, and Kaliboon appeared, screaming at the king. Another Kylix soldier appeared out of nowhere as their mask was removed, crumpling to the ground. Ziri appeared next, reaching for the mask from the fallen soldier. In one swift move Vanarzir yanked it away, threw it on the ground, and smashed it.

"Don't worry." Kaliboon said, turning to Rafik. "We took care of the others wearing these Ravohka."

The four ganged up on Vanarzir, but he still couldn't be touched. His strength and swordplay were nearly unstoppable. Finally, as Kaliboon tried slashing at him from behind, while Ziri, Rafik, and Xeo attacked from the front, they got a passing glance at his armored chest. The strike rejuvenated the four, and they pressed on the attack. Vanarzir began to step back, losing ground from the constant barrage of attacks.

All around the Kylix were being defeated or surrounded. The Kylix could have taken one of the armies, but the Fohdorsha and Soniky at the same time? It was quickly being proven they couldn't. An ear-splitting roar tore through the air, and in the distance Rafik could see it. The king laughed as he got to his feet, brushing himself off. The familiar fear filled him, and he could no longer move. Petrified by what was coming. The last time he saw it was in the Biodlay Desert. The Obsidian Dragon.

It roared, and as it grew closer blew fire, scorching the ground and anything caught in it. The dragon wasn't attacking anyone, but creating a burning wall between the battle, and the Sampra Tribe. There was no returning or retreating to the tribe quickly with the inferno raging. The black dragon circled back and dove, landing on the ground with such force it caused the battlefield to shake.

Immediately the Samprans surrendered and bowed, chanting in their own language. Even Kaliboon stood awestruck. "You don't understand." She said. "These great dragons are supposed to be extinct. Especially the Obsidian Dragons."

With burning orange eyes, the dragon whipped his head around and glared at the Soniky, who all broke free from their petrifying fear and began to flee.

"You never stood a chance when I have a dragon." Vanarzir laughed. "And not a moment too soon, Rathsa. Your master is pleased."

The black dragon, Rathsa, grumbled and glowered at the king.

Rathsa flew over the battlefield, scorching the lands as he saw fit. Most Soniky fled northward as fast they could. A few, like Shallon, stuck around and fought who they could. The Kylix were overtaking everyone now, and it was a futile effort. After the awe of Rathsa's arrival, and seeing his allegiance to Vanarzir, the Sampran warriors stopped praising it, and returned to fighting. Their path back home was blocked, so none retreated. They fought against the Kylix, but with Rathsa flying above, it seemed to rejuvenate the Kylix's spirits.

Kaliboon joined the fight against the Kylix, forgetting Vanarzir. Ziri, Xeo and Rafik charged at the king, but were blocked by a sudden wave of Kylix soldiers. It was chaos, and nobody could see which side was truly winning.

"Try to stop the dragon!" Rafik yelled.

Xeo nodded. He was wearing his mask but hadn't been using it. In the beginning of the battle too many arrows whizzed passed him or spears narrowly missing. He decided he would be less of a target on the ground. He glanced up at Rathsa and saw him making another round overhead. When they were face to face, he would freeze up in fear. If he could come up from the side or behind, maybe he stood a chance. He waited for the Obsidian Dragon to fly overhead before launching into the air. One Kylix soldier clung to his leg, but Xeo kicked free.

The beating of the wings made a strong wind to fight against, and the blasts of fire made the air feel like he was in an oven. At the last moment he reached the tail and clung to it with all his might. Rathsa gave a fleeting glance at Xeo before whipping his tail back and forth. Xeo held on, slowly climbing up the monster's tail. The rough scales weren't much to grip but gave him enough that he wouldn't slide off.

He inched up the dragon, finally getting to his body. Panting, he paused before standing up. If Rathsa didn't make any sudden movements, he could reach its head. The dragon didn't pay attention to him, and soon he was running along the back of Rathsa. He hoped his sword would be strong enough to pierce the dragon's scales. At the base of the neck was an empty saddle. He cut the straps and watched it fall to the ground. If there was a weak spot, it had to be here.

Xeo raised his sword and drove it down as hard as he could. The sword bent and he lost his grip. It clattered against Rathsa's back before it fell into the sky. Rathsa roared and began flailing. Though the attack didn't even leave a scratch, it got his attention. The Obsidian Dragon rolled in midair, and Xeo slipped into the sky. The ground was getting closer and closer, but Xeo used his mask, and swooped back into the air just before meeting the end of one of the Kylix soldier's spears.

Rafik watched what he could while fighting off the Kylix and made his way towards Xeo. "Are you alright?"

Xeo whooped, screaming in the air, and pumping his fist. "That was amazing!"

"It would have been more amazing if you succeeded!"
Rafik shouted, smiling. It was when Xeo wasn't making jokes he
had to worry. He and Ziri continued fighting their way to King
Vanarzir as Xeo tried again to subdue the dragon.

Then, it happened. A blinding light so few had ever seen
before. Twice a year, on the spring and autumnal equinoxes, at the
moment the day was the exact length as night, the Black Wall
would disappear. The sky overhead was already darkening, and the
sunset in the west was a breathtaking array of pinks, oranges, and
purples. The flash happened so fast, so few saw it. Even fewer
recognize what they had seen. The flash was brief, but long enough
the fighting paused. Silence fell over the fighting armies as they
stared from one to the other, wondering if they had seen the same
thing. Even those who hadn't noticed, crazed, and taken with
bloodlust, froze as they noticed everyone had stopped.

Rathsa screamed as if in rapture, and flew westward,
abandoning the battle. King Vanarzir yelled for the dragon's
return, but it didn't listen. The flash was gone, and the Black Wall
returned. Moments later, as the confusion faded and Vanarzir's
rage echoed through the valley, the battle resumed. The air in the
Kylix soldier's sails was gone, and a new flame had ignited within
the Sampra Tribe as they cheered and praised the return of
dragons.

With the sudden shift in energies, the Soniky returned, and
started boxing the Kylix in again. The fight didn't last much
longer, the Sampran warriors were easily subduing the Kylix. King
Vanarzir called for retreat, and the Kylix fled westward. Rafik and
others chased after the Kylix, as they made their way into the
nearby forests, trying to lose the victors' trail.

Rafik weaved in and around trees, ignoring everyone else
around them. One Kylix soldier tried swiping at him. Rafik just
sidestepped and continued running. He could see the golden figure
of the king in the middle of the bone army. The king suddenly
turned, heading towards the foothills. Rafik followed, along with
the Kylix that weren't in front of him.

They came to a stone outcropping engulfed in shadow, penned in by sheer cliffs on either side. The Kylix screamed, claiming they were doomed. The Sampran warriors and Soniky wouldn't be far behind. Rafik caught up to the king just as a familiar fog rolled into the clearing.

"It can't be." Xeo said, landing beside his friend.

Rafik's face paled. "Impossible. She's dead."

Ziri appeared beside the two, equally stunned. "Does this mean…?" She trailed off, and her body beginning to shake.

The violet streaks within the fog pulsed faintly. The sound of stone grinding against stone echoed in the clearing. Deep in the darkness, two shadowy stone pillars grew from the ground. Between the two pillars was a wrought iron gate. Each pillar was topped with a skull, violet flames glowing from within their eyes. The gate creaked open, and a loud and familiar roar echoed throughout the clearing. Before Treshna could appear, Vanarzir ordered everyone to enter. Without looking or waiting, he dived in. Rafik, Xeo, and Ziri watched as the Kylix disappeared through the gate. Where they went, they didn't know.

The gate closed, and the three could move again. Most of the Kylix fled through the gate. The remaining ones were taken captive. Seeing the gate and hearing that roar petrified them, and they had a feeling this victory wouldn't last long. Their nightmare was just beginning.

Chapter 30: The Bordin Witch

Tahlbiru Ocean, Alutopek

Nightmares plagued Anza. She was drowning in the depths of the Tahlbiru. Taktors swam around her, gnashing their serrated teeth and eagerly waiting for her to perish. The next moment she was back at Dragon's Roost reading ancient books with Izamar. Opening another book, she was sucked in and back at the Sarason Fortress. She saw Gorik fighting Skage along with shadowy soldiers she didn't recognize. Gorik plunged a sword into the necromancer's chest, and the tower began to fall apart. With his last movement before death took him, Skage grasped Gorik, refusing to let go. Her uncle watched the tower crumble, waving to the others to move on. They fell into the Tahlbiru where Anza flailed and screamed as the icy water took her breath. Massive stones sank around her, and a large one came crashing down on top of her. She screamed, seeing Gorik try to swim out of the wreckage, but to no avail. A Taktor swam up from the depths and pulled Gorik into the abyss of the ocean. Their fangs digging into his arm.

Anza shot up, gasping for breath. Her eyes darted around as she reached for the surface. "Whoa, whoa." A voice said, rushing over to her. Her eyes focused and she saw Inakus comforting her. They were no longer near Datz but in the hull of a ship. Waves of water crashed against the ship, rocking it back and forth. She was lying in a hammock, swaying in rhythm of the ship. "Just a bad dream. You're safe."

"Where are we?" She asked. "I don't remember getting on a ship."

"You've been asleep for nearly three days." Inakus explained. "I guess you needed the rest. Even through your nightmares we couldn't wake you. I brought you on board with me. Welcome aboard the *Fallen Order*."

"I'm on a ship?" Anza asked.

Inakus nodded. "I couldn't just leave you there. Spring may have just started, but it's still too cold to leave you out there even if I wanted to."

"Where are we going?"

"The captain hasn't told me that." Inakus said. "I'm about to be leaving. Just had to make sure you would be waking up first. But don't worry, you're safe here." He added after noticing a tiny glimpse of fear in her eyes.

"I need to find Rafik." Anza said. "Does the captain know that?"

"The captain only knows you're on board." Inakus said. "I'll let her know you're awake. You stay here."

Anza nodded. As Inakus went out of sight she slid out of the hammock. Everything swayed back and forth. She could hear the sea crash against the ship, and the torchlights strung from the ceiling were dim. It was hard to see too far ahead. Some sailors moved about while others shouted and gambled at a table. One hobbled worse than her, clinging a bottle. She turned another corner and found the stairs leading to the deck of the ship.

Atop the stairs she bumped into Inakus. "Anza?" He asked, clutching her before she fell down the stairs. "I told you to stay in the hammock."

"I fell out." Anza lied.

Inakus gave her a quizzical look. "Anza, this is Captain Farra."

Captain Farra stared at Anza. Her cold, dark eyes matched her hair streaming down from beneath a large, feathered hat. "So, you're Anza."

Anza nodded. "Nice to meet you."

Inakus fidgeted, glancing towards Anza and then to his feet. He wringed his hands, slowly stepping away from the two women. "Now that she's awake, I will scout ahead." He said, cutting into the greetings. "I'll be back soon with a full report."

Before Captain Farra could say anything the Taktor had spun around and was dashing to the rails. He dove in and disappeared into the depths. "What's gotten into him? He's usually

334

more polite than that." Captain Farra said. She turned her attention back to Anza. "Did he tell you anything about how I run things?"

"He didn't even mention you." Anza said.

Captain Farra nodded. "He told me he found you in the ocean. Revived you, and you fell asleep. Wasn't sure if much else happened."

"We talked a bit first. I learned his name, and he told me how my uncle died in the battle at the Sarason Fortress." Anza explained.

"Gorik?" Captain Farra asked.

Anza nodded. "How did you know?"

"There were only two people who died in that battle. And only one was old enough to be an uncle, if you ask me." Captain Farra said. "It was a tragic night across the Nyler, though. Even if we took the victory."

"At least we won." Anza said, smiling.

"Indeed." Captain Farra agreed. "Inakus didn't say much about you. Where are you from?"

Anza scanned the horizon. There wasn't land in sight. An endless ocean went in every direction as far as the eye could see, before hitting the Black Wall that covered the sky. "Um…" Anza stammered. "I'm from a small village you probably haven't heard of. But I go by Anza Bordin."

"Anza Bordin?" Captain Farra asked. "Two names? Nobody has two names. They're their name, plus where they're from. Like I'm Captain Farra of Trinkit."

"I do." Anza nodded.

"I want two names." A deep voice growled, making his way above deck. Anza noticed his arms were covered in tattoos of corpses and treasures. He was mostly bald, only having a short, thick, crimson mohawk. His eyes were like pools of seawater and had a scar running down from the bottom of his left ear to his neck. Though Farra was taller he had an air about him she knew she didn't want to cross him. "How about Rahgo Bloodthirsty?"

"That just sounds silly." Captain Farra said. "Just stick with Rahgo. If people don't know who you are by one name alone, you don't have a good enough reputation yet. You don't need a second name."

"What does your name mean?" Rahgo asked.

"Anza means grace." Anza said.

"No. Your second one. Your last name." Rahgo said.

"Bordin means non-magical."

"Gracefully non-magical." Rahgo scoffed. "Sounds boring. No wonder you need two names."

"Better than what 'Rahgo' means." Anza said, smirking. She was lying, but he didn't need to know that.

"And what's that?" Rahgo barked.

"It means rancid meat." Anza said and Captain Farra burst into laughter. "I'd much rather be a graceful boring person, than advertise how disgusting I am."

"What did you just say?" Rahgo snapped. He grabbed Anza's collar, pulling her towards him. He balled his fist and glowered just inches away from her face.

"Relax, Bad Meat, you asked for it." Captain Farra said. She put her hand on Rahgo's shoulder. After a moment he finally released her.

"I don't like her." Rahgo said.

"She has fire." Captain Farra said. "Reminds me of the boy."

"Aye." Rahgo grumbled. "Probably why I hate her, too."

Captain Farra shook her head. "Anyway, Anza. There are rules within my crew and on my ship. If you're to be a part of it, you will abide by them."

"And what are the rules?"

"The first being that you are to remain on this ship until you can be trusted." Captain Farra said. "That means it can be years until you take a step on land."

Anza frowned. She had to find out if Rafik was still alive, where he is, and continue her training on Fang-Elsea Island. "Is there a way to speed up the trust process?"

"It doesn't help when you don't tell me where you're from." Captain Farra said.

"You have somewhere to be?" Rahgo barked. "Tell us."

Out of the corner of her eyes she saw two sailors tossing a body overboard. On the ground was a pile of Kylix armor. She looked to Rahgo, his clothes torn, making him appear even more intimidating and powerful. Captain Farra's clothes were much more put together. She wore baggy pants and long leather coat. Her white blouse was also baggy but had flecks of red across it. *'Was that blood?'* She thought to herself. Both had swords ready at their hip. "Inakus didn't tell me you're pirates." She spoke.

"Will that be a problem?" Captain Farra asked. "I can't imagine a young girl who was found in the middle of the Tahlbiru has many...reputable opportunities."

Anza shook her head. "Quite the opposite, really. I noticed you're tossing bodies overboard, and they're near a pile of Kylix armor. You're not Kylix, which means it's likely you came across some. Maybe this was their ship, and you took it?"

Captain Farra's eyes widened, and her brow raised. "Very perceptive. What makes you say that?"

"Kylix always wear their armor. Even in the middle of the desert they're required to. I can't imagine it any different on the sea if they have a navy now. Which tells me you aren't them. You're not wearing anything to signify where you're from or where your allegiance lies. That means you fly under your own colors." Anza elaborated.

"For being named non-magical, that's quite the skill you have." Captain Farra said, smiling. "Very impressed. I'll have to keep my eye on you."

"May I ask where you're going?"

"*We* are sailing east. Until I can trust you more, that's all you need to know."

Anza nodded. "I guess we'll go the long way around."

"Long way to what?" Captain Farra asked.

"Oh, it's nothing, really. I'm not sure if you'd be interested." Anza said.

"Tell us, girl!" Rahgo spat, taking a step forward.

It took all her strength to not cower or take a step back. Anza merely smiled. "Well, getting yourselves tangled up with the Kylix can draw attention to yourself. And I'm trying to avoid that. You see…can I trust you?"

Captain Farra nodded. "Until you betray my crew, or me, you can."

"Fair enough. You see, I'm hunting for treasure."

"Treasure?" Rahgo asked, a greedy glint in his eye.

"Yes. A big one. Hidden from Vanarzir and past kings for ages." Anza said.

"How do you know of this treasure?" Captain Farra asked.

"I was tending to my cousin, Izamar." Anza explained. "He was dying of a sickness. In his final breath he told me of a treasure on Fang-Elsea Island. He told me to seek out my Uncle Gorik to help me find it. He could get me there. Last we heard he was in Datz. Travelling closer I guess I misheard that he was at the Sarason Fortress, not died there. I made a small raft and rowed out. I didn't see the tower everyone described, so I thought maybe it was hidden underground. But my raft sank, and that's where Inakus found me."

"This…treasure." Captain Farra said. "You can find it?"

Anza nodded. "It's buried beneath a boulder between two hills. West of the boulder is a river that runs red like blood. And it's beyond a forest that whispers in the shadows, threatening to snatch you, and feed you to the eagles that even dragons are afraid of." Even she was impressed by her lie.

"That's a tall tale you have there." Captain Farra laughed. "Almost had me for a moment."

"No, no." Rahgo interrupted. "I think I remember hearing about a treasure like that when I was a lad."

"You did?" Captain Farra and Anza asked in unison. Captain Farra eyed Anza, narrowing her eyes.

"Izamar told me it was a family secret." Anza hurriedly blurted.

"Could be why you have more details than me." Rahgo shrugged. "Farra, can you imagine if we find it?"

338

Captain Farra growled. "I will consider this, before agreeing. We will continue heading to where I've already decided."

Anza nodded. "I understand. I hope during that time you can learn to trust me."

"Me too, child." Captain Farra said, inspecting Anza from head to toe. "If it's a family secret, why are you sharing?"

"Uncle Gorik is dead." Anza said. "And I need to find this treasure. Izamar asked me to. And I don't want to let him down. He was like a father to me. If I'm not stuck on this ship, I guess my best bet now would be to suggest going there. Must be easier, or at least safer, than taking on the Kylix."

"We'll talk more." Captain Farra said. "Until then, go to the galley and get yourself something to eat."

"Do you mind if I explore the ship as well?" Anza asked. "I've never been on one so big before, but I don't want to upset you."

Captain Farra waved her hand as she turned away from her. "Fine, fine. Stay away from the brig and we won't have any problems. Rahgo, follow me. Be prepared to work tomorrow, Anza. Everybody pulls their weight on my ship, including children."

Anza bowed as the two turned. She swiveled back to downstairs, smiling. It worked. "Thank you, Cousin Izamar." She giggled.

Anza had been on boats before. Her Uncle Gorik would often take her and Rafik sailing along the shores of Datz. But she had never been on a ship like this. Two giant masts, and a massive hull. As she returned below decks it was like a labyrinth. The first floor was the galley, sitting area, and sleeping quarters. At one end of the ship there was a shaft closed off by a grate at the top, and a railing stopped her from falling deeper into the ship.

On the second level windows covered by loose boards tied to a string. Next to each window were small barrels of arrows and bows beside them. A handful of sailors shooed her away, saying it wasn't a place for little girls. She didn't argue and made her way to the third floor.

She peered around one corner and saw iron bars. A handful of people were sitting against them, whispering to one another. One of them turned, glaring at Anza. Before the prisoner could say anything, she hurried the other way and found what she was looking for. There were barrels and boxes stacked to the ceiling. There was a small channel between a couple that she slowly squeezed her way through.

There weren't any guards or anyone else who could stop her. More than once she heard the skittering of rats, but that was it. The ship didn't seem to rock as much this low as well. She weaved her way throughout the cargo before finally coming to a dead end. If she could jump high enough, maybe she could continue climbing atop everything? She shrugged and managed to kneel.

'Ako tinda bisini.' She thought in her head before pausing. While speaking to Captain Farra and Rahgo she had the strongest feeling to return to the mirror and ask Izamar for some advice. How to proceed from here. But as she was kneeling, about to recite the spell, she stopped. Would Izamar help her? If she went back so soon, what would he say? She could easily lie and say she'd been gone for longer. Would he know she was lying if she tried?

She imagined what Izamar would say. "A plant cannot grow if you always dig it up to check on the roots. "Great. Now my conscience sounds like you." Anza shook her head and got back to her feet. Now wasn't the time to go back and ask for help. Less than a day out of the mirror. Well, less than a day of being awake. She couldn't rely on him. Not for every little thing like this.

It felt like it was easier squeezing and pushing her way into the cargo than it was getting out. One wave hit the ship, causing some of the boxes to shift, nearly crushing her foot. After that near miss she hurried out of the tight maze, popping out without anyone noticing. She was surprised there wasn't anybody else down here. Especially with prisoners. But then again, where would the prisoners go if they escaped?

Knowing she was alone, she no longer tiptoed, and walked gingerly back to the stairs. "Psst." A voice whispered loudly from the brig.

Anza looked up and saw a large, hairy, dark-skinned man staring at her. The devilish grin sent shivers down her spine. "What?"

"Come here."

"No." Anza said, shaking her head. "Captain Farra said not to talk to you."

"Ah. I thought you were different. Not another filthy pirate."

"I'm not one of them." Anza snapped.

The man chuckled, raising his hands. "Alright, alright. Take it easy. Just a friendly man looking to chat." A few of the other prisoners chuckled as he said it.

"What could you possibly want to chat about with me?"

"For starters, if you're not with them, where did you come from? Where are we?"

Anza shrugged. "All I know is we're on the Tahlbiru, going east. They picked me up near Datz."

"Near Datz." The man said, nodding. "Interesting."

"Why?"

"Curious, is all." The man said. "And your name?"

Anza hesitated. Was it safe to give them her name? Realizing she should probably keep the same name as the one she gave Captain Farra, she replied. "Bordin. Anza Bordin."

The man's eyes widened for the briefest of moments, and a wry smile grew on his face. "Nice to meet you, Anza Bordin."

"I wish I could say the same." Anza said.

"You're feisty. Though I'm not surprised."

"Why?"

"Being Rafik's sister, I'd imagine you'd have to be."

"Rafik?" Anza gasped. "You know my brother? Where is he? Did you hurt him? I swear to the gods if you even laid a finger on him, I would make you wish you were never even born."

341

"I already wish that." The man laughed. "I didn't hurt him. I overheard him mention you on this very ship, in fact."

"He's here?" Anza asked, excitement exuding from her voice. She craned her neck to the stairs, making sure none of the sailors were coming down to investigate her sudden burst of happiness. "Is he in there with you?" She tried peering around the large man but didn't recognize the other faces in the prison.

"Calm down." The man said. "He's gone. Long gone from here."

"Where did he go?"

"To find you. Two years ago, in fact."

"But he's alive, right?"

"The last I saw him he was." The man said, nodding. "Though I have heard stories."

"Stories? What stories?"

"Of a boy named Rafik who escaped execution in the Sekolah Fortress at the hands of King Vanarzir, only to die while vanquishing the necromancer Skage. You know, the newest legend in Alutopekan mythos."

Anza shook her head. "You're lying. He didn't die."

"Maybe. Maybe not." The man shrugged. "He escaped death once. Perhaps he could do it again."

"Where's the Sekolah Fortress?" Anza asked. "Why was he there?"

"My guess is the same reason every other child is. To be trained to be part of the Kylix."

"He was captured?" Anza whispered.

"Where have you been for the last two years?" The man asked. "Your brother is a legend."

"He can't be dead." Anza shouted. "He can't be!"

"I'm sorry to be the one to break the news to you. Thought you knew already."

If the man had said anything else, she didn't notice. She stood there, almost like in a trance. How was this possible? Her brother gone. She still saw his mischievous smile. Could hear his laughter echoing in her ear. His eyes full of hurt and sorrow but

342

lighting up when he saw her. As her body felt numb a tear streaked down her face. "It's my fault. All of it."

"How? You weren't there?" The man said.

Anza walked away, not saying another word nor noticing anything else. Her body just moved on its own accord. It wandered through the upper decks before returning to the wall of cargo she had managed to slip through earlier.

She leaned against the wall and cried. It was like a dam had been broken. They streamed out of her, and she couldn't stop it. Her heart ached and somehow the entire world just felt hollow. Even the light appeared dimmer.

'At least he died a hero.' She thought. *'He's my hero. Now all Alutopek know he is. But what's left for me?'* The man had said he cheated death before. By King Vanarzir, no less. Could he have escaped again? She didn't want to give her hopes up. No, what she had to do now was become the next hero. Protect those who can't protect themselves like Rafik always did. "I'm going to Fang-Elsea Island." She got to her feet, clenching her fists. "I'm going to bring magic back to this world greater than before."

Blood trickled down her closed fists, her nails digging into her skin. With her index finger she traced a design into her palm with the blood coming out of her cuts. It glowed a dark green before fading back to crimson. "*Hembir.*" Heal. She spoke. Her cuts vanished. Seeing her skin knit itself back together gave her a sort of energy boost. Almost feeling unstoppable.

She walked out of the storage area with her back straight, shoulders pulled back. There was a glint in her eye now. One of not just determination, but revenge. Skage might be gone, but Vanarzir wasn't. How could she hurt him? How could she make him pay for making everything turn upside down?

It wasn't an easy decision. So many believed they could take on Vanarzir, and so many have failed. She wasn't going to be like them. As she climbed the stairs, she wasn't paying attention to the sailors suddenly stopping from their duties. They all huddled along the rail at the deck and watched with eager anticipation.

There was a flash in the sky that caught Anza's attention. Finally pulling her away from her thoughts, she gasped.

The Black Wall was gone. The brightness of the sun was blinding, but so beautiful. The pinkish sky touched the waters as the sun was setting in the west. Faint stars glimmered in the darkening sky. It was the spring equinox. One of only two times a year where the Black Wall disappeared for just the briefest of moments.

Sure enough, a moment later, the sky was gone. The gorgeous swirl of colors became a hazy brownish tinge of twilight from the Black Wall. She could still make out slightly where the sun was disappearing, but the glory she saw was gone. She had heard people claiming to have seen this, but it happened so briefly few really saw it. None could really absorb the beauty and allure of what was beyond the Black Wall.

With that realization, she knew what she was going to do. She was going to destroy the Black Wall.

Chapter 31: Korban's Finger

Bomoku Mountains, Alutopek

Kryn awoke to a gentle nudge to her gut. She slowly opened her eyes, only to yelp and scramble to her feet a moment later. It was still alarming to be woken by a shadow. The only bright side was within mere seconds she was ready to start the day. It was worth it, though, getting a full night sleep. One benefit of being stuck as a shadow was that Nekvaz never had to eat, drink, or sleep. It only seemed to bother him if Kryn and Junla were cooking something he used to enjoy.

"One day I'll eat that again." He'd say, taking a long and loud sniff of the air.

"I didn't know shadows could smell." Kryn said.

"This one can." Nekvaz replied. "I don't think most shadows can talk either."

The three had been traveling for a few days now. Tonight was the Spring Equinox. Just as Kryn had expected, they were nowhere near the Nassir River. She wondered what was happening during the battle. Had her friends made it in time to the Nassir River? Were they still alive? Her heart always told her yes, but that didn't stop her from worrying.

After meeting Nekvaz he led the two girls deeper into the Bomoku Mountains. He said he learned of a place near the Morvar Ruins that he wanted to take them to.

"There's a reason why the Obsidian Tribe settled where they did." Nekvaz explained. "The Pearl Tribe is settled on the eastern edge of the Bomoku Mountains. Said to have the greatest warriors, they guard the way into the mountains. The Lepal, or Water, Tribe is near the Vinsen Ocean where they feel most at home. The Morvar Tribe is more like Sampra. We chose to settle where we were needed rather than where we wanted. We became guardians."

"Guardians of what?" Kryn asked.

"Climb this mountain and find out." Nekvaz said. "I'll meet you at the top. And no helping." He pointed at Junla and the two imagined a scolding look on his nonexistent face. Before any protests could be made the shadowy figure sprung onto the mountain side and slithered upward.

"I hate it when he does that." Kryn groaned.

"You're just envy-jealous." Junla laughed.

"You would be too if you had to climb this thing!" Kryn shouted as Junla launched into the air. She spiraled upwards, slowly getting higher and higher thanks to her mask. She stared at the red rock of the mountain and cursed. "Ya shire."

They were higher than most mountains now. The climb getting steeper, air thinner, and vegetation giving way to the red rock. There was loose gravel and sand, but nothing alive. Kryn was surprised to see being so high the Black Wall above her still looking so far away. Maybe there wasn't really anything beyond the wall? She shook her head at the thought. Even in Nekvaz's journal he talked about faraway lands not part of Alutopek.

Before starting the climb, she scanned the horizon. To the southwest was Mt. Korban. It still stood magnificently above everything and loomed over her. It was the tallest mountain she had ever seen. While flying along the flatlands with Junla, when she would glance up the mountain, she swore she could see the peaks, scraping the clouds. Now there were clouds even beneath her. Craning her neck upward, it appeared that the mountain just continued. It was no wonder that mountain was used for the Dragon Riders. How else could one get to the top? She made a mental note to ask Nekvaz if anyone had climbed to the top before.

Far below it was just color. The forests surrounding Mt. Korban were coming back to life, being an olive shade in color. The flatlands were a paler green with splotches of violets and pinks. Even the mountains were varying shades of reds, grays, and browns as spring hadn't yet quite reached there yet. The entire area was a breathtaking portrait she would never forget. A faint yell echoed from above. Kryn squinted her eyes, held her hand to her forehead to avoid the glare, and saw a small outline of Junla. Again, Kryn cursed.

She reached as high as she could, grabbed hold of the mountain, and pulled herself up. It was difficult climbing. The mountainside was smooth, offering little foot or handholes. There was a part where she even had to wedge her fingers between a long crack between stones as a grip, climbing upwards. She stopped to catch her breath at one precipice, where a small outcropping of a boulder allowed her to sit down.

As she rested, she felt grooves in the stone. She traced the markings, and soon recognized them as letters. Some were in the common language that she knew. Others in what she assumed was the Fohdorshan letters. Most had been worn away she couldn't make out what any of them said. She followed the messages, scrawled all over the boulder, and followed it back to the wall. At the base, in small writing, was a message she could read. "We don't quit." She read aloud.

Others had taken this journey. But where it went, she still hadn't a clue. Why the Morvar felt like they needed to guard this mountain peak, she wasn't sure. The climb alone would stop most. "We don't quit." She repeated. She clapped her hands and stood up against the wall. She wasn't going to give up now.

The climbing in this section seemed easier. The mountain was more potted, allowing easier reaches and grips. It didn't last long, though, as the potted area gave way to an even smoother area than before. More than once Kryn had to climb downwards, just to try another route. On the fourth try, she came to a thin ledge. It didn't look like there was any other way of climbing up this mountain. She began to think maybe she even started climbing at the wrong point and would have to go all the way back to the beginning and start again. Pushing down those negative thoughts, Kryn swiveled herself, back against the mountain side, and slowly inched across a thin ledge she had just noticed. The wind howled, nearly pushing her off, and cold began creeping into her bones. Her teeth clattered as she fought off the rest of her body shivering.

She imagined herself shivering so much she shook herself off the mountain itself.

With that thought, she glanced down, and saw how high she had climbed. A sense of vertigo overtook her, and she pressed hard against the wall, closing her eyes tight. "We don't quit. We don't quit." She repeated over and over. As the sense faded, Kryn tilted her head up and opened her eyes. She wasn't going to look down again. Inch after inch, she pressed forward. The ledge eventually gave way to another large boulder jutting out of the mountain side. Junla waved from atop the mountain, and Kryn smiled, waving back. "You cheater." She smiled.

There wasn't much mountain left to climb. Kryn took a couple deep breaths and climbed some more. It was nearly evening when she finally made it to the top of the hill. She rolled onto the top ledge, groaning. "That hurt!"

"It didn't look fun-enjoyable." Junla said.

"It wasn't." Kryn said, still trying to catch her breath. She rolled onto her stomach and tried pushing herself up with her arms, but they were like jelly. They wobbled and shook violently, not even getting Kryn off the ground by an inch.

"Any higher and I don't think you would have made it." Nekvaz said. "Congratulations."

"Thanks." Kryn said, accepting Junla's help in getting to her feet. Even on them, she leaned on Junla to stay upright. "Where are we?"

Junla yelped, as she opened her mouth. Nekvaz was covering her mouth faster than lightning could strike the ground. "A sacred place." The shadow said. "I learned of this place long ago and didn't put it in my diary. This place has been lost to time, and I don't want the monsters of this world discovering it."

Nekvaz paused, turning to admire the mountain top. They were on a large plateau, but on the other side were two rocky walls stretching and arching, but not touching. The sky could be easily seen between the two. It was like an arch with the center missing, although it extended for a long way, like the maw of something large. Or a cave not quite sunken into the earth. The rock formation was peculiar but didn't seem like anything worth guarding.

"It's pretty." Kryn said.

"Dragons are wild animals. Monsters from an era where they ruled all Amlima, and humankind hid away in caves. As man started standing up for themselves, the dragons took notice and made a pact with them. A select few dragons and a select few of man would be chosen to watch over and protect one another. A treaty, if you will. This pact gave rise to the Dragon Riders." Nekvaz explained. "For any new Dragon Rider, it starts here."

"What's so special about here?" Kryn asked.

"You'll see." Nekvaz said. "Every spring and autumnal equinox the light hits this cavern just right. It's as if for a fleeting moment, the gods themselves reach down, and point to your destiny. The Dragon Riders called it Korban's Finger."

Kryn was about to roll her eyes until she remembered everything she had seen. Two years ago, she saw the dead come back to life. She has seen a monster from Soboribor terrorize and hunt her and her friends. She set foot on an island guarded by a beast said to only exist in legend. Found a tomb of a fallen god. Maybe this wasn't so farfetched after all. "Do I just wait, then?"

"At the spring equinox, enter the cavern." Nekvaz said.

Junla's eyes lit up. "Does this mean-signify what I think it means?"

Nekvaz didn't say a word. He stood silently, his shadow slowly fading into the darkness as evening came through. Kryn wasn't sure if this would work, with the Black Wall up. But sure enough, just a few minutes of waiting, and the edges of the cavern began to glow. Another moment, and the entire channel was glowing with light, while the rest was shrouded in darkness. It looked like a golden arm came down from the heavens and pointed downwards at the far end of the cavern. Nekvaz nudged Kryn to move.

Kryn slowly inched forward. Her legs were still wobbly from the climb, and her balance was shaky. Bit by bit, inch by inch, she stepped forward. Now within the cavern she noticed on the ground masks. Half buried in the sand, scattered about, were Ravohka. And on the far end, directly downward from where the finger was pointing, was a large, oval shape.

A voice in her head told her to take it, and with shaking hands she reached out and snatched the stone. The light was so bright, she wasn't sure what she had grabbed. She turned and walked out. Junla gasped, and Nekvaz ordered for her to enter. Kryn stared at the stone, not taking another step. The oval was rigid, being covered in dark green scales. On one side, just above the center in the middle of the egg, was a large purple gem. Is this…is this what I think it is?"

Nekvaz nodded. "Kryn, you have been chosen."

She stared in awe at the egg. It was heavier than it looked, but still much lighter than what it should be. The intricate detail of the scales on the egg was magnificent. It was like a crocodile's but somehow much more glorious and beautiful. The purple gem glowed. As she brushed her hand against the gem, Nekvaz snapped.

"Don't touch that." He warned. "Not yet."

"Why?" Kryn asked.

"If an egg is taken from Korban's finger during the spring or autumn equinox it alerts all dragons." Nekvaz explained. "In ancient times that isn't a big deal. But now…when there's only one known dragon to be alive…"

"They'll come to investigate." Kryn finished.

"Yes." Nekvaz said. "And Rathsa is with Vanarzir. If he comes, he could force servitude on you and the draglings as well."

"Draglings?" Kryn asked.

"Baby dragons." Nekvaz said. "And we don't want that. I want you to be safe. Go hide."

Kryn tried protesting, but to no avail. The shadowy form of Nekvaz kept pushing and nudging her away from him. "Fine, I'm going, I'm going." She finally said, no longer digging her heels into the dirt.

"Get back into the cavern and hide there. Don't come out. No matter what." Nekvaz said.

As Junla stepped out, a smile stretching from ear to ear on her face, holding a similar egg, but copper in color, Kryn hurried back to her. "We need to hide." She said, tugging at Junla.

"Why?"

"Nekvaz said so." Kryn said. "He warned us not to come out no matter what."

Junla nodded and followed Kryn back into the cavern. They both hid behind large stones jutting out of the ground. Darkness crept into the land, and the finger of light faded from existence. Every time one of them moved Nekvaz screamed at them to stay still. The night was freezing, and the two huddled together for warmth, but dared not move. Finally, what seemed like hours later, a sudden gust of wind pummeled the plateau.

There, standing and roaring in front of them, was a massive black dragon. Spikes ran across its back from the base of its neck to its tail. Its eyes glowed a burning orange and the scales were like glimmering pieces of shadow, even in this darkness. Massive spikes jutted backward protecting its neck, and leathery wings flapped blowing away some of the smaller rocks off the mountain.

"Rathsa." Nekvaz said. "We're finally united again."

The dragon growled and grumbled. If it meant anything, Kryn and Junla didn't understand it.

"I know. It was the only way. I'm sorry. I'm ready to go back. We'll face him together." Nekvaz said. Rathsa roared, making the girls cover their ears it was so loud. Kryn even thought his roar was louder than any rumble of thunder she had ever heard. The black dragon lowered its front half like a bow, and Nekvaz sprinted and jumped, using one of the dragon's spikes to hoist himself up. Without saying another word or glancing back, Rathsa ran and jumped off the mountain, flying eastward. The two disappeared into the night.

"What now?" Junla asked.

"Wait until morning, then climb down the mountain, I guess." Kryn said. "You got one too?"

Junla's smile lit up. "A voice-call told me if I wanted one, I had to give up-lose my Ravohka. I thought that would have been a harder decision-choice."

"You still got one and didn't have to climb the mountain?" Kryn laughed. "You cheated."

"Nekvaz told me after I got-arrived up here I probably wouldn't get one. I realized-knew where we were once I was up here." Junla said. "I would have been so jealous-envious of you."

"Great." Kryn sighed. "I'm glad you have one too, but now we need to climb down with these things. I was hoping you could fly us down."

Junla smiled, petting the egg. "It's worth it." The two huddled together beside the boulder they were hiding behind. They each held their dragon eggs tight. The jewel on each of the eggs pulsed with a faint light like a heartbeat.

Kryn awoke to a slight punch in the face and a loud yawn she recognized instantly. Junla was waking up and stretching. "Watch it." She snapped, rolling over. As she did, she felt the large, round, rigid egg still wrapped in her arms. The thought of what she held woke her up instantly. It was more than just a dream, this was real! Her eyes sprang open, and she sat up, holding the egg out for her to examine.

It was just as beautiful as last night. Varying shades of dark forest green scales rippling down the egg. In the center was a purple gem. As it grew brighter, the light of the gem faded from view. The egg was warm to the touch, and she wondered how long until it might hatch. She stared at the purple gem, wanting to touch it. Nekvaz had told her not to yet. After considering it for a moment, she decided to wait and examine it further once they were off the mountain.

She turned to Junla, as she stretched with one hand, her other was wrapped firmly around her own egg. Where her egg had scales in shades of dark green, hers were beige and copper. The purple gem on Kryn's was crimson on hers. Both radiated with magnificence that one couldn't just look away once they started

352

staring. "Morning." Junla yawned, snapping Kryn out of her trance.

"Morning." Kryn replied, holding the egg tighter.

"Last night was like a dream-wish." Junla said, stumbling to her feet. She held out her egg and marveled at it, twirling it around. "Do you know what's inside-hidden?"

"I have an idea." Kryn laughed. "Our eggs are different colors."

Junla nodded. "During the Age of Monsters, way before humankind was around, there were 12 breeds of dragons. Most are gone now, but the egg could be from any of them."

"Where did they come from? They just…appeared." Kryn asked.

"Magic." Junla shrugged. "It has to be."

Kryn had seen the dead come back to life, several peers she grew up with have talent, and lived part time in a room hidden within an ordinary bag. Yet the thought of an egg, let alone a dragon egg, suddenly appearing seemed off. "I don't know. Maybe somebody else was here."

"Maybe." Junla said. "I don't care. We have-possess dragon eggs. The first in centuries. Probably even longer from Korban's Finger."

"What about Rathsa?" Kryn asked.

"If the stories are true-believable, Nekvaz found him at the bottom of a swamp." Junla said. "Another reason why so many don't believe-trust Rathsa is alive."

Kryn gently placed her egg against the boulder and slowly walked away, not turning from it until she was several paces away. She stood on the ledge of the plateau and nearly gasped at the beauty. The only thing taller than where she was at was Mt. Korban itself. The Black Wall glowed above them in the eerie twilight she had grown used to. But the view looking down, was breathtaking. The red rocks of the Bomoku Mountains blended with the greens of the trees and fields. Everything looked peaceful and calm. Like a portrait. There wasn't a sign of danger in any direction. Just endless natural beauty.

"How are we getting down?" Junla asked, coming to stand beside her.

"Carefully." Kryn sighed. "I have no idea. It was hard enough climbing up without holding onto the egg. And I don't want to drop it."

The two paced back and forth across the plateau, periodically returning to the eggs to ensure they were still there. There was nothing up here. Not a tree, a bush, flower, or even a stream. It was just rock, sand, and boulders. Peering over the edge, they did see larger birds soaring through the sky, but they even seemed tiny from so high up. As the day ended, the only bit of warmth the sun on the Black Wall provided faded.

"It's going to be a cold-freezing night." Junla said.

"Let's go back into the cavern." Kryn suggested, not waiting for her friend before returning to their only shelter. The two each grabbed their eggs and huddled together behind the boulder.

"I think we're stuck-trapped up here." Junla said. "Or we abandon-leave the eggs."

"Neither of us want that." Kryn said, shaking her head. "There has to be another way."

The grinding of stone echoed through the large cavern. The mountain rumbled and shook, and the two believed it was about to collapse back to the ground far below. As soon as it started, it had ended. Where the finger of light pointed the night before to the eggs, the gap in the walls now pointed to a hole in the ground. Kryn was the first to examine it. Just wide enough for them to squeeze through single file. She held the egg above her head as she shimmied into the hole. It extended, slowly widening and spiraling downward. Soon the walls and ceiling weren't just a shoulder length apart, but two full grown men could walk through the tunnel. Then three. Then four. As it widened the walls were no longer barren. Large pieces of art and letters Kryn didn't recognize covered it in an endless tapestry.

"History." Junla whispered beside Kryn, oohing, and awing at the walls. "Dragon Rider history."

"Maybe we can read it one day." Kryn said. "But we need to get out of here."

The two weren't sure how far they had descended before coming to a fork in the road. To the right it seemed to go deeper into the mountain. To the left there appeared to be light not far away. "Which way?" Junla asked.

"Let's get some fresh air." Kryn said, pointing to the direction on the left.

Junla nodded and took the lead. "I don't like it down-below here." She sighed. "Remind-prompts me of being stuck-trapped back home."

Kryn smiled but didn't say a word. They had made it off the mountain, she was holding a dragon egg, and everything just felt right. Junla disappeared into the light, and Kryn was just a few steps behind her. The bright light was the eastern light reflecting off the Black Wall. They had been traveling and walking down the inside of the mountain all night. Fatigue washed over her as the realization hit her, and she slumped against the wall. Sleep sounded good right now.

A cracking of a branch alerted her, and Kryn bolted up right, albeit a little wobbly. A familiar voice laughed at her. As her vision came into focus, she saw Junla first. She was on the ground, not moving. Hurik stood over her, laughing. There was a sword in one hand, and Junla's egg in the other. "I had a feeling you'd lead me to something. Might not be a Ravohka, but this will do nicely." He stared at the egg out of the corner of his eye, a thin smile spreading on his lips. "But two of them? Well, that would be even better."

"You're not having either egg." Kryn snapped. "Give hers back."

The thief shook his head, his white hair coming loose from the dark jacket he was wearing. If he had been wearing that the whole time, they could have walked past him without realizing it. Hurik laughed. "I don't think I will. And I don't think you can stop me this time."

"I'm going to try." Kryn gently placed her egg on the ground behind her, not turning away from Hurik. She brandished a sword in one hand, and a knife in the other. Hurik took a couple steps back before gently placing the egg on the ground. The two circled Junla, not saying a word, or taking their eye off the other. More than once Kryn wondered if this was a ruse, and some of his friends were snatching the eggs as they prepared to fight. Finally, she couldn't take that thought anymore and glanced back where her egg was. Noting it was still safely there, Hurik lunged with a murderous growl.

Kryn parried the blow but was quickly pushed into the brush and trees of the forest. Being away from the eggs was too risky. She sidestepped instead of parried which gave her time to return to the mountain. Their eggs were still there, as well as Junla, still lying on the ground. Kryn spun around, holding her sword up to block a blow she knew was coming, but with her other hand stretched forward with her knife.

Hurik jumped backwards, losing his footing, and Kryn pressed onward. She was on the offensive now, and she wasn't going to let up. The two dueled throughout the nearby trees and clearing by the mountain. At one-point Kryn would have the advantage, only for Hurik to snake in and take it a moment later.

'If only I still had my fire.' Kryn thought to herself, blocking another blow. The two were evenly matched, but Kryn's tired body was giving way. She could feel her moves slipping. Almost too late to block a blow. Too slow to take the advantage. She envisioned driving her sword into Hurik's chest, but it seemed more and more likely it was nothing more than a dream that could never happen.

As Hurik swung his sword down, and Kryn blocked it at the last moment, he spun around, swung his sword one way, and dropped it, as he swiped his leg from the other direction. The sudden move caught Kryn off guard, and she fell onto her back. From his boot Hurik yanked out a small knife and held it to Kryn's throat.

"I expected more from you." He sneered. "Accept defeat and I'll let you live."

Kryn shook her head. This couldn't be the end. She watched as Hurik drove the knife down into her chest. It was a small blade, but she still felt it dig into her. The rags she had for clothes offered little protection. She gasped and pawed at the knife as Hurik got to his feet.

"You can keep the knife." He laughed, pulling it out and tossing it to her side. He walked to the eggs, not looking back, whistling a merry tune.

She glared at Hurik, feeling blood pool up around her chest. She gasped, coughing up blood. Again, she felt the cold and longed for warmth. Hurik picked up Junla's egg first. Then hers. He laughed again, turned, and winked at Kryn.

Kryn tried speaking but just coughed up more blood. Her attacker laughed once more, shook his head, and started to leave. There was a spark. A warmth spreading from her heart and into every part of her body. At first, she hadn't noticed, being so focused on wanting to stop Hurik as he had the eggs. The spark grew. It was more than a sudden light now. As if something had struck. The spark grew to a small ember, nestled in kindling, and just waiting to start. The next moment she felt it. The light returning. In an instant her small ember grew from a fire to a raging inferno.

She screamed as she held her hand over the hole in her chest, burning and fusing the hole shut. The sudden scream caused Hurik to freeze and slowly turn. His pale skin now almost transparent. His cotton white eyes widened with fear.

"Give me the eggs." Kryn demanded, spitting out the last of the blood. The fire within her was burning everything within. Her body was like a furnace. There was nothing more she wanted than to protect those eggs. It was like something primal woke up in her, and this monster was going to do all it could to protect them.

"I'll give you yours back." Hurik said in a shaky voice.

In response Kryn hurled a fireball at his feet, causing him to yelp. "Both eggs."

357

"Be reasonable." Hurik said. "She doesn't need it."

Kryn snarled. "Give me the eggs!"

"Alright. Alright!" Hurik said. He slowly bent over and placed each egg on the ground. Once his hands were free, he raised them into the air and stepped backwards, inching his way into the forest. Kryn roared, throwing two more fireballs in his direction. As the smoke cleared, he was gone.

She hurried to the eggs, grabbing them both. Her fire was back, and she was going to protect them. As she thought this she fell beside the eggs, exhaustion finally taking her. Regaining and using the fire had taken a lot out of her.

Kryn groaned, feeling small bits of pressure all over her body. It was like a kitten crawling on her. But where the cat's paws were soft, these feet were rough, scaly, and a bit sharp. She tried ignoring the strange kitten crawling on her, but it kept nudging her. First in the hands, and then on her neck. It finally spun around like a dog trying to find a spot to lie down a couple times before laying down on her chest.

A moment later she felt warm breath tickling her nose. This cat, dog, or whatever it was, was staring at her. Begrudgingly Kryn squinted. All she wanted to do was rest, not give love and attention to some stray animal that found her sleeping body a worthy bed. Her eyes came into focus as they shot open at the sight of this 'cat.' Staring at her behind yellow, cat-like eyes and covered in shimmering green scales, was a dragon.

Chapter 32: Return of a Monster

Sampra Tribe, Bomoku Mountains, Alutopek

Once the Soniky and Sampra had finished rounding up the remaining Kylix soldiers, Rafik and Xeo hurried westward back to Tragi. If Treshna had returned, who knew what became of him. Ziri and Kaliboon stayed behind to help clean the mess up. Xeo was holding Rafik from under his arms and flying as fast they could. It was hard to tell where they were exactly with night being upon them.

Rafik stared up at the moon, glowing through the Black Wall. He wondered if that was the same glorious orb he saw for the shortest of moments at the height of the equinox. That was proof there was a world beyond the Black Wall. Gorik had mentioned seeing a flash of light beyond the wall a time or two while out at sea but being surrounded by toppling ruins of a once great city, not many saw it. Most believed it to be nothing more than tall tales from a sailor.

Thinking of Gorik brought back memories of his father. He was part of a rebellion he would soon be joining. A smile crept on his face realizing this. It felt like he was slowly becoming the man his father was.

"There it is." Xeo said, pulling Rafik away from his thoughts.

Just up ahead was the mirage tree with trimmed vines and branches. A dark blot on the land showed where the pit was. Xeo lowered Rafik with a couple of feet of a drop, and he landed on the ground with a stride, and stumbled. Xeo flew on ahead and landed, running to the rim of the pit. At the bottom, against the far side of the hole, was Krista and Tragi. They were sleeping, leaning on one another, but Valkayto's body was missing.

"Wake up." Xeo shouted. The two sputtered incoherent noises and scrambled to their feet ready to fight.

"You're alive!" Tragi smiled. "I'm so glad you're alive!"

"Me too." Xeo said. He jumped into the hole, using his mask to land softly, and embraced his brother. "I thought you were a goner."

"Why would I be?" Tragi asked. "I've been here. Away from battle."

"What about Treshna?" Rafik asked.

"Wasn't that your sister?" Krista asked? "She's dead."

Tragi nodded. "I buried her. In the center of this pit. Thought we'd fill up the hole before we moved on."

Xeo nodded. "When did you bury her?"

"When it was still light out." Tragi said. "Why?"

"During the battle we heard her roars. She's not dead." Rafik explained.

"We need to dig her up." Xeo said. "Where is she?"

"Is this necessary? We've been here the whole time." Tragi argued.

Xeo shook his head and Tragi sighed.

"It's over here." Krista said. Just feet from where they were standing was a mound of dirt that appeared more disturbed than the rest. It could barely be seen by the limited light.

"Let's start digging." Rafik said, grabbing the nearby shovel.

Within moments Valkayto's corpse could be seen peeking through some of the dirt. "See, she's right there." Tragi said, pointing. "Do you want to go any further desecrating our sister's grave?"

"No." Xeo said, sighing and sitting down. It was like the wind was knocked out of him with how he collapsed. "I thought she was back."

"We heard the roars." Rafik said. "Maybe there's more than one?" Fatigue was taking him now too. From the battle, to chasing King Vanarzir into that strange gate, and hearing the roars of Treshna, he could finally relax.

"Did you see her?" Tragi asked.

"Maybe it was a ruse to help the Kylix win?" Krista suggested. "You know, like a trick."

"Oh, they didn't win." Xeo laughed.

"Does that mean the king is dead?" Tragi gasped, a smile growing from ear to ear. "Congratulations!"

Rafik shook his head. "Don't celebrate too soon. He got away. Escaped through this magical gate. Most of the Kylix did too."

"The roars were coming from inside the gate. But we couldn't see anything." Xeo said. "So, we hurried back here thinking Kay was still alive."

"That makes sense." Tragi said. "I wish she were."

"Me too." Xeo said. "She would have been proud of me today. I fought a dragon."

Tragi gasped. "No, you didn't! That's impossible."

"It's true." Rafik confirmed. "Didn't win, though. Flew off at the equinox. Did you see what happened?"

Krista shook her head. "We weren't there. What happened"

"No, the Black Wall." Rafik said. "It disappeared. My uncle said he saw that happen a time or two while out at sea. Most didn't believe him."

"Nope." Tragi said. "If that happened, we didn't see it. It's starting to sound a little too fantastical now. Xeo fighting a dragon, you two fighting the king and him escaping through some magical gate where Treshna is roaring out of, and now the Black Wall disappearing for a moment or two."

"It's true!" Rafik insisted. "We're having a feast to celebrate tomorrow night."

"If it is all true, where's Ziri? Where's Kaliboon?" Are they alright?" Tragi asked.

"What about Taygin?" Krista asked.

"Taygin stayed away from the battle." Rafik started. "But the other two are fine. A little banged up like the rest of us, but still in one piece. We'll see them tomorrow and they'll confirm everything we said."

Tragi yawned. "Then I'm going back to sleep." He walked away, leaning against the wall. Krista followed, holding his hand.

Rafik and Xeo exchanged glances, but didn't say a word, only silently giggled.

Xeo walked with the others instead of flying in the morning. Their stomachs growled, but none of them wanted to stop and search for food. With how Rafik and Xeo described the Sampra Tribe, Tragi and Krista were eager to arrive and have a decent meal. Nearly there, and they found Taygin. His face was pale, sweat streaming down his face. He was clutching something beneath his shirt, rubbing it and muttering to himself.

"There you are." Taygin said, his voice slightly higher. "I thought you two were that way?" He asked, looking at Rafik and Xeo and pointing to the east.

"We came back for Tragi and Krista." Rafik said. "We didn't see you."

"Must have." Taygin laughed, darting his eyes from Rafik to Xeo. "I heard we won."

Rafik nodded.

"We did, yes. That's what heroes do you know? Go into battle. Win. Not cower on the sidelines." Xeo said.

"Xeo stop." Rafik said, glaring at him.

"No, it's alright." Taygin said. "I deserve it. From now on I'll be much braver. Probably braver than either of you."

Xeo burst out laughing. "I fought a dragon. Try being braver than that."

"We're going to be hearing about this a lot, aren't we?" Tragi groaned.

"Yep!" Xeo said, flashing a cheesy grin. He held the mask against his side, with his arm pinning it in place. He patted it with his free hand. "I think I made the best choice, flying."

"This'll be more annoying than hearing him whine about the masks." Tragi said.

The group laughed, and continued their trek to the Sampra Tribe, enjoying each other's company and the first full day of spring.

The fires surrounding the Sampra Tribe had been put out, leaving a blackened scar along the ground. With the ivory-colored towers stretching into the sky behind the burns, it was an impressive sight. Even Krista remarked how extraordinary the Sampra Tribe appeared. The streets were made of white granite and even the sides of buildings were encased in a white plaster. Pearls and faint pink stone accented the white in intricate designs. It looked out of place when compared to the area of red foothill mountains and forests. Pillars touched the sky with statues of a Sampran warrior, or a dragon. At the base of each pillar were small plaques naming the figure above.

"Welcome to the Sampra Tribe." One man said, bowing to Rafik and Xeo. "We saw you in battle. We're glad you survived" Unlike in the Lepal Tribe, most Fohdorshan were wearing masks. And the majority were wearing the same one. A star shaped mask with rounded off edges instead of points. The upper prong was sheared off, and shorter than the rest. There were two vents below each of the eyes, but no sign of a mouth. Though all of them could be heard as if a mask wasn't blocking their mouth.

Xeo shrugged and donned his mask. "Happy to be here." He exclaimed.

There were other Fohdorshan members within the tribe, most recognizably because of the different color of Ravohka they wore. Each of them bowed their heads as Rafik and Xeo walked by. Another pointed for them to continue climbing up the foothill and deeper into the tribe. They finally arrived at a great building held up by twelve pillars on either side. Atop the roof was a large, fat dragon. Its belly nearly drooped over the sides of the hall, and its head pointed upward. The nostrils billowed clear smoke, almost like steam.

As the massive doors opened for the five of them echoes of shouting erupted from within. Once inside, the five gasped. White chandeliers hung down by different colored chains that were wrapped in pearls. Row upon row of tables had the Soniky warriors feasting and laughing among the Fohdorshan. The room was so large it was hard to see the other side. It didn't help that everything was a polished white and glowed from the torchlight.

"Are we dead?" Xeo asked. "Because I kind of feel like I'm dead right now."

"The white is a bit much." Tragi whispered, moving his hand to shield his eyes from the reflecting light. "Makes me feel very…dirty." He said, noticing his dingy clothes and rubbing at his dirty face.

"We aren't the only ones." Rafik smiled. A lot of the warriors, including the Fohdorshan, were dirty.

Ziri ran up to them, smiling. "I saved you a seat." She said, turning and hurrying back to her own.

Sure enough, there were empty seats beside Ziri. Across from her were Shallon, Kaliboon, and others Rafik recognized but didn't know their names of. "So, he's the one?" A man asked sitting next to Kaliboon. He had gray eyes and a similar face to Kaliboon. His hair was gray but had faint traces of blue if the light hit it a certain way.

Kaliboon nodded. "Xeo, this is Jessux, my brother. He saw you take on Rathsa."

"Very brave." Jessux said, nodding.

"He almost was angry you were wearing a Ravohka." Kaliboon said. "He's part of the group who hunts down fallen or stolen Ravohka. Not many kolinda have the privilege you do."

Xeo smiled. "I'm honored." Before he could say much more a large plate of food was brought to him. His stomach growled, and he eagerly wolfed it down, forgoing most manners.

"I see you survived." Shallon said to Rafik.

Rafik nodded. "It wasn't easy. And King Vanarzir got away."

Shallon shrugged. "No good thing ever is. Did you find your father?"

"I did." Rafik said. "Why couldn't you tell me?"

"Would you have preferred if I did?" Shallon asked.

"No." Rafik smiled, shaking his head. "It's hard, seeing his final memories. But it's one I'll never forget. For a moment, I thought he was alive again."

"Your talent is a great one. Use it well." Shallon advised.

Rafik frowned, lowering his head. Any sort of pride he felt now shifted to shame. "I-I don't have talent anymore."

Shallon's eyes widened. "What happened?"

Rafik shared of his adventures from the Bruin Fortress, and what led them to this point. He didn't leave out any details. He was one of his father's friends, and he knew he could be trusted. "Do you know if there is a way to get talent back?"

Shallon shrugged. "I'm sure there is, but I wouldn't know it. Maybe a strong witch or wizard. But those are long gone. If there is a way, though, I don't doubt you'll find it. You made it here after all."

"Thanks." Rafik smiled.

"The queen really is dead?" Shallon said. "There were rumors."

"Well, they were just rumors until Taygin killed her." Rafik said, glancing in his direction. He was on the other side of Ziri, silently eating, and smiling if he made eye contact with anyone. With his other hand he continued rubbing what was hidden beneath his shirt on his chest.

"Very strange times, Rafik. The Flash usually isn't that noticeable." Shallon said.

"The Flash?"

Shallon nodded. "There was a reason the Soniky chose the spring equinox for battle. For short moments at the spring and autumn equinox the Black Wall disappears. We believed if people saw even a bit of that, coupled with people fighting back the Kylix, they would be inspired. But it usually doesn't last that long."

"Does that mean anything?" Rafik asked.

"I'm not sure." Shallon said. "I first thought that it meant Vanarzir's power is slipping. Most Fohdorsha are celebrating saying dragons returned, and that was why. A few are saying magic is returning. At this point, I don't really know. What I do know, is that word of our victory will spread. The rebellion is starting."

Rafik smiled. "And once I go to the tomb of Tulang, I'll be part of the rebellion."

"You deciphered the code." Shallon noted, smiling. "Great job." At that moment somebody Rafik didn't recognize approached Shallon and whispered into his ear. His smile faded and he politely excused himself, hurrying out the door.

Rafik watched Shallon rush out the door and finished eating his meal in silence. Ziri sat next to him but was laughing with the others, deep in conversations of their own. As he stood up, though, he saw it under the table. The club Shallon used, and his sword. Rafik's eyes noted the familiar shape. This was the moment. He had been fighting the urge for two years wanting it. As he saw it at the Bruin Fortress his hunger for the sword increased but faded as they travelled across Alutopek. Seeing it just yesterday, and now today, the craving returned tenfold. He didn't want the sword. He needed it. He could use it. After all, Shallon didn't even try using it during the battle. And his own talent was gone.

He finally made up his mind, and inched down, trying not to bring attention to himself, and grabbed the sword. The familiar voice echoed in his mind, and a sense of calm rushed over him. If he didn't have talent, at least he had Blaridane.

'You again.' It hissed, scouring Rafik's mind like a loose dog hunting and sniffing for its prey.

'Me.' Rafik said, smiling.

'I knew you'd be back.' Blaridane said, laughing. 'You need me.'

Rafik nodded. 'I do.'

Shallon returned a moment later, rushing past Rafik and the others. He walked briskly to the far end of the hall and whispered something into a man's ear. The man stood up and the hall grew quiet. "We earned a well-deserved victory yesterday and made new allies. For ages, the Fohdorsha have kept to themselves. But even then, the Soniky have shown they aren't like other outsiders, like

366

Vanarzir and his Bone Hunter army. The Fohdorsha will continue aiding the Soniky in fighting back the Kylix and defeating the king who swept across the Bomoku Mountains, causing so much pain, suffering, and chaos. From this day forward, the Soniky have a home among the Fohdorsha, and we are allies."

The hall began to cheer, but the man raised his arms to quiet them once more. "For centuries, the Sampra Tribe has grown strong, guarding the eastern gate to Mt. Korban. We started sharing our prosperity, opening the gates to the other tribes. But for the first time since the Great Fall, all tribes are welcome. Delegates have been sent to our brothers and sisters living in hiding and fear. Now is not the time to continue building walls, but tables. We must help our neighbors. Only then will we be able to defeat this new evil once and for all."

"What does that mean?" Xeo asked.

Kaliboon stopped cheering and clapping to answer Xeo. "The disgraced and exiled tribes are allowed back home. It's a big deal."

"And the Soniky just got a lot more allies." Tragi said. "We might actually win this thing."

Rafik didn't say anything, just reveled in the feeling of being back with the cursed sword, too distracted to fully understand what was happening around him. But hearing Tragi's response, he smiled. *'Good news old friend.'* Rafik finally said, welcoming the voice. It was like a piece of him that was missing had now been found. *'We are going to war.'*

Blaridane said only one word in response to that. It screamed it in his head with that familiar, hateful, and arrogant hiss. *'War!'*

367

Glossary

PEOPLE and ANIMALS

A

Agam – (Ag-uhm) An Immortal. Master of Fire.

Amsahvi Tribe – (Am-saw-vee) Fohdorshan Tribe of earth.

Anak-Turin – (Uh-knock Toor-in) Dark Immortal and king of Mahparry.

Annorla – (Uh-nawr-lah) Famed blacksmith and heir to a blood metal ring. Aunt to Kryn.

Anza – (An-zuh) Sister to Rafik, daughter of Tamra and Drane. A quick learner who is naturally curious. From Datz.

Arzir – (Ahr-zir) Former king of Alutopek. Father to Vanarzir.

B

Bahsha – (Bah-shuh) Elderly woman of Lynn

Bantrita – (Ban-tree-tuh) Former historians. A sect of people dedicated to the truth, able to view past events. Now glorified storytellers and outlaws.

Bone Hunter – Extinct race of man that came from the Rantyak Islands.

Brohl – (Brohl) Member of the Soniky. Friend to Drane

C

Cavernous Lazywing – Great dragon said to be extinct.

Crimson Shroud – Great dragon said to extinct.

D

Dahsho – (Dah-show) Son of Kaliboon.

Dragon Rider – Legendary order of people who tamed and rode dragons.

Drane – (Dreyn) Sailor from Datz. Father to Rafik and Anza, husband to Tamra, best friend of Gorik. Died nine years ago. Everyone was told he fell overboard while drunk.

E

Emerald – One of the Four Kings, or Four Jewels, of Alutopek. Bone Hunter Prince of the Rantyak Islands. It's also a town hidden with the Timlin Forest.

F

Farra – (Fahr-uh) Pirate from Trinkit. Current captain of the *Fallen Order*.

Fohdorsha – (Foh-dohr-shaw) In common tongue they're called the Dragonborn, though they hate that term. Original inhabitants of the Bomoku Mountains, and Alutopek. Most fear them and stay away whenever possible. Because of this, countless misconceptions have emerged.

Frosted Tangle – Dragon originating from the Sampra Tribe. Mostly used to pull carriages now.

G

Gorik – (Goh-rik) One of the best sailors of Datz. Best friend of Drane, surrogate uncle to Rafik and Anza. Member of the Soniky.

Grothel – (Growth-uhl) Minotaur guardian to the Hall of Heroes. 10 feet tall, very wide, and covered in mattered brown fur.

Gyre – Water Immortal.

H

Haloro – (Huh-lohr-oh) A Kylika Soldier who has the talent of speed. From the Ohmrang Field.

Haxama – (Hacks-uh-muh) From Drugahn. Former acquaintance to Izamar.

Hushrin – (Huhsh-rin) Captain of the Tahmlo Tribe Guard

I

Immortals – One of two cursed races of men. Bodies of man, massive wings protruding from their backs, beaks, and feathers blend in with their hair. They have control over one of the elements of Amlima. Their true name is taboo; nobody is allowed to hear or speak of it, except for other Immortals.

Inakus – (In-ahk-uhs) A warrior of the Taktor race.

Izamar – (Ahy-zah-mahr) Former wizard. His spirit now resides within mirrors in his library at Dragon's Roost.

J

Jessux – (Jess-ucks) Brother to Kaliboon and part of the Fohdorsha.

Jinuk – (Ji-nook) The new Kylix commander from Borlo who is squirrelly, cowardly, paranoid, and filled with bravado.

Junla – (Joon-law) Fohdorshan from the Amsahvi Tribe.

K

Kaliboon – (Kal-ih-boon) A Fohdorshan living in the Lepal Tribe, mother to Dahsho and sister to Jessux. Dark hair with grey eyes.

Kangor – (Can-gore) A former god of the Rhine-Pa religion, said to have fallen from grace and has since died.

Korban – (Kohr-bin) The first Dragon Rider.

Krista – (Kris-tuh) Kylika soldier from Haitu. Has the talent of healing.

Kristol – One of the Four Kings, also known as the Four Jewels, of Alutopek. The only woman of the Four Kings, and the leader of the raiders that became the Four Kings. Rumored to be the wife of Emerald. It's also a village on the western side of the Nyler Peninsula.

Kryn – (Krin) From Sysinal. Orphan. She is overconfident and has the talent of fire, and the first in history to have that ability.

Kylika – (Kai-lick-uh) Special group of Kylix soldiers. From the Bone hunter language meaning 'powerful soldier.' Wears a bestial helmet instead of the standard human skull helmet.

Kylix – (Kai-licks) Name of the army of Alutopek. Comes from the Bone Hunter language meaning 'soldier.' They wear skeletal armor to honor the Bone Hunter heritage.

L

Lepal Tribe – (Leh-pawl) Water Tribe of the Fohdorsha

Lortimo – (Lohr-ti-moh) Chief and village elder of the Lepal Tribe.

Lonesome Abyss – One of the Great Dragons of the Lepal Tribe, rumored to be extinct.

M

Mahlix – (Mah-licks) From Haitu. A Kylix commander.

Menjua Tribe – (Men-joo-uh) One of the Fohdorshan Tribes. Translates to the Ashen Tribe.

Morvar Tribe – (Mohr-var) One of the Fohdorshan Tribes. Translates to the Obsidian Tribe.

Muirinda – (Myoorin-duh) Granddaughter to Bahsha

N

Nayflin – (Ney-flin) Former Kylix soldier. (Deceased)

Nehran – (Ney-ren) Captain of the Day Runner

Nekvaz – (Nek-vaz) Friend to King Vanarzir and member of the Morvar Tribe.

Neypa – (Ney-puh) Air Immortal.

P

Palok – (Pal-uhk) An archer part of the Tahmlo Tribe Guard.

Paris – (Par-is) Member of the Bantrita.

Pokoto Tribe – (Poh-koh-toh) One of the Fohdorshan Tribes. Translates to the Forest Tribe. It's also a location. (See location section for more.)

Q

Quellor – (Kwel-or) Mythological hero. Constellation encompassing the north star.

R

Rafik – (Raf-ik) Son of Drane and Tamra, brother to Anza. Talent of psychometry. Fiercely protective of his sister and friends. From Datz.

Rahgo – (Raw-goh) Member of Captain Farra's crew. From Trinkit.

Rathsa – (Rath-suh) The last of the obsidian dragons.

Roobino – One of the Four Kings, or Four Jewels, of Alutopek. It's also a town in the Lahmora Swamps.

S

Safsil – One of the Four Kings, or Four Jewels, of Alutopek. It's also a town in the Ohmrang Field.

Salina – (Suh-leen-uh) One of the three ruling council members of Datz. She is vindictive, jealous, selfish, and heir to the Datian throne.

Sampra Tribe – (Samp-ruh) One of the Fohdorshan Tribes. Translates to the Pearl Tribe. Their tribe rests on the eastern foothills of the Bomoku Mountains. (See locations section for more.)

Samron – (Sam-ron) Former lead trainer of the Kylix army. Now commander of the Kylix. From Borlo.

Savage Husks – A small dragon from the Tahmlo Tribe.

Sayros – (Sey-rohz) An Immortal. A life tracker from the Dark Tribe with orange eyes.

Shallon – (Shal-in) Member of the Soniky. Tall, large, and quiet. Has an emerald embedded in his right hand, and a tattoo of a half moon over his left eye. From the city of Emerald. Member of the Soniky.

Skage – (Skeyj) Necromancer (Deceased) Was defeated two years ago by Rafik, Xeo, and Tragi.

Soniky – (Soh-nik-ahy) Secret and ancient organization of rebellion. First formed to overthrow the Four Kings. According to legend, they lurk in the shadows ready to overthrow any unjust ruler.

Swayfir – (swey-fur) Friend of King Vanarzir. From Detnu.

Syrus – (Sahy-ruhs) Mythical being in the Rhine-Pa religion said to have saved humanity. The soul of a fallen god embodied in a man.

T

Tahmlo Tribe – (Tom-low) One of the Fohdorshan Tribes. Translates to the Fire Tribe. Also a location. (See location section for more.)

Taktor – (Tak-tohr) One of two cursed races of men. Taktor are bound to the sea.

Taygin – (Tay-jin) Kylix soldier. Eager for power, and envious of those with talent. A brown-noser, selfish, but wanting to always prove himself worth more than he has. From Haitu.

Teller – Chief and village elder of the Amsahvi Tribe.

Tiris – (Tir-is) An Immortal of the Dark Tribe, now nothing more than the embodiment of fear.

Tragi – (Trey-jahy) – Twin brother to Xeo, and brother to Queen Valkayto. From Kristol.

Treshna – (Tresh-nuh) Known as the Hound of Soboribor. A monster cursed to snatch the souls of the living and take them to the underworld, no matter what. It's appearance it's usually the body of a bear, the head of a bison, ears of a wolf, and legs of a deer.

V

Valkayto – (Val-kay-toh) Meaning 'Daughter of Kayto.' She is the sister to Xeo and Tragi. From Kristol.

Vanarzir – (Van-ahr-zir) Meaning 'Son of Arzir.' King of Alutopek. Creator of the Black Wall

X

Xeo – (Zee-oh) Twin brother to Tragi, and brother to Valkayto. From Kristol.

Y

Yomin – (Yawm-in) Commander at the Bruin Fortress. Bald with sagging cheeks.

Yon – (Yawn) Dockmaster of Lynn.

Z

Ziri – (Zir-ee) Has the talent of poison. From Trinkit.

PLACES

A

Akitung – (Ack-i-tuhng) Jungle region in North-East Alutopek.

Alutopek – (Uh-loo-toh-pek) Name of the continent.

Amlima – (Am-lim-uh) Name of the world.

Amsahvi Tribe – (Am-saw-vee) A hidden tribe of Fohdorsha near the Lepal Tribe on the western edge of the Bomoku Mountains. It resides with trees and their roots, hidden from the outside world in exile. Also a tribe of Fohdorsha. (See the people and animals section for more.)

Anirats – (An-er-ats) City of Secrets. Hidden somewhere within the Gateway Mountains.

B

Biodlay – (Bi-oh-dlay) Central desert region of Alutopek.

Black Wall – Ebon dome surrounding Alutopek. Created by stealing talent and magic of the people.

Bomoku Mountains – (Boh-moh-koo) Southern mountain range of Alutopek. Home of the Fohdorsha. Shrouded in mystery and superstition.

Bruin Fortress – (Broo-in) Meaning fortress of bears, it is the Kylix Fortress between the southern border of the Nyler Peninsula and northern border of the Biodlay Desert. Looks like a lower jaw sticking out of the ground.

D

Datz – (Dats) City of ruins. Rests on the eastern shore of the Nyler Peninsula. People here are known to be the best sailors in Alutopek.

Detnu – (Det-noo) The eternal city. Oldest city in all Amlima, resting on the western foothills of the Gateway Mountains. Capital of Alutopek.

Dragon's Roost – Secret hideout and library of Izamar. Located in the heart of the Biodlay Desert.

Drugahn – (Droo-gon) City of Myths. One of two known villages around the Opal Lake.

E

Eko River – (Ek-oh) Named after the canyons resting on this river that create echoes. Eko is the ancient language name for echo. It's the only river that runs South to North, from the Bomoku Mountains to the Tahlbiru Ocean.

Emerald – A town hidden within the Timlin Forest. Founded by, and named after, Emerald, one of the Four Kings of Alutopek. Known as the City of secrets.

F

Fang-Elsea Island – (Fang-el-see) Largest island in the Vinsen Ocean.

G

Gateway Mountains – Named because of the vast canyon between two major mountain ranges, blocking off all western Alutopek to the rest of the continent. The only safe passage is through the canyon.

Golden Gate –Kylix stronghold at the mouth of the Eko River.

H

Haitu – (Hey-too) City of sand. Rests on the banks of the Eko River. Home of the Kylix army.

J

Junsharri Fountain – (Joon-shar-ee) A fountain in the center of Drugahn. Depending on who you ask, depends on the superstition and lore surrounding this great fountain.

K

Kristol – Town built in the rolling hills on the western portion of the Nyler Peninsula. Founded by, and named after, Kristol, one of the Four Kings of Alutopek. Known as the safest city in Alutopek because of the guard there.

L

Lahmora Swamp – (Lah-mohr-ah) The South-Eastern region to Alutopek.

Lepal Tribe – (Leh-pawl) Village of the Fohdorsha, located on the western side of the Bomoku Mountains near the Vinsen Ocean. Also, a group of people. (See people section for more.)

Lynn – (Lin) City of the Gods. City settled at the mouth of the canyon in the Gateway Mountains, and on the edge of the Biodlay Desert. Home to most temples and shrines to the gods of all religions.

M

Mahparry – (Mah-pahr-ee) The world beneath the world. Home to Immortals.

Morvar Ruins – Ruins east of Mt. Korban lost to history. Once home to the Morvar Tribe.

Mount Korban – (Kohr-bin) The tallest mountain in Alutopek, located in the heart of the Bomoku Mountains.

N

Nyler – (Nahy-ler) Most commonly known as the Nyler Peninsula, the northern most region in Alutopek. Comes from the Bone Hunter word meaning 'north.'

O

Ohmrang Field – (Ohm-rang) Western region of Alutopek.

P

Pond of Memories – Pond in the center of Datz where a temple once stood. At the bottom is a trapdoor that leads to Mahparry. Datians use this pond as a place of reflection and mourning.

Pokoto Tribe – (Poh-koh-toh) A Fohdorshan Tribe located south of Mt. Korban. Also a group of people. (See people and animals section for more.)

R

Rohz – (Rows) A long lost kingdom. One of the first in mankind's history.

Roobino – Town built in South-Eastern Alutopek. Founded by, and named after, Roobino, one of the Four Kings of Alutopek. Known as the city of magic.

Ruins of Kangor – (Can-gore) The tomb of Kangor, God of Protection. Said to only reveal itself to travelers in need or who are in peril. Resides at the bottom of the Gateway Mountains on the western edge of the Biodlay Desert.

S

Safsil – Town built along the shores of Alutopek in the Ohmrang Field. Founded by, and named after, Safsil, one of the Four Kings of Alutopek. Knowns as the city of life.

Sampra Tribe – (Samp-ruh) Fohdorshan Tribe on the eastern foothills of the Bomoku Mountains. It's a city that hasn't been conquered in millennia and flows with wealth. It is also a people. (See people and animals section for more.)

Sarason Fortress – (Sair-uh-suhn) Former stronghold of Skage. Now destroyed and the ruins are sunk into the Tahlbiru Ocean.

Savage Tavern – Tavern in the Tahmlo Tribe named after the Savage Husk dragons.

Sekolah Fortress – (Sek-oh-lah) Fortress in Haitu and place all Kylix soldiers are trained.

Soboribor – (So-bohr-ih-bohr) The underworld in the Rhine-Pa religion. Realm where the most evil and foul of people go.

Sysinal – (Sis-in-uhl) City of warriors. Resting on the edge of the Biodlay Desert and the Akitung Jungle. It was once a massive coliseum that people would come far and wide to watch games. Now the coliseum has become the city itself.

T

Tahmlo Tribe – (Tom-low). A Fohdorshan Tribe northwest of Mt. Korban within the Bomoku Mountains.

Tahlbiru Ocean – (Tawl-bur-oo) Name of the northern ocean surrounding Alutopek and the Rantyak Islands. Comes from the ancient words tall and cold, meaning 'deep freeze.'

Trinkit – (Tring-kit) City of pirates. Founded by Datians before the Black Wall, it's always been a town of ne'er-do-wells. Home of the 'Pirate Alley.' Located on the northern edge of the Biodlay Desert on the shore of the Tahlbiru Ocean.

V

Vinsen Ocean – (Vin-sen) Name of the southern ocean surrounding Alutopek. Comes from the ancient words meaning

THINGS and LANGUAGE

A

Ako tinda bisini. Ako basana – (Ak-oh tin-duh bih-see-nee. Ak-oh buh-sah-nuh. An ancient language spell that translates to 'I'm not here, I'm there.'

B

Blaridane – (Blair-i-dane) Cursed and ancient blood metal sword.

Bordin – (Bor-din) From the ancient language meaning non-magical or powerless.

Byta Kuduhlli fro sah – (Bit-ah Koo-duhl-lee Froh Saw) Ancient language that means "switch places with me."

D

Day Runner – Captain Nehran's ship.

Dransbian Steel – An extraordinarily strong, expensive, and sought-after metal. Said to be able to pierce dragon scales.

E

Elemental Stones – Legendary stones of fire, water, air, and light. Harnessing one grants the user limited control over the element.

Endless Bag – A magical bag that has a secret room hidden inside.

F

Forteek – (Fohr-teek) Bone hunter word for husband.

Forteka – (Fohr-teek-uh) Bone hunter word for prison.

H

Hembir – (Hem-bir) A spell from the ancient language meaning 'to heal.'

I

Iospa Diamond – (Ee-oh-spuh) Legendary diamond of loyalty said to once be owned by dragons.

K

Kolinda – (Koh-lin-duh) Fohdorshan word for outsider.

Kymu-Guiden Talisman – (Kai-moo gahyd-in) An ancient and mysterious talisman. Hexagonal in shape with a ruby red spider embedded on the beveled top. It amplifies the user's power.

M

Magic Most Marvelous – Oldest book in the Dragon's Roost library. Gives the basics and history of rune magic.

Master's Books – A collection of four legendary tomes in Immortal mythology. Said to control life, peace, death, and chaos. Reading from any gives you the power of a god.

Mentor's Mirror – A mirror Izamar created. Anybody who has encountered the mirror can be summoned after death to help the living.

O

Omurahi – (Oh-moo-raw-he) A spell from the ancient language meaning 'wild fire.'

P

Perjong – (Purr-jong) Fohdorshan for truth. Also the name of the Ravohka that when worn and making eye contact, the user can detect if others are lying.

Q

Quellor – (Kwel-or) Constellation encompassing the northern star. Named after a mythological hero.

R

Ravohka – (Ruh-voh-kuh) Fohdorshan for mask. Comes from the words ra, meaning power, and vohk, meaning face. Fohdorshan wear these masks that were once their talent.

Rhine-Pa – (Rahyn-paw) Polytheistic, and most common, religion in Alutopek and Mahparry.

T

Talent – A mysterious power granted by some at birth, during grim times, or at puberty. The power isn't the same for everyone, i.e., Ziri has the talent of poison while Rafik has the talent of psychometry. Talent was stolen and the Black Wall was created, however some are gaining powers back.

Y

Ya shire – (Yuh shai-ur) A cursing phrase in the ancient language. Commonly used to mean 'dang it.' A popular cursing phrase in the Nyler Peninsula and among sailors.

__Acknowledgements__

Before thanking anyone else, I need to thank the amazing artist, Dragolisco, for once again doing amazing work. His work never ceases to amaze me, and it captures fantasy that leaves me in awe. I love his work and cannot express enough gratitude towards him. I highly recommend you check out his other artwork and even boardgame! I promise you won't be disappointed.

This story had been cooped up inside my head for so long it's nice to finally have Treshna out of it! So many people have encouraged and urged me to continue writing. But a special thanks to the Tuper-Giles and Kirchoff families, for being my rock and support, even when I don't believe I deserve it. And it also goes to the Clegg family. You have a special place in my heart I can only describe as genuine family. I love you all. And Riot, I hope this book wasn't too predictable for you.

A huge thank you and all my appreciation goes to Pauline. She is by far the main reason you read any of my work. She has pushed me to do and be my best and encouraged me to break out of my comfort zone. Pauline continuously keeps me on track to get my work done, and to get it out there for others to read. She is the true hero, and I can't give enough praises to her. Thank you so much, and I love you!

Gus and Rowdy are horrible animals who still strive to achieve my complete, utter, and undivided attention. They succeed often and are the true monsters and villains of my life that I can't live without. I love them both immensely.

Most importantly is you. The person reading this book! Reading this one probably means you read the first as well. Hopefully, you have enjoyed it and can't wait for more. I've always wanted to share my stories and inspire others. I am so thankful you took time to read my story. I appreciate that and look forward to sharing more stories in the future with you as well.

About the Author

Growing up in haunted houses, exploring forgotten forests deep within mountains, and spending the last ten years writing and sharing fantasy and horror stories online, T.S. Colunga has a unique way of storytelling. She is best known for her fantasy series (Regin of Shadows), YouTube channel (Terra's Tales), and her e-book horror short story series (Lakewood Stories). She lives and works from home in a small town tucked away at the bottom of the Uintah Basin in Utah. Although she sees herself as quite independent, she gets bossed around by her two dogs, Gus and Rowdy, daily.

If you would like to contact her, email her at tscolunga@gmail.com.

Author Notes

In a reading group online I'm part of I heard several expressing how interesting it would be if authors put in 'author notes' at the end of the book like a director's commentary on a movie. I thought this was a fun idea, and figured I would give it a whirl. I hope you enjoy this further insight into Alutopek, and this story.

Dragons

I've always been fascinated by these mythical monsters. Big or small, smart or dumb, I enjoy them all. After reading a guidebook by Dragolisco, the cover artist for this book, I started thinking of different species that could be found in Alutopek. Writing these I felt like I was writing a nature documentary on dragons!

In a future project I'd love to write a dragon compendium with each of these magnificent beasts.

Fohdorsha

The Fohdorsha are inspired by my favorite story of all time, BIONICLE, as well as masks from Japanese and African cultures. Masks have always fascinated me, and this has been my favorite part of world building was developing their culture, history, and region. In an earlier draft I went into way too much detail with them. Maybe in a future story we can delve deeper into their world. I hope so.

The names for the Fohdorsha are a mixture of Indonesian and Swedish terms, combined with a language I developed for them.

I knew I wanted to include two separate journeys for Rafik and Kryn through the Bomoku Mountains, and I thought including the banished tribes would be interesting. Though I wasn't entirely sure where some were, or how they would react with newcomers or their surroundings. After playing with the writing tool and games 'The Story Engine' and 'Deck of Worlds' it all kind of flowed together. If you have writer's block, or just want a fun time writing and world building, I highly recommend these. They've helped get the brain juices flowing when nothing else would.

Sadly, I had to cut a lot of the Ashen Raiders out. I hope to explore these rapscallions again in the future.

Korban's Finger

This sacred site has been in my mind since I was six or seven. While hiking with one of my sisters in St. George, Utah I randomly came across this impressive and awe-inspiring place. All that was missing was the pedestal with the egg. From then on, I knew this place had to be in my books, especially since it seemed to be a real place. I'm so happy it worked out to become the cover of my book.

Treshna

I've always been fascinated by mythical creatures and wanted to make one of my own. Treshna was the product of an overactive imagination from a teenager trying to create a North American hybrid to rival the griffin. Of course, if it's supposed to be a monster from the underworld cursed to hunt you, it needs to have the ability to grow and adapt to become even more of a nightmare. Her back story was inspired by the 'Weeping Woman,' La Llorona.